*by* WILLI HEINRICH

---

THE DEVIL'S BED
THE CRUMBLING FORTRESS
THE LONELY CONQUEROR
RAPE OF HONOR
MARK OF SHAME
CRACK OF DOOM
CROSS OF IRON

# THE DEVIL'S BED

by

## WILLI HEINRICH

*Translated from the German by*

*HANS KONINGSBERGER*

THE DIAL PRESS

*NEW YORK 1965*

# THE DEVIL'S BED

# 1

While she was waiting for Bentley, she remembered how once upon a time she had played with the thought of killing him. But that had been half a year ago and there were more subtle ways for a woman to get even with a man.

She watched Major Green light his pipe for the fifth time in ten minutes. He had an aversion to her, and she knew it. She had known it even before she had entered the room. The general had had the same aversion, but the general had been a well-educated gentleman— polite and patient. Major Green did not have those qualities. But what American woman could have blamed him, only four months after the end of the war.

"Are you here alone, Mrs. Brazzi?" she heard him ask.

"Yes."

Major Green forced a smile. "I admire you," he said without enthusiasm. "I don't know anybody like you."

"Just assume that I have nothing else to do," Helen answered. She walked over to one of the four high windows. The blinds were drawn because of the noontime heat. Pressing down one of the slats, she looked out into the sunny street.

"In Sicily the heat is easier to bear," Major Green said. "Have you ever been in Sicily before, Mrs. Brazzi?"

"No." Her eyes were dazed by the light in which the town seemed to drown. "My husband used to tell me about it," she said.

"Of course," Major Green answered.

She heard the door open and then, again, the voice of the major: "This is Lieutenant Bentley, Mrs. Brazzi."

For more than six months she had waited impatiently for this moment, but her heart did not beat any faster. She turned toward the lieutenant.

He was young and tall with a thin, freckled face, light eyes, and reddish hair, and his uniform was covered with ribbons—several more than Major Green was wearing. He did not look at all the way she had imagined. Worse: he seemed sympathetic.

"You know what this is about, Lieutenant," Major Green said listlessly. "Mrs. Brazzi would like to hear the whole story once more from you." He turned to Helen. "Perhaps it would interest you that Lieutenant Bentley is also from Toledo, Ohio."

"I have already been told that," Helen said.

Bentley looked at her with a mixture of curiosity and shyness. He had once seen her picture in the paper: that of a slender woman around thirty-five. Now in the soft light of the room her face still seemed very young, regular, and a bit bony; her mouth touched with pale lipstick; her eyes strikingly large with long lashes. Her wide-brimmed hat flattered her. There were few women who could wear a hat like that; Helen Brazzi was one of them. Impatiently the major began talking again: "Mrs. Brazzi knows most of it. Tell her what happened that night."

"Yes, sir," said Bentley, addressing him. "We were lying in front of Palmigano—"

"I know the story," Major Green interrupted. "Address yourself to Mrs. Brazzi!"

The lieutenant blushed. "Yes, sir."

He now felt so shy that even the simplest words came with difficulty.

"It must have been the fifth of August 1943," she said to him.

Bentley nodded. "That's right, ma'am. Our attack on Palmigano had already started on the first of August. On the fifth of August the Germans counterattacked . . . in the middle of the night. We were overrun by them and a part of our company was cut off."

"Not you?" Helen asked.

It sounded like a reproach to Bentley. "Not me, ma'am."

"I don't understand that," Helen said. She had a deep voice, which

*8*

"I'd like to discuss that with Lieutenant Bentley," Helen said. "If it's all right with you, I will expect him tomorrow morning in my hotel." She looked at Bentley. "Of course if that suits you, Lieutenant?"

"Certainly, ma'am," Bentley said and blushed again. "At what time?"

"Around nine o'clock. Good day, Major Green."

She was at the door so quickly that Bentley had no chance to open it for her. He turned around and looked at Major Green, who hadn't moved. Then he went to the window and looked down to the street. After a short wait he saw Helen Brazzi leave the house and cross the street.

"You can go, Lieutenant," Major Green said without turning around. "Lieutenant Warnick can take over. Don't stay away longer than four days."

"Yes, sir," Bentley said and left. In front of the door he stopped and lit a cigarette.

## 2

Two years had passed since Genno Brazzi had been posted as missing —time enough for a woman to get used to the idea; time enough when the missing man had been a Sicilian farmer's boy whose parents, only thirteen years earlier, had lived in one of these godforsaken little hamlets in the mountains between Catania and Caltanissetta and who, when they had finally scraped together the money for the voyage, had emigrated and joined their relatives in Toledo, where even the poorest Sicilian had a chance to make his way. Of course not all of them had the additional luck to catch the demanding daughter of a family of the American moneyed aristocracy, but Genno Brazzi had made it. A little Italian spaghetti eater had married one of the most desirable women in Toledo.

And now here she was, four months after the end of the war, coming from Toledo to Naples to settle in her mind what she should not really have needed to settle because of the way things were. Perhaps she was as hysterical, Bentley thought, as that woman from Cleveland who had mutilated her face with a razor, after the death of her husband on the Monte Casino front, to prevent herself from ever being tempted to dishonor the dead with a new marriage.

It would not be an easy thing to convince Helen Brazzi that she faced something which money could not change, and while Bentley thought about that, he wondered why she had chosen him, particularly, to accompany her to Chiesa.

It was a big hotel. Before the war only rich tourists, from all over the world, had lived there. Now most of the rooms were empty. The doorman sent Bentley up to Helen's room.

In his imagination Bentley had developed a romantic image of Helen; he was almost disappointed when he didn't find her in a negligee. Although it was very early in the day, she was properly dressed in a simple, dark suit. He hadn't remembered her medium-length blond hair. He realized that she had been wearing a hat the day before. Because of her he had lain awake half the night; he had never before fallen in love at first sight.

She greeted him with a nod. "I expected you at nine," she said. "Did you have any breakfast?"

Bentley smiled. "Two hours ago, ma'am." He had come half an hour early because he couldn't wait any longer to see her. "If I'm too early . . . "

She interrupted him. "I would have let you know through the doorman. How much leave has Major Green given you?"

"Four days, ma'am."

"That's not very nice of Major Green." She smiled. "Wait a moment." She went into another room.

Although the events of the last few years had left their traces, the apartment was still luxurious. Only the rugs and the silk upholstery showed wear. Between two large windows was a door to the balcony.

Waiting for her to return, Bentley remembered that it had always been his desire to marry a woman with experience, although he had half expected to meet a young creature and forget his decision. But now he was feeling something of a different order. He was attracted by Helen Brazzi's character, her self-assurance, and also by the injury to her spirit which he guessed she felt, because if her spirit wasn't wounded, why would she have come to Naples? The cool mask, behind which she hid, was penetrable. She wasn't eccentric. She was simply obsessed by an idea, a flood of feelings which had been channeled in the wrong direction. What a task she presented, even for a man who knew what he wanted!

"I put in a call, Lieutenant," she said when she returned. "Why don't you sit down? Do you smoke?"

At least the cigarette case was the way he had expected it. He felt less shy; offering him a cigarette was the first personal gesture she had allowed herself toward him.

"You have already helped me a lot, Lieutenant Bentley," she said behind the drifting smoke of her cigarette. "Before I saw Major Green yesterday I wondered whether there was any sense in what I was doing."

"I was wondering about that, too," said Bentley. "If you don't promise yourself too much . . ."

He was immediately sorry he had said it. In his situation it would make more sense to go along with her, but Bentley tended to say what he thought.

She looked carefully at him. "What did you mean when you said that?"

"I am thinking of your husband. If you want to find out what happened to him, I think you have a chance. You are very brave, Mrs. Brazzi."

Helen smiled. "And you are very young, Lieutenant Bentley. Twenty-five?"

"Twenty-nine," Bentley said. People always thought he was younger. He didn't like that.

*13*

"My mistake," Helen said. "But would you nevertheless keep your advice to yourself in the future?"

"As you wish, ma'am."

The last woman who had talked to him that way had been his teacher in Toledo. But he accepted it quietly. He would not allow his sensitivity to dilute his desire for her.

"At first I was not prepared for a mystery," she said. "There was nothing mysterious about my husband being missing. It was not much different from a death notice. That's how I felt about it at first."

"I understand," Bentley said carefully.

She looked at him without emotion. "It only became mysterious when Corporal Hopkins came to see me. He told me that my husband had been kidnapped by Italian collaborators and might still be alive."

Bentley felt the blood drain from his face. "Corporal Hopkins came to see you?"

"Does that surprise you?"

"A little," Bentley murmured. He began to understand why she had chosen him to go to Chiesa. "He lives in Portland," he said rudely, "twenty-five hundred miles from Toledo."

"He didn't forget to mention that," said Helen. "I paid for his trip. Perhaps even a bit more."

"That's just like him." Bentley felt himself becoming angry. "When did he come to see you, Mrs. Brazzi?"

"It must have been at the beginning of March."

"I see. Yes, Hopkins was wounded in October and was home on leave. But then you already knew the story when we met yesterday . . ." He stopped himself and shook his head. "It was irresponsible of him."

"I don't agree with you," Helen said. Since she had met Bentley, she had begun to think that Hopkins' suspicions were without foundation. But now Bentley's confusion seemed to confirm them. She was determined to use every means to get the truth out of him. Major Green would not tell her the truth.

"Corporal Hopkins' visit," she said quietly, "helped me very much. You're not married, Lieutenant?"

"No, ma'am."

*14*

"Then you don't have to consider what your wife would have done in my place."

"That's right, ma'am," Bentley said. He had recovered his composure. "As long as money is not a problem . . ."

She interrupted him. "It took more than money, Lieutenant Bentley. You also need at least one senator—with good connections in the Pentagon—who agrees with you that there are worse things than a simple notification of death. I am telling you this so you won't wonder any longer why Major Green, in spite of his objections, has given you leave. Have you known Major Green for a long time?"

"Three years, ma'am."

"Corporal Hopkins told me that Major Green was company commander in Sicily."

"That's right, ma'am." Bentley said.

Helen smiled. "I always imagined company commanders much younger. Major Green looks as if he should be at least a colonel. There is my call!"

When she went to answer the phone in the adjacent room, Bentley walked to the window, trying to arrange his thoughts. The hotel was near the beach, with a wide view of Vesuvius. Bentley was familiar with it. From his post he saw the mountain every evening, bathed in red light.

He wondered why she had told him about her senator. Perhaps she wanted to intimidate him. At the time of Brazzi's disappearance Hopkins had been acting platoon commander. He had known more than the others. Nevertheless it was unlikely that he had known everything; he could have found out only from Major Green.

And so what! Bentley thought bitterly. He hadn't wanted this damned war. He had wished a hundred times every day that it would be over, and when it was he had been drunk for a week. But you couldn't be drunk all the time, and afterwards he had been so sober that he had wanted to bury himself in the ground. It was as if his world had come to an end, and the worst thing was that he didn't know what to do with himself anymore. Whether he picked up a book or went to a movie he could never lose the depressing feeling of banality. Ten times a day he had wanted to run away, because every-

15

thing that excited people disgusted him, and he couldn't explain this to anyone.

He looked out again onto the town. Compared with Naples, Toledo was ugly, but two years was a long time for a man whose family lived in Toledo. Two years of disillusionment and involuntary exposure to dirt, heat, hunger, and poverty. Perhaps it had been different before the war. He didn't know. He only knew that he was sick of it. Every time he walked through the town he had a senseless feeling of guilt because nowhere in the civilized world were there so many dirty, half-starved people as in Naples. Nowhere were there so many women for sale on every street corner, and so many slum children, and nowhere was the air more corrupted with the smell of spoiled fish, faded flowers, and invisible corpses. Only in the night, when the wind rose from the sea, carrying the fresh smell of salt water, did the fetid odor diminish.

He heard Helen Brazzi end her conversation, and he returned to his chair.

"What were we talking about?" she said as she came in.

"About your senator," Bentley said bluntly. If she was trying to intimidate him, he would force her hand.

She sat down and smiled at him. "We were talking about Major Green," she said, "but if you're interested I do want to tell you that knowing a senator is not an everyday affair. There aren't that many. Especially not the kind who have good friends in the Pentagon."

"I'm impressed, Mrs. Brazzi," Bentley said. He was now certain that she was trying to intimidate him.

She looked at him curiously. "I had forgotten that you're from Toledo," she said, although she most certainly would not have forgotten. "But even in my case it required a considerable campaign contribution before my senator was willing to listen to me. Anyway, your superiors have agreed that you can be my guest for longer than just four days."

"Did you phone Major Green?" Bentley asked quickly.

"I could have, but after yesterday's experiences it seemed better to phone directly to headquarters."

She went to a little desk and took out some papers. "Perhaps you are surprised," she said without looking at him, "that I am telling you so much about myself. It's just that I don't want you to have the wrong impression about my trip."

"I realize it's not a pleasure trip," he said and stood up. "When do you want to leave, Mrs. Brazzi?"

She walked over to him and looked up into his face. "Tomorrow morning. We have a direct connection to Palermo. In Palermo we will try to rent a car. If you will be here at eight o'clock . . ."

"Yes, ma'am." He put his cap on and went to the door.

"Lieutenant Bentley," Helen said.

He stopped at the door and took his cap off again.

"You have a nice uniform," she said with a smile, "but do you also have a civilian suit?"

"Three, ma'am."

"Would it be possible to leave your uniform here?"

"If you wish, ma'am."

"I would be very happy if you did," Helen said.

When he was gone, she sat down and looked at herself in the mirror. Perhaps she would dream of him again tonight. She recalled how he had said that she was brave. She had never been brave. She had decided on this trip the way one decides on an operation which can no longer be postponed and the success of which is uncertain. She had decided because even the most senseless activity was better than the lasting uncertainty. But it had nothing to do with courage. Perhaps this voyage was not much more than an escape from herself, from being alone, from the absolute void which Genno's death had left behind: a flight from the feeling of being superfluous, from the temptation to forget him—a flight from the temptation to blot out his memory in bed with the first comer. She was the daughter of McShane. She was his daughter at home, on the street, in the theater, and at parties and receptions. Whatever she did, she was the daughter of Mc-Shane. In New York, Chicago, Philadelphia, he had been a little star among big stars, but in Toledo he was a myth. Big McShane! and she was the daughter of Big McShane. It had its obligations even when she was sick of being the daughter of Big McShane. She had already been sick of it when she met Genno Brazzi, when she, the daughter of McShane, married a nameless American citizen of Italian descent, a little uneducated Sicilian with bad manners and dirty fingernails. Was it love? Was it pride? Was it to thumb her nose at the conventionalities of Toledo society? Was it to show them that she was immune to their suspicions, their whispers? She, the daughter of the great McShane!

She stared at her face in the mirror with disgust.

## 3

She seemed unable to register any emotion. The town, with its palaces, cathedrals, and Byzantine buildings, did not move her. She walked beside Bentley as quietly and indifferently as if she were shopping in Toledo, Ohio.

After Bentley had tried for the third time to draw her attention to one of the views, the Palazzo Bonagia, then the Monte Pellegrino, gleaming red in the reflection from the setting sun, he gave up. He wasn't too interested in it himself, really, and he was glad to have her near him. During the crossing she had not once come out of her cabin, and he had not counted on seeing her again after supper—until she had knocked on his door fifteen minutes earlier and asked him to take a walk to the port with her.

For Bentley every step was full of memories. Memories of Lieutenant Hall, of Lewis, Porter, Heath, Cooper, Brownfield, and whatever their names had been. Those men were not waiting to go home anymore.

When darkness fell, the crowd in the narrow streets became even thicker: soldiers, sailors from Morocco and Algeria, women in rags with heavy makeup, slum children carrying boxes with mussels or shoe polish kits, between strikingly beautiful girls in gay dresses, young men in white shirts and red ties, typically south Italian from their pomaded hair to their highly polished shoes. Only at the waterside was it quieter at this hour. The throng of barges was new for Bentley. Two years ago warships had been here. Everything else had changed too. The uniforms of the Allies had almost vanished from the scene; instead, everywhere one saw the uniform of the carabinieri. The new government under Parri seemed determined to get things in Sicily back to normal. There was still many burned-out ruins near the coast —signs of the invasion. Here nothing had changed in two years.

Bentley did not understand why Helen Brazzi had wanted to go to the port. At the next street corner she suddenly turned back to the hotel. He could have sworn that she hadn't even glanced at the harbor.

Her talent for ignoring everyone around her—even the most persistent beggars who recognized her as an American and offered her all sorts of services—fascinated Bentley as much as the cool resignation with which she stepped away from two drunken sailors. When he moved to talk sharply to the two, she pulled him away by his sleeve.

The crowd became thicker, the darker it got. It was as if a thousand doors had been opened and an unending stream of noisy people had come pouring into the streets. They stood in heavy clusters in front of bars and restaurants or streamed down small side alleys, and pushed through the Corso Vittorio Emanuele, to vanish again into the hidden depths of the town. In front of the houses scantily dressed women talked on the steps and on chairs. The smell of salted fish mixed with the various smells that came from all windows and doors, and the sour smell of sweaty people, and the ever present smell of the sea.

Bentley had feared that Helen wanted to go back to the hotel, but she did not. They came to a quieter area with beautiful gardens and villas on both sides. The road led toward a hill on which a palace stood. It was surrounded by a large park—a massive square building with a beautiful façade.

"There is the former palace of the king," Bentley said. "From the park you can see the whole town. Would you like to climb up to it, Mrs. Brazzi?"

"It might be better than a sleeping pill," she said.

Her voice sounded different, tired and somewhat resigned. Bentley wondered whether he would ever fathom her mind. He was already prepared to forget all his principles for her.

The park was grandly designed, and well-kept roads crisscrossed through it. There were stone balustrades and old trees under which it was cool and quiet. They met no one.

They found a bench with a view overlooking not the town but the harbor and the sea, spread out beneath them. The horizon was lit up as if decorated with pearls of colored glass. Monte Pellegrino, high and steep against the sea, deepened the dusk with its shadow and towered over the town like a monument of bare stone. Its naked back reflected the last rays of the sun.

"*Conco d'oro!*" Bentley said. "Can you translate that, Mrs. Brazzi?"

Helen nodded. "Golden shell. What is it?"

He had noticed earlier that her Italian was even better than he would have expected from someone who had been married to a Sicilian.

"That is the name of the bay," he said. "When I heard it for the first time, we were waiting at dawn for our landing. None of us knew at that time that it would be so difficult to get to Rome."

"Have you been in the Army for long?" Helen asked. She realized, without pleasure, that she enjoyed listening to him.

Bentley smiled. "Too long, ma'am. God only knows where I ever got the idea that I wanted to be in uniform. I don't think I'll stay in much longer. When I was fifteen I wanted to be a mountain guide. Imagine that in Toledo!"

He smiled and looked toward the horizon, where the sky became yellow, then purple and finally orange. "I never really knew what I wanted," Bentley went on. "I don't think about it too much. It's as if you had to pick one dish from a hundred menus in a few seconds."

"I don't understand that," Helen said with her deep voice. She was sitting so close to him that their shoulders touched.

"You don't have to understand it," he said and offered her a cigarette. She shook her head and he lit one himself.

"It's only the war which has made me understand," he said. "The connection isn't right anymore."

She still didn't understand. "Which connection?"

"The connection between what you tell yourself and reality. Do you love flowers?"

She looked blankly at him. "Why not?"

"I never cared for them," Bentley said with a smile, "until we came to Monte Casino. We attacked ten times in vain, every time along the same road. I've never seen as many flowers in my life as along that pasture. Perhaps I'll become a gardener when I get out of the Army."

He's trying to make an impression on me, Helen thought. Since she had realized that she liked him, she had begun to hide behind her reserve.

"Monte Casino?" she asked. "That was much later, no?"

"Much later, ma'am." He nodded. He knew what she meant.

"I thought about it all yesterday," Helen said slowly. "You told me that your company had been cut off?"

"Two companies, ma'am. But we managed to fight back to our battalion."

"And you left your wounded behind," Helen said.

Bentley tossed his freshly lit cigarette to the ground and stepped on it. Since he had seen her, a day earlier, in the hotel, he had been waiting for her to take up the subject again.

"It was very dark, ma'am," he said as quietly as possible. "Why does that interest you so?"

"I just wonder," Helen said, "why the Italians took my husband with them."

"They took someone else with them too."

"I knew that already from Corporal Hopkins. He thinks that they were caught by the Italians while they were attending to the wounded. My husband and the other man couldn't have been wounded. The Italians wouldn't have bothered with the wounded."

"That's possible," Bentley said distractedly. "It was war, Mrs. Brazzi. We had no time to worry about it too long. Whatever we could do, we did."

"Afterward," Helen said and stood up. She walked over to the balustrade and looked down. When Bentley came over to her, she turned and leaned her back against the stone. It was now so dark under the trees that she could not see his face.

"What do you mean when you say 'afterward'?" he asked.

"Nothing special," Helen answered.

"Of course you mean something special," Bentley answered. "I don't want to play with hidden cards, Mrs. Brazzi. I don't know what all Hopkins has told you. He always talked too much and tried to act important. You shouldn't take him too seriously."

"No more seriously than I take you, Lieutenant Bentley," Helen said. "If I understand you correctly," she went on, "you don't want to stay in the Army?"

"No, I don't think so."

"Don't you like it anymore?"

"I'm sick of it," Bentley said. Although he was still suspicious, his voice became lighter. "Perhaps I'm too old for it. From a certain day on you realize how time runs away from you. In the Army it's like sitting in a rowboat while everybody else is flying by in expensive yachts. Rich people affect me. I would like to get somewhere before it's my turn."

"Don't you get somewhere in the Army?"

"If you are lucky and you have protection. Even then you only end up with a motor instead of oars. You still don't get onto the expensive yacht."

"That's quite a philosophy," Helen said with a little laugh. "Is it your only one?"

"Do you know a better one?"

"Well, all the same, you have helped to win the war," Helen said.

Bentley sat down beside her on the balustrade and swung his legs back and forth. "That's for historians. I won't be mentioned in their books; I can't even buy a copy of *Time* with that war I won. Look at that place there." He nodded in the direction of the trees, where, hardly visible in the dark, the outline of the palace stood out. "How much do you think that costs?"

"I understand," Helen said. She was more impressed than annoyed by his openness.

Bentley laughed. "Perhaps you don't understand."

"I understand you quite well," Helen answered. "And I think you know exactly what you want."

"Then you know more than I do. I can't wait to get back to Toledo. It's been two years since I've been back, though I know after six months I will give my eye teeth to be back in Italy."

"That's the way it is," Helen said.

Bentley nodded. "With only the small difference that *you* can get back to Italy anytime you feel like it."

The idea that she might come back to Italy one day with another man while he, Bentley, would be thousands of miles away from her training some stupid bunch of recruits in some stupid barracks seemed unbearable to him.

When he suddenly pulled her toward him and kissed her, he was only doing what he had already thought about for a long time. Yet it wasn't the result of a clear thought but more an unexpected reflex; and it was done in the almost instinctive expectation that by kissing her he could extinguish the memory of Genno Brazzi between them —the way one extinguishes a fire before it becomes dangerous.

She didn't resist because she was so surprised. Her lips were moist and cold. Only when he loosened his grip on her did she turn her face aside and take a deep breath.

Bentley came to himself. He let go of her and absent-mindedly wiped his mouth with the back of his hand. "I guess you'll send me back to Naples now," he said in a hoarse voice. "Maybe it's better."

"You would like that," Helen said but not in her own voice. It seemed someone else's.

Bentley looked at her, surprised. He had had enough women in his life—yet none of them had gotten under his skin as this one had. During the war he had, but for a few exceptions, acted like a cool and brave officer. Yet Helen Brazzi instilled fear in him.

"You don't want me to go back to Naples?" he asked.

"I need you," Helen heard herself say. "Ever since Corporal Hopkins came to see me, I've known that you and I, and no one else, would go to Sicily. Did you know that my husband volunteered for service?"

Bentley nodded; he couldn't quite speak.

"I could have talked him out of it," Helen said and looked down again on the town and the lights reflecting in the sea. "But I never managed to resist any of his wishes. He was determined to free his country from the Fascists. Let's go. We have a difficult day ahead of us tomorrow."

Bentley didn't move. "What did Hopkins tell you?"

She turned slowly toward him. "Didn't you just say that he was a stupid talker?"

"You don't want to tell me?"

"Not here."

This seemed to confirm what he had suspected all along. "I think maybe I'll go back to Naples," he said.

"Are you afraid?"

"Of what?"

"Then you don't have any reason to go back to Naples," Helen said. "Lieutenant, it's no little matter for me to let myself be kissed by an almost complete stranger, but compared to what I have ahead of me it's nothing, and I'm not going to have it endanger the success of my trip. I have already invested too much. Does that explain it?"

Bentley didn't answer. Later when he was walking beside her toward the hotel, he was still fighting with himself. He was a man from a lower middle-class family. His parents had worked hard even to let him go through high school. There had been no money for college. He had never had any grandiose ideas about his future, but the discrepancy between what had seemed possible a few days ago and what seemed possible now was oppressive, and sufficient to make a man like Bentley forget his principles and self-protective reserve. His decision was made, even before he said good-by to Helen Brazzi in front of her hotel-room door.

# 4

The rent for the car would have been enough to buy one like it. It was an old Fiat with bad tires, bad springs, and dirty seats, but of all the cars which Bentley had looked at in Palermo it was the only one with a sound engine. There were no spare parts, no new tires. Bentley had to pay another two hundred dollars for ten jerry-cans of gas and a filled tank. Helen had refused to travel by any of the many trains or buses.

They had left quite early, but it was noon when they came to Chiesa. The drive along the mountain roads, partly unpaved and full of holes, had cost a lot of time and had been very difficult. They alternated driving. All of Bentley's attempts at conversation soon floundered. When Helen did respond, she was so curt that he soon lost his impetus. During the whole trip she stared intensely at the landscape or followed the road on a map. She had obviously not forgiven him for the incident of the night before.

The village, high in the mountains, below a ruined castle, was a narrow gray sea of houses stuck to the rock like a beehive. It was indistinguishable from the many mountain villages they had passed earlier on their trip. A narrow dirt road followed the formation of the mountains in dizzy curves. When they reached the first houses, the water in the Fiat's radiator was boiling.

"It looks even worse than I remembered," Bentley said. "Where do you want to stay, ma'am?"

"I didn't know you could be funny, too," Helen said. She was horrified by the dark and decrepit houses.

Bentley continued. "There are three inns in Chiesa. Before the war it was a well-known tourist place."

The street ended on a square occupied by old trees and a well. Behind it was a street too narrow for cars, with steps in it, which led under an arch into a village. The houses were all the same shape and size, with windows so small that they looked like firing slits in a bunker. In the shadow of the well two cats were sleeping.

"People don't live here," Helen said in a wry tone.

Bentley smiled. He knew what she was thinking. He would have liked to stay in the hotel in Palermo too. You will only see them in the evening when they come back from the farms," he said. "There is one of the inns!"

She had already discovered it herself. It was the only house with a real window.

"If you don't mind, I'll have a look at it," Bentley said. "The other inns can only be reached on foot."

"I'm coming with you," Helen said.

They entered a small room with a low, curved ceiling, little niches, and lanterns. The chairs and tables were crudely put together and painted dark brown. There were three large windows in the room.

"I'll go look for the owner," Bentley said.

Under the windows was a wooden bench. Helen sat down at the table and looked through one of the windows at the wild mountain landscape with its steep peaks, deep valleys, and lonely roads. If Bentley hadn't been there, she would have been tempted to leave. She heard steps somewhere in the house, voices over her head, a door opening, and then steps on the staircase. A moment later Bentley returned with a little man who spoke softly and gestured broadly. When he saw Helen, he fell silent and looked surprised. His face appeared as if it had been carved out of wood.

"Two double rooms," Bentley said. "I don't think any of the other inns will be any better. We could go on in the car to Nicosia . . ."

"We are staying here," Helen heard herself say.

The three of them climbed a dark staircase to a small corridor with three doors. "You take this one, Mrs. Brazzi," Bentley said. "It has a larger window than the other."

The room was small and clean and the bedding looked neat. On the washtable stood a bowl and pitcher of white enamel; at the window was a table with two chairs. It was better than Helen had expected.

"If you want to bathe, he will bring you a tub and hot water."

"Why is his Italian so strange?" she asked.

"He speaks a dialect."

"Are you taking the room?" the innkeeper asked. He was wearing dark velvet pants, a white shirt, and boots. His little red eyes were barely visible under his bushy eyebrows.

"We will take both," Bentley answered.

The innkeeper looked at them without understanding. "Both double rooms?" he repeated.

Bentley smiled. "Both double rooms. Do you want to eat something, Mrs. Brazzi?"

She was as hungry as she was tired, and she nodded. "In an hour. Would you get me my things?"

"Yes, ma'am."

Bentley left the room. The innkeeper followed him like a shadow.

Alone in the room, Helen lay down on the bed, folded her arms beneath her head, and closed her eyes. She didn't know what she had expected of this trip, and since the night before, she no longer knew how to behave with Bentley.

She heard him on the stairs. He opened the door, brought a suitcase in, set it down beside the closet, and approached the bed.

"I'm afraid he recognized me," he said.

Helen looked at him, surprised. "The innkeeper?"

"When we came to the village two years ago, we stayed here. I immediately remembered his face. By morning the whole village will know."

"That doesn't matter. Tell him that I will pay a thousand dollars to anyone who can tell me anything about my husband."

"You're not serious!" Bentley said.

"Why not?"

"You won't get anywhere that way with these people. I know them."

His resistance annoyed her. "I know them. Don't forget that my husband came from Sicily."

"I haven't forgotten, Mrs. Brazzi, but he hadn't lived here very long."

27

"His parents had. Ten years ago they would have sold me their soul for a thousand dollars. Do as I tell you."

"As you wish, ma'am." Bentley left the room, admiring her in spite of himself. Helen lay on the bed thinking about their conversation. She felt as if she had repeated the lines of a bad play. Smiling at herself, she got up and began to hang her clothes in the closet.

She was still unpacking when Bentley returned with her other suitcases.

"Did you already talk to him?" she asked.

"He doesn't know anything. He claims he's never heard your husband's name."

"I wouldn't have expected anything different. What else?"

Bentley shrugged. "When I asked him whether Salvatore and Pietro had any relatives, he acted as if he didn't know what I was talking about and vanished into the kitchen. There is something wrong there, Mrs. Brazzi."

His tone of voice worried her. She sat down on the bed and looked up at him.

"I told you already," he said, "that we interrogated the families of both—"

"You didn't tell me that," Helen said quickly. "Why do you mention it?"

"We interrogated them and other people in Chiesa. It was war, Mrs. Brazzi. We didn't exactly treat them with kid gloves."

This time she understood. She felt her hands become moist. "Are you afraid?" she asked.

Bentley grinned. "I knew where I was driving with you, Mrs. Brazzi."

She looked thoughtfully at him. "Was either of them married?"

"No."

"That doesn't make it any simpler," she murmured. "Do you mind putting my empty suitcase on the cupboard?"

Bentley did as she asked. The image of her lying on the bed stayed in his mind.

"Do you still need me, Mrs. Brazzi?"

"Later. Thank you very much, Lieutenant. Would you pick me up in half an hour for dinner?"

28

"O.K., ma'am."

Bentley went back to the car and drove it into the shadow of the trees. Both cats had vanished from their place beside the well. As he got out of the car he caught sight of the landlord of the inn hastily climbing the steep path that led into the village. Bentley watched him until he had vanished around the corner of a house; then he took his own luggage out of the car.

In his room he removed his heavy Army pistol from his suitcase and checked to be sure it was loaded. His hands were steady. He felt no fear, but he had decided that it would be an ignominious ending for an officer who had survived the invasion of Sicily, and Monte Casino, to be found dead four months after the war in a dark house in Chiesa. He put the pistol in his pocket. Then he heard Helen's steps next door. He carefully tapped against the wall with his finger. Wood. Compared to what had separated them a week ago, it wasn't much. For the next few minutes he busied himself with his belongings. The door of his closet squeaked. She would hear it as clearly as he heard her. The noises seemed to him like an invisible bridge between them.

He opened the window and looked at the landscape. The hotel stood above a steeply descending mountain edge. Far below he saw the road curve up the mountain. Across the valley the horizon was studded with an almost infinite number of mountaintops, sharply silhouetted against the blue, lightly clouded sky. Somewhere in those mountains, he thought, the bones of Genno Brazzi were lying and it was hopeless to look for him. He had not been a bad soldier. He had been disciplined and withdrawn, almost shy. He must have been at least five years younger than his wife, which was no handicap. He had looked good, the type women like, something different from the red-cheeked young men of Toledo. Possible that a young American girl would have thought him interesting, but it still didn't explain why she had married him. Her father was one of the best known men in town. It wasn't likely that he hadn't resisted his daughter's wild step.

It was time. He washed his hands, put on a clean shirt, and went out into the corridor. Helen was waiting for him outside of the door to her room.

"What's the matter?" she asked when he looked at her without speaking.

Until now he had only seen her in dark dresses with high collars. Now she was wearing a sleeveless orange dress with a low-cut neckline.

"Quite a change," Bentley said. "You should always wear dresses like that."

Without answering, she went down the stairs in front of him.

The innkeeper was waiting for them. He had put on a white apron and was standing in the door of the restaurant. "Are you satisfied, madam?"

Helen nodded. She didn't like the way he looked at her.

A table had been laid, and next to a stone wine bottle stood a vase holding a few flowers.

"He knows what a lady should have," Bentley said. "Perhaps those flowers are what he was after."

"I don't understand," Helen said.

"About an hour ago I saw him running up the path to the village. By the way, his name is Rigido. What would you like to eat, ma'am?"

"What does he have?"

"Spaghetti con Sarde and rice. The rice balls are a specialty of his."

"Let's try them," Helen said.

Signor Rigido smiled, revealing two rows of very bad teeth. "Fish soup?" he asked.

"I can recommend it, Mrs. Brazzi," said Bentley.

Helen sat down and looked at Bentley. "What did you think when you saw him running toward the village?"

"I'm not too sure. If he was just after flowers, he wouldn't have been running."

"We are his only guests," she said.

"Possibly." Bentley picked up the bottle and filled the glasses. "Marsala," he said after he had tasted it. "He serves a good wine, ma'am."

She put her hand on her glass. "I'm very glad that you have come, Lieutenant. Do you have a first name?"

"Two, but Clyde will do."

"All right, Clyde. As long as you are sensible you can call me Helen."

"What do you call sensible?" he asked, trying to hide his disappointment.

"The same thing I told you in Naples; something I should have repeated last night. This is not a pleasure trip for me."

Bentley nodded. "I know what you must think of me, but my feelings are more than you suspect."

"More than what?"

"More than the usual."

"It's always only the usual," Helen said. "If it weren't the usual, you wouldn't have been in such a hurry. Or do you always kiss women the first day you meet them?"

He wasn't so much hurt by being regarded in this light as by her ironical tone of voice. Worse, his motives looked cheap, and he knew it.

"If I remember right," he said in an annoyed tone of voice, "you didn't want me to go back to Naples yesterday. Perhaps you didn't mind what I did as much as you do now."

She looked coolly at him. "I don't know why you tell that to yourself, Lieutenant. I haven't discovered anything in you so far that would make you irresistible to any halfway civilized woman."

Bentley stood up. "There's only one answer to that," he said and left the dining room.

She hadn't wanted that. She had been trying to barricade herself against both him and her feelings, behind a wall of resentment and coolness. She had overshot her target. She couldn't risk his going back to Naples and leaving her alone in Chiesa. Without him she felt helpless and uncertain of herself in these strange and primitive surroundings. And as long as she didn't have definite proof that he was responsible for the death of her husband, the inner conflict which meeting him had created in her would become steadily more unbearable. She had to find out the degree of Bentley's responsibility as quickly as possible. It seemed to her now as if this was even more urgent than learning the actual fate of her husband. She sat at the table and considered this until she was sure of her feelings. Then she got up and went to Bentley's room.

She found him packing. Pushing the door shut behind her, she stood and looked at him.

"You want to leave with the car?" she asked.

Bentley didn't answer.

"Don't forget that I paid for it," she said. "You would get into trouble, Lieutenant."

He shrugged.

"It isn't fair, Clyde. You know that I need your help."

"You knew that before, too." Bentley said. He had everything in his suitcase now and closed it.

She went toward him and stood so close to him that he could feel her breath on his face. "I didn't mean to hurt you, Clyde," she said quietly.

There was a vague scent of perfume around her; her face was pale and quiet. His mind commanded his hands and feet, but they would not obey him. He tried to look away from her, but her eyes held him. He stood in front of her bound in a web of contradictory feelings. When he put his face on her shoulder, he disliked himself, but he could not help himself.

# 5

After lunch Helen pleaded a headache and disappeared. Since the village lay at an altitude of twenty-five hundred feet, it seemed plausible.

Bentley spent the afternoon in his room. He started a letter to his parents but didn't finish it. From his window he watched the peasants return from their fields, riding on mules and horses without reins, huddled figures, dark and silent as the landscape behind them. Between them walked the women wrapped up in black clothes.

The steady clatter of feet on the cobblestoned street must have wakened Helen, because he heard her bed creak as beds did in all hotel rooms from Chiesa to Palermo to Naples.

Half an hour later she knocked on his door. He had anticipated it, but he waited a short while before he opened it.

"I would like to see the village," she said.

Bentley only had to put on his jacket. She looked at him. Something seemed to have changed about him but she could not pinpoint what.

The way out led through the restaurant. At a table there were now four men playing cards. Their unshaven faces looked inimical. None of them looked at Helen and Bentley. The innkeeper wasn't around.

"They are just here to watch us," Helen said.

Bentley nodded. "Don't show anything."

At the door he gave a quick look back and saw four pairs of eyes focused on him. The innkeeper was standing in the door of the kitchen. Bentley didn't mention it to Helen as they climbed the narrow street that ended in the narrow labyrinth of alleys flanked by dark, decrepit houses, piles of garbage, and gray stone arches.

They passed many people who walked by without greeting them or showing curiosity. Men in black on horses, some with rifles on their backs; women and children bent under heavy burdens; girls of striking beauty carrying water jars, their breasts sharply delineated. In front of the houses between half-naked children and pigs and goats covered with mud, old men were sitting wrapped in dark coats. Mules loaded with firewood labored up the narrow streets. From the open doors came a smell of wood fire, spoiled milk, and urine; a mixture of poverty, dirt, and dark little streets which led finally to the wall of a house.

"Pietro lived here," Bentley said and pointed to a house that looked as dark and decrepit as the others. "He has two brothers and five sisters. It looks as if he isn't living here anymore. Don't stop. That would draw attention."

"I want to draw attention," Helen said. "Where did Salvatore live?"

"He lived higher up . . . in a cave. You will see it. Do you want me to ask after Pietro's family?"

Helen nodded. Where they were walking the street was not more than six feet wide. Gradually men and women began to appear in the doors of the houses, looking at them steadily and quietly. Helen felt the palms of her hands growing moist again. She looked at Bentley. He had stopped to talk with an old man who was crouched on the ground a few feet away holding a homemade cigarette between his lips. His eyes stared into space.

"That's what I was afraid of," Bentley said, coming back to her. "They have moved."

"Where to?"

"He doesn't know."

"Let's try Salvatore," Helen said.

Bentley touched her arm. "I don't think you will get anywhere this way. People know exactly why we are here now. Just look at their faces."

"Someone will talk," Helen said. "I will pay him well enough to get him out of this terrible place."

Her words betrayed feelings which she had hidden behind her apparent indifference since they had left the inn. She was now in a sudden hurry to leave the gallery of dark and inscrutable faces behind her. Only when they came to the next side road did she slow her pace.

"I had a feeling they were going to kill us," she said. "I guess I'm hysterical."

Bentley smiled. "I had the same feeling, and I'm not hysterical. What did you expect, flowers?"

"We didn't do anything to them."

"You didn't."

"Then it was a mistake to bring you along."

"It's too late, ma'am," Bentley said and took her arm. She did not pull away.

The steep steps in the street led under an archway and ended at the base of a vertical wall of rock with doors, windows, and balconies, at some places four stories on top of each other. Helen looked from the wall to Bentley.

34

"What is that?"

"The caves," Bentley said. "They've carved the rock into a regular beehive. Don't be fooled by the windows. They're stuck on. It's pitch-dark inside."

He pushed a door open. Behind it was blackness. When her eyes adjusted, she could make out a crude stairway which seemed to lead to a higher story. "Most of them aren't inhabited anymore," Bentley said. "The government has made them illegal. But it would take two days to search through all of them. They have cross-connections and corridors. Once you're inside you can't get out without a compass."

"Did Salvatore have brothers or sisters?"

"Three. His two brothers were killed in the war. The sister should be about twenty now."

"Please take me to him," Helen said.

Bentley smiled. "You do impress me; you're not easily intimidated."

"You may be a good soldier," Helen said, "but you don't understand much about women."

They followed the road along the base of the wall of rock. It was stony and steep, and led away from the houses. Along its opposite side was an abyss, in which agaves and aloes were growing. Their leaves looked like bared swords.

Further on there were fewer caves. The rock was wilder. The wind had risen; it blew the clouds together into huge balls. Shadows filled the valley.

"It doesn't look as if people still live here," Helen said.

Bentley laughed. "You'd be surprised. When strangers appear, the people make themselves invisible. They may think we've been sent here by the government."

"Are they punished?"

"When they're caught. In the twentieth century, Italy cannot afford to have cave dwellers. Think of Michelangelo."

"I was thinking of the houses in the village."

"Nobody in Rome thinks about them. It's a matter of individual achievement. I am an American and I don't feel responsible. Do you feel responsible?"

"Not personally," Helen said. "Where are you leading me?"

"We're there. It's better that I go in alone first."

Helen looked at the exterior of a cave that stood before them. The entrance was at the level of the road and sealed with a wooden door. If it hadn't been for the rock wall rising above it, it would have looked like a little house. Over the door was a small hole from which blue smoke billowed.

"Somebody lives here," Bentley said. "Perhaps the right people. What did you want to say to them?"

She didn't know yet. She didn't have a definite plan, but she had a thick wad of bank notes in her pocketbook.

"Something will come to me," she said.

Bentley nodded. "I hope it will be the right thing."

He had regained his self-assurance during the last fifteen minutes. As he opened the door he put his right hand in the pocket of his trousers.

Helen didn't have to wait long; he came back so quickly that she was ready for a disappointment. Then she saw his face. He smiled contentedly.

"She is there. Her mother too, and a young man. Perhaps she is married to him."

It was a big cave, cut out of the rock in the shape of a cupola and full of smoke. When Helen's eyes got used to the dark, she was able to make out the inhabitants and the way it was furnished. Next to a big stove stood a woman in black who was putting corncobs into the hot ashes. From a rusty chain suspended from a wooden arm above the stove hung pots and pans. Next to the stove, on a kind of platform of wood, tomatoes, cheeses, and corn were stored.

The young man sat on a bed covered with goatskins. It was made of raw wood. Next to it were a big wooden baking trough, wobbly, dirty chairs, benches, and a table. A wooden wall divided the room in two. Half a dozen goats were penned in the smaller half. In the back a small passageway led to a second cave. From a rusty hook on the wall hung a Madonna statue and two shotguns; apart from these the walls were bare.

Helen turned toward the girl who was standing in the middle of the room, facing the door, in a posture that expressed fear and suspicion.

"I would suggest that you talk to her outside," Bentley said. "We can't stay in here very long."

Helen nodded. The smoke had already brought tears to her eyes.

"Leave it to me," Bentley said. "I'll bring her outside. Do you also want to talk to the mother?"

"No. I don't expect much from her," Helen said.

Outside, she took a deep breath. Goats were new to her, especially their smell.

Moments later Bentley came out with the young girl; the young man came too, staring at his hands.

"Her name is Piera," Bentley said to Helen confidentially. "Look at her dress. It is certainly not cheap."

It had struck Helen already in the cave. She had only seen such dresses in Naples and Palermo. The girl looked older than twenty; her figure was that of a woman of twenty-five. She had a beautiful regular face with black eyes and a full mouth. On her wrist she was wearing a golden bracelet, undoubtedly worth a fortune in Chiesa.

"How beautiful," Helen said to the girl, indicating the bracelet. "Where did you get that?"

"From my fiancé."

Helen looked at the young man. He was poorly dressed, had an indifferent, rather stupid face and very dirty hands.

"Shall I send him back in?" Bentley asked.

"He doesn't bother me." Helen turned again to the girl. "I want you to give a message to your brother," she said.

"I don't know where he is," the girl answered.

"Of course you know," Helen said. "I live at Signor Rigido's and I would like to talk with your brother. He shall send me word where I can meet him. Will you tell him that?"

"I can't, signora," the girl said. "We haven't seen Salvatore in three years."

"Because the carabinieri are looking for him. But I am not a carabiniere." Helen opened her pocketbook and took out a packet of bank notes. "Here are five thousand dollars," she said. "Do you know how much money that is?"

The girl nodded.

"How do you know?"

"I don't know," the girl said quickly.

Helen smiled. "Your brother will know. If he tells me a place to meet him, I will come alone and there won't be any carabinieri."

"They have sent you," the girl said inimically.

"Who?"

"The carabinieri who live in the town hall."

Helen looked at Bentley, who hadn't taken his eyes off the girl. "Do you understand that?"

"Not quite. Ask her how long the carabinieri have been here."

"For eight days," the girl said in reply to Helen's question.

"I have only been here for two days," Helen said. "I have neither been sent by the carabinieri nor talked to them. I don't know any of them. What do they want here?"

The girl didn't answer.

"Fine," Helen said. "Whatever they are looking for, I am not interested in. I want to talk to your brother, and when I have talked to him, I will give him five thousand dollars. That's all, Piera."

She put the money back in her pocketbook and said to Bentley, "I think we can go."

"I think so too," Bentley said and looked at the sky. The sun was already low over the mountains. "Back to the inn?"

"Where does this road lead to?"

"To the castle."

"Let's have a quick look at it," Helen said. "I need some air."

"I do too," Bentley said.

After walking about fifty feet, Bentley looked back. Piera and the young man were still standing in front of the cave. The mother was with them too now. They were staring after Helen and Bentley without expressions on their faces.

"I don't think he'll show," Bentley said. "With the carabinieri after him. . . . Perhaps Piera has given away more than she wanted to."

"Why?"

"I was just thinking," Bentley said, evading her question. He laughed. "You should have been a lawyer; you caught her nicely. Where did you learn that?"

Helen didn't answer. She felt like an actress after her first performance.

The road ended at the foot of some steps which seemed to ascend endlessly and steeply toward the gray ruins of a castle.

"Can you still make that?" Bentley asked, indicating the steps.

She didn't answer. "Did the girl recognize you?"

"I guess so. Her mother certainly did."

"You prove to be more and more of a stumbling block for me," Helen said and stopped walking. She turned to look at the village, deep below her. It appeared as a picturesque sea of roofs from which, like a giant bubble, the dome of a baroque church swelled toward the sky.

"Earlier today you thought differently," Bentley said. "Would you like to get rid of me?"

"You could wait for me somewhere," Helen mused. She hadn't forgiven herself for following him to his room, and now she wished, half consciously, to weaken the impression she must have made on him by doing so.

Bentley remained quiet. He had decided not to take her sudden moods too seriously anymore. "I could," he said. "But do you really think I would leave you alone in Chiesa?"

"You planned to, this afternoon."

"I didn't know what you were going to do then. I couldn't let you risk your head."

"That's crazy," Helen said impatiently. "What gives you the idea I'm risking my head?"

"It could also be called suicide," Bentley answered. He hadn't expected much to come from Helen's meeting with the girl, but now he suddenly saw an opportunity of making himself indispensable to her.

"Perhaps Salvatore will not let the five thousand dollars escape him," he said. "But he may not let you escape either. From now on I won't leave you alone for another minute."

"You are ridiculous," Helen said and started up the steps. He had scared her more with his words than she wanted to admit.

At the top of the steps they came to an arch with an indecipherable inscription on it. Across a decrepit bridge they entered the inner part of the castle of which only a few walls remained. The ground was carpeted with tall, thin blades of grass. From this point they could see almost the entire island—mountain chains and mountaintops in the soft red of the sunset; white roads and gleaming rivers; and to the east the snowy point of Etna.

"You don't look very impressed," Bentley said, wiping his face. "Perhaps it's tactless to ask you if you are ever impressed by anything outside yourself."

"I'm impressed by your lack of tact," Helen answered and looked around for a spot to sit.

"Take my jacket," Bentley said. He spread it in the tall grass and watched her while she sat down on it and opened her pocketbook. She took out a cigarette and put the open pocketbook on the grass next to her.

"Do you always carry your money with you?" Bentley asked.

"Do you know a better place?"

Bentley grinned. "No, not for you." He sat beside her and looked around him at the old walls. "Ruins awe me," he said, "They make me feel small. Lewis once said 'they make you feel the breath of eternity.' "

"Who is Lewis?" Helen asked.

"Somebody who once existed. Did you ever think about it: why people are so crazy about their cultural monuments?"

"Not much," Helen answered.

"I did. When we were finished fighting in Sicily, we visited the temples in Agrigento. After, I understood why people need such things. They reaffirm existence; people flee from their own lack of importance behind cultural monuments. They write long theses in order to achieve eternity, if only by the back stairs, because they have helped decide what is eternal."

"And where are you fleeing to?" Helen asked.

She was sitting so close to him that he could once more smell her perfume. He looked at her with a smile. "Behind you. I like you, your face, your hands, and your way of being. I know I won't be the same man because of knowing you."

To Helen it was probably the strangest confession ever made by a man. She carefully put out her cigarette in the grass.

"Do you always speak that way?" she asked.

"Only to you." Bentley answered. In truth, he had never before met a woman to whom he could have said a thing like that. "I think you're more remarkable than the temples of Agrigento," he said. "But nobody will write a thesis about you. People of all generations have gotten writer's cramp over the temples of Agrigento. Perhaps they will write as much one day about the Lincoln Tunnel or the Empire State Building, when the temples are no longer fashionable. They will always find something to look at with awe, even cemeteries, but none of them will write about you."

"That's terrible," Helen said. And for a moment she caught herself thinking that it really was.

Bentley lay back in the grass and looked at the high empty sky over the castle.

"It is indeed terrible," he said. "And it's even more terrible that one knows it's terrible. Do you remember how you looked when you were a little girl?"

His sudden tack amused her. "More or less."

"With pigtails," he said. The picture of her suddenly came to him. He started to laugh.

Helen frowned. "Why is it so funny?"

"I guess the thought seems incongruous," he said vaguely. "You know, the years between five and ten are the only ones I would like to live again. Something was especially impressive to me during that period—maybe my first ice skates. I think girls between five and ten are at their sweetest. After that they become silly geese."

"That's a bit harsh," Helen said with a smile.

Bentley shrugged. "What do you want? When they're geese they're harmless, at least. When girls reach seventeen, they become dangerous, especially for men over fifty. They become the embodiment of missed chances. They represent the past, the way the temples of Agrigento do. And when they are thirty, they begin to become dangerous for men of any age."

"Like me?"

"Like you . . . for me," Bentley said, and reached up and put his hands on her shoulders. He pulled her back toward him, turned her around, and kissed her. He touched her face, her back, and suddenly his senses whirled. When he cupped his hands over her breasts, she stiffened, jumped up, and walked away from him.

Bentley remained on the ground. He hadn't wanted it to happen. Not here. He had simply lost control and now he was regaining it, especially when he noticed her pocketbook, which had spilled, and saw the pistol which was lying among her things.

"Why did you bring that?" he asked quietly.

At first she didn't know what he was talking about, and then she saw what he was looking at. She moved so quickly that he couldn't have stopped her if he had wanted to. She put the pistol and the other things back in her pocketbook, closed it, and turned her back to him. Her hair was messed up and her face pale.

Bentley stood up, thinking that he had misjudged her. And yet she hadn't resisted him at all during that first minute. He lit a cigarette and watched the sun, which was beginning to sink behind the mountains.

"You have two choices," he said. "You can send me away. Or you can forgive me for wanting you very much."

"Perhaps there is a third possibility," Helen said.

Bentley turned toward her. She was sitting on a section of wall, looking in her pocketbook.

"I don't have any more cigarettes," she said.

Bentley mused that any other woman in her place would have worried about her appearance first. He walked to her and gave her a cigarette.

"Do you want me to go back to Naples?" he asked.

"No."

"Why not?"

She didn't answer.

Bentley sat down beside her. "Even if I want you, I'm not crazy enough to think that you packed that pistol for fun, and you can't tell me either that you are going to give five thousand dollars to the man who killed your husband."

"How do you know my husband isn't alive?"

"Is that why you're here?"

"Why else?"

"Then I can't help you," Bentley said.

The air had become cool from the gathering fog, which was beginning to obscure the landscape. Only Etna remained clear against the horizon.

"You can't understand," Helen said. "The time since my husband disappeared has seemed like two years in the waiting room of a railway station. I couldn't stand it anymore at the end."

"Other women have to stand it."

"I'm not interested in what other women have to do."

"That is not your only mistake," Bentley said. "He was just a man."

"At least he wasn't after my money," Helen said.

Nothing could have hurt Bentley more. "I know he wasn't after your money," he said in a hoarse voice as he stood up. "He just married you for love, even though you were five years older, and even though, after he joined our outfit in Tunisia, he went to a soldier's brothel every night. For love of you."

He was sorry he said it even before he had finished. He would have liked to bite off his tongue.

"Who says that?" she asked, her face going pale.

"I'm sorry. It doesn't have to be true," Bentley mumbled in despair. "I only heard it the day before yesterday."

"Who told you?" she asked, still very pale.

Bentley sat down again beside her and put his hand on her arm. "I told you it doesn't have to be true, and if he did once or twice . . ."

"I asked you how you know," Helen repeated. Her tone of voice was even harder to stand than the expression in her eyes.

Thinking that he had made his second unforgivable mistake, he said angrily, "from a man who saw it."

"And you didn't?"

"I was his company commander. If I had bothered about the personal lives of all my men . . .

"If you didn't bother, you didn't know," she said, throwing her cigarette on the ground and extinguishing it with a twist of her foot. She stood up and turned to leave.

"Idiot," Bentley hissed at himself.

# 6

Helen had stayed in her room with the door locked for twenty-four hours and refused to answer Bentley's knocking. He told the innkeeper that she wasn't feeling well. When she came down to dinner that evening, he had the worst day and the worst night of his life behind him. Her face was composed and indifferent, as before. She asked him if he had already eaten dinner and when he said no, she suggested that they have it served in her room.

Bentley went to tell the innkeeper. He didn't feel like eating in the restaurant anyway. It was full of noisy men playing cards and drinking wine from large bottles, but as Bentley walked in it became as silent as a church.

After he had talked to the innkeeper, he returned to his room, changed, and stood at the window for a while. Ever since he had learned that she was carrying a pistol, he had worried. He had lain awake half the night. Now he thought he knew what he had to do. When he heard the innkeeper on the stairs, he went to her room.

Rigido served tuna fish, spaghetti with sardines, and a cheese plate. He was a bit more loquacious than he had been the day before; he recommended a white wine from Monte Erice and asked after Helen's health.

Helen just nodded in reply. She didn't speak much during dinner either. She ate little, although Bentley knew she hadn't eaten breakfast, and she drank much more. When Rigido came to take the dishes away, she had finished two glasses of the heavy wine.

Bentley watched the innkeeper put the dishes on a tray. "You're not from here," he said to him.

Rigido shook his head. "I took over from my brother-in-law, Signor Bentley. I used to live in Catania."

"But do you know the area around here?" Bentley asked.

"I only worry about my guests," the innkeeper said.

Bentley gave up and shifted his tack. "Do you have many guests?"

"Before the war, signore. But the last five years, nothing doing."

"It's going to be better again," Bentley said. "We've heard that there are carabinieri here."

"I don't know anything about that," Rigido said, and bade them good night.

Bentley smiled. "He's an even better liar than Piera. Tomorrow I am going to the carabinieri and have a talk with them."

"No, you won't," Helen said. "If Piera's brother hears about that, he will think that we are involved with them."

"Are you still going to talk to him?"

"Yes."

Bentley looked at her across the table. The neck of her blouse was cut so low that he could see where her breasts rose. The faded light of the electric bulb made her look pale and tired.

"I have another suggestion," Bentley said. "Why don't you go back to Toledo?"

"Are you scared?"

"Not for myself. Shall I tell you what will happen if you go on like this?"

"I am not curious," Helen said, and lit a cigarette.

"I don't believe you," Bentley said. "You can't be indifferent to the idea of being as dead as your husband within a week. As long as I am with you, I'm going to try to prevent that."

He stood up and went to the bed, where her pocketbook was lying. Realizing what he was going to do, she came after him, but she was too late. He removed the magazine from her pistol, put the pistol back in her pocketbook, and turned toward her. Her face was distorted with anger. When she tried to take the magazine out of his hand, he gave her a push which made her fall back on the bed.

"You always make the same mistake," he said. "I may not understand anything about women, but they don't understand any more about men. Don't forget; I'm stronger than you."

*45*

He put the magazine in his pocket, went to the table, and filled a glass with wine. He drank it off in one gulp. For the first time in three days he felt satisfied with himself.

He had become warm. He opened the window and looked out for a few seconds at the sky; then he turned again toward Helen.

She was laying on her stomach, her face buried in the pillow. He walked over to her and sat down beside her. "I am responsible for you," he said quietly. "I'll take you back in one piece to Naples, even if they court-martial me for it. You'll be grateful one day."

"You will go back to Naples before me," Helen said and stood up. She hadn't cried. She looked almost gay. Perhaps he would never learn to predict her reactions. As far as she was concerned he most certainly did not understand much about women. Marriage with her would certainly never be monotonous.

He watched her as she closed the door, removed the key, and quietly walked to the window.

"I think you are intelligent enough to know what I am talking about," she said. "If you don't give me back the magazine of my pistol, I will throw the key out of the window."

"That's an original idea," Bentley said, astonished. "What do you think it will accomplish?"

"There'll be a little scandal. When the innkeeper hears my cry, he will find the door locked. He will call the carabinieri. The carabinieri will call the military police, and tomorrow evening you will be back in Naples."

Bentley became serious. "That's something from a movie," he said. "Nobody would believe it."

"You forget who I am," she answered coolly. "I leave you exactly enough time to put the magazine back on the table."

After all he had been through with her, he readily took her at her word. He took a moment to consider the situation. He could be a good loser, because he was a fair man and he admired anyone who was cleverer than he. Moreover, in this case he was more afraid of being separated from her than of the seriousness of her threat.

He took the magazine out of his pocket and put it on the table. "You win," he said. "Where did you learn that?"

"In the movies," Helen said. "Also I was corrupted at an early age. I guess you realize that I could always do this again."

Bentley nodded. "Don't worry, you win."

"You can never be sure with a man," Helen said. Yet she felt so sure of herself that she didn't bother to put the magazine away. She sat down at the table and quickly drank two glasses of wine. When she reached to pour a third one, Bentley moved the glass away.

"Do you often get drunk?" he asked.

"Don't talk to me that way. Why are you still in my room?"

"I enjoy talking with you," Bentley said, humoring her. "I never enjoyed talking with a woman so much. You said just now you were corrupted at an early age."

"Does that surprise you?"

"Knowing you now, it does," Bentley answered. "You hardly seem corrupt."

She shrugged. "You only know me as McShane's daughter. Before he came to the Rojas-Overland Corporation he was unemployed for a year. People still talk about that. I didn't grow up in high society."

Her tone of voice surprised Bentley. "Aren't you liked by Toledo society?"

"Are you?"

He grinned. "I'm not the daughter of McShane. But I'd think people would look up to you. I admire your father, and I know his story as well as anyone else's in Toledo. How he started as an engineer in Detroit, how he was moved to Toledo, and how he introduced some radical ideas to the business. People started watching him. He's among the few people I admired when I was young. I still admire him."

"I do too," Helen said in a tone of voice which didn't make quite clear what she meant. She was silent for a moment. "Shortly after his third promotion he had a car accident. It wasn't his fault. My mother was sitting beside him."

Bentley nodded. He had heard about it. "How old were you?"

"Sixteen."

"That's bad," Bentley said. "Too old not to understand and too young to handle it. He didn't marry again?"

"No. And I would never have forgiven him. I had a governess.

47

After a while I found out that she was bringing her boy friend into the house behind my father's back. I used to spy on them until after a few weeks she caught me at it and offered me fifty dollars not to tell my father."

"I was just wondering why you hadn't told him before," Bentley said carefully.

Helen looked at her hands. "I was seventeen. I was a little animal and I was curious. First I thought that she was going to look for another job, but I didn't want that. She was more or less in my power and I used it. I threatened to tell my father why she wanted to leave. She wouldn't have gotten another job as a governess, and she was still young. She must have felt trapped."

Helen took her glass back and Bentley didn't stop her.

"Perhaps it's better not to talk about these things," he murmured.

"You wanted to have a conversation!" she said. "I wouldn't tell you if a few hundred people didn't already know. What would you have done if you had been the governess?"

"I'm not a woman," Bentley said. "Perhaps I would have killed you?"

"She did better," Helen said. "She made me her accomplice. One day when my father was on a trip she gave a birthday party for her boy friend and she invited me. They gave me so much to drink that I didn't know what I was doing anymore, and I . . . I joined them."

"My God," Bentley said.

She looked at him with a grimace. "Why not? Later I liked it."

Bentley looked at her dubiously.

"That's the way it goes," Helen said thickly. "He was fourteen years older than I and very experienced. Everything was all right until my father caught us. He beat them both up, and he sent me to a boarding school for difficult girls."

"He should have sent you there right after the accident," Bentley said.

"He didn't want to be separated from me. When I came back from boarding school there was another governess, an old lady. After a year I began to feel like I was in a prison. My father had less time for me. He left everything to the governess."

"I can imagine her type," Bentley murmured. "It must have been bad."

She looked at him without expression. "You just wait. Two years later my father brought a young man to the house. Nice, rich family; good college. I liked him, we became friends until suddenly he stopped coming. It turned out that my father considered it his duty to tell him about my 'past.' The young man didn't want that kind of a girl for a wife."

"What a fool," Bentley said with disgust. "Was he the one who spread the story?"

"He certainly told his family and his family told their friends; they had to explain why the engagement was broken. They couldn't make them think there was something wrong with their nice son. So the story spread and in the end my father's friends found out too. It gave them a chance to get even with me, because they had always felt that I didn't quite take them seriously, and they didn't like that."

Helen walked over to the bed. "I have a headache," she said. She lay down and put her hands behind her head.

"That's when you met your husband?" he asked.

"Two years later. He worked in an office in my father's firm. By that time my father had made it. He used to send his employees to the house on errands."

"Genno Brazzi," Bentley said softly. He was becoming the first dead man Bentley had ever hated.

"He told me about Sicily," Helen said. "It didn't take long before we started meeting outside the house and at his home."

"The boss's daughter," Bentley said.

"So what?"

He realized he had made another mistake and he tried to take the sting out of his remark. "I mean, that didn't make it any simpler for you."

"It didn't make any difference," she said coolly. "When I told my father that I would marry him or no one, he agreed. Perhaps he felt that he had to make up for something. Genno was ambitious and intelligent. He would have made it without connections."

"If it hadn't been for the war?"

"Yes."

"Now I understand more," Bentley said.

She laughed contemptuously, "That's what my father thought. I know what you're thinking, but you're wrong. If it had been only sex, I wouldn't have married."

"People often tell themselves that," Bentley said.

He took a sip from his glass, went over to the bed, and sat beside her. "I'd say it's a good point of departure. It's about as important as anything else. After all, what did you have to talk about? Sicily?"

"You have a disgusting character," Helen said.

"I didn't choose it," Bentley said. "I'm surprised that you still allow me to be here."

She didn't answer.

"You must have a reason," Bentley went on. "You never do anything without a reason. Or do you just keep me here to pity you?"

"You're a fool, Clyde."

Bentley smiled. "To each his own, Helen."

When he touched her it was only because he wanted her to forget her husband. She wasn't quite drunk, but she wasn't quite sober either. He sensed that she knew that what she had told him would upset any man but that it would also make her more desirable. She was a somewhat desperate woman—desperate enough to carry a pistol in her handbag; perhaps obsessed enough to shoot somebody, maybe herself. Bentley wasn't quite clear on the degree of her feelings. Nevertheless, she had put all her cards on the table, and in the morning she would be sorry she had.

She allowed him to kiss her, to open her blouse, and to fondle her breasts. For that, too, she would probably never forgive him. At that moment he was still aware that it wasn't fair to exploit her passing mood; that she wouldn't forgive him or herself. For a few minutes of pleasure he would be throwing away a unique chance. Unique if she were the woman he guessed she was behind her cold mask—

But suddenly, Bentley's doubts no longer mattered. Nothing mattered except his burning curiosity, the excitement of discovery, endless discovery. The blind feeling, the thrilling touch of nylon and of her soft hair. Then nothing existed except the sweet fragrance of her hair, the strange and soft fragrance of her body—the blend of perfume and her powder. Nothing existed except the overwhelming, all-devouring lust to lay bare, to touch, to see. Nothing mattered, until he lay beside her and she looked at him with a strange mixture of hate, fear, and curiosity.

And then she said, "Hopkins told me that he is on your conscience."

"Who is on my conscience?"

"My husband, and eight others with him."

He had suspected that she thought this from the first moment he had met her. Now he knew. He lay beside her a few more seconds, then he took his hands off her and stood up. He went to the table, emptied his glass, and looked at it. "How much did you pay him for that?" he asked.

She didn't answer him. She hadn't stirred. He covered her with the sheet and carried the empty glass to the table.

"If you want it in writing from me," he said, "I'll have to disappoint you."

"I want to hear it from you."

"And then?"

"That's all."

Bentley nodded. "It's well paid for, but I have to disappoint you all the same."

"The key is on the table," she said. "Tomorrow morning we are going to Palmigano."

"What do you think that will accomplish?" Bentley asked.

She didn't answer. He went to the door and unlocked it. "When do you want to go?"

"I'll let you know," Helen said.

"Just knock on the wall."

"The same goes for you," Helen said coldly.

Bentley grinned. He went out, closed the door behind him, and leaned back against it.

Most people visited Taormina, or the ruins of the Greek theater, or the Temple of Himera. But she wanted to visit Palmigano. The last time Bentley had seen it, it had been a smoking pile of ruins.

# 7

When Bentley returned to her room, she had already had her breakfast. She called him in and asked him where he had been.

"I went for a walk," Bentley said. "I thought you were still asleep. I knocked on your door before I left."

She looked at him. "You didn't. I heard you get up and leave the inn."

"Then I must have forgotten," he answered. Her room had already been cleaned. Through the open window he could see the mountains, silvery clear in the morning sun. He sat down at the table and looked up at her. She seemed more beautiful to him than ever before. "I've been to the carabinieri, you'll be delighted to know."

"I told you not to go to the carabinieri," she said sharply.

"True, but aside from the fact that I didn't feel bound by that, I think that after what I've heard, I worked in your interest."

She sat down across the table from him. She wasn't acting any differently than usual; it seemed as if last night had never happened. Perhaps nothing *had* happened. He had let himself be fooled, and knowing now how she looked without clothes on didn't help him very much. On the contrary, everything seemed even more hopeless.

"Two weeks ago," he began, "there was a bank holdup in Nicosia. Four men. They killed a clerk, but then the carabinieri chased them. First they fled in a truck, and then between Cerami and Palmigano they switched to horses and escaped to the mountains."

"Is that all?"

Bentley looked at the tablecloth. "Those are the bare facts. Some people said that the men were armed with M-1's."

"That's very interesting," Helen said impatiently. "Perhaps you can tell me what an M-1 is."

"It's a semiautomatic carbine. We used them in 1943."

She looked at him. "Who are *we?*"

"Our Army," Bentley answered. "It's an American Army rifle."

This time she reacted. The frown on her forehead was deeper than he had ever seen it, and she did not move for a full minute.

"There's something else," he said. "The carabinieri think that it was the same bunch that robbed a jewelry store in Cefalù a few weeks ago. It's been the fourth successful holdup within a year. Since the local people can't deal with them, they sent for the carabinieri from Palermo. They are posted in Chiesa, Palmigano, and Cerami. . . ."

"A jewelry store?" Helen remarked.

Bentley realized she wasn't listening to him anymore. She looked distracted. She went to the window and stared out, then she walked to the cupboard and finally she sat down again.

"Did you tell the carabinieri why we're here?"

"I thought I'd better."

"Did you also tell them about Piera?"

"No, and not about the bracelet either, if that's what you're getting at."

"That's what I was getting at," Helen said. For the first time since she had arrived on Italian soil she felt excitement. "If it turns out that your talking to the carabinieri was a mistake, I will send you back to Naples. I promise you that."

"I don't think it was a mistake," Bentley said. "The girl made a mistake when she suspected us of having sent for the carabinieri. That let us know that there's a connection between her brother and the gang. That's more than I had hoped for yesterday. The lieutenant of the carabinieri would like to meet you; his name is Gastone, and he plans to call on you this evening."

Helen frowned. "What gave him that idea?"

"He is curious," Bentley said with a smile. "He is an ambitious man and he speaks perfect English. He thinks that the gang is hidden somewhere in the mountains here; if he knew what we knew, he

*53*

would hang Piera and her mother upside down from a tree until they told them where the gang is hidden."

"Only you could tell him about the connection," Helen said.

"I don't think it would serve any purpose. As far as I can tell, that gang won't take any risks. They won't be stupid enough to make their security depend on a young girl."

"Four men, you said?" Helen asked distractedly.

Bentley shrugged. "There could be more. One must have brought the horses. The truck was stolen two weeks ago in Palermo, which shows that it was well plotted. If their bank robbery was fouled up by the carabinieri, I guess they would like to lay their hands on five thousand dollars now."

"I think you're right," Helen said.

He looked at her. The memory of the evening before had become abstract in the light of day.

"What are you going to do?" he asked.

She stared past him. "Nothing."

"I'd be surprised," Bentley said. "Did you sleep well?"

"Why do you ask?"

"Is it so unusual to ask?"

"When you ask it. Had you expected me to sleep badly?"

Her tone of voice irritated him. "Not really," he said with bitterness. After his good news, he had hoped she would be more kindly disposed to him.

"As far as I can judge it," she said coolly, "you had a good time last night. You were free to end your amusement in the usual way."

"Maybe that's not the way I want you."

"That's your problem."

The whole business had become so confusing to Bentley that he could no longer find a way out. He had hardly slept the night before and he felt exhausted and depressed.

"Hopkins is a stupid fool," he said. "Major Green can testify that it was not my fault."

"I believe Major Green as much as I believe you."

"Did Hopkins tell you about him too?"

"Why don't you ask him yourself?"

"Because he's in the United States," Bentley said and stood up. He walked around the table and took her face between his hands. He kissed her mouth and her eyes. Then he knelt before her on the floor, put his head in her lap, and moved his hands along her thighs and her legs. He began to lose awareness of what he was doing.

"Why don't you shoot me if you think it was my fault that he was killed?" he muttered.

"I think you will shoot yourself," Helen said.

Bentley looked up incredulously. She was staring him full in the face with the same expression of hate, curiosity, and fear that she had had the day before.

"Did you take me along for that?" he asked.

She nodded. "You would have found out anyway."

Bentley walked to his room but he couldn't think clearly. He smoked two cigarettes but it didn't help. Finally he started to pack. After half an hour he still wasn't ready. He started again and realized he was being clumsy on purpose. Then he gave up. He sat down on his bed beside his suitcase and looked at the door.

For the first minute he had hoped she would come after him as she had the day before. Then, out of pride, he had gone on packing. But now he was drained of pride. It was too late for him to run away and she knew it. Nothing she had done or not done during those three days had been without purpose, and now she had almost reached her goal. There was no point in fooling himself about that. He waited another two minutes and then he went back to her room. She was still sitting at the table in the position he had left her.

At first Helen had been mad when she heard him returning, but then she began to feel uncertain again: the same feeling of uncertainty which had come over her the evening before. She would have been glad now if he had left, but she no longer had the strength to send him away.

"Did you think it over?" she said without looking at him.

"I need you. I don't care what you want of me."

"Then we will now go to Palmigano," Helen said. "Please wait for me downstairs."

The only person in the restaurant was Rigido. He was reading his paper. When Bentley came in he put it aside.

"Beautiful weather, signore," he said. "Going out?"

"A little trip," Bentley said sourly. "You don't have to wait for us for dinner. Do you run the restaurant alone?"

"Since my wife died, signore. It doesn't pay to have help."

"A bit lonely," Bentley said.

Rigido walked to the door with him. "Not too bad, Signor Bentley. Everyone is alone here. Where are you going? To Palermo?"

Rigido hadn't shaved yet, and his wooden face looked sleepy and uglier than usual. Bentley offered him a cigarette.

"We are going to Palmigano. The lady wants to see the place where that business with her husband happened."

"That was a terrible story," Rigido said.

Bentley looked at him curiously. "This morning I saw the carabinieri come by again. I am surprised that you still haven't heard that they are in town."

"Lots of things happen here that I don't hear about," Rigido said, eagerly drawing on the American cigarette. "That's good tobacco, Signor Bentley. I would pay you any price for a pack."

"I'll give you ten cartons for free," Bentley said, staring at the sunny square. The two cats had returned and were lying under a wagon.

"Ten cartons," Bentley repeated. "Maybe more. Do you have a place where I can store my jerrycans?"

"In the cellar, Signor Bentley."

Rigido walked with Bentley to the car and watched him open the trunk. "Fifty gallons!" he exclaimed.

Bentley grinned. "You're an expert. We will leave two jerrycans in the car."

While they were putting the cans in the cellar they didn't talk. When they returned to the car, Rigido said, "An old model, signore— 1931 or 1932. Did you buy it?"

"I rented it."

It was cool and shadowy under the trees. Bentley sat down on the wall of the well and looked up the empty village street.

"How can you stand it here?" he asked.

"I'm used to it," Rigido answered and wiped his forehead with a red handkerchief. "When we came here, my wife was still alive. I'm too old now to mind."

He muttered something Bentley couldn't understand. His reddish eyes looked sad.

Bentley gave him a pack of cigarettes. "For your help. Have you thought over my offer?"

"I'm ready to do any kind of business with you," Rigido said, "as long as it is business. The people here are poor, Signor Bentley, but they live the same as you and I do. How many cigarettes can I buy for a thousand dollars?"

Bentley didn't answer.

"I know no man," Rigido went on, "who wants to die for a thousand dollars. I have so few guests that I should be glad that you're here."

"Aren't you?"

"I like the lady," Rigido said and looked up into the trees. "It would make me unhappy if something happened to her."

Bentley pushed his cigarette out against the wall. "If anything happens to her, there will be a lot of unhappy people in Chiesa. Remember that, Signor Rigido."

He went to the car and started the engine. He watched Rigido vanish into the inn, shuffling his feet as if he were carrying a heavy burden.

Five minutes later Helen appeared. Her dress was blue and white. A bit too elegant for Chiesa, Bentley reflected. She was wearing low-heeled shoes and looked like a teenager.

As they were driving down the valley she turned to Bentley. "Did you have a chat with the innkeeper?"

"Maybe," Bentley said. "He helped me carry the jerrycans to the cellar."

"What did you talk about?"

He wondered whether she could have overheard and decided it was impossible. "He likes you."

"There's something frightening about him," Helen said. "When I came downstairs he looked as if his wife had just died."

"Maybe he sees things," Bentley said. "If I lived here for more than two weeks I would see things."

When they had come to the bottom of the valley and reached the highway, he drove faster. They passed few people—several goat herds, two farmers riding a cart, and an old woman crouching at the side of the road.

The road led steadily deeper into the mountains, threading through sparsely vegetated passes and past fields of dark thorny bushes. Only in the valleys was the land cultivated; there men and women in black labored, filling baskets with fruit.

Eventually they reached Cerami, which looked like a stage setting. A vista of crowded rooftops, ending with the high cupola of a baroque-style dome, stretched out between the bare mountainsides. Beyond, high mountaintops rose against the sky.

"The Nebrodi!" Bentley exclaimed. "If the carabinieri are right, the gang is hiding somewhere in that direction between Monte Ambola, Monte Pelalo, and Monte Soro. They are each five thousand feet or higher."

"How are they going about finding them?"

"The lieutenant showed me a map. He's divided the area into squares and they're checking one every day. They are turning over every stone."

"Stop a moment," Helen said. When Bentley had drawn up at the side of the road, she got out of the car and looked at the mountains. Cerami was now behind them. Ahead, to the left, lay a small valley, its trough a dried-out river bed. Alongside it was a road, climbing up and vanishing behind a curve.

"How far is it to Palmigano?" Helen asked.

Bentley looked at the map. "Still about ten miles."

"Then we have time. Where does that road lead?"

The road didn't show on the map. "It can't go far," Bentley said. "I would think that that valley ends somewhere between Monte Ambola and Monte Soro."

"Let's go down it a piece," Helen suggested. "As soon as it gets too difficult we can turn around."

"What do you expect from that?"

"I want to make myself familiar with the landscape. Are you afraid?"

"You've asked me that twice before," Bentley said. Her moods didn't surprise him anymore. Nevertheless, he had to admit to himself that there were few places in the world he was less eager to see than Palmigano.

He steered the car onto the side road. After about five hundred yards it became narrower and so steep that Bentley had to shift into first gear. The road hugged the steep mountainside; after half an hour, it suddenly came to an end behind a huge formation of rock, part of which overhung it like the eave of a roof. From that point on, only a footpath led up the edge of the mountain, on which little olive trees grew.

Helen got out of the car, climbed up the path a few feet, and then came back.

"Let's look down on it from above," she said. "I want to know how it looks from the other side."

They left the car in the shadow of the rock and followed the path. It was ten o'clock in the morning, but already it was quite warm, and Bentley took off his jacket. His heavy pistol slapped his side at every step. He slipped it into the pocket of his jacket, which he carried over his arm.

It took them ten minutes to get to the olive grove. The little leaves of the trees shone like silver in the sun. It smelled of exotic gardens, of the late summer, and of the sea.

From a point above the olive grove they could see the land stretch out toward the north: empty valleys, huge bodies of rock, and the bluish labyrinth of the picturesque mountain terrain, with peaks, holes, cones, and abysses, crowned above by the mighty limestone mountain of Monte Soro to the northeast, and the steep rocky peaks of Monte Ambola and Monte Pelalo to the south and west; an empty sea before the blue infinity of the horizon.

"If the carabinieri aren't going to leave any stone unturned," Bentley remarked, "they have found themselves a lifetime job. I don't give them a chance."

"I hope you're right," Helen said.

Bentley smiled. "Yesterday that remark would have surprised me. You obviously still don't know what you really want."

"I want to talk with Salvatore. Do you really think he would let himself be caught alive by the carabinieri?"

"That's unlikely," Bentley said and stopped smiling. "If he is as clever as I think he is, he will not risk his head, not even for ten thousand dollars."

"One has to try. I don't have much time any more. As far as I know, my father is already on his way to Naples."

Bentley looked at her, surprised. "Does he want to get you back?"

"Put yourself in his place," Helen said. "I left him only a rather confused letter. If I had discussed it first, I would still be in Toledo. I prepared this trip alone and I went alone, but I can't afford to go back with empty hands. You are in my way, Clyde. As long as you stay with me in Chiesa, Salvatore will think it is an ambush. He might think he can fool the carabinieri, but he won't risk taking on the United States Army."

"Do you want to send me away?"

"I have to. If you make trouble, I will call headquarters and ask for your recall."

Although he had counted on it the night before, her statement now caught him by surprise.

"You wouldn't have me recalled because of Salvatore," he said. "He must know already that I'm here. If I were to vanish suddenly, he would really be suspicious. You want to get rid of me, that's all."

"And suppose I do?"

Bentley fell silent. He sat down on the ground, laid his jacket beside him, and lit a cigarette. Now that what he feared most was happening, he was completely quiet. His situation was similar to hers: he didn't have much time anymore, and if this was his last chance, he would use it.

"I'm not forgetting," Helen said, "that I wouldn't have gotten this far without you. Do you mind if I sit on your jacket?"

She did so before he remembered his pistol. She twisted aside, put her hand in his pocket, and pulled out the pistol.

"I knew already the day before yesterday that you had this," she said. "It's too heavy for me. Mine is quite sufficient. I can hit a tree at sixty feet. Is that good?"

He hadn't considered that she could also be naïve. "Where did you try?"

"We have a country house on Lake Erie."

Bentley had thought as much. All rich people in Toledo had a country house on Lake Erie. "Do you also have a pistol permit?"

"No, I didn't have time to get one. Will you get me a cigarette?"

She stared at a cloud sailing slowly over the top of Monte Pelalo. Small shafts of light filtered through the olive leaves and danced in her hair. Her white dress outlined her body perfectly. Bentley looked away.

"Maybe you're making a mistake telling me right now that you want to get rid of me," he said. "It might occur to me to take myself the little souvenir from you I didn't take the other night."

"I thought about that," Helen said. "You may have it now if you tell me the truth."

She still held his pistol in her hand, pointed toward the ground. When she lifted it and aimed at his stomach, his heart fluttered, only half from fear.

"Is it loaded?" Helen asked.

"Sufficiently for a murder. Is that your plan?" He didn't sound as casual as he would have liked to. He watched her put out her cigarette with her left hand and release the safety catch with her right thumb.

"Perhaps we don't even have to go to Palmigano," she said. "Perhaps I won't even have to send you back to Naples. Perhaps I'll even allow you to continue your amusements."

"In exchange for what?"

She looked coldly into his face. "Tell me, Clyde. Is my husband on your conscience or not?"

Bentley didn't answer. As he saw her steady the pistol at him, he felt sick. He was as afraid as when he was fighting at Monte Casino. She was a reckless person and she might do anything. Still he couldn't speak a word.

"As you like," Helen said and put the pistol beside her indifferently. "You look pale, Clyde. Do you really think I wanted to shoot you?"

"One can't be sure with you," Bentley said. He felt perspiration dripping down his back.

She looked at him with cold eyes. "As long as you don't give me any special reason, I don't intend to shoot you. Besides I'd rather satisfy myself by telling my father, which won't give you less than five years in a military prison."

"I don't understand a word," Bentley said. "What 'special reason' are you talking about?"

"I'm talking about that little souvenir you wanted to take from me," Helen said. "If five years weren't so short I would aim for that even if you did. Anyway, I'd like to be able to look at your face before you are court-martialed."

Bentley stared at her. At times in his life he'd behaved without much consideration for women—as long as he felt that their resistance was only a well-played maneuver. After all, many liked it that way. But Helen Brazzi was different from anyone else in his experience. He suspected that the memory of having her would leave him with a shadow of frustration.

He put the pistol in his pocket, got up, and put his jacket on. "I guess you now want to drive to Palmigano," he said shakily.

She shook her head. "Not today. Perhaps tomorrow."

"But tomorrow you wanted to send me to Naples."

"You still owe me an answer," Helen said and allowed him to pull her up; but she knew even while she was saying it that it was only a pretext not to have to send him away. She was afraid to be alone with her thoughts. Since he had told her two days ago about her husband, some of the glamor of the memory of Genno Brazzi had faded. For two nights she had weighed the explanations and alibis which a woman can think up for a man who cheats her with a whore, but she could not convince herself.

As Bentley walked beside Helen back to the car, although nothing showed on her face, he guessed that she had just suffered her worst defeat. He felt almost sorry for her.

# 8

After lunch she retired to her room. She sat motionless at the table for half an hour; then she put a scarf on her head and walked out into the hall. The toilet was at the end of the corridor in a shabby room with sloping walls. When she came out, she slammed the door behind her, opened the door of her own room, and slammed it equally hard. She waited a few seconds, then she took off her shoes and went barefoot into the corridor and down the stairs. At the bottom of the stairs she put her shoes back on.

She walked out of the inn without meeting anybody in the restaurant. The square lay quiet in the sun. In the heat of the day the town seemed deserted. In front of one house two donkeys were bound to an iron ring. The shadow of decrepit walls, dog, cats, and goats lay peacefully dozing together. A woman vanished into a doorway with a water bucket. Helen quickened her pace. In the quiet which enveloped the village like a glass dome her steps sounded like small explosions against the walls. Cool air from shadowy archways hit her face, and behind a wall a dog started to bark.

She took the most direct route to the caves. It struck her that a few of the entrances were open. It indicated that people had talked about who she was. Walking along, she saw old men and women sitting on the ground weaving baskets. Children were helping them. A little girl came out and stared curiously at her, her finger in her mouth. Helen nodded at her with a smile.

The door to Piera's cave was closed. She had counted on the possibility, but it took her a couple of seconds to master her disappointment. Considering her next move, she looked back at the village, which was hardly discernible in the sunlight, its gray roofs and walls blending into the rock. Two dark birds of prey floated motionlessly in the air currents of the high empty sky.

She waited for ten minutes and then she began to climb up toward the castle. A cool wind from the sea blowing down across the mountains made the heat more bearable. The contours of the rocks were hazy in the blue September sky. Only Etna was clearly distinguishable; its snow fields glittered in the sun.

About two hundred feet below the castle a few goats were grazing on a gentle slope which Helen had not noticed previously. When she looked closer, she discovered Piera, sitting with her back toward the ruins and holding a stick in her hands.

Further up the steps Helen discovered a small path which led between the rocks toward the southern slope of the mountains. At some spots the weeds were so thick that they covered the path.

After she had walked a little way along the path, she heard a voice. Not knowing whether it was a woman or a man calling, she proceeded carefully around a large boulder which blocked her view of the castle. Then she saw a man kneeling in the weeds with his back toward her. Lying in front of him, with her dress pulled up to her waist, was a young girl, not older than twelve years. She was watching the man and laughing.

He was not touching her; he was kneeling in front of her, bent over, gesticulating and stammering strangely. The girl continued to laugh with pleasure. Then her eyes caught Helen, and she jumped up and ran away.

The man turned around. Helen had seen his type before; but she could not remember seeing a more frightening expression of evil on any man's face. He was bearded; his black hair grew low over his eyebrows; he had small, sharp eyes, which glared moodily at her and would have frightened her, even under less revolting circumstances. In spite of the heat he was wearing a hunting jacket with black patches, a dirty pair of trousers, and an equally dirty cap. His feet were naked and filthy.

As he got up and walked crazily toward her, she put her hand in her pocketbook. At that moment he turned around and ran after the girl. Helen heard him call; it sounded like the cry of an animal.

She leaned back against the rock. For a few seconds she thought she was going to vomit; then she saw Piera standing in front of her looking startled at the pistol. Helen put it back in her pocketbook.

"I caught a man," she said breathlessly. "He had a little girl with him. Do you know him?"

Piera shook her head.

"He has a dark beard," Helen said.

"Oh," the girl said. "That was Vito. He is dumb. He can't speak." The girl laughed. "He always does that. He doesn't do anything to them, signora. Vito can't do anything to any girl. Everybody in Chiesa knows that."

"You mean you tolerate him?" Helen asked, surprised.

"He is harmless," Piera assured her. "He just looks at girls and does like this." She imitated the movements of the man's hands and laughed again. "He is so comical when he does that."

"Has he done that with you too?" Helen asked.

"When I was very small," Piera said. "All the little girls run after him. He only likes little girls."

Helen was lost for words. "I want to tell the carabinieri, Piera. That man belongs in an institution. Did you talk with your brother?"

"I don't know where he is."

She sounded defiant and hostile. She was no longer the little fearful girl of the previous meeting. She had taken off the golden bracelet; now she looked almost exaggeratedly poor.

Helen looked sharply at her. "You told me that the day before yesterday. If I tell the carabinieri that he belongs to the gang who held up the bank in Nicosia, they will lock up both you and your mother."

The girl's face changed color. "That's not true."

"That they will lock you up?"

"That my brother . . ." She stopped and looked past Helen at the bushes behind her.

"I am alone," Helen said. "You don't have to be afraid of the American officer. I brought him along so that he could lead me to you. As soon as I want, he will go away."

"It wasn't my brother," the girl said. "Why do you think it was him?"

Helen opened her pocketbook and took a few bank notes out. "I know. The carabinieri will believe me that your brother was involved in this, and they will ask you where you got your gold bracelet and the beautiful dress. You won't be able to lie to the carabinieri, Piera."

The girl did not answer. In spite of her tan, her face had turned gray.

"Tonight the lieutenant of the carabinieri is coming to see me," Helen said. "He will want to know what I'm looking for here. If I haven't talked to your brother before tomorrow evening, I will tell the lieutenant everything."

"What do you want from my brother?"

"I am Helen Brazzi, the wife of Genno Brazzi. Give your brother this money. It is five hundred dollars. The rest I will give him myself."

She held out the money. When the girl hesitated, Helen stuck the bills in the top of Piera's dress and said, "You are pretty, Piera. This money will buy you more pretty dresses than you can get for yourself. Tell Salvatore that I won't give him five thousand dollars, but ten thousand dollars. Don't you have a father anymore?"

"No."

"Then you will be able to use the money well," Helen said and turned away, leaving her standing there.

She headed back the way she had come. After she had gone about fifty steps, a man stepped in front of her. It was Bentley. He was waiting where the path crossed the steps of the castle. Helen remembered how Piera had looked past her at the bushes; she must have seen or heard him.

"Where are you coming from?" she asked angrily.

"I heard you leave your room," Bentley said.

The idea that he had been following her the whole time, that he had probably laughed at her efforts to get out of the house unobserved, made her burn with anger. She walked past him and went down the steps.

"I was worried about you," Bentley said behind her. "It isn't that I was just spying on you."

"You will never do it again," Helen said.

He followed her like a puppy. "I was doing it in your own interest," he insisted. "I didn't hear everything you said to the girl."

Helen stopped and turned quickly around.

"Were you eavesdropping?"

"I didn't mean to until I heard that guy cry. Then I saw him running up the slope after a child. When I looked for you, Piera was already with you. I didn't mean to listen in."

"But you did," Helen said a bit more quietly. "When I want your company I will let you know. You won't ruin this for me, Clyde."

Bentley nodded. "I don't intend to. Was that man crazy?"

"He just likes girls under twelve."

"Did you catch him at it?"

"Piera says he never really does anything. But what I saw was enough for me. The people here know about him and they don't mind."

He had never seen her so angry, not even when she just now discovered him. "Don't take it too tragically," he said. "In Naples during the war they sold their children for five dollars. When a whole family sleeps in one hole, the children soon know those things about babies being made and born; when they are fifteen they start on it themselves. By the way, I'm afraid you made a mistake this time."

"When?"

"When you threatened Piera with telling the carabinieri that her brother was in Nicosia. You better face the fact that their cave will be empty tomorrow."

"That's my worry," Helen said and continued down the steps. Threatening Piera had been an impulse of the moment, an irresistible need to do something to regain her lost self-esteem and to get rid of her doubts—perhaps even to have an excuse for being with Bentley.

Bentley followed close behind her. She wasn't wearing stockings; he caught himself admiring her slim legs and hips.

"That's my only quibble," he said. "Everything else I couldn't have done better."

"You would have done worse. Do you know what solidarity is?"

Bentley smiled. "I may have heard the word in school. Why do you ask?"

"The carabinieri are Italians," Helen said. "They won't be so interested in delivering two of their own people to the United States Army. If the carabinieri arrest him, in a year or two Salvatore will be as free in Sicily as you and I."

Bentley looked at her, squinting. "That is to say, of course, if he isn't sought by his own people as a holdup man," he said. A trace of admiration appeared in his face. "You're pretty sharp. If he accepts that it's up to you whether the carabinieri will find out about it or not . . ."

"Up-to-who-else would it be?"

"I don't know," Bentley said.

## 9

In the afternoon she decided to take a bath. Rigido brought a huge wooden barrel and seven buckets of hot water to her room. Bentley could hear them talking through the thin wall. When the innkeeper had gone, he locked his door. Lying on his bed, he followed her movements in his mind. It was intolerable. He went to the window and opened it. He had the feeling he was choking. He remembered how she had looked at him as she said good-by at her door, with patient curiosity, like a psychologist awaiting the results of an experiment.

But he was not quite ready to give in. He was still absorbed in watching his own psychic collapse—the agony of his crumbling pride and principles—with a kind of detached irony. He was no longer worried about what Hopkins might tell. It was not a matter concerning himself, and perhaps his conduct would appear less sensational than she imagined.

He heard steps on the stairs, then Rigido's voice and a knock at Helen's door. He couldn't hear her answer. The innkeeper came to his room. His dwarflike face expressed worry. "An officer," he said, "wants to see the signora." Bentley felt his heart skip a beat.

"An American officer?" he said.

"No, an officer of the carabinieri. He says—"

Bentley felt too relieved to bother with the rest of the sentence.

"Send him up," he said.

Lieutenant Gastone was a head shorter than Bentley and soft and thin. His little mustache failed to offset his femininity. In his impeccable uniform and highly polished boots he looked like a star in a musical.

Rigido appeared with a bottle of wine and three glasses and put them on the table; then he vanished. The carabiniere never looked at him.

"We expected you tonight," Bentley said as they sat down. "Have you had any success?"

"Not yet." The lieutenant smiled. He had crossed his legs and was smoking one of Bentley's cigarettes. "For a change, we are going to try at night."

Bentley looked surprised. "Won't it be a bit dark?"

"It's a full moon," the lieutenant explained politely. "I hope my visit to the signora is not too inconvenient."

"She should be here any minute."

"An interesting case," the lieutenant said, picking up the bottle and looking at the label. He pursed his lips and put it back on the table.

"I've been on a little side trip to Nicosia," he said. "The officials there remembered immediately. The case of the two soldiers was in the files. The officer in charge thought it highly unlikely that after all this time the case could still be solved. His guess is that those two men had vanished to Turin or Milan."

"That's possible," Bentley said.

Lieutenant Gastone flicked his cigarette. "I'm not a Sicilian, Mr. Bentley. I came to Palermo only ten days ago. As soon as this job is finished, I am going back to Rome."

"I figured you were from Rome," Bentley said.

Lieutenant Gastone smiled. "My ancestors settled in Rome four hundred years ago. I don't want to discourage the lady. As long as I don't find out differently, I will work on the assumption that one should look for people where one least expects to find them. The idea that all missing Sicilian criminals are hidden up north makes life simpler for the authorities here, but it is not necessarily true."

"Mrs. Brazzi will be glad to hear your theory. I think I hear her coming." Gastone stood up and opened the door. Helen looked fresh and rested, and allowed the carabiniere to kiss her hand.

"Lieutenant Gastone," Bentley said listlessly.

The officer smiled. "A sincere admirer of your great nation, signora. If I were given a choice between living in your country and mine, I would need a week to think it over."

"In that case I had better save you that struggle of conscience," Helen said.

It struck Bentley how charming Helen could be when she wanted. "Lieutenant Gastone was in Nicosia today," he said. "They think it unlikely that Salvatore and Pietro are still in Sicily."

"That's interesting," Helen said as she sat down. "You speak English beautifully, Lieutenant Gastone, or does one say Signor Gastone?"

"Just say Gastone," the lieutenant answered lightly. "I know that people in America aren't as conventional as we. Before I joined the carabinieri I was an exporter, then an interpreter, and then an officer at division headquarters. I had already learned my English in school."

"You must have had a good teacher," Helen said and turning to Bentley: "Please get us another chair from my room, Clyde. I think it would be better if we didn't go down to the restaurant."

When Bentley returned, Helen was already telling the lieutenant her adventure with the mute.

Bentley put the chair down and opened a bottle. While he was filling the glasses Helen noticed that the lieutenant was making notes. His face was still polite and attentive. He asked a few more questions and then he closed his notebook.

"I will look into it today, signora," he said. "Unfortunately such cases are not rare. That man is probably impotent. In an institution they will find some more harmless way to keep him occupied."

"I don't understand why the parents of the children don't do anything about it," Helen said. "Can you explain that?"

Lieutenant Gastone stared at the table top. "There are many explanations, signora. The right one in this case I can probably tell you tomorrow. Do you perhaps know the name of the girl with whom you talked about this?"

She threw a hasty glance at Bentley. "No. I think it was just a young woman who happened to be passing."

"It's not important, signora. Your statement is enough. I'm sorry that you got such a bad impression of our country. But Sicily is not Italy; the real Italy begins north of Naples."

"In Rome," Bentley said, feeling increasingly annoyed with the lieutenant. The way he talked, the way he pressed his fingertips together, his habit of tapping his boot with his little whip, all annoyed him equally. Gastone seemed so certain of his irresistiblity that he could not even stop to enjoy its effect.

"You must have been very young when you were in the export business," Bentley said, with an effort at irony.

Lieutenant Gastone maintained his polite smile. "I had a good start, Mr. Bentley. An uncle of mine is the owner of one of the largest textile businesses in Italy. Yet for me it turned out not to be the right thing in the end. A person has his personal ambitions."

He turned again to Helen. "I have already told Mr. Bentley that your case interests me very much, signora. If you need my help, please count on me completely. Have you already made a start?"

Helen shook her head.

"You won't hear much from the relatives of those two," Lieutenant Gastone said. "Pietro's family is now living in Ragusa. We have nothing against them. Salvatore has a mother and a sister here. Right now I cannot investigate them more thoroughly because I have no authority to do so and it is not connected with my present job. I could, of course, if some connection were established."

"What do you mean?" Helen asked quickly.

Once more Gastone pressed the fingers of one hand against those of the other and looked at her with a smile. "No one knows the place where those two are living, signora. Now, if I had some reason to connect them with the holdup criminals we are looking for, it would

71

provide me with the grounds to make a thorough investigation of those relatives. I've had good experience with that kind of thing."

"I wouldn't like that," Helen said sharply.

Even before the polite smile vanished from his face, she realized she had used the wrong tone of voice. She corrected herself. "I mean, I don't think it would be a good idea. Piera and her mother . . ."

She had made another mistake and it annoyed her. "Lieutenant Bentley told me about them."

"Lieutenant Bentley?" The carabiniere was smiling again. "I thought that you were here as an American officer, Lieutenant Bentley. Did you have reason not to mention your acquaintance with the local citizens until now?"

"That's right," Bentley said.

Lieutenant Gastone stood up briskly. "Excuse me, signora," he said. "We have a hard night ahead. If you will permit me, I will pay you another visit tomorrow or the day after tomorrow. And please don't hesitate to call on me if you need my help."

"I don't think that's likely," Helen said shortly.

Lieutenant Gastone kept smiling. "I won't be in the way of your investigations, signora." He bowed, gave Bentley a friendly nod, and walked to the door. Gracefully and amiably, with his whip tucked beneath his arm, the compact man turned, nodded his head slightly, and was gone.

"You should have left him to me," Bentley said. "He is more dangerous than ten snakes. Furthermore, he knows more than I had guessed."

"He knows it from you," Helen said sharply. "It was a mistake to look him up."

"Since everybody in the village knows why we are here, he would have found out anyway. You may not think it possible but everyone in this little hole-in-the-wall knows more about you than you can imagine. You can't arrive in Chiesa as an American lady and think you will go as unnoticed as if you were a peasant from Cerami, dammit!"

"Don't speak to me that way," Helen said furiously.

Bentley stared at her. He hadn't meant to let himself go so far. He grabbed the bottle but saw that the glasses were still filled—even Lieutenant Gastone's.

"Don't underestimate him," Bentley said quietly. "If he has been sent from Rome, there must be a reason. This business may be a matter of prestige to him. People like him cannot bear not to succeed; he will try everything. But at the moment he isn't that sure of his case."

"He will be after this conversation," Helen said. "I gave myself away."

For a moment she looked like a little girl who had not been able to get her way, and Bentley felt tempted to pat her on the head consolingly. But his feelings had grown too complex for such a gesture. He had reached a level deeper than mere sexual excitement. He was becoming afraid of her obsession—afraid that she had lost control of herself—and it depressed him. Since his last conversation with Rigido he had begun to think that even his worst expectations did not do justice to the real danger which Helen Brazzi had put herself in.

# 10

Piera came when Helen was already in bed. Helen put on a dressing gown and opened the door. It was past eleven.

"I expected you tomorrow," she said calmly. "Sit down."

"I have to go in a moment," Piera said. She looked quickly around the room and then at Helen's face. "You are to come tomorrow evening at nine o'clock to Cerami, signora . . . without the officer."

"I can't do that," Helen said. "He will stay in the car while I talk to your brother. Will Salvatore be in Cerami?"

"You will see him," Piera answered. "He will stand at the roadside. But if you bring the officer, you will not see him, signora."

There was something different about her. When Helen thought about it, she noticed that Piera was wearing heavy shoes and wool stockings.

"Couldn't you have told me that tomorrow?" Helen said.

"No."

"Why not?"

The girl didn't answer.

"Are you going away?" Helen said.

"The carabinieri were at our house."

"When?"

"Tonight. They said it was forbidden to live in the caves."

"Didn't you know that?"

"Sure. But the carabinieri from Nicosia have never bothered us about it."

Helen sat down at the table. "I didn't send them to you, Piera. Is your mother leaving too?"

The girl nodded.

"Where are you going?"

"An uncle of mine lives in Cerami. He has room for us."

"That is good, Piera," Helen said and looked her straight in the face.

"You are coming?"

"Yes."

"Without the officer?"

"Yes."

"Good night, signora," Piera said.

Helen stayed at the table. When Bentley came in, she turned slowly toward him. "Were you eavesdropping again?"

"The walls are so thin that I couldn't help it," Bentley said. He was wearing only a shirt and trousers. He sat down next to her. "You won't go," he said slowly and grimly. "I would sooner burn the car."

"Don't talk nonsense," Helen said. She looked slightly pale and unusually thoughtful.

Bentley lit her cigarette. "That damn Gastone," he said. "What he said about the caves was just a gimmick."

"Perhaps now you realize it was a mistake to go and look him up," Helen said.

Her voice sounded unusually conciliatory and he remembered that she had tried at first to convince Piera that she had to have him along.

He took her hand. "I'll admit all my mistakes as long as you don't go alone. You won't come back, Helen."

"Piera's brother wouldn't dare try anything."

"For people like him there's nothing to dare anymore. Take me along, Helen."

She looked at his hand. "Perhaps, if you'll tell me the truth."

"Is that the only thing you ever think of?" he asked in a subdued voice.

She pulled her hand away. "It's important."

Bentley stood up. "If your husband is still alive, I'll be very sorry. You think he's still alive?"

"And if he is?"

"I'll beat you to him," Bentley said. "As soon as I see the guy I'll kill him."

He walked out of the room so quickly that she didn't have time to answer.

The evening was warm. Helen opened her window. It was a clear night. The black silhouette of the mountain range stood out sharply against the night sky. She watched the moon rising. She was afraid; for the first time in her life she felt consciously afraid of dying.

Four days earlier everything had been so simple. Only in Naples had she begun to doubt, and with doubt came the beginning of equivocation and the first compromise and compensation. For the first time in years her feelings had been forced to assume dimensions, and she had had to abandon the comfortable flatness of illusion.

And now she found herself trying to escape into a new frame of self-deceit. Was it a substitute for the belief she had forced herself to sustain for two years? Was she desperately trying to ignore the fact that she was falling in love with a man whom a week earlier she had hated more than her own weakness? And how could she do without him as long as she was in Sicily? Not for a moment since she had been in Chiesa had she really counted on meeting Salvatore. Not for a moment.

The silence of the room hummed in her head. The palms of her hands were moist. She wished Bentley had stayed.

After ten minutes she could no longer bear it. She dressed, put a scarf around her shoulders, and went out into the corridor. When she walked down the stairs she heard Bentley behind her.

The restaurant was dark. Bentley walked past her to the door. Outside he turned toward her.

"Do you want to take the car?"

"I didn't call you," Helen said.

"I'm not assuming you called. What are you planning to do?"

"Nothing."

"I know that feeling," Bentley said. "I used to feel that way before we went into an attack."

It was so clear outside that he thought of Lieutenant Gastone. He wouldn't find Salvatore, even with a full moon.

Helen turned toward the village. As she walked beside Bentley up the steep steps she noticed that in spite of the late hour lights were burning in most of the houses. Men and women were sitting in the doorways talking in low voices. They fell silent as soon as Bentley and Helen approached them. Helen felt their eyes in her neck. She could feel the silence spreading before them as if the village was being evacuated. A group of young boys and girls was barring the street in front of a bar. As Bentley and Helen approached, it collapsed into two files on each side of them and formed again behind them. From the bar came the tinny music of a little radio.

Helen wanted to turn back, but the idea of having to run the gamut of all those eyes again prevented her. She didn't protest when Bentley chose the road toward the caves.

"Perhaps we'll meet Salvatore," he said grimly. "We know he is somewhere around here. If not, the girl couldn't have come to you so quickly."

"She had nine hours," Helen said. "But perhaps you're right."

Bentley laughed shortly. "She's not going to Cerami with her mother. Every family in Chiesa would be ready to take them in until

76

the carabinieri are gone. Actually I think Salvatore got cold feet and took them somewhere."

"Because of me."

"I don't think the carabinieri alone would have scared him. He wants to take his sister out of the firing line before he starts his duel with you."

"Don't be dramatic," Helen said nervously. "I have no intention of dueling with him."

"Then why did you get yourself a pistol?"

"I just found it in my father's drawer. Why do you assume that Salvatore is the right man anyway?"

"The right man?"

"Let's assume that my husband was really killed. You told me in Naples that seven or eight Italians were involved."

"Salvatore was certainly in on it," Bentley said. "But I still don't understand what you expect from a meeting with him."

She didn't answer.

"I don't assume that you expect him to make a teary-eyed confession. And if it's just that you want to be sure, there would be a cheaper and less dangerous way to find out."

"This is my affair."

"It is all your affair," Bentley said. "But if I may give you a piece of advice . . ."

"What's the matter?" Helen said.

"Nothing. I just hate to hear steps behind me at night."

She stood stock-still and turned around. Outside the village it was even lighter. In the light of the moon the contours of the houses were clearly visible. Every detail of the steps from the village stood out.

"You must have made a mistake. I don't hear anything."

"Perhaps I didn't," Bentley said, not really believing himself.

"Do you want to go to the castle?"

The road to the castle led past the caves. The idea scared her. "What else can we do?"

"We can turn right before we get to the caves, but I don't know where the road ends."

It was another fifty feet to the road, which climbed gradually across the mountain slope. They followed it for about three hundred

77

yards before they realized that it led to the south side of the mountain.

Bentley said, "This must be the road on which you met Piera today. It goes around the mountain. Do you want to turn around?"

"Later."

Grass and wildflowers interspersed with weeds covered the ground. They had left the caves behind them; they were now above the village. At their backs loomed the vertical wall of the castle.

Helen spread her scarf on the ground. "You'll catch cold," Bentley said. "Here, take my jacket."

"The grass is warm. Give me a cigarette."

She pulled her knees up under her arms and looked around. The valleys lay in darkness. They resembled rivers of white smoke streaming in the moonlight between the phosphorescent shores of the mountains. The silhouettes of the peaks were black gaps in the starry sky.

"There he is," Bentley said.

Helen saw the man at the same time. He was walking carefully up the road. When he had come within twenty feet of them he turned around quickly and stepped back into the shadows.

"He must have seen our cigarettes," Bentley said. "Wait here."

"I'd prefer you to stay here," Helen answered quickly.

He had expected her to object, but there was a difference; she was afraid and she wasn't even trying to hide it.

"It certainly wasn't Salvatore," he said. "He's Italian and he'll keep his word with a lady. That is, he won't kill you until tomorrow evening. I just want to know if that man is going back to the village."

He found his suspicion confirmed. After about a hundred yards he reached the spot from which he could see the steps toward the village. He saw a figure running quickly toward the houses. He tried to follow him with his eyes, but he vanished into the blackness of the street.

Helen was waiting for him where he had left her. He sat down beside her and lit a cigarette. "He's gone," he said. "I saw him vanish into the village. He was probably just a voyeur."

"A voyeur?"

He wasn't at all sure that he was right about the shadowy figure, but he didn't want to make her unnecessarily afraid. He laughed. "That's people who watch their governesses through a keyhole. I still don't know why you told me that story. It doesn't suit you."

"That I told you?"

"Did you tell it to your husband?"

"You are not my husband," Helen said.

Bentley nodded. "There's nothing worse than not being your husband," he quipped. "I don't believe in hell, but that's how I imagine it."

He paused and looked up at the stars. His voice had changed when he continued: "All right, perhaps your husband is on my conscience. For five minutes I had gone to pieces, if you know what that means. It was in the middle of the night and the Germans were everywhere. Instead of worrying about my men, I ran away. In fact, a whole battalion ran away, except for the wounded and the two men who stayed with them. I only missed them when we organized ourselves again at company headquarters."

"Is that all?" Helen asked after a long pause.

"As far as I'm concerned, yes. I wanted to form a reconnaissance force and see if they could be saved, but Major Green wouldn't let me. He was a captain at the time."

"Why did he forbid you?"

"He thought it was useless. I didn't agree. Perhaps he would agree now, but at the time he'd also gone a little to pieces. We had four bad weeks behind us and very little experience in battle. Without the war, men like Green would have been on pensions ten years earlier."

Helen looked at him. She had waited for this moment for six months and now she almost hated him for telling her. "Then my husband was one of the two who stayed with the wounded?"

"Probably."

"Even though he must have cracked as much as anybody and even though he had as little experience as you?"

He had known she was going to make this point, and he also knew that there was no rational answer.

"Why are you telling me this now?" she asked in a flat voice.

Bentley shrugged. He had followed an impulse, and he was sorry now.

79

"You promised to take me with you tomorrow evening if I told you the truth."

"Is that all of it?"

"Yes."

Helen didn't answer. It was just a confirmation of what she had already known for six months. Nevertheless, she was surprised at the indifference with which she had heard it. The meeting with Salvatore loomed like a huge door in her mind and allowed her to feel nothing but fear and uncertainty. She felt like a little girl who had climbed a tree and didn't know how to get down.

"Now what will you do?" Bentley asked. "Will you talk to your senator?"

"I'll think about it," Helen heard herself answer.

Bentley jammed out his cigarette briskly. "They can't do much to me, especially not what you may wish. A young company commander can lose his nerve in battle. We won the war; that's all they asked of us. What do you expect to happen tomorrow evening?"

"I hadn't thought too much about it," Helen said truthfully and got up.

"If he waits for you at the roadside," Bentley said, "he won't see me in the dark until he gets very close to the car. Let me go with you, Helen."

"I guess I'm afraid not to," Helen said. "What would you feel if you were me?"

"Probably the same," Bentley said quickly. "One knows that one has to die one day, but one prefers to put it off as long as possible."

"As long as possible," Helen said.

# *11*
-------

The following day he saw her only twice—at breakfast and at dinner. The rest of the time she stayed locked up in her room. He could hear her pacing up and down.

In the afternoon it had clouded over. From his window Bentley watched the clouds hanging over the mountains. A cool wind rose from the valley and blew leaves across the bare mountain side.

He walked back to his table and picked up his pistol, as he had already done a dozen times. He released the safety catch, weighed the weapon in his hand, and then put it back in his pocket. He would rather have had a rifle.

Shortly after five he heard the voice of Lieutenant Gastone. He was already in Helen's room, and with occasional spasms of his polite little laugh he chatted with her about the weather. It occurred to Bentley that he had never met an Italian who wouldn't use the smallest cloud in the sky as an excuse to talk almost endlessly about the Italian climate.

"I think we're getting rain," was the first thing Gastone said when Bentley entered Helen's room. "It will make our expedition much more difficult."

Bentley grinned. "When it rained, we always postponed the war. Obviously the full moon hasn't helped you much."

For one second the smile vanished from the face of the carabiniere. "We are not at war, Mr. Bentley. How long did it take your army to get to Rome?"

Bentley enjoyed the reply, even from a man he didn't like. "Indeed, a bit longer," he answered. "Are you bringing us any news?"

"Yes," Gastone answered, and directed himself again to Helen. "Vito, your child molester, has vanished; nobody in the village knows where he is."

"I don't understand," Helen said, perturbed. "Were you in his cave?"

"He probably lives in a different one every day. He is somewhat of a mascot to the people here, it seems. They hide him. I'm afraid that he won't show up until we have gone. Anyway I will tell my colleagues in Nicosia so they can keep an eye on him."

"How can people hide him?" Helen said. "He seduces their children."

"The mayor assured me that he is harmless."

"Because he isn't quite able to rape twelve-year-old girls?"

Bentley was pleased to note that the lieutenant was shocked. But in his shock was a measure of admiration.

"Why don't you get a chair from your room, Clyde," she asked impatiently. "You make me nervous standing there. You have permission to sit on my bed too."

"Thank you, ma'am," Bentley said with a smile.

He still wasn't sure that he had acted right in telling her the truth the night before, but he felt a bit more at ease. The past night, for the first time in five days, he had slept well. He realized that she had spoken even less than usual at the meals they had had together, but that she still let him eat with her, after what he had told her, was amazing enough. Still, he couldn't help but feel that she hadn't said her last word on the subject.

"To be quite frank," Lieutenant Gastone said, "I don't understand the people either, signora. The way things are now, perhaps it wouldn't be in your interest if we started hunting Vito."

Helen frowned. "Why not?"

"It might earn you enemies," Lieutenant Gastone answered. "The woman who talked to you may have told other people. You haven't seen her since?"

"No."

"She would have been able to help us, I guess," Lieutenant Gastone said. He stood up. "As soon as something new turns up, I will let you know immediately, signora. By the way, we also found out that Piera and her mother have vanished too, but you probably already knew that."

She looked at him candidly. "From whom?"

"Right." Lieutenant Gastone looked at her, amused. "I forgot you are only interested in the brother. Forgive my distraction, signora!" And he took his leave with a smile.

"He always makes a nice exit," Bentley said admiringly. "He should have been an actor. If I were Salvatore, I would now slowly begin to worry."

"Me too," Helen said. "I would like to drive to Cerami."

"Now?"

"It doesn't do any harm to see the road once more by daylight."

"It's not a bad idea."

Bentley went back to his room. He put his pistol in his pocket and went out to the car. Helen joined him as he opened the door. They drove into the valley, encountering many men and women with horses, mules and carts, lugging olives, lemons, and vegetables. Unlike the previous drive, their car created enormous curiosity. In the rearview mirror Bentley could see the men turning around and staring after the car and the women putting their heads together.

"I'm afraid that everybody in the village already knows about your meeting with Salvatore," he said. "I still hope you'll change your mind before tonight."

"It's too late," Helen said.

He looked quickly at her. She was paler than he had ever seen her before. "You just say that," he insisted. "If you really think it has to be, why don't you let me go there alone. You can bet he'd tell me as much as he'd tell you."

"Are you trying to relieve your conscience?"

"Dammit!" he cried. "I know a general who has five divisions on his conscience, if not more, and he is as famous now as Abraham Lincoln. He has thrown away more lives than you will find in all of Toledo just to capture one mountain—a mountain which didn't make the war end five minutes sooner. Compared to that general, I'm just small fry. How long are you going to go on kicking small fry?"

She didn't know what to answer. Before she knew him it had been easier to hate him. As far as she had made any plans for him, she was

*83*

satisfied with the results. But she was confused now and beginning to wish they had never met.

"You have three possibilities," Bentley went on. "You can tell the senator about me or you can send me back to Naples."

"And the third one?" Helen asked.

"Give me a chance and leave Salvatore to me. If your husband is still alive, he will tell me."

"I want to speak to him myself," Helen said.

When they reached the main road it started to rain. The clouds were hanging so low that they obscured the sides of the mountains. Quickly the holes in the street filled with water. Bentley switched on the windshield wipers, but they were stuck.

"Italy is never prepared for rain," he said. "Perhaps it's a fuse." He cursed as he got out of the car.

Helen watched him as he lifted the hood. The street was empty in the early dusk. A cold wind chased curtains of rain through the valley, tore the clouds apart, and skimmed them in strange shreds across the mountains.

"It's not the fuse," Bentley said, getting back into the car. "Perhaps we can find a mechanic in Nicosia. We can get there in forty minutes."

"Can you go without me?" Helen said. "I want to go back to the inn."

He saw that she was shivering in her thin dress. "Do you want my jacket?"

She nodded.

As he hung it over her shoulders, his wallet fell on the floor. He bent over to pick it up. "We still have three hours," he said. "I'll be back before eight."

"Perhaps it will stop by tonight," Helen said.

"Not in the mountains. I know the area. Without windshield wipers, we won't see five feet in front of us tonight."

In spite of the rain he drove quickly, and they were back at the inn in ten minutes.

"You wouldn't have seen much in this weather anyway," Bentley said, helping her out of the car. "I have some magazines in my room. You can get them if you want to."

She gave him back his jacket. "Where are they?"

"On the table. Here's the key to the room."

Signor Rigido was standing in the door of the restaurant. He was wearing a heavy jacket and a woolen scarf. He looked frozen.

"Terrible weather, signora," he said, a worried look on his face. "Isn't the signore coming?"

"Later."

He followed her to the steps. "When do you wish to eat dinner tonight, signora?"

"As always."

Then she stopped and looked at him. "Why?"

"I thought," murmured Rigido, "because the signore . . ." he stopped, blinked, and went back to his kitchen.

Helen bit her lip, waited a few moments, then went to her room to change. She found the room comfortably warm, and discovered a valve in the chimney through which warm air flowed into the room. She went to the window and saw that it was raining even harder. The mountains were now completely hidden by the clouds. A little later she saw the little Fiat roll down into the valley. She watched it until it disappeared on the main road.

Although she didn't really feel like it, she went to get the magazines. She picked one up and opened it listlessly. Between the pages she discovered a letter. She sat down in the chair and started to read it.

It was addressed to Bentley's parents and sounded like a letter written by a teenager more interested in his relatives than in girls, and whose curiosity about the world had in no way been satisfied. It had the same tone of wonder that Helen had felt and had gone on feeling even during the three years of her marriage—the keyhole curiosity of a bright child, full of the instinct to play with fire. Bentley hardly fitted the framework that she had prepared for him. It was the letter of a nice boy to his parents, punctuated by concern about their health, a desire to see them soon, greetings to uncles and aunts. It was so incongruous that she felt uncomfortable with her former image of him.

She carefully put the letter back in the magazine. Then she noticed two books. They were Italian language books. She tried to recall if his Italian had improved in the last few days.

She went back to her room and sat down listlessly. At the same moment, she heard hurried steps on the stairs. A few seconds later someone knocked at her door.

It was Bentley. "I forgot to take money with me," he said, looking around her room. "Did you get those magazines?"

"Not yet." She gave him back his room key. "Would you bring them to me?"

She waited at the table. When he returned, she thought he looked relieved. "I'm sorry that I had to come back."

"You should keep your money in your wallet," Helen said. "Or did you forget your wallet, too?"

"No, not my wallet." Bentley said.

Now she saw that he not only wrote letters like a teenager, but that he could also blush like one.

She waited motionlessly until she couldn't hear his steps anymore. Then she opened the magazine which had contained the letter. As she had expected, it had gone.

She caught herself smiling at the thought of him for the first time.

# *12*

He returned so soon that she still had an hour to wait before her meeting with Salvatore. The windshield wiper had been rusty; a few drops of oil had fixed it.

"The man didn't want to take any money for it," Bentley told her during dinner, which was served in her room. "There were about twenty cars in his garage, but he has no spare parts to fix them. When I gave him two packs of cigarettes, he wanted to give the car a complete tune-up. I had trouble stopping him. As long as you're not after their countrymen, they don't know how to help you enough. Why aren't you eating?"

"I'm not hungry," Helen said and pushed her plate away.

"It's not your last meal," Bentley said. "You didn't eat anything at lunch either. How long do you want to keep that up?"

"I'll try tomorrow," she said.

Bentley wiped his mouth. "Perhaps. Don't get your hopes up. Even if Salvatore talks with you, he may not tell you the truth."

"Not even for ten thousand dollars?"

"That depends on you. How do you propose to make sure he tells the truth?"

He didn't wait for an answer but got up and walked to the window. It was still raining. The panes were steamed over. He wiped one with his handkerchief, but he could make out nothing of the landscape. The night had covered it as if with a black blanket.

"I know how it goes," Bentley said. "You get involved in something and you can't get out of it. And what will you do when you have found the truth?"

"That depends on the kind of truth."

"I see," he said and sat down again at her table. "And what have you decided about me?"

She was silent.

"What happened to me with your husband has never happened to me again. I have reproached myself for it a long time. The next morning I lost another dozen men, only this time it wasn't my fault. You get used to it. I had ordered a group to dig themselves in. Two did, but the rest just sat down in a large bomb crater. When the shells began to fall, they were buried right there. If they had followed my orders, they might still be alive."

"Didn't my husband follow your orders?" Helen asked.

Bentley shrugged with exasperation.

Rigido came to get the dishes. "I'm inconsolable, singora," the innkeeper said. "Didn't you like the fish?"

"It was splendid," Bentley answered for Helen. "The signora has to get used to the climate. Do you lock the house at night?"

"Not usually, sir. But if you wish, I will . . ."

"No, don't bother," Bentley said.

He waited until Rigido had left the room, then he looked at his watch.

"Fifteen minutes to go. If Salvatore is a gentleman, he will come alone."

She looked startled. "You mean he might bring the others?"

"If he is not a gentleman. Four or five men, each of them armed with an M-1. They could knock out a whole company of carabinieri. I'm surprised you never thought about that."

"Are you afraid?" she asked, her face pale.

Bentley smiled. "No more than you. Since you want to go anyway, it doesn't make any difference."

He walked around the table until he stood behind her; he put his lips against her neck.

She shivered. "Stop that!" she said sharply.

"I had to do it," Bentley said. "It's one of those evenings when you have to obey your impulses."

She heard him leave and heard him moving around in his room. Then all she could hear was the beating of her heart. If Bentley had asked her once more to give up the trip, she would have done so.

Ten minutes later he came back. He had put on his coat and stood waiting for her at the door.

"If I may give you one more piece of advice," he said, "don't bring all the money. Five thousand will do it."

"I don't have ten thousand," Helen said.

"Very good. And as long as I haven't figured out what they're planning you better stay in the car. Don't let them talk you into getting out."

"If he sees you . . ."

"He won't see me," Bentley said.

Below, in the restaurant, a few men were playing cards. Rigido was sitting behind them. When Helen and Bentley walked through he got up, an uncertain look on his face. "You are still going for a drive, signora?"

Helen just nodded, betraying her dislike for him.

"He's becoming too inquisitive," Helen said when they reached the street. "You shouldn't chat so much with him. It encourages him."

The rain had lessened, and only large drops were falling from the trees. In the car she lit herself a cigarette. He noticed that her hands trembled. He was on the verge of asking her once more to change her mind, but he knew that she would only ask him again whether he was afraid. He could not afford to show less courage than a woman he loved.

When they were in the valley, Bentley drove. The road was slippery and he nursed the car slowly through the dangerous hairpins. About a hundred yards before the main road, he turned off the lights and stopped.

"What are you doing?" Helen asked.

"A little change. I tried it out in Nicosia."

He got out of the car and pulled the back seat forward. Behind it was a large space. He left it leaning forward and climbed back behind the wheel.

"It's a bit complicated," he said. "But it's the only way I can get out of the car unnoticed."

"Could you be more specific?" she asked nervously.

Bentley smiled. "I went to the movies, too, when I was a kid. If you see a man with a machine gun standing in the road, you can always try to race past him, but I wouldn't advise it. Just do as I tell you."

He changed places with her. She drove slowly. Leaning intently forward to watch the road, her face looked waxen in the dashboard light. Although it had stopped raining, patches of fog on the road made the driving more and more difficult. The contours of the landscape became formless.

"The battery is on its last legs," Bentley said. "We won't see him until he is standing right in front of the car. What will you say if he demands the ten thousand dollars?"

She didn't know. She only knew that nothing in the world would have made her go on if Bentley hadn't been there. The thought occurred to her that if something happened to her it would be on his conscience exactly as her husband was. It made her feel a wave of self-pity. But she would face even greater danger rather than show him that everything she had done in the last few days had been an act, that she had maneuvered herself into a role she didn't wish to play and which she now had to play to the end.

Her hands were moist. She wiped them on her coat. Bentley handed her a lighted cigarette.

"Maybe you imagined all this more simply," he said. "When you came to Naples you didn't know about Salvatore."

A few times before he had guessed her thoughts, but she wasn't in the mood to show him that he had done so again. "I had several reasons for coming," she said shortly.

"Yes, I realize that. If it would help, I'll give it to you in writing that I have your husband on my conscience. Once I thought you wanted to kill me, but you're not the type. I made a mistake."

"You're making a mistake now," Helen said and stopped the car. She opened the door and looked up and down the road. Then she drove on toward a little hill which was just barely visible about fifty yards away. To the right of the road, weeds were growing; to the left was farmland. She stopped the car again and got out.

Bentley hadn't noticed anything. He put his pistol back in his pocket and climbed out of the car too. "What are you doing?" he said. "I didn't see anything. Why did you get out?"

She didn't answer. For a moment she had thought she was choking. Fear was coming out of her like an eruption. She couldn't suppress it.

"For five thousand dollars you could have made him come to the inn," Bentley went on. "Why are you making it so easy for him?"

"How far is it still to Cerami?"

"Not more than three miles. We have already been driving for twenty minutes. Do you want to go back?"

"Perhaps."

Bentley smiled, relieved. She misunderstood the smile, thinking it was at her expense. She climbed back behind the wheel. Almost at the same moment Bentley spotted a boy crossing the hill.

He was wearing a dark coat and an old cap, and he carried a stick. Although he seemed to have seen the car, he continued toward them.

Helen now saw him too. She got out again and watched him approach. His face became visible in the headlights.

"What do you think?" she asked nervously.

Bentley took his hand out of his pocket. "Anyway, it's not Salvatore. Perhaps he sent him."

"He looks like a shepherd boy."

"Perhaps," Bentley said. He waited until the boy was near. His coat and cap were soaked with rain. His young face showed more curiosity than fear.

"Where do you come from?" Bentley asked.

The boy stopped and pointed over his shoulder. "From Cerami, sir."

"Do you live in Cerami?"

"In Chiesa, sir. My uncle lives in Cerami. I watch his goats."

"But you sleep in Chiesa?"

"Only today, sir. Tomorrow is Sunday. I don't have to watch for the goats."

It sounded plausible. Helen turned impatiently toward Bentley. "Why do you bother with him?"

Bentley didn't know. "I guess I'm suspicious. I've heard stories about uncles in Cerami. It sounds as if he's learned it by heart."

"You're imagining things."

"Did you meet a man?" Bentley asked the boy.

"On a horse, sir."

"Where?"

"Riding toward Cerami."

"When?"

"Half an hour ago."

"Stop it!" Helen said. Now all she wanted was to get back to the inn. "Can't you see that he doesn't know anything?"

Bentley became uncertain. "Do you want to go back with us?" he asked the boy.

"To Chiesa?"

"Yes."

The boy smiled. "If I may, signore."

This made Bentley even more unsure, because he hadn't expected the answer. But before he could ask any more, Helen got back into the car. Bentley nodded at the boy. "Perhaps we will see you when we come back. We have to go to Cerami first."

"Thank you, sir," the boy said with a smile. He walked on quickly.

Bentley watched him until he had vanished in the dark. He suddenly felt sure that he had made a terrible mistake.

"Let me drive," he said to Helen.

"Why?"

"You'll see."

Although the road was very narrow, he managed to turn the car around. He went fast, with his bright headlights on. After three minutes he slowed down. The boy had disappeared.

"Do you understand?"

Helen didn't answer. She didn't understand, but she didn't care. Going back to Chiesa, all she felt was enormous relief.

"He's a very clever devil, that Salvatore," Bentley said admiringly. "If you had been alone, the boy would have taken you to him."

"You think he went back."

"Sure. When he saw us come after him, he must have hidden himself somewhere in the dark until we passed. Now he's taken the shortest route to Salvatore. I guess we might as well forget it."

"I think so too," Helen said, managing to sound indifferent.

Bentley looked at her. "I'm sorry your rendezvous didn't come off. I never thought of the possibility that he might send a boy ahead."

"On what possibilities did you count?"

"On almost all of them."

"I'm not impressed," Helen said. She had already regained enough confidence to speak to him in her usual way. "What would you have done if Salvatore hadn't come alone?"

"That's hard to say," Bentley answered. Now that he thought about it, his plans seemed too optimistic. "I was going to get out of the car through the trunk. Inside the car I would never have been able to stand up to them. Outside of the car I might have been able to do something."

"How brave of you," Helen said, but it didn't sound as ironical as she had meant it to.

Bentley shrugged. Now that he knew she talked that way even when she was afraid, he didn't mind anymore. He had found more human traits in her during these last few hours than he had expected. Living through crises with her was a way of getting to know her, and the more he knew her the more desirable she seemed to him. That his own position was becoming more and more difficult didn't bother him as much as the aching fear that she might suddenly vanish from his life, which was what had weakened his decision to be completely honest with her about her husband. Leaving her to her unrealistic hopes seemed the only way to keep her with him for a bit longer, and it would be stupid not to use it. Bentley was not going to lose any such chance. It seemed to him now as if his life depended on it.

## 13

That night the thought of Bentley kept her awake. She was worried at the idea that she might be in love with him. She didn't want that; yet she couldn't put him out of her mind.

Finally she fell asleep. After what seemed like minutes, she was awakened again by the sound of church bells. She remembered that it was Sunday and tried in vain to fall asleep again. Later she heard Rigido come up the steps. She didn't answer his knocking. She heard him go to Bentley's room and she could hear the murmur of their voices. She waited until Rigido had gone downstairs and then she got up and went to the window.

She had already realized that the sun was shining. The sky looked as if there had never been a cloud in it. She opened both windows and looked across the valley at the mountains, which stood brightly and festively in the morning sunshine.

The water in the jug was ice-cold. She poured some in the basin and splashed some on her face, her arms, and her breasts and rubbed her skin until it burned. Then she put on her robe.

She was still doing her makeup when she heard the innkeeper come up the stairs again and go to Bentley's room. He stayed there only for a moment, and then she heard Bentley knock on her door. She called to him but as he didn't answer, she opened the door.

"I'm sorry to disturb you," he said and pushed past her into the room. "The innkeeper brought me breakfast. He wants to go to church and he couldn't wait any longer. Do you want to have breakfast in my room?"

"In ten minutes."

"In ten minutes the coffee will be cold," Bentley said. "You don't have to get dressed for my sake. Did you sleep well?"

"Yes."

"I didn't."

"Should I say I'm sorry?"

"Why should you if you don't feel like it." His sharp tone bothered her. "Do you know what you are doing?" Bentley went on.

"What are you talking about?"

"About your robe," Bentley said. She was only half a foot away from him; it was the first time that he had seen her in her red velvet lounging robe. In a burst of emotion—a physical reaction to her unexpectedly unfriendly, almost hostile, attitude—he stepped closer to her and pulled her robe open. For a second her body was revealed to him completely nude. Then she pushed him away so vehemently that his back hit the door.

"Without clothes you look more human," he said and walked out.

Back in his room he sat down at the table and tried to think. Although Rigido had brought him the message from Piera, he had not made a decision. He only knew that there were factors to be weighed. That was as far as he had gotten when Helen came in. Her robe was tied now, and she let him pour her a cup of coffee.

"Tomorrow we are going back to Naples," she said.

Her face was blotched and she looked unhealthy. Bentley had never seen her so perturbed. He did not doubt for a moment that she meant it, and he realized that unconsciously he had already prepared

94

himself for her decision. He had regarded her as a gamble from the start, and he had never abandoned the possibility that he might lose—partly because he had never been completely free of scruples. Even if he were to make love to her she would still be Genno Brazzi's wife and nothing in the world would change that.

"You're getting sensitive," he said. "Of course, until yesterday you were pursuing a definite and limited goal. You know, you could have had me much cheaper, but . . . ."

"But what?" Helen asked.

"Maybe you didn't want me cheap," Bentley said and looked at his watch.

She turned pale. "Are you serious?"

"I still don't know," Bentley said and got up, put his jacket on, and left the room.

She heard him go down the stairs. It struck her that not even her own husband had ever pinpointed her feelings so precisely. One day he would tell the story in an officer's club, not to brag, but just as a man who, having fallen short of his goal, needs to fill the void with talk. The same was true of her. After the fifth or sixth drink she always needed to complete the unfinished circles with talk. Come to think of it, she had started talking to him after only two glasses of wine. After what had existed and not existed between them, he wouldn't feel any loyalty. Why should he?

She had no choice but to go after him.

When she realized that, it occurred to her that she still needed an alibi for going after him.

She went back to her room. Her face was burning. She lay down and stared at the ceiling. Going back to Naples was no way out. She remembered how he had sat beside her two days ago and kissed her. She was afraid that she would still remember in two years.

When the door to her room opened she was still lying on her bed staring at the ceiling. She heard the door and it struck her that she hadn't heard any steps. But she was so certain that it was Bentley that she didn't look up. At the same moment she realized that she hadn't locked her door on purpose. Only the odd silence made her turn her face toward the door. A strange man stood before her.

95

"I am Pietro. Salvatore sent me," the man said. "You wanted to talk to him, signora."

For a few seconds she lay motionless, staring at him. She could feel the blood running to her face. Then she slowly sat up and pulled her robe together. It had been open by unconscious design.

"Why doesn't he come himself?" she asked mechanically.

Pietro smiled. It was a little smile around his mouth which didn't reach his eyes. "He will be sorry that he couldn't come, signora. What do you want from him?"

She went over to the table and lit a cigarette. Now she could think clearly again, and she felt calmer, perhaps because she expected Bentley to come back any moment.

She sat down and looked at Pietro. He was about Bentley's age, a man of average height with a dark, hard face and curly hair. He was wearing corduroy trousers, a black jacket over a white shirt, and boots of raw, undyed leather. His eyes were black and cold and didn't leave her for a second.

"I guess you know what I want from him," she said finally. "I told Piera who I am."

"We knew it already before then," Pietro said.

She had to admire his style. He didn't seem to be at all concerned by the fact that less than half a mile away were a dozen carabinieri with no other thought than catching him and his companions.

He went over to the table, took a cigarette, and put her cigarette case in his pocket. "You are looking for your husband," he said, lighting his cigarette with her lighter. "How much is it worth to you?"

She stared at him.

"We thought fifty thousand dollars would be a fair price," he said, looking past her through the window. "When can you have that?"

"Where is he?" Helen asked. She felt as if all the blood had been drawn from her head.

"With us. Do you have fifty thousand dollars?"

She shook her head.

"Perhaps your father has," Pietro said, going to the door. He locked it, went to the night table, and picked up her pocketbook. He opened it and emptied it on the bed. His movements were so

96

coolly natural that it didn't occur to her to try to stop him. Since he had locked the door, she was beginning to feel panic.

She watched him take her pistol, examine it, and put it in his pocket. Then he started counting the money.

"This is only four thousand five hundred," he said without looking at her. "Where are the other five thousand?"

"In a bank." Her own voice startled her.

He looked at her sharply. "Where?"

"In Naples."

"That's too bad, signora," Pietro said. He put the money in his pocket, took a dress from her closet, and threw it on the floor in front of her. "Get dressed."

She didn't move. He hit her in the face. The blow was so sharp that she fell from her chair to the floor.

"I don't work this way usually, signora, but we have little time. Don't wait for your friend. He is still busy. Get up."

She could feel blood trickling from her mouth and she was groggy, but she knew that she could still think. She also knew that he was serious.

"You don't have to be bashful," he said. "I know how a woman looks."

He watched her as she scrambled up and took off her robe. She was so stunned by fear and pain that nothing seemed to matter.

"Wash off your mouth," he said and went over to the closet. He opened her suitcase, threw a few things in it, and turned around. She was dressed.

"Your mouth," he said.

She went to the table, poured some water, and washed her face.

"That's enough, signora," he said. "If you are sensible, you will be back here in a few days. And don't try to shout. Nobody will hear you."

He opened the door, took her arm, and pushed her through in front of him. Bentley was standing on the landing of the stairs.

"Tell him to throw away his pistol," Pietro said dropping the suitcase and pulling her close to him.

"Throw away your pistol, Clyde," Helen said tonelessly.

Bentley backed toward the steps. "If something happens to her, you won't get out of this house, Salvatore."

"You talk too much," Pietro said and fired at him past Helen's hips. When he fired the second time, Bentley was already on the stairs. He dashed through the restaurant and out into the street.

The square in front of the inn lay abandoned in the sun. Bentley stood behind a tree, waiting for Helen and Pietro to come out.

"You won't make it, Salvatore," he shouted when they appeared in the doorway. "If you send the lady back to her room, I will let you go."

"Go to the car," Pietro shouted at Helen.

"You won't make it that way either," Bentley called. "I'll shoot up your tires. Go up the street with her. Send her back after fifty steps. That's a fair offer, Salvatore."

Pietro nodded. "Stay where you are." He took Helen by the arm and walked under the arch up the empty street into the village. After fifty steps he looked back. Bentley was standing under the arch.

"Stay here," Pietro said to Helen. "We will see you again, signora. Think about your husband."

"You are lying," she said. "He is no longer alive."

Pietro just smiled. This time the smile was in his eyes too.

She watched him jog away and vanish around a curve. Then she sat down on a stairway beside the street and waited for Bentley.

He arrived out of breath. "Did he hurt you?"

She shook her head.

"I couldn't risk more because of you," Bentley said. "If I'd only known if the carabinieri are here . . ."

"Not now," Helen said. "He was not Salvatore. Take me back, Clyde!" The street lay as empty as if the village were a ghost town.

"They are all in church," Bentley said. "He picked a good time. Did he take your set of car keys?"

"He took everything," Helen said. "My car key, my money, and the pistol. He even took my cigarette case."

Bentley swore. "Why didn't you tell me sooner?" he asked.

"It wasn't worth it."

In her room she lay down on her bed. Bentley brought in her suitcase. She was still deathly pale.

"Did you say it wasn't Salvatore?"

"Salvatore had sent him. His name is Pietro."

"Where were you?" Helen asked after a moment.

Bentley laughed angrily. "In the castle. When the innkeeper came up the first time, he told me Piera had been here and asked me to meet her there at nine."

"You didn't tell me that."

"I wanted to, but at breakfast I was mad at you. When she hadn't shown up at nine o'clock I ran all the way back. I never have premonitions, but this time I did. They must have made a little mistake in their timing. They didn't figure I'd suspect something and get back so quickly."

"I'm surprised you fell for the trap at all," Helen said.

He was surprised himself, but after Helen had told him that she wanted to go back to Naples the following day he had hoped that a meeting with Piera might make her change her mind. He sat next to her and looked at her face. It was completely calm. Most women would now be suffering a nervous collapse, but she was already talking in a normal voice.

Looking at her closely, he realized that the left half of her face and her mouth was swollen. He took her lower lip carefully between his fingers and pulled it forward. Her mouth was full of blood.

"Did he hit you?" he stammered.

She nodded. "I had to get dressed before his eyes," Helen said and swallowed the blood.

"I don't want to get separated from you again," he said with a voice full of anger, "but now I think you better go as quickly as possible to Palermo."

"And you?"

"Perhaps I can help the carabinieri. What did this man say to you?"

"That my husband is still alive. They want fifty thousand dollars."

"From your father? It wasn't hard to guess. I've been afraid of this since yesterday. More reason for you to go to Palermo."

"I still have three thousand dollars," Helen said. "He didn't see my second pocketbook."

# 14

Lieutenant Gastone showed up after dinner. He apologized for the delay and expressed satisfaction with the fact that the rain had stopped. Then he turned toward Helen. "If you ever need a good dentist, signora, I can give you an address in Nicosia. One of my men had a tooth pulled there three days ago."

"Mrs. Brazzi doesn't need a dentist," Bentley said. "Did you come back just now?"

"Ten minutes ago," Gastone said and studied Helen's face. "If we are not lucky soon, we will be sent back to Palermo."

"Perhaps we can improve your luck," Bentley said. "I think they gave you the message that we asked for you?"

"As soon as I came back," Gastone said. "I'm sorry I couldn't come sooner."

"That's all right. What we have to tell you will be as interesting now as it would have been in the afternoon. We know that Salvatore and Pietro are the same people who held up the bank in Nicosia."

Lieutenant Gastone smiled. "We already discussed this possibility once, Mr. Bentley. I think we knew it before you."

"How?"

"My colleague in Nicosia gave me a little tip. But what we need is proof. We don't have enough proof to involve the relatives of those two in our investigations."

"We can give you that proof," Bentley said and started to relate the incidents of the last few days.

The lieutenant took notes for a while; then he stopped, interposed a few questions, asked for descriptions of people, and then fell silent. He turned to Helen, who hadn't said a word.

"As long as you don't leave the inn, signora, I can guarantee your safety. It would be even better if you decided to move temporarily to Nicosia."

"I even suggested Palermo," Bentley said. "She insists on staying."

"Do you have any special reasons, signora?"

"She wants to see the man hanged," Bentley answered for her.

Lieutenant Gastone stood up. "That would go beyond my authority," he said without smiling. "But you will be satisfied. I don't like it when ladies are beaten up."

He went to the door and turned around once more. "You have done me a great favor. It is a pity you didn't decide to do it sooner. Will you still be needing Signor Rigido this evening?"

"I don't think he has anything to do with it," Helen said quickly.

"I don't think so either, signora. It's a routine matter. Tomorrow morning he will be at your service again. Good night, signora, Mr. Bentley." He saluted with his riding whip and walked out.

"I can't get used to his face," Bentley said. "If it suited his job, he would arrest his own mother. Is there anything else you'd like now?"

"I'm thirsty," Helen said. "Can you get us something to drink? I would love a brandy."

"You deserve one," Bentley said.

He was gone a long time. Helen went to the table and washed her face carefully with a cloth and looked at herself in the mirror. The swelling had receded. She touched her mouth, and then she went to the door and locked it. She undressed, put on her morning coat, paused in front of her closet and finally put a nightgown on under the morning coat.

When Bentley returned she was sitting at the table. He didn't comment on her outfit. He put a bottle and glasses on the table.

"It took awhile," he said. "I had to wait for Signor Rigido to send his customers home before leaving with the carabinieri. They were waiting for him at the door."

"Lieutenant Gastone too?"

"No, that kind of job he leaves to his infantry. They must have come with him. They couldn't have gotten here that quickly. Rigido was on the verge of a collapse."

"I am sorry," Helen said and watched him fill the glasses. "I'm not so sure he's involved."

Bentley smiled. "I thought you didn't like him. Well, if he is involved, Lieutenant Gastone will make him talk. Does your face still hurt?"

"No." She sipped from the glass, savored the brandy in her mouth for a moment, then swallowed it. "I forgot to thank you," she said.

"It was my fault," Bentley said. "I shouldn't have left you alone. You behaved wonderfully."

"I don't think so." She thought back on the experience and felt like choking.

Bentley reached into his pocket and brought out two twisted scraps of lead. "While you were sleeping I pried them out of the floor with a knife. He missed on purpose. I guess he didn't want to get in trouble with the United States Army. These aren't from your pistol."

"How can you tell?"

"By the caliber. It's not an Army pistol either. They must have quite a collection."

"I wonder why he came alone," Helen said, looking at the bullets.

"I don't know. Maybe they didn't want to make too much of a stir," he said. "Suppose they try it again during the night . . . "

She looked up, startled. "You think they might?"

"I think they're liable to do anything," Bentley said. He took her hand across the table. "Think about my suggestion. In Palermo you would be safe."

"Lock the door," Helen said.

Bentley obeyed. His mouth felt dry. His legs would hardly move. He had thought he might have a chance this evening, but he hadn't thought it would be that simple.

He could hear her going to the bed. When he turned around she had taken off her dressing gown. He could see the outline of her body through her nightgown. She lay down on the bed, put her hands behind her neck, and looked at him.

"Tell me about yourself," she said softly. "Don't you have a girl friend?"

"The way you have a girl friend when you're twenty-nine."

He got the bottle and the glasses, put them on the night table, and sat down beside her. "Since I met you, I've grown up," he said. "I am two hundred years older now."

"Is she rich?"

Bentley grinned. "As rich as I am."

"That's why you don't want to marry her," Helen said. "You're waiting for a rich woman. I'd be ideal for you. That's what you are waiting for, isn't it?"

Bentley caught his breath. "When we came here," he said with difficulty, "you told me that I was just after the usual thing."

She made him give her a cigarette and blew the smoke in his face. "First the usual thing and then the money. The usual thing you can have. You earned it today."

He didn't know why she said it; he hadn't expected any serious resistance anyway. But he wanted to fight for her—even if it was no longer necessary to fight.

"I don't give a damn what you think about me," he said and kissed her. He drew up her nightgown and caressed her body until her breathing grew heavier.

"You can't tell me that you don't mean more to me than that," he said with his mouth close to her face. "Maybe I'm wrong, but it's just because you've been able to fool me that makes you something special to me. You're my type, whether you like it or not."

Her hips were small, almost bony. When he bent over her she locked her legs. "You said yourself that you wanted a yacht," she said breathlessly. "Perhaps my father will give you one. Leave the light on."

Bentley took his hand from the light switch. She would never stop baiting him; not even when he had finally made it. But he was determined now not to let anything come in his way.

"I don't like presents much," he said and stood up. "Did your husband like them?"

"What do you think?"

Bentley took off his jacket. "When I was a little boy I believed in hell. Now I think it's silly to resist temptation. For a woman like you I would even be happy in the Army, or being a messenger boy for your father."

"Two months," Helen said. "Then you'd be sick of it."

She watched him put his jacket over the back of a chair, unlace his shoes, pull his shirt out of his trousers. "Give me a bit more time," she said.

Bentley stopped. "Do you want me to go back to my room?"

"No. Just give me a bit more time."

He had never met a woman more difficult to understand. He went to the other side of the bed and took off his clothes. She had turned her face toward the door. When he lay beside her she was trembling.

"I won't touch you if you don't want it," he said and he was serious, perhaps because it was becoming so complicated. From a certain moment on all he had wanted was to lie beside her and caress her. Now that he was lying beside her he felt as if he had just been through a sleepless night.

"You ought to cover yourself," he said.

She turned toward him and he saw that she had tears in her eyes.

"It isn't fair that the woman suffer from war, too," he said in a husky voice. "I have never met a woman who wanted war. They should try to stop this business. It's nice to believe in heaven, but you can't take anything with you, nothing of what you have done or haven't done. Did I ever tell you the story about Lewis?"

She shook her head, keeping her eyes on his.

"He was a student of theology," he said. "All his life he never touched a girl. Before we landed in Sicily, we were in Tunisia. One of those women who waited every night for us to give them chocolate was after him. One evening he came back to camp and cried on my shoulder. She had nearly gotten him. He had run away at the last second, literally. After that he never left the camp, but he couldn't sleep at night. After two weeks he looked like a corpse. It was impossible to get a sensible word out of him. The others told him that the woman was waiting for him every evening. I still don't know how he held out. When we landed in Sicily, he was one of the first to get killed. I have never seen anybody look so satisfied being dead. Even when we were burying him, he looked satisfied."

"Was he a friend of yours?" Helen asked.

Bentley saw with relief that her eyes were dry again.

"I've never been so close to anybody since," he said. "I didn't want to be; too difficult—like a whore falling in love with her clients. If there really is a heaven, he got a very good spot there. I still tried to believe in heaven then. I couldn't bear to believe that he had been torturing himself all his life for nothing."

"Don't you believe in it anymore?" Helen asked.

"I've tried to a hundred times, but I always get stuck somewhere. If what I feel with a woman would stop me from getting to heaven, I'm not so sure I want to get to heaven. Do you believe in heaven?"

Helen nodded.

"You should," Bentley said. "Otherwise you couldn't stand your present life. If I started believing in heaven again, it would be for your sake."

She smiled.

He saw that she was looking at his body, and he pulled up the sheet. He hadn't felt embarrassed in front of her for a moment, not even when the wave of restlessness had swept over him. Now the feeling was gone, and it struck him that she hadn't done anything to make him feel that way in the first place. She had lain quietly the whole time. She was still an ambiguity—an ambiguity turned flesh, but he was satisfied lying next to her and talking to her the way one talks to one's wife in the intimate atmosphere of a bedroom—in the relaxed intimate state of two people with nothing to hide from each other and who have told each other everything. The suspended state of her emotions affected him so powerfully that in response his own pulsing desire had become suspended, and it struck him as not at all strange—quite natural, in fact. A few days with her had surmounted and obliterated the experiences, the passions, and the frustrations that had accumulated during two years of war.

He leaned over her and turned off the night lamp. For a moment he felt her body stiffen in anticipation, but then he lay down on his own side of the bed and laughed lightly.

"If it's good for your nerves, I'll stay with you tonight," he said. "I don't think I snore. Would it bother you?"

She didn't answer. He felt her moving closer to him under the sheet. It wasn't quite dark in the room; the window framed a square of clear moonlight, which fell at an angle across the floor.

"You must think I'm crazy," Helen said, "but I can't explain my feelings to you."

"Of course not," Bentley said. "After all, you think I have your husband on my conscience."

"That's not it."

"It isn't?"

"Not just that," Helen said.

Bentley nodded in the dark.

"I'm not a whore," she said.

"No, you're not."

"I tried," she muttered, "but I'm not a whore."

It was so terribly logical and illogical at the same time and so terribly hopeless he couldn't think of anything to answer. He felt for her hand under the sheet and took hold of it. Later he realized that she was asleep.

# 15

When she woke up in the morning, he was gone. His place next to her was still warm. She missed him.

The window was wide open. She looked at the blue sky and the mountains. The sun was shining warmly into the room. She looked at the room, the sheets, the cupboard, and the terrible little paintings on the wall as if she were seeing them for the first time.

She had slept well. Her head was clear. The swelling on her face had vanished. She felt fresher and more rested then she had felt for a long time.

But Bentley's absence worried her. She couldn't hear any sound from his room. She stood up, washed hastily, and got dressed. Her nervousness increased when she discovered that her door was locked from the outside. She was about to start beating on it with her fists when she heard steps. A moment later the lock turned, and Bentley came in with a breakfast tray.

"You scared me," Helen said.

Bentley smiled. "This time it wasn't a bogeyman. I had to find breakfast myself. Signor Rigido hasn't come back. But there's a carabiniere at every door. Lieutenant Gastone really meant it when he said he was guaranteeing your security."

"Why did you lock my door?"

"Carabinieri are just men," Bentley said and put the tray on the table. "Did you sleep well?"

She blushed slightly. "Yes."

"I didn't," Bentley said. His face looked pale and haggard. "You snore," he said.

"Well, tonight you can sleep in your own bed," Helen said and looked at the breakfast tray. "Did you cut this bread?"

"Why?"

"It looks as if it had been done with a saw."

Bentley sat down. "It must have been the knife. The carabinieri told me that they looked through all the caves last night."

"Did they find something?"

"No."

"But Pietro has to be somewhere in the neighborhood," Helen said, tearing off a piece of bread. "He came by foot."

"That doesn't mean anything. He could have left a horse somewhere; he probably wasn't alone anyway. One man stays with the horses in case something goes wrong. They were probably ready for anything."

"But not for you," Helen said. "Do you still have the other set of keys?"

Bentley took it out of his pocket. "I have lost a rifle, fifty dollars, and a new hat, but never car keys. Do you have a checkbook?"

She looked at him without understanding. "For my bank?"

"Yes."

"Sure, but not here. Why do you ask?"

"You should have a checkbook on an Italian bank. When I had my car fixed, I asked around a little. There's only one big bank in Nicosia, the Central Bank. I think you ought to open an account there in your own name."

"Why on earth?"

"Just in case," Bentley said vaguely. "Since I couldn't get you too enthusiastic about Palermo, I'd like at least to do something about my insomnia. You have now lost five thousand dollars. Deposit the rest in an account. It's safer than your pocketbook. After that we can have dinner in Nicosia and look around. It will change your mind; there are a lot of things to see on this island. Before the war every civilized American tried to have a look at it at least once."

"What do you think an account at the Central Bank will gain us?"

"The gang will try to withdraw the money. That will give me a lead to you."

"To me?"

Bentley stared at the smoke from the cigarette. "It was just an idea," he said. "Perhaps we'd better look at the sea after we eat. I feel as if I haven't seen it in ten years. I don't mind mountains, but here they're so crowded together I feel like I'm in a mousetrap."

Helen was silent. He had made her more nervous than she wanted to admit to herself.

"How far is it to the sea?" she asked after a while.

"If we go by way of San Stefano, forty miles."

She nodded. "Come and get me in half an hour."

Bentley looked relieved. "How did you like the coffee?"

"Terrible."

"Same here," Bentley said. He took the breakfast tray with him and went down to the restaurant. At the door he met Lieutenant Gastone and Rigido, who was standing behind him, looking perturbed.

"I hope you didn't miss him, Mr. Bentley," Lieutenant Gastone said, laying his whip on the table.

"I didn't, but Mrs. Brazzi did. The coffee I made was terrible."

"I'm so sorry," Lieutenant Gastone said. "I didn't count on you getting up early today. Did you have an undisturbed night, Mr. Bentley?"

Bentley didn't like the way he said it. He looked in the smiling face. "You ought to know. Didn't you send us a lifeguard?"

"Just a precaution, Mr. Bentley. I have given sharp instructions not to bother you."

Now Bentley was sure. One of the carabinieri must have noticed something. Perhaps he had even been standing in front of Helen's door during the night. He watched Rigido go over to the bar and busy himself. "Did you get anything out of him?" he said confidentially to Gastone.

"Nothing of importance," the lieutenant replied. "I'm really only here to tell you that Vito was seen in Cerami yesterday, but we lost track of him there."

Bentley smiled with difficulty. "I'll have nightmares about Cerami someday. Did you hear anything from Piera?"

"She doesn't have an uncle in Cerami. That much we did find out, and there is also no boy living in Chiesa who comes to Cerami to take care of his uncle's goats."

"Do you have any idea where Piera could be?" Bentley said.

Lieutenant Gastone knocked the ashes off his cigarette. "If I knew, Mr. Bentley, I would also know where her brother hides."

Bentley noticed that he was looking at the door. "Mrs. Brazzi isn't ready yet. You can pull back your lifeguard for a while. We are going to San Stefano."

"Beautiful area," Lieutenant Gastone said. "I've had a little business to do there once or twice." He stood up and put on a pair of leather gloves. "Give my regards to the signora, Mr. Bentley. Perhaps I'll drop in this evening. When do you think you will be back?"

"I'm not thinking about it."

"Perhaps you can send me word through Rigido. I assume that you don't want one of my men to come with you."

Bentley nodded. "You assume right, Lieutenant. Are you concerned?"

"That's my profession," Gastone said, putting the whip under his arm. "Perhaps you would like to know why the people here have never done anything against Vito: they believe he chases bad spirits from their houses."

Bentley looked at him. "That's a nice medieval notion."

"In Sicily the Middle Ages aren't over yet," Lieutenant Gastone said, and took his leave.

It had the faint sound of a warning. Bentley looked after him angrily. If it were up to him he would have gone straight to Palermo with Helen.

It was very bright and warm in the restaurant. The sun burned through the large window. From the kitchen came the sound of running water.

Bentley turned to Rigido, who was busy with the espresso machine, and said, "I'm sorry you were bothered."

"I will be bothered more," Rigido said moodily. "How long do you think you are going to stay here, Signor Bentley?"

"Would you like to get rid of us?"

"I can't send you away, sir. But they questioned me half the night and locked me up in a dark hole."

"But I can't tell the carabinieri what to do and what not to do," Bentley said impatiently. "And after all, the signora was almost captured in your house."

"I was in church, sir."

"The whole village was in church," Bentley said. "I never suspected there were so many pious people in Chiesa. Still, I'd bet that quite a few of them will find themselves in hell one day. I would like to go for a drive with the signora. Can you give us a thermos bottle of tea?"

"If you give me the bottle, signore. Will you be back for dinner?"

"If nothing happens in the meantime," Bentley said. He stared thoughtfully at Rigido's disgruntled face. "You ought to know. Do you think we would be safer in another inn?"

"In another inn it wouldn't be my problem," Rigido answered. "I shouldn't worry anyway. The lady treats me like a dog. But I don't wish the trouble on her I would have if I did know something. One day the carabinieri won't be here anymore, Signor Bentley."

"Salvatore isn't immortal either," Bentley said, and went to get the thermos bottle.

# 16

West of San Stefano the road became empty of traffic. The vineyards and the vegetable plots vanished too. Instead, red oleanders and peach trees lined the road, which was well paved and followed, through many curves, the formation of the coast with its rocks, cliffs, sandy peninsulas, and hidden caves. Further inland, on the other side of the road, rock formations jutted toward the soft blue sky, which was reflected in the sea.

It was unbearably hot in the car. Bentley drove with his jacket off. Helen had pulled her dress up over her knees to cool her legs. Distracted and silent, Bentley concentrated on the curvy road. Further on, at a point where the road curved away from the sea, a small sandy lane wound through high bushes and stubby trees toward the water. Bentley remembered it. It looked more or less the way he had imagined. He stopped the car.

"Do you want to?"

"What?"

"Rest a bit. We have plenty of time."

Helen nodded. Bentley steered the car down the lane. After about two hundred yards it became so narrow that they had to stop the car. He took the thermos bottle and a blanket from the back seat. The road led to a steep wall of sand overlooking a little quay with a smooth sandy beach. The sea lay as calm as a lake.

"How wonderful," Bentley said. "I don't know why people always want to go to Honolulu. Have you ever been there?"

"Yes."

"I should have thought so. Without the war I wouldn't have even made it to New York."

He helped her down the steep slope, spread the blanket on the sand, and tested the water with his hand. "Lukewarm," he said. "I'm sorry, but since you told me in Naples that this wasn't going to be a pleasure trip, I didn't bring a bathing suit. Can you swim?"

"Not in the nude."

He smiled. "I wouldn't look. I promise you—"

"Don't bother," she interrupted him shortly.

Bentley shrugged. He took his clothes off and waded into the water. When he looked back once, she was leafing through her new checkbook. He floated on his back for a while, then he swam back to shore, walked to where Helen was lying, and fashioned his shirt into a loin cloth. Since the night before, he didn't feel it necessary to bother, but the way she looked at him made him shy.

He lay down beside her in the sand and opened the thermos bottle. "Do you ever lie in the sun?" he asked.

"Not lately."

"I understand. I used to play chess with Lewis every night. Since he died, I haven't felt like it anymore."

She let him fill the cup with tea. "You really don't want to swim?" he asked.

There wasn't any other point to being on the beach, but she didn't want to show herself to him without clothes.

Bently got up. "I'm going to the car. If you want to, you can have a swim in the meantime."

He dressed and climbed back up the slope. Near the car he sat down in the shadow of a little tree and stared at the mountains. It was getting late in the afternoon. Here and there the shadows of the mountains already reached the beach. The peaceful atmosphere began to work its effect on Bentley. He smoked a cigarette and watched a flock of little birds floating through the air like tiny arrows.

Fifteen minutes later he walked back to Helen. He found her wrapped in the blanket. Her skin was still glistening with water.

"Where have you been so long?" she asked.

"I was meditating," Bentley said and leaned over her. The salt water had washed the makeup from her face, but she still looked pretty. As he kissed her she closed her eyes. He put his hand under the blanket and caressed her breasts. Only when he began to pull the blanket away did she begin to resist.

"Not here," she said. But she continued to tolerate his caresses. She had spent half the day thinking about them, and she had reached a compromise with herself.

"You are becoming a problem for me, Clyde," she said. "I didn't come to Italy to find a new problem. What do you expect from me, marriage?"

"It would solve the problem," Bentley said. "I love you."

His remark made no impression on her. "I have already told you once that you have helped me a lot," she said impatiently. "Today that's even more valid than a few days ago. Perhaps some day we can see each other in Toledo."

That was more than he had hoped for. "If you want to," he said hesitantly. "Was your father there when Hopkins . . ."

"You wouldn't meet him," Helen said quickly. "I was thinking about our weekend house."

Bentley nodded. He felt disappointed. "Do you go there often?"

"If you'll be sensible and not propose marriage to me anymore."

"I understand," Bentley said and took his hand off her. "You can't forgive me."

"That's not the point," Helen said. "I just don't want to spend my whole life with a reminder."

"I understand," Bentley repeated. "So every now and then you'll throw the dog a little bone to keep him from barking."

He was making it more difficult for her than she had feared. She began to wonder about her compromise.

"Are you blackmailing me?" Helen asked.

"The bishop of Toledo could find out about me," Bentley said. "Or didn't you go to church every Sunday with your husband?"

Helen was silent.

"I'm beginning to think you're stalling me," Bentley said.

He wasn't hurt because she had refused him again but by the cheap way she was trying to pacify him. So he was to look forward to a meeting in Toledo—where another alibi would keep him under control until she could get rid of him without complications.

"You won't risk antagonizing me, will you?" he said. "Little Clyde might talk. He might even get the notion of writing something nasty in some kind of true confessions magazine, say the story about your governess. Why did you tell me that? To impress me? You didn't tell it to your husband. Were you afraid he might run away like the other one?"

She turned to him. "He would have married me if I had told him a dozen such stories," she said loudly. "Whatever he became was thanks to me."

"Of course," Bentley said as loudly as she. "A little lap dog on a golden leash! The trouble is, when he didn't have the leash anymore, he forgot his training and joined the other little dogs."

She had never hated him as much as at that moment. She stood up. As she threw off the blanket Bentley stood up, too.

His face was distorted. He put his arms around her, pulled her to the ground, and for one moment she lay next to him, bewildered, in the warm sand. Then she began to resist him again, kicking him and turning her face aside, and when he twisted her arm to force her on her back and crushed her under his weight, she started to scream with anger and hatred.

He let go of her quickly. She lay on the sand with her eyes closed and screamed. She went on even after he had walked away from her. He had never heard a woman scream like that. When he couldn't bear it anymore, he threw the blanket over her head. Then he put his jacket on and walked to the car without looking around.

He sat down near the car, under the same tree, and watched the twilight rising from the sea and covering the mountains. When Helen approached, Bentley's face was wet with tears.

She stood still in front of him and looked at him, but she felt no pity for him. She hadn't stopped hating him; she only had forgotten for a while.

She sat and waited for him in the car. She watched him out of the corners of her eyes as he arose, climbed behind the wheel, started the engine, and backed the car up the lane. His face now looked petrified.

It became darker. San Stefano could only be recognized now by its lights. The rock on which it lay seemed to be transformed into a Christmas tree with little candles.

They drove on toward the mountains. Again they passed people returning from the fields, peasants on horseback, mule carts blocking the road, trucks, and the local buses. Only when the road started climbing steeply beyond San Stefano did the traffic thin.

Helen was smoking. The more she thought about the latest episode with Bentley, the less she understood it. She was mostly worried about her own behavior. She hadn't screamed because of fear. She had heard herself scream the way one hears another person. Perhaps she had been hysterical, although she had never before known symptoms of hysteria in herself.

No, she thought, it wasn't hysteria; it was some kind of physical allergy. Still, she hadn't felt that way about his earlier caresses. She had been curious then—she had felt the curiosity of a woman who has lived three years without a man. She had often tried to imagine how it would have been with this man or that man, but she had evaded all opportunities. She knew her own weaknesses and she was afraid of opportunities. She knew that at crucial moments her curiosities and weaknesses tended to be stronger than her willingness to suppress them. With Bentley the opportunities could not be avoided because of the proximity of their lives, and the insistence of his erotic attacks. Bentley had never been repulsive to her as a man. Perhaps she was no longer young enough to exist without feeling wanted every now and again, but if her repugnance to intimacy was not confined to this particular man, she had better see a psychiatrist as quickly as possible.

She now felt like an epileptic after an attack; she began to be afraid of herself.

After a while they reached Nicosia, a spacious town surrounded by four high peaks of rock. Helen had liked it at first sight, and as they drove through the wide main street, she wondered whether it wouldn't be better to move into one of its nice hotels. She had seen one earlier. But a last remnant of pride kept her from it.

Bentley's total silence began to concern her. It created an abyss between them and she was tempted once or twice to say a few conciliatory words, but she couldn't. She was almost glad when the lights of Chiesa showed in the night sky.

The square in front of the inn lay abandoned. The only light came from the windows of the restaurant and fell faintly on the trees. It was a familiar scene for this hour of day. As Bentley turned off the car's beams, two men left their places under the arch and walked toward the car. Helen became aware of their steps a moment before they reached the car. Each opened one of the back doors simultaneously and got in. It happened so fast that she didn't understand. Bentley didn't either, but he realized that he had made a mistake.

"Drive down the road," said the man behind him.

Helen recognized his voice. When she tried to turn around, the other man put his hand on her shoulder.

"Don't move, signora," he said softly. "I wouldn't want to hurt you."

She heard him laugh softly, and as Bentley drove the car down into the valley he was still laughing.

"Turn right at the crossroads," Pietro said to Bentley, "the way you just came."

"To Nicosia?" Bentley asked.

"To Nicosia," Pietro said politely, "and don't do anything unless I tell you to. How much gas have you left in the car?"

"Half a tank," Bentley muttered. His mind was working again. He could have killed himself for being such a fool.

"That's enough," the second man said and laughed again. "She has nice hair," he said to Pietro. "You hadn't told me about her hair."

"She has other nice things," Pietro said and, addressing Helen, "He loves blondes, signora. You don't have to be afraid of him."

Helen was silent. She felt frozen with fear.

They met no one on the dark mountain road. The moon rose and it became lighter. Although Bentley drove slowly, nobody commented. It confirmed his impression that they were waiting for something. Even though he didn't know exactly what they were up to, he didn't think there was any immediate danger. Their captors would know what consequences any violence would have for the entire population. He was surprised by the lack of concern he felt for himself. Only an hour earlier he had been determined to go back to Naples the following day. After his latest experience with Helen he was convinced that his efforts to get closer to her were hopeless. He felt that being separated from her would be easier than being with her under these conditions. His disappointment was so great that he felt an almost senseless satisfaction with the present situation. Somehow it might provide him with a chance to make himself useful to her and thus conquer her resistance.

He had no plan. The pistol in his pocket seemed useless. He wished it weren't in such an obvious place, even though the two men had not yet thought of searching him. The way they were sitting, it wasn't necessary.

Sooner than Bentley expected, he found a chance to get rid of the pistol. When they had covered about half of the twenty-five miles to Nicosia, Pietro ordered him to back into a side road that angled off to the right of the main road. During the few seconds that the two men were concentrating on his driving, Bentley succeeded in taking the weapon out of his pocket.

For a moment he was tempted to gamble everything, but he didn't want to expose Helen to any danger. He dropped the pistol between his legs to the floor of the car. The noise of the impact was concealed by the sound of the engine.

"Turn off your lights," Pietro said.

Bentley obeyed. He expected to be told to get out of the car. Instead, Pietro bent over and carefully went through his pockets. Bentley almost laughed. He felt the pistol with his foot and pushed it as close as possible to the door of the car.

"Do you want a cigarette?" Pietro asked. There was enough light for Bentley to recognize his own cigarettes in Pietro's hand. He took out two, gave one to Helen and held up his lighter for her.

"There's not much I can do at the moment," he said to her in English. "Just do whatever they tell you to."

Helen nodded. In the light of the flame her face looked surprisingly calm.

"Talk as much as you like," Pietro said from behind in English. "My friend doesn't understand English."

He said something to the man beside him, who started to laugh again. When Pietro's companion lit one of Bentley's cigarettes, his face became visible for the first time. It was round, chubby, and friendly-looking, with soft black eyes, a little mouth and faint lines in the cheeks. It was the vace of a village priest.

"It should have been here by now," Pietro said.

The chubby-faced man stopped laughing and nodded. He held the cigarette between a thumb and finger and looked at it. "I can't get used to their taste," he said. "Why do they perfume them so much."

"Perhaps their wives like it," Pietro said and nodded toward Helen. The chubby-faced one started to laugh again. He bent over and touched Helen's neck with the tips of his fingers. When he started stroking her hair she felt a shiver of fear run across her back.

"Stop that!" Pietro said without changing the tone of his voice.

The chubby-faced man drew his fingers back. "Just her hair," he said. "It's like touching silk."

"You say the same thing about your horse," Pietro said. Then he saw the headlights of the bus. It came from the same direction they had come, and it approached them very quickly. As it went by they could see the ticket collector standing beside the driver, and behind him three seated passengers.

"That's the last one for today," Pietro said to Bentley. "If you hurry, you can be back to Chiesa in four hours. To Nicosia it isn't quite that far."

"Maybe you haven't made any mistakes so far," Bentley said hoarsely, "but this time you've made a big one."

Pietro got out and opened the door at Bentley's side. "One never knows in advance," he said indifferently. "Get out, signore."

He stood next to the door, watching Bentley's hands.

It was almost hopeless. Bentley had known it when Pietro had gotten out of the car before him, yet he had one last chance. As he got out he kicked the pistol out of the car. It fell close by on the road. The rain had made the earth soft and there was no sound. When he was out, he stepped on it and ground it as deeply as possible into the soft earth.

"If something happens to the lady," Bentley said to Pietro, "you'll have ten thousand men on your tails, I promise you."

"It's up to you, signore," Pietro answered. He reached behind

*118*

Bentley and switched on the headlights of the car. "As long as you don't tell the carabinieri, the signora has nothing to fear."

Bentley could hardly speak from anger and frustration. Through the windshield he could vaguely make out Helen's face.

"Don't forget the book," he said to her. "Within three days I will be with you again."

"What are you talking about?" Pietro said sharply. "What book?"

"A pocketbook," Bentley answered in Italian.

Pietro looked puzzled, then he turned to Helen. "Let me see it."

She gave it to him; he held it in his left hand and pointed with his pistol toward the road. "Get over there, signore, on the other side!"

Bentley obeyed. He hadn't quite reached the spot when the car began to move. For a moment Bentley felt the glare of the headlights in his eyes, then the car was by him, accelerating quickly.

Bentley stared after it until the red taillights vanished, then he walked to the spot where the car had stood. It took him five minutes to find the pistol. He wiped it off with his handkerchief, and put it in his pocket mechanically.

Back on the road, he looked at his watch. It had become so light by now that he could easily see the dial. It would be about twelve miles to Nicosia. Even if he walked quickly, he wouldn't get there before two o'clock. Four hours of empty mountain landscape—yet it didn't bother him as much as the question of why the car had headed toward Nicosia.

He still hadn't found the answer when, exactly four hours and twenty-five minutes later, his legs aching, he reached the first house in Nicosia.

# 17

Helen got no answer to that question either until about two hours later, when they had gone thirty miles from San Stefano, following the coast east until they finally turned onto a bad road leading southward into the mountains. Although she did not have a good sense of direction, she guessed that they had gone in a circle and were heading to the road between Chiesa and Nicosia.

She had now had about three hours to get used to the situation and she had calmed down somewhat. It seemed a paradox, but since Bentley was no longer with her she felt her self-confidence returning, and the farther away she got from him, the surer she felt. Perhaps it was partly the almost exaggerated politeness with which the two men treated her. They offered her cigarettes and asked every fifteen minutes whether or not she had to out; the man with the chubby face had put a blanket behind her back. She also found herself somehow relieved that the man beside her was Pietro and she was surprised at her reaction. The chubby-faced man was called Antonio. She could not have thought of a better name for him. She no longer feared him; when he stroked her hair again she found herself weighing the possibilities that her attraction to him might provide. She wasn't used to their dialect yet, but she understood scraps every so often.

Like Bentley, she had reached the conclusion that they wouldn't risk hurting an American. They wanted the money, that was everything. She wasn't worried about the size of the sum. For a man like her father it would not be an insoluble problem to find the cash.

In fact, when she thought about the shock it would give her father, she felt almost gay. She had succeeded only twice in her life in shocking him, and this would probably be better than the business with the governess and the marriage with Genno Brazzi.

The more she thought about it, the more the whole affair seemed a romantic caper. She was nearing the precise objective of her trip to Italy, which made the situation more amusing and gave her her first sense of accomplishment. She began to feel as if she had never veered from her original goal.

The road became worse the farther they got into the mountains. It was unpaved and full of holes and not much wider than the car. On both sides were dark ruins of abandoned houses, occasional trees and bushes, and deserted wells. The mountains seemed to bask in the clear moonlight; the landscape was as strange as ever. If she were right in thinking that they had gone in a circle, they would soon be back on the road to Nicosia.

Her head ached from the sudden changes in altitude. She had a bottle of cologne in her pocketbook, but Pietro hadn't returned it to her; it was in the back of the car. When she asked for it he exchanged a few words with Antonio. She heard him open the pocketbook and rummage through it, then the light in the car went on.

"What's the matter?" Pietro asked.

"A checkbook," Antonio said. "The Central Bank of Nicosia."

"How much did you deposit, signora?"

For a moment she hesitated, but then she remembered that Bentley had put the receipt in his pocket.

"Fifteen thousand," she muttered.

Antonio lifted his head. "Fifteen thousand dollars?"

She nodded.

"Let me see," Pietro said. He took a hand off the wheel and took the checkbook from Antonio. "When did you deposit this, signora?"

"Today."

"Cash?"

"I had it transferred by wire," she said quickly.

Pietro looked at the checkbook and gave it back to Antonio. "Can anyone draw money from it?"

She shook her head.

"You're lying, signora," Antonio said. "It's a regular account.

Anybody can take out money as soon as you have signed the check. Don't lie to us, signora, and don't assume that we're stupid."

Although he hadn't raised his voice, she felt another shiver of fear run down her back.

"Too dangerous," Pietro said, distracted. He turned off the light in the car and looked sideways at Helen's face. "Why did you have it sent to you?"

"I had no more money," Helen said.

Antonio bent over. "They won't know yet what has happened. Tomorrow morning would be the best time."

"Do you want to do it?" Pietro asked.

"Carmelo. I'll drive him there."

"Carmelo only knows about horses," Pietro said.

He concentrated again on the road, which climbed steeply.

When they had reached the top Helen saw Monte Soro. It seemed to fill the entire horizon. She also recognized Monte Pelalo and Monte Ambola. She was now seeing them from the other side, but she could never have mistaken them for other mountains, these two heavy bodies of rock looming in the bluish moonlight.

It couldn't be but a few miles as the crow flies to the spot where she had sat with Bentley and looked at the mountains for the first time. And to the right was the pyramid-shaped mountain where Chiesa was. By car she could be back at Signor Rigido's inn in half an hour. She realized that she was on the verge of crying. The caper was not so romantic that she wouldn't have rather been in her bed at that moment.

The road descended again through many curves toward the valley, which, as far as Helen could see in the dark, stretched between Monte Soro and Monte Ambola toward the south. Gradually the valley narrowed and she couldn't see more than a few hundred yards ahead. After about three miles, they reached a fork. The road turned toward the southwest, and toward the southeast was a narrow valley with steep sides. The bottom of the valley consisted of nothing but a dried-out mountain stream.

"Here we are, signora," Pietro said and stopped the car. "It's not exactly what you are used to, but we have prepared a bit for your visit."

She looked at him. "Where are we?"

"Home," Pietro said, and turning to Antonio; "Look at the gas."

He waited until Antonio got out and then he looked at Helen's feet. "May I see your shoes?"

He sounded so polite that she took off her shoes without protesting. Pietro examined the thin heels, tested them with his hand, and then broke them off. "You wouldn't have gotten very far with them," he said and gave them back to her. He put the heels in his pocket, got out, walked around the car, and opened her door.

"We have some way to go on foot," he said. "Do you want to bring the blanket?"

She nodded.

Antonio approached. "It should be enough," he said. "About two gallons. Have you thought about cashing a check?"

"Too dangerous," Pietro said again and turned to Helen. "Come with me, signora."

Antonio stayed in their way. He was a bit smaller than Pietro, with muscular shoulders.

"It's fifteen thousand dollars," he said quietly. "I will discuss it with Giuseppe and Lucio."

"I have to think about it," Pietro said and took Helen's arm. "Stay close behind me, signora."

He led her into the narrow valley. She heard the car start again and go on in the same direction. They picked their way along the rocky bed of the stream. Although the moon had risen over the mountain, it was difficult going, and she had to hold on to Pietro at the difficult spots. The path climbed narrowly and they had to make their way around huge boulders.

Further on, the valley became a bit wider, and the going got easier. It looked to Helen as if the valley ended at the foot of a high mountain, which they were approaching. With each step she felt her newly regained self-confidence crumbling away. The only thing which kept her from panic was her curiosity over how, in this labyrinth of rock bathed in blue moonlight, any trace of human habitation could exist.

"Only fifteen minutes more, signora," Pietro said encouragingly. "Do you want to take a rest?"

She stopped immediately. She could feel every stone through the thin soles of her shoes, and her feet already hurt excruciatingly.

"Where are you leading me?" she asked breathlessly.

123

Pietro put the blanket on the ground and waited until she sat down. "There are three little caves here," he said finally. "The Germans made them during the war. You will sleep as well tonight as at Signor Rigido's."

"You think so, do you?" Helen said. She looked at him sideways and saw that he was smiling. He looked almost sympathetic, and for a moment he reminded her of her husband. Then she recalled how he had hit her the day before.

"How long are you going to keep me?" she asked. "Until the money is in your hands?"

"Perhaps."

"You don't know yet?"

"There's a problem," Pietro said. He fished a crushed cigarette out of his pocket, lit it, and stared at the valley behind them. "A few of my friends feel that fifteen thousand dollars is too little. They want a hundred thousand. At first I wanted to do business with you alone, signora, but since it didn't work out yesterday, I was obliged to bring my friends in. It would have been better if I hadn't had to do that. For you too, signora."

"Because they want a hundred thousand dollars," Helen said.

"That's not it so much," Pietro said, drawing on his cigarette. "You see, I don't care much about Sicily and I don't care much about my relatives; the sooner I get out of here the better. But my friends feel a bit different. Some of them have their families. And Antonio wouldn't leave Cerami even if he didn't have any relatives. He likes Cerami."

Helen felt the blood draining from her face. She asked as quietly as she could, "Why would he leave Cerami?"

"Because of you, signora. As soon as we set you free, you will go to the carabinieri. I don't care. I have nothing to lose, but some of my friends have more to lose. They expect me to stop you from going to the carabinieri."

Helen was silent. She looked up at the moon and continued quietly, "You want to kill me?"

"Not me, signora."

"Aren't you the boss?"

Pietro smiled. "We don't have a boss. We are seven men and any one of us can do as he pleases."

"Why don't you then?"

As he didn't answer, she turned toward him. "Because they are your friends?"

"I'm not sentimental," Pietro said. He stubbed out the cigarette and got up. "At the moment, I can't promise you anything, signora. Incidentally, you haven't asked me about your husband."

"Has that something to do with it?"

"Only to the extent that he isn't alive anymore."

She had known it before, but now that he had said it, she resisted the knowledge. She let Pietro help her up, and as she climbed up the path beside him she felt completely dizzy. She couldn't feel her feet touch the ground. She couldn't feel the pain, she could feel only the strange giddiness compounded of cold and fear.

The valley ended beyond a sharp curve to the left, at the bottom of a steep slope which led to a completely vertical wall. There were cliffs on three sides of them.

"Give me your pocketbook," Pietro said. "You will now need both hands. Four days ago the carabinieri were here. At this spot they turned back. Do you see anything?"

Helen shook her head.

"The carabinieri didn't either," Pietro said. "The caves are behind the wall. When the Americans fired on the Germans, there was an avalanche of stones. Now the caves have only one entrance. They can't even be seen from the air."

Helen stared distractedly at the mountain. He realized that she wasn't listening and asked, "What are you thinking about?"

"I'm wondering if you killed my husband," Helen said.

"If I did, I wouldn't tell you, signora," he said softly.

"Do you know who did?"

"We were eight Italians," he said. "Salvatore and a man from Sperlinga were wounded in action. Your GI husband and his buddy helped us to carry the wounded men home."

"Did you take them with you because of that?"

"Not just because of that. Antonio . . ."

"Was he there?" Helen asked quickly.

Pietro hesitated, then he shrugged. "You will probably find out anyway. Antonio was a sergeant in the Italian army. He wanted to use the two GI's as hostages in case we met Americans on the way."

"I see," Helen said. She sat down on a rock and stared ahead of her.

"I had nothing to do with it," Pietro said softly. "Most of us lived in Sperlinga and Nicosia. We also had a wounded man from Sperlinga and so your husband and his pal had to carry him to Sperlinga. Salvatore and I stayed in Chiesa. What happened in Sperlinga wasn't our business."

"And what happened in Palmigano?"

Pietro stood motionless for a few seconds, then he took her arm and pulled her to her feet. "How do you know about Palmigano? From your friend?"

"Know what?"

"About . . ." He stopped, smiled again, and released her. "You're wondering about the wounded Americans? It was their own fault. We just wanted their arms. One of them fired the first shot and hit Salvatore. We were at war and we were sick of Americans, signora. They treated us like dogs."

"A year ago there was no war," Helen said.

He stopped smiling. "A year ago?"

"Mr. Bentley told me how a year ago in Palmigano a man was killed. I guess that wasn't your business either."

She could see him flush, but his voice didn't change. "I would shoot him again, signora. He betrayed us to your compatriots for two cartons of cigarettes. Without him everything would have been different. Now, come on!"

The climb was not as hard as Helen had feared. The rocks were piled up like the steps of a staircase, though some were so high that she wouldn't have managed them without Pietro's help. When she looked back, the sight made her dizzy again.

At the end of the path they were greeted by Vito. Helen recognized him before they got close to him. He was crouching at the edge of a broad hollow, which Helen only noticed when she stumbled into it. If Pietro hadn't caught her, she would have fallen, and for a moment she felt herself held against his chest, smelling his odor of sweat and horses. Then she found her footing again. "Did you hurt yourself?" he asked.

She shook her head. The unexpected meeting with Vito had given her a fright. She watched Pietro talk to him. She could see Vito's terrible face quite clearly.

She looked away from him to the far side of the hollow, where the entrance to the cave lay: a dark square, with its top and sides supported by beams. She could see now why Lieutenant Gastone hadn't been able to find this hiding place.

"They didn't expect us so soon," Pietro said. "Are you hungry, signora?"

"No."

"Piera will make you an espresso. Wait here for me."

He ducked into the entrance of the cave. While Helen waited for him, she realized that the knowledge of Piera's presence had relieved her a bit, although it hadn't surprised her. The day before, Bentley had already said that she was probably hiding in the same place as her brother.

A noise in back of her made her turn around. Vito was standing with his feet apart, muttering unintelligible sounds and pointing first down the slope and then at her. She stepped back. He shook his fist at her and his mutterings changed to a furious howl. She was paralyzed with fear and disgust. Then she heard Pietro's voice behind her. He passed her so quickly that she only saw his back. She heard a sound as if a piece of wood had been broken, a dumb cry, and then Pietro's voice. "I'm sorry, signora. He's angry at you. When he gets one of his attacks, one can't talk with him. Come with me."

She couldn't bring herself to look back to where Vito had been standing. She followed Pietro through the small entrance of the cave, trembling throughout her entire body.

The cave was much larger than Helen had expected. It was a long room with a curved roof and vertical walls, roughly hewn out of the rock and primitively furnished. On a table an acetylene lamp was burning with a blue flame. The first thing she saw was Piera, who was standing by a doorlike opening in the right wall. She was half dressed, with her hair in disorder. As she saw Helen, she hesitated a moment but didn't speak, and walked past her to a tile stove, in which ashes were still glowing.

"Piera was already asleep," Pietro said, sitting down. "When she is disturbed in her sleep she is unbearable. And this is Salvatore."

Helen had already discovered him. He was lying on a narrow cot at the back of the cave. When she looked at him closely she almost burst out laughing. The young man, hardly twenty, looked so different from the way she had imagined him that the reality seemed ironic. He had a narrow bony face with hard, unpleasant lines around his mouth and thin lips. Only his eyes were beautiful. They were Piera's eyes, almond-shaped and gleaming. He was covered to his waist with a blanket and wore a dirty T-shirt.

"Glad to meet you, signora," he said with a grin. "I would have loved to come for you myself, but my damned legs don't work. Did you have a pleasant trip?"

Helen didn't answer. She watched Piera put some wood on the fire and pour some water from a bucket into an iron pot. The stove had a makeshift chimney, next to which hung various pots and pans. On the bare rock floor goatskins had been spread and in one corner were two bundles of straw. The air in the cave was surprisingly cool and dry.

While Helen looked around, she felt Pietro's eyes watching her. His dark, hard face had a strange expression.

"Not quite your taste, signora," he said with a smile. "Not ours either. We came here for two years. Look at Salvatore. The bullet hit him in his back. It wasn't nice to shoot an eighteen-year-old boy in the back, not even if he was trying to get hold of an American rifle. He ought to go to Palermo. There is only one surgeon in Sicily who can get the bullet out. But, unfortunately, he is close to the Americans and charges a fortune for it."

"As soon as I can walk again," said Salvatore, "I will kill the surgeon. He's the first one I'll kill."

Pietro nodded. "And after that the doctor in Nicosia, and the American commander, and the American Military Police and the new members of parliament in Rome and who else, my boy?"

"The Pope," Salvatore said with a grin. "And the Bishop of Milano. And then I'll wed Piera to a bigshot in Palermo and I'll be a gentleman. A gentleman like Genno Brazzi," he said with a little laugh. "And what was the matter with Vito?"

"Vito doesn't like the lady," Pietro said lightly, and noticing that Helen was still standing in the entrance of the cave, he pointed at a chair. "Why don't you sit down, signora? Piera makes the best espresso in Sicily."

Helen obeyed. She could hardly stand up anymore anyway. She wished that she could hide in a dark corner and not see or hear anything more.

"Vito is a barbarian," Salvatore said, still grinning. "How can he have anything against the lady? If you ask me, I like her." He turned to Piera, who was crouched in front of the stove blowing into the fire. "Why didn't you tell me that she was pretty?"

"Pietro has told you a dozen times," Piera answered harshly.

Salvatore laughed. "She is jealous," he said to Pietro. "Watch out for her. If you make any passes at the signora, she will go into a nunnery." He looked at Helen. "Did you already ask her how she knew we did that job with the bank?"

"There is time," Pietro said. "Or do you want to tell us now, signora?"

Helen hesitated. If she told the truth, it would be an indictment of Piera, and she would make an enemy of the girl, which she wanted to avoid. She was glad Piera was there. All alone with the men she would have felt more lost.

"We found out from the carabinieri," she said, turning to Pietro.

"In Chiesa?"

"Yes."

Salvatore whistled. "I didn't know they were that smart. Was it that lieutenant?"

Helen nodded.

"I don't understand," Pietro said. For the first time since Helen had seen him, he looked worried. He watched Piera come to the table with the coffee, fill a cup, and put it in front of Helen. "Did he also tell you how he found out?" he asked.

"Through a colleague in Nicosia," Helen said. "But they don't have any proof yet."

"They have now," Salvatore murmured. He looked at Pietro, who was chewing his lip. "What do you think of it?"

"Nothing," Pietro said.

"They would have found out sooner or later," Piera said, sitting down at the table. All she was wearing was a skirt and a thread-worn blouse. "Don't let your espresso get cold, signora. Would you like some sugar?"

Helen shook her head. She remembered she had liked Piera from the first moment, and she felt much better sitting down with her and drinking her coffee. It was bitter, but since she hadn't had anything warm in more than twelve hours, it perked her up. The cup was dirty and the table too. It looked as if it had never been wiped.

"Do you like the espresso?" Piera asked her.

"Very good," Helen answered.

Pietro smiled. "I told you she makes the best espresso in Sicily."

He had pulled himself together and looked calm again. When Helen observed him closely, she realized reluctantly that he was handsome. He had a long, narrow head, a regularly shaped sun-tanned face, and black oval eyes which only changed expression when he smiled. He was still wearing a white shirt, with a jacket and corduroy trousers.

When Helen had finished her coffee, he got up. "You must be tired," he said. "I will show you where you sleep."

"On a mattress!" Salvatore added. "He brought it all the way from Cerami for you. You must have made a wonderful impression on him, signora. Now that I have met you, I must say that your husband was a fool."

That was the second mention of her husband. Before she could answer, Pietro came between them. "Come with me, signora. He has had two years of practice at annoying people."

He took the lamp from the table and led Helen through the opening in the right wall into a smaller cave filled with crates, saddles, and other objects. In the back two mattresses with blankets lay on top of a pile of straw. A small entrance led to the next cave. It was bigger than the middle one. In the back was a table with a lamp and two chairs, and next to it a stand made with three pieces of wood. The bed consisted of a mattress, a pillow covered with a white pillowcase, and three blankets on top of a wooden frame.

"It's all we could do in a hurry," Pietro said, lighting the lamp on the table. "I hope you will sleep well all the same. Under the blankets you will find a nightshirt of Piera's. I guess you need some other things."

Helen laughed. "I don't even have a toothbrush."

"I will get you one tomorrow. And about the other things, don't worry for the time being. I think everything will be all right."

"You mean about you killing me," Helen asked as lightly as she could.

He stared at her. Then he smiled again. She hated herself for it, but every time he smiled she felt her heart beat faster.

"That too," he said. "It would be a pity. Good night, signora."

"There's one thing I don't understand," she said quickly.

He looked at her.

"Why did Salvatore say my husband was a fool?"

"Most men are fools," Pietro said and left, taking the second lamp with him.

Helen sat down and opened her pocketbook. Everything was there except her checkbook. She took out the cologne and daubed her forehead. The cave was lower than the outer one—less than seven feet high—and it gave Helen the feeling of being closed in. She scrutinized it carefully. Its entrance was at the opposite end from her bed, but at one of the side walls she saw a second opening which was supported with a large crate and stones. She remembered vaguely that Pietro had talked about an avalanche. It must have buried the old entrance to this cave.

Sitting immobile, she suddenly recognized her cigarette case on the table. Pietro had taken it yesterday. It was still half full.

Of all the men she had met in her life, none had made such contradictory impressions on her as he. Already the day before she had realized how much he fascinated her and that her revulsion for him was fed more by a barely conscious curiosity than by indignation over his brutal behavior. Their latest encounter hadn't altered her feelings. She was unable to sort out her impressions nor answer the question how much she could trust him. After all, he had at least one murder on his conscience, (by his own admission), a holdup, and four or more other crimes. And his role in her husband's fate was still unclear. But it was precisely his shocking frankness which made her think that he was indeed not, apart from his general involvement, one of the real culprits in the case, about which, she realized, he hadn't told her the whole truth yet.

But she was beginning to doubt whether she really wanted to know the whole truth. Apart from the fact that her present situation gave her enough to worry about, she had felt something like fear from Salvatore's little hints, fear of what she might still learn about her husband. After all that had happened, she didn't quite feel like learning more than what Bentley had already told her; at the moment it certainly didn't weigh heavier than her concern about her own predicament.

She stood up and felt the mattress. It wasn't as soft as Rigido's mattresses and the woolen blankets were rather rough—as rough as Piera's nightshirt. But unless she wished to sleep in her clothes, she had little choice.

Before undressing she turned the flame of the lamp low. In her location at the back of the cave she wouldn't have to worry about being watched by Pietro. Still, she had never been more completely at a man's mercy.

She blew out the lamp and found the bed in the dark. Lying down, she remembered that she had forgotten to look at her watch, perhaps for the first time in fifteen years.

She felt the rough cover against her skin. She could almost feel the mass of the mountain over her and the depressing silence of the blackness around her. They combined to form a breathless threat. She would have liked to cry. Her fatigue was gone. She suddenly felt wide-awake and terribly abandoned. If Pietro had come in now, she might almost have felt relief; but Pietro did not come that night.

# 18

Piera woke her the following morning. "Please get dressed, signora," the girl said. "Antonio is waiting to talk to you."

Although she had slept deeply, Helen knew immediately where she was. As if struck a blow, she recalled the events of the past day.

"You slept for a long time, signora," Piera said. "Antonio has been waiting for an hour."

Her voice sounded friendly, and as Helen looked at her she even smiled.

"What time is it?" Helen asked.

"Ten," Piera said. "I brought you a bowl of warm water and some soap I have had since the war. My mother gave it to me. It smells so wonderful that I have never used it. It's from Paris."

"Then I don't want to take it away from you," Helen said.

"If I give it to you, you are not taking it away from me. Pietro said you shouldn't agree with everything that Antonio demands."

It sounded like a conspiracy. Piera was again wearing the good dress which had drawn Helen's attention at their first meeting. Her hair was carefully done. She looked like a young lady, only her rough shoes didn't fit into the picture.

"Do you have secrets from Antonio?" Helen asked.

"He thinks he's terribly clever," Piera said with contempt. "That bank was his idea, too. He always says it's all for Salvatore, but actually he is only thinking of his own profit. Giuseppe and Lucio are the same. They need money for a tractor."

That was the second time Helen had heard those two names. "Do they belong with you?"

"Only when something is up. They are relatives of Antonio. They live four mountains away. We really don't want to have anything more to do with them. Giuseppe is the one who killed the bank clerk. Hurry, signora, Antonio is already impatient."

Helen waited until she had gone, then she stood up and quickly washed her face and her hands. She was dressed by the time Piera came back.

"You can have your coffee later," she said. "Antonio wants to know if you have a fountain pen."

Helen mumbled, "Why?"

"You have to fill out the check. Is it simple to cash it?"

Helen looked in her face. "Are you supposed to cash it?"

"Yes. I've never cashed a check, signora. What am I supposed to do?"

"You have to sign it on the back," Helen answered. Her heart beat fast and she sat down. "Why are they sending you?"

"They think I would be the least likely to draw attention. I have a good dress. Since that business with the bank they don't dare go to Nicosia during the day."

"Would they be recognized?"

"I don't think so, signora. They were wearing scarfs over their faces. Pietro doesn't want me to go to the bank, but the others say it's not dangerous. Do you think it's not dangerous too?"

Helen was at a loss. She had no reason to be considerate, but she didn't want to put the girl into a difficult position. Piera had done nothing except what she had been asked to do, and the idea of making a business deal out of Helen's meeting with Salvatore was certainly not hers. But Piera's position wasn't what made it difficult for Helen to decide. She was more concerned with trying to figure out what opportunities it would give Bentley if Piera cashed a check. After what she had seen and heard so far, she doubted that it would help her much. Furthermore, she was afraid of making her own situation more difficult.

"I don't know if it's dangerous," she said hesitantly. "Suppose something happened to you?"

Piera smiled uncertainly. "You have to ask Pietro, signora, but I don't think it would be good for you. Carmelo is coming along too. He's supposed to keep a lookout."

"Is that your fiancé?"

"He's here to care for the horses, signora. If something happens to me, he will tell the others. They are waiting outside now."

"Aren't you afraid?" Helen asked.

"Yes, I am afraid, signora, but we need the money, and if it's not dangerous . . ."

"I didn't say it wasn't dangerous," Helen interrupted her quickly. She had made her decision. Bentley's plan might work in principle, but there were too many uncertainties in it—for him as much as for her. "It's possible that the bank has been warned since my disappearance," she said. "By my friend, if you want to call him that."

"Pietro said that too," Piera said. She stood still for a few seconds, then she looked in Helen's face. "I won't cash the check, signora," she said with a warm voice. "Why did you warn me that it was dangerous?"

"I suppose I don't want you to be arrested. Where's your mother?"

"With my uncle."

"In Cerami?"

Piera blushed. "I was lying, signora. He lives in Messina. My mother is often with him. She has tuberculosis and the air isn't as raw there as in the mountains."

"Has she been here?"

"Yes, often, signora. But Salvatore doesn't like it. It's too much of a strain on her, and, after all, they have me here."

Helen found herself liking her more and more. "It can't always have been easy for you," she said quietly.

The girl looked at her with surprise. "Before the war I had three brothers, signora. Two of them never came back." She took the dirty water and carried it out.

Now, with the girl gone, Helen was not so sure she had done the right thing. But the longer she thought about it, the longer she was certain it was better for her to depend on herself than on Bentley and the carabinieri.

She sat down at the table, pulled a little mirror out of her pocketbook, and took care of her makeup. She was as careful as ever. It was the one thing she would not give up unless she was forced to. The better she looked and the better Pietro's impression of her was, the better for her.

Pietro came in, startling her so that she dropped her compact.

"I didn't mean to scare you, signora," he said seriously and sat down at a corner of the table. "Shall I hold your mirror?"

Helen nodded mechanically. She couldn't understand why she hadn't heard him approaching. He must have come in on tiptoe.

"I've always wondered how a woman makes herself up," he said. "Giuseppe and Lucio are impatient to meet you. I told them you have blond hair, blue eyes, and a good figure." He picked up her little eyebrush and held it against the lamp. "What's this for?"

Helen explained.

"May I see how it's done?"

Holding her mirror for her, he watched her with interest. Seeing him with a serious face and looking with such concentration, she suddenly started to laugh.

"I can't do it with you staring at me," she said.

"I'm sorry," Pietro said, disappointed. "I would like to watch. The women of Chiesa have no notion of things like this. They smell of goat's cheese, don't wear underwear, and age very quickly."

Helen laughed. She leaned back in her chair and looked at his immobile face. "All of them?"

"All of them as far as the smelling and growing old are concerned. The other depends on the weather."

He took her hand and looked at it. "You have beautiful hands, signora. I like to see women with beautiful hands. The hands of our women are not beautiful. They don't do anything for them and they work too hard." He was silent for a moment. "Piera told me that you advised her not to cash the check. What makes you think that your friend has notified the bank?"

Helen closed her compact. "He's not my friend," she said in an annoyed voice, surprising herself. "He was commissioned by his commander to accompany me to Chiesa."

"He can still be your friend even if he just accompanied you to Chiesa," Pietro answered. For a moment it seemed that he was suppressing a smile, but his expression changed so quickly that Helen couldn't really tell. "Was he there when you deposited the money and got the checkbook?"

She nodded.

"Perhaps he's forgotten," Pietro said thoughtfully. "Anyway, Antonio will take the risk. We are agreed on the principle, just not on the means. Come, signora. Salvatore is still sleeping. He had a bad night."

He took the lamp with him. As they walked through the adjoining cave Helen saw Vito lying on the straw. He was snoring with his mouth wide open.

When she entered the outer cave, she noticed that the table and the chairs were gone. Salvatore lay on his cot with his back to them. It wasn't as dark here; some daylight fell through the opening.

After ten hours inside, she felt relieved to get out in the air. Four men were waiting for her there. She knew two of them: Antonio and the young man in Chiesa whom Piera had called her fiancé. She remembered his name—Carmelo.

He was sitting with another man about his age at the edge of the hollow, which was still in shadow. In the center of the hollow were the table and chairs. Two thick bottles and some glasses were standing on the table.

Antonio, in a pair of worn-out trousers and a very ragged shirt, was sitting at the table, looking thoughtful. Across from him sat a gaunt man, with thin lips and deep-set eyes. He had a little mustache and was at least five years older than the man next to Carmelo, but Helen saw that they looked very much alike.

Seeing the hollow for the first time in daylight, she realized that it was larger than she had thought—about forty-five feet long and twenty feet wide. In its center, where the ground was lowest, one could not see over the edge.

Antonio greeted Helen with his usual little laugh. "We have been waiting for an hour, signora. Pietro is a really polite man. He didn't want us to wake you before. How do you like it with us?"

"I hadn't expected it to be so cozy," Helen managed to say.

Antonio began to laugh. "She has a sense of humor," he said to Pietro, who remained beside Helen and stared indifferently at him. "Did you know that Americans have a sense of humor?" Antonio asked.

"I am not interested in their humor," the man with the mustache said. "We have lost enough time."

Helen looked at him more closely. He was wearing a dark velvety jacket, gray trousers which vanished into high boots, and under his jacket a heavy pullover with a turtleneck. His age was hard to determine; she guessed he was about thirty. He looked extraordinary with his carefully groomed hair and his half-closed eyes. He seemed very unsympathetic toward her.

"Don't take Giuseppe seriously, signora," Antonio said gaily. "He was a difficult child." He turned to Pietro. "Why don't you get her a chair? If she sits down I can see more of her legs. I would rather look at a beautiful woman's legs than eat a good dinner."

"Don't choke," Pietro said and walked back to the cave. Helen realized that she was looking after him. She wondered where Piera was; she hadn't seen her in the cave.

"Let's get to the point," Antonio said importantly. He pulled the checkbook out of his pocket, put it on the table in front of him, and examined it as if it were a rare stamp. Then he looked at Helen and laughed. "So you think it's dangerous to cash a check. Why do you think so, signora?"

Although she couldn't afford to, she felt angry, not only because she had been forced to stand there like a schoolgirl but also because of the man's aloofness. "I guess you're intelligent enough to know that yourself," she answered coolly.

Antonio looked surprised, then he started laughing again. "Did you hear that! She thinks I'm intelligent enough to know for myself."

"I'm not deaf," the man who was called Giuseppe answered. He regarded Helen as if she were a horse. "If you get fresh, you will be whipped," he said in a normal tone of voice.

"By you?" Helen heard herself ask, although her fear had grown stronger than her anger.

For a moment no one said a word. Then Giuseppe got up slowly, his eyes wide.

She had never before looked into such murderous eyes; instinctively she turned around and ran toward the cave.

At the same moment Pietro came out carrying a chair, and as she passed him he dropped it, grasped her by the arm, and pushed her behind him into the entrance of the cave. To Giuseppe he said, "If this is a new game, I want to play too. Sit down and rest your rear."

Giuseppe changed color. "Don't talk to me that way," he said hoarsely. "Who are you, to talk to me that way."

"You're a shitty guy," Antonio said with contempt. "Don't talk so much. Sit down!"

"This isn't settled, as far as I'm concerned," Giuseppe said, but he sat down and took the bottle and filled his glass. He emptied it in one gulp and said to Antonio, "If I'm not needed here . . ."

"If you weren't needed here, I wouldn't have called you," Antonio said. "This is a serious matter. Within a week there will be two carabinieri in front of each house between Nicosia and Randazzo. Save your breath to tell me how to cash the check. If Piera doesn't go, one of *us* has to go."

"Why doesn't Pietro go?" another man asked. His name was Lucio. He was also wearing a shirt and trousers. He was shorter than Giuseppe, dark and thin. He had a face like a mouse—with little beady eyes. He stood up from his seat by Carmelo and moved to the table. "I'm in favor of him putting his cards on the table," he said. "What kind of a way is this to treat your friends!"

"There is time," Antonio answered. He looked from one to the other. When Antonio's gaze reached him, Pietro picked up his chair and went to sit by Carmelo. "What is the matter with you?" Antonio said.

Slowly Pietro looked at him. "Are you talking to me?"

"I never knew I was cross-eyed," Antonio said. "Why don't you get that woman out of here?"

"Why?"

"We want to sing a little duet with her," Giuseppe said with suppressed anger. He looked at Pietro, who leaned toward Carmelo and whispered to him. Carmelo nodded and fixed his dark, penetrating eyes on Antonio.

"What's going on here?" Antonio asked after a moment. "Are we cashing a check or aren't we cashing a check?"

"If we only knew . . ." Lucio murmured and picked up the checkbook.

Antonio grabbed it out of his hand. "Wash your dirty hands first," he said furiously. "They would see immediately that something was wrong with such a check."

"My hands aren't any dirtier than yours," Lucio answered, looking at them. Then he looked again at the checkbook. "If it wasn't a matter of fifteen thousand dollars . . ."

He stopped and licked his lips.

"I don't like it either," Antonio said, more quietly. "They have never had anyone withdraw fifteen thousand dollars. The whole bank will come to watch."

"We should try for less first," Giuseppe said, filling his glass again.

Antonio picked up his thought. "Let's try five thousand. If it works, we will try another five thousand."

"But it is fifteen thousand," Lucio said, still staring at the checkbook.

"Holy Mother of God!" Antonio swore. "What are we talking about!"

"I just meant . . ." Lucio murmured and hesitantly turned away from the checkbook and looked at Pietro. "What do you think?"

"I think you have a tractor in your head instead of brains," Pietro answered contemptuously. He walked over to the table, took the checkbook, and walked into the cave. He found Helen sitting on her bed in the dark. Pietro turned on the lamp and looked at her face in the light.

"You don't have to be afraid," he said quietly. "Will you fill out the check for me?"

She stood up and took her fountain pen out of her pocketbook.

"Make it out to your friend."

She stared at him. "To Bentley?"

"Isn't that possible?"

"I don't know if he'll cash it for you."

Pietro smiled. "That's our problem, signora. Fill in twelve thousand dollars."

"I can't."

"Why not?"

She saw the suspicion in his eyes but thought it better to follow through now. The night before she had still thought that Bentley's plan could work if she made the amount of money in the bank sufficiently tempting. Now she wished that she had bitten off her tongue instead of bluffing.

"There's only three thousand dollars in the account," she said slowly.

Pietro frowned. "Last night you said fifteen thousand."

"I lied to you."

"Why?"

"Perhaps I thought . . . " She stopped. It was useless to lie.

"What did you think?" Pietro asked. His eyes were as coldly expressionless as they had been when he had come into her room.

"I don't know anymore," she mumbled. "If you want a hundred thousand dollars, it doesn't make much difference what I said last night."

"It makes a difference to me," Pietro said and took her arm. He sat down at the table, pulled her close to him, and looked at her. "What did you think?"

He held her arm as in a vise. As he pressed harder she felt tears coming into her eyes, but she didn't utter a sound.

"Did you want to trap us?" he asked.

She shook her head as the tears started running down her face. Then she felt the pain stop, and she looked up and saw that he was staring at her. It was the first time that he had looked at her that way. She remembered that she was wearing a deeply cut sleeveless white dress. He let go of her, pushed her aside, and got up.

"Make out the check for three thousand dollars," he said. His voice sounded different—husky and breathless.

When she began to write, she felt his eyes on her neck. Her arm hurt, but she felt some sense of satisfaction too. It was encouraging to know that at least in one regard he was the same as other men.

She put the top on her pen, placed it in her pocketbook, and turned around.

"I haven't thanked you yet," she said, giving him the checkbook. "Your friend must have misunderstood me before."

Pietro didn't answer. He looked at the check, tore it out of the checkbook, and put it in his pocket.

"Perhaps he misunderstood me on purpose," Helen continued. "Is he married?"

"Why does that interest you?"

She smiled innocently. "He seems to be one of those men who occasionally forget that they're married."

Pietro looked at her with narrowing eyes. Then he nodded. "I'm glad you told me that, signora. Wait here."

He went back outside, where the men were sitting around the table drinking. Only Carmelo had not left his place at the edge of the hollow. He was making himself a cigarette and staring into the valley.

"You took a long time," Antonio said, annoyed. "If we want to cash this check today . . . "

Pietro interrupted him. "The American will cash it." He lay the check on the table and watched them stare at it.

"Why only three thousand?" Antonio asked without looking up.

"She had the rest transferred to a bank in Naples," Pietro answered.

Antonio slowly looked up. "She didn't know that last night?"

"She forgot."

"She forgot that she sent twelve thousand dollars to Naples?"

"Yes."

"She forgot that she sent twelve thousand dollars to Naples?" Antonio repeated.

Pietro stepped back and put his right hand in his pocket. He looked past the others to Carmelo, who laid his tobacco on the ground and leisurely got to his feet.

"Where is the checkbook?" Antonio asked, the color drained from his face. As Pietro took the checkbook from his pocket and tossed it on the table, no one stirred. "Only one check is missing," Pietro said with contempt. "It is made out to her friend. He is the only man who can cash it for us without causing suspicion. He will cash the hundred thousand too; he is her fiancé."

"Fiancé?" Antonio asked.

"Yes."

Antonio looked at the checkbook, leafed through it, and threw it back on the table. "Perhaps so," he said finally and looked at Pietro. "Was this your idea?"

Pietro nodded.

"When will we see him?"

"As soon as I find out where he is. Carmelo will take care of that."

"Good," Antonio answered, and he, Giuseppe, and Lucio all picked up their glasses. The tension disappeared as if an earthquake had passed. They talked among themselves. Finally Antonio stood up and took Pietro aside.

"You are a difficult man at times," he said reproachfully. "Why didn't you tell us right away that you wanted to use the fiancé?"

"I hadn't made up my mind about it," Pietro said.

Antonio thought a moment and cleared his throat. "It won't make it any easier," he said. "He will not leave a stone unturned to find her. But I want to know if we're still agreed?"

"Agreed about what?" Pietro said, looking without expression at Antonio's round sweaty face.

"You know what I'm talking about," Antonio said. He measured Pietro for a moment. "What have you suddenly got against Giuseppe?"

"You're barking up the wrong tree," Pietro said. "He and Lucio have given us nothing but trouble."

"If the American woman hadn't shown up, we would have never managed without them. Anyway, a hundred thousand dollars is enough for all of us. Or did you know half a year ago that she would show up?"

"I've waited for her for thirty-one years," Pietro said and walked away. He went over to Carmelo, who was sitting down again.

"You can get Piera," Pietro said and looked away into the valley lying bare and empty in the sunlight, its floor and walls textured with protrusions of rocks and shadows of crevices. On the far side a low mountain range stretched from east to west, half hiding Monte Ambola, which rose in the cloudless sky.

"What are you waiting for?" Pietro asked.

"I would rather that you sent Vito to get Piera," Carmelo replied.

"What's the matter?"

"She hit me."

"Why?"

"I tried to kiss her," Carmelo said.

Pietro smiled. "They often do that the first time. Once we're in Switzerland and you're a rich man, she will no longer hit you."

"She says she'd prefer you," Carmelo muttered, then turned his gaze to Antonio, who was talking intensely with Giuseppe and Lucio. "She says she would rather have Vito than me."

"A woman never says what she thinks," Pietro answered dryly. "I'll send Vito to her. He's slept long enough. Wait for me with the horses. We have to go to Chiesa."

Carmelo didn't stir. "Are you interested in her?" he asked.

"No."

"If I could only buy a house in Switzerland," Carmelo muttered. "She says she would only have you if she could get a house in Switzerland."

"She's told me that too."

"Would you buy her one?"

"Since I'm not interested in her, I won't buy her a house either. Does that satisfy you?"

"You've never lied to me," Carmelo said, still watching Antonio. "Antonio's quick with a knife, but he's not as quick as I am. He should watch it."

He turned around, climbed out of the hollow, and descended the slope beyond it. Pietro looked after him, then turned and went to the entrance of the cave, where Salvatore asked him, "What time is it, fellow?"

"Are you hungry?"

"No more than always. Are the others here?"

"They are already leaving," Pietro answered. "You can have breakfast with the signora. I am riding to Chiesa with Carmelo."

"They'll catch you one of these days," Salvatore muttered. "When they catch you, I'll kill myself."

"You make me cry," Pietro said and turned away quickly. First he awakened Vito and then he went to Helen. She looked as though she had been waiting for him.

"It will take a bit longer," he said. "Piera will make you breakfast. I am sorry you had to wait so long, signora."

"I'm not hungry," Helen answered. She watched him sit down at the table and light a cigarette.

*144*

"I told my friends that you had transferred twelve thousand dollars to a bank in Naples," he said. "They wouldn't have believed your story. I don't know if I believe it myself. In case Giuseppe, Lucio, or Antonio ask you, you are engaged to marry your friend."

Helen stared at him.

"I'm talking about your friend in Chiesa," Pietro explained. "It's part of my plan. Do you need anything else beside a toothbrush?"

"Toothpaste," Helen answered mechanically.

He smiled. "I'll explain it all to you later. Personally I would rather not have you engaged to him."

"Why?" she asked and blushed a little.

"Egoism," Pietro said. "Perhaps I can get you some of your things tonight."

She looked up quickly. "Are you going to Chiesa?"

"Yes." He said it as indifferently as if he were planning a stroll.

"If you are just going to get my things . . . " Helen said and stood up. It was ridiculous but suddenly her heart started beating fast. "I mean . . . it isn't that important."

"It is to me," Pietro said. "I would like you to have everything here you need."

"And if they catch you?"

"Salvatore asked me the same," Pietro said, sitting up. "It's only one of two possibilities, signora. Would you mind?"

She didn't answer. But when she looked at him, she realized that she was sorry he had killed a man. Everything else could at least be explained.

"I don't think you would mind," he said with a smile. "I was a little rude to you the day before yesterday. Do you want me to apologize for it?"

She couldn't tell how he meant it, but he sounded sincere. "Why?" she asked quietly.

He nodded. "I asked myself that too. I don't have much experience with women. I've never minded before, but I mind with you."

His words echoed in her ears after he had left her.

# 19

The Fiat was standing in its usual place in front of the inn. Bentley saw it before he got out of the police car. In the door of the restaurant, half hidden in the shadows, he made out the uniform of a carabiniere.

He handed the driver of the police car a pack of cigarettes and walked toward the inn, looking at the Fiat on his way past it. The carabiniere saluted. "The lieutenant is waiting for you in the restaurant, signore," he said in a friendly voice.

Lieutenant Gastone wasn't alone. There were also two carabinieri and Rigido. The carabinieri had posted themselves beside the door and Rigido was sitting gray-faced at the table. He was being interrogated by Lieutenant Gastone. When Bentley came in, Gastone stopped talking and walked toward him.

"Are you doing anything?" Bentley asked immediately.

Gastone shook his head. "I haven't because you asked me not to. I must point out that you alone are responsible for that, Mr. Bentley."

"You wouldn't be of any help to Mrs. Brazzi," Bentley said and looked at Rigido. "Did you get anywhere with him?"

"He doesn't know anything. It's possible that the gang saw you leave with the signora. All they had to do was wait for you to come back."

"Under the noses of the carabinieri?"

Lieutenant Gastone looked uneasy. "I warned you, Mr. Bentley. May I remind you that I offered you an escort."

"I'm not blaming you," Bentley murmured. He hadn't slept in

thirty-six hours, he had hardly eaten, and he had not had a quiet moment. He had made a dozen plans and abandoned them all. Two hours earlier he had telephoned Lieutenant Gastone from his hotel room in Nicosia and asked him to send a car. He still had not thought of anything.

"Did you find the Fiat?" he finally asked.

"One of our patrols discovered it a mile behind Nicosia on the road to Sperlinga. The ignition key was still in the car. When you hadn't come back by eleven o'clock last night, I notified my colleagues in Nicosia and San Stefano."

"The mountains to the west of Nicosia don't belong to the Nebrodi," Bentley said. "You have been looking in the wrong direction for two weeks."

Lieutenant Gastone sat down and stared at his hands. "Perhaps. Perhaps not," he said after a while. "They have given me thirty carabinieri, Mr. Bentley. What I need is a hundred carabinieri. I don't know where the gang is hiding, and I don't know how strong it is. We have searched every house in these two weeks, and every possible hiding place in the Nebrodi. We have questioned a few hundred men and women and we have been in Ragusa and questioned Pietro's family. They all say they haven't seen him in two years and haven't heard from him. They couldn't even give me a picture of him. All I have to go on is what you've told me, and if your description is accurate, it doesn't fit Pietro at all. In fact, your description has the disadvantage of fitting half the men in Sicily. It's fighting windmills, Mr. Bentley. What are you going to do now?"

"I don't know yet," Bentley said. "Perhaps they will try to cash a check. Three thousand dollars is a fortune to them."

"Not if they can get fifty thousand with less risk. You underestimate them. If I report this in Rome, I will get as many carabinieri as I . . ."

Bentley interrupted him. "We already discussed that on the phone. Mrs. Brazzi wants to talk with Salvatore. She has a chance now. I warned her often enough."

"If I understand you correctly . . ."

"You understand me right," Bentley said. "I was told to take Mrs.

Brazzi to Chiesa. I did as I was told. What she is doing here is her own business."

Lieutenant Gastone looked shocked. "You mean you would leave her?"

"Officially. Unofficially I will take two weeks leave. The United States Army is not responsible for the extravagant ideas of American women. As long as possible I will keep this from becoming official business. Is the Fiat O.K.?"

"The tank was empty. We filled it."

"Then I will go to Nicosia again tomorrow morning. If they haven't tried to cash a check before evening, I will give up on that."

"And if they do?"

"My hotel is two minutes from the bank. They will notify me and stall the man until I arrive."

"And then?"

"That depends," Bentley said and looked at Rigido, who was sitting immobile, a small, ugly bundle of humanity. The two carabinieri were leaning against the door and showing their boredom. They hadn't understood a word of the English conversation.

Lieutenant Gastone pressed the tips of his fingers together. "Perhaps you'll be lucky," he said after a while. "If I give you some of my men . . ."

"Better not," Bentley said. "We should avoid anything that would put Mrs. Brazzi in danger. We are pursuing different goals, Lieutenant. You want to catch the gang, and I am interested in Mrs. Brazzi's safety. It is hard to combine those two objectives."

"And if something happens to the lady all the same?" Lieutenant Gastone asked.

Bentley looked into his eyes. "Then you won't see a hundred, you'll see a thousand carabinieri around. I trust the gang to know that as well as you and I do. Did you find any clues in the car?" he asked.

"No. If you are thinking of fingerprints . . ."

"I don't read whodunits," Bentley said impatiently. He jerked his chin toward Rigido. "What are you going to do with him?"

The lieutenant shrugged. "I could lock him up for two or three days, but not more. There are surely people in Chiesa who know more than he does. My problem is not that they don't know anything. It would be easier to make a stone talk."

"Because they're afraid?" Bentley asked.

"That too," the lieutenant said. He crossed his legs and stared at the ground. Bentley looked at him questioningly.

"Perhaps it sound farfetched," the lieutenant said, "but it could be called solidarity of the poor. I'm not sure you would understand."

Bentley got up. "Why not? There is also solidarity among gangsters. Please thank your colleague in Nicosia for the lift. I sent the driver back."

"One moment!" Lieutenant Gastone said, and his face was suddenly more serious than Bentley had ever seen it. "I won't do anything officially," he continued, "but you can't expect me to stop my search because of the lady."

"I don't expect you to."

"Good." The lieutenant smiled. "Let me be frank, Mr. Bentley. I need to gain some time, the same as you do. As long as you don't notify the military people in Palermo, I won't report the matter to Rome. We are in occupied country. There could be political consequences and it would stir up quite a lot of dust in Rome. It would make the police in Palermo responsible, and they would pass the buck to me. Do you understand what I am talking about?"

Bentley frowned. "I guess so."

"I want to convince you," Gastone said, "that the signora is as important to me as to you. I want to make sure at all costs that nothing similar, nor even anything worse, happens to you. The gang will take your American citizenship into consideration only as long as you don't bother them."

"I'll remember that," Bentley said. "Leave Signor Rigido here. He can make me some dinner. Good night, Lieutenant."

He was already at the door when Lieutenant Gastone called him back. "It was the Central Bank, wasn't it, Mr. Bentley?"

Bentley turned around. "Why do you ask?"

"Just a routine question."

Bentley went to his room. Everything was exactly the same as when he had left it and gone to Helen's room, to drive her to San

Stefano. It was hard to imagine that no one knew what had happened to her during the last twenty-four hours.

He opened the window, lit a cigarette, and stared at the dark silhouette of the mountains. Although he didn't want to admit it, he realized that it was senseless to go to Nicosia again. The check hadn't been cashed that day, and it wouldn't be cashed the following day. The night before, it had seemed a real possibility and he had held on to it like a drinking man to a lamppost, but now he didn't believe it anymore. If he was going to make one more try, it was just because he needed to do something.

He didn't like the taste of his cigarette. He threw it out of the window and got up to wash his hands. The room in Nicosia had been better and the service wonderful. The hotel owner had even loaned him pajamas and a razor. If he hadn't felt compelled to return to Chiesa, it would have been nice to stay there. But he realized now that there had been at least one reason why he had returned which had not been quite rational. When Rigido came with the dinner, Bentley expressed that reason.

"I want to move to Mrs. Brazzi's room," he told the innkeeper. And then he added, as if to explain: "It has the larger window. Do you have a second key?"

Rigido nodded. "I have two keys for every room, Mr. Bentley. I will bring you new bed linens later."

"That's not necessary," Bentley answered. He sat down and stared at his dinner.

"Eggs and bacon," Rigido said. "Since you just asked for something light . . ."

"Yes, that's all right. Bring me the key for the room, please."

He started to eat. Then he realized that Rigido hadn't stirred. He pushed the plate back and looked at him. "What else?"

"I should have told the lieutenant," Rigido muttered, "but the man said that if I did, the lady would die."

Bentley stared at him. Rigido seemed to shrink and shrink until his face looked like a squeezed lemon.

"Which man?" Bentley finally asked. It had taken him at least a minute to regain his voice.

"He was here before," Rigido said unhappily. "He drank a glass of wine and told me that I was to give you a message, that if I didn't give it to you, they would burn down the house and hang me from a tree."

"Did you know him?"

Rigido's eyes blinked for a moment. "No, signore. I never saw him before."

Bentley stood up. "What were you supposed to tell me?"

"You must pack some things for the signora—dresses and anything else she might need—and take them in a suitcase to Nicosia tonight at eleven. The man also said that nothing will happen to the lady if you don't tell the carabinieri and if you bring the suitcase for the signora."

"He didn't say anything else?"

"No, signor. I mean, I told him you hadn't come back and then he said, if you didn't come back tonight, you should bring the suitcase tomorrow evening."

"Did he come on foot?"

"I don't know, signore. Before he left he told me to go to the kitchen."

Bentley looked at his watch. He still had two hours. For a few seconds he wondered whether he should tell Gastone, but then he rejected the thought. Salvatore and his friends would be prepared for that.

He searched for a cigarette and lit it. After the initial surprise, the message seemed almost a relief. It was strange and revealing that the gang would take such a risk for such a purpose, and it relieved him that they seemed to be trying to make Helen's involuntary stay as easy as possible. After the night before, he was no longer worried about his own welfare.

"Bring me the key," he said to Rigido. "I'll bet you did know that man."

"May I drop dead . . ." Rigido began.

"You can do that if something happens to the lady. It's possible that in the next few days her father will come. If I am not here, you must tell him that the signora is on a trip with me. Do you understand?"

Rigido stared at him. "Her father is coming here?"

He looked so upset that Bentley became suspicious. "Does that bother you?" he asked.

"He is supposed to be a big shot," Rigido muttered.

Bentley nodded. "So big he could put this whole town in his pocket."

He stubbed out his cigarette and sat down again. He wasn't hungry but he forced himself to eat and drink a glass of wine. Before he was quite finished, Rigido brought the key to Helen's room.

"Put it on the table," Bentley said. "Has the lieutenant left the carabinieri behind?"

"I didn't see one, Signor Bentley," Rigido said.

"Good."

Bentley finished his meal, took the key, and went to Helen's room. He waited a minute in the doorway and stared at the table and the bed. It seemed to him as if she had only left her room for a moment.

He went to the cupboard, opened her suitcase next to it, and started to pack her lingerie. He packed a few other items that she might need, and when he had finished, he had to light another cigarette. He went over to the washstand and studied the little creams and bottles. Since he didn't know which ones to pick, he put them all in the suitcase. Then he added some dresses and a raincoat. The suitcase was so full that he couldn't close it. He repacked everything; then he realized that he had packed only one pair of pajamas. Under her cover he found her nightgown. It was the same one she had worn two nights earlier. He sat on the edge of the bed, spread the nightgown on his knees, and stared at it. He put his hand under the transparent material and looked at it. He clenched his hand and he looked at his fist through the nightgown until he felt dizzy. Then he wiped his eyes and put the nightgown with the other things in the suitcase. He hesitated, and then took it out again and put it under the blanket on the bed. He had only an hour left to make a plan.

## 20

Salvatore greeted Helen with a conspiratorial grin. He was lying in an old deck chair in the shadow of a tarpaulin made from an American Army tent, which was hung above the entrance to the cave from rusty nails and a wooden plank. As before, he was covered up to his waist with a woolen blanket. Only his feet stuck out; they were bare and dirty. Piera was at a table leafing through an old magazine. When Helen came out of the cave, she looked up.

"You may have breakfast right away," she said, putting the magazine aside. She had changed in the meantime to a cheaply made dress of thin material which reached only to her knees and fitted her thin muscular body like a glove.

Helen sat down next to her at the table, which still held the empty glasses and bottles. The table was standing exactly in the middle of the hollow. Helen looked up at the wall about her. It was so high that it seemed impossible to guess its dimensions. It appeared to be slightly concave.

"It won't come down," Salvatore said, watching Helen's expression. "Only a little stone avalanche now and then. If it hits you while you're sitting here, you'll be dead."

"He's just trying to scare you," Piera said and stood up. When she began clearing the table, her long black hair kept falling in her face. Helen caught herself trying to imagine her as Pietro's mistress. Then she realized Salvatore was watching her and she turned toward him. In the light of day his face was less repulsive than the evening before. And when he smiled, he looked like a fifteen-year-old boy.

"You are terribly pretty, signora," he said sincerely. "I really don't understand what your husband saw in my sister."

Helen felt her heart skip a beat. She looked at Piera, who shrugged indifferently. "Don't listen to him. He's just trying to annoy you."

"Why not, if she lets herself be annoyed," Salvatore asked with a grin. "Are you easily annoyed, signora?"

Helen didn't answer. She *was* really annoyed, but only because he had bluffed her for a moment. She watched Piera vanish into the cave with the glasses and bottles. Perhaps she shouldn't expect compassion from a man like Salvatore.

"You could at least tell us something about America," she heard him say. "Is it true that American girls take a bath twice a week in milk?"

She made a face at him. "Who told you that?"

"My mother. When she was still young, she read a lot. Her brother wanted to be a teacher but there wasn't enough money. He is a fisherman in Messina now."

"Piera tells me that she is ill."

He nodded with an unhappy face. "My father too. They always told them in church that God wants them to have as many children as possible, but they didn't explain how to feed them. Did you have a quarrel with Giuseppe?"

"Is that the man with the little mustache?"

"He nurses it like a baby," Salvatore said. "Giuseppe always had an easier life than we. When his father died a year ago, he left him more sheep and goats than he can count with his stupid head. Now he wants to have a tractor too. He would be the first man in Sperlinga with a tractor!"

Helen looked at him. It might have been chance, but because Pietro had mentioned Sperlinga the night before, the name alerted her. "Does he live in Sperlinga?"

"He and Lucio. They are brothers."

"I thought so," Helen said. "Have you known them long?"

"We met during the war," Salvatore said. "Lucio and I were wounded at the same time."

"In Palmigano?"

"Yes."

"I didn't know," Helen muttered. She looked distractedly at the spots of wine on the dirty table. If that were the case, Giuseppe and

Lucio would have to know her husband's murderer and if they did, it was a safe assumption that Pietro knew too. When he had talked with her about it the night before, he hadn't mentioned Lucio and Giuseppe. There seemed to be only one explanation for that and she felt her hands tremble as she thought about it. She asked as calmly as she could, "Didn't my husband help to carry a wounded man to Sperlinga?"

"That's possible," Salvatore said.

"Was it Lucio?"

He turned toward her and stared. "What makes you think that?"

Before she could answer, Piera came with the breakfast. She put everything on the table and said to Helen. "We don't have butter and milk, signora. It wouldn't keep in the heat. I brought you jam and two eggs. Is that enough?"

Helen nodded. She watched the girl cut a few slices from a large loaf of bread, fill her cup with black coffee, and pour some more coffee in a plate. She broke up three slices of bread in the plate and put it next to Salvatore on the top of a crate, which she propped up on the arm of Salvatore's deck chair.

"Eggs for the signora," he said with a grin. "Why don't I get any?"

Helen couldn't hear Piera's answer. Salvatore laughed and whispered something to her. She blushed and came back to Helen. "Don't listen to him," she said. "It's not good for a man of his age to be bedridden."

She sat at the table with Helen and watched her open her eggs. "We have another deck chair," she said. "If you want to, you can sit next to Salvatore in the shade. It's rather hot in the sun."

It was hot. Helen felt as if she were sitting in a steam bath. As she ate she looked at the hollow and the piles of stone again. It puzzled her that the top of the well, which jutted out over the hollow, had not screened the old entrances of the cave against the stone avalanche. She mentioned this to Piera.

"You can only see why when you come up from the valley," the girl said. "About a hundred feet above us a huge chunk fell away from the mountain wall. It fell right in front of the cave. You can't see where it came from now because of the piles of stone. When it happened the Germans were supposed to have had a command post here."

"Was it buried under the stone?"

"I don't know, signora. Do you know?" she asked Salvatore.

He shrugged. "Probably. Otherwise they wouldn't have blown out a new entrance to the cave."

"We couldn't have found a better place for Salvatore," Piera said. "Giuseppe found it by chance. He was after a buzzard he had shot, and he found a nest right here."

"How did you get your brother here?" Helen asked.

"On a horse."

"Right through the American lines," Salvatore said. "The last five hundred yards Carmelo and Pietro carried me. Don't ask me how I felt."

"It hurt terribly," Piera said and stood up. "Now I have to take care of Vito."

"Where is he?"

"He is on guard against the carabinieri," Piera answered and went into the cave. She came back with a deck chair, which she put next to Salvatore. She took the coffee pot and the bread from the table and climbed out of the hollow with it. Helen looked after her and wondered what would happen if she were to run away. It was not more than half an hour to the road.

She turned and looked at Salvatore. There was something about his eyes and his attitude which warned her. He had both hands under his blanket and as she looked at him he pulled out a heavy pistol.

"Made in U.S.A.," he said. "Twelve millimeter. It's a good substitute for bad legs, signora. Why don't you sit down."

Helen obeyed. She shouldn't have underestimated him. Moreover she didn't know where the other men were. The two deck chairs were so close together that she touched Salvatore's shoulder when she sat down.

"I could shoot a bird out of the sky with this," he said and put the pistol back under his blanket. He was still wearing the dirty T-shirt of the day before and as she stared at it, he blushed.

"I know I'm not as elegant as you," he grumbled. "Neither would you be if you lived here for two years."

"It must have been bad," Helen said. "Couldn't you have stayed in Chiesa?"

"People were afraid. When your friend and the soldiers went through the village, we were in the cellar. We could even hear their voices. If they had caught us they would have marched out the whole village. Pietro also thought it was dangerous to stay in Chiesa. Somebody would have given us away someday."

"How old is he?" Helen asked.

"Pietro? Thirty-one. Do you like him?"

She didn't answer.

"I wouldn't have made it without him," Salvatore said. "He could have gotten away a hundred times in those two years and put himself at ease."

He looked up and stared at the edge of the hollow against the cloudless sky. "He always dreamed about going to Switzerland," he went on. "Now he is too old for that. Switzerland only wants very young people. He lost too much time because of the war."

"Has he learned a profession?"

Salvatore grinned, but his face was empty. "In Chiesa one learns to herd sheep, signora. He tried to get a job for eight years before the war, but when you come from Chiesa, all they do in Palermo and Messina is shrug. They know we still live in caves and they think we are primitive and lazy. I think he likes you, signora."

"Did he tell you that?" Helen asked, annoyed at her own excitement.

"I can see it, signora," he said. He put his hand on her knee. His bony, thin, boy's face suddenly looked feverish. "I like you too," he said in a hoarse voice. "If you give me a kiss, I'll tell you a secret."

She stared at him. "I don't think it would be worth it."

"I'm sure it's worth it. I can tell you what Pietro is planning."

Helen was silent. What Pietro was planning she could find out from him. But there was something else she might find out from Salvatore, and while she looked hesitantly at him she had a thought.

"Perhaps you can also tell me who killed my husband?"

His face closed up. "I don't know, signora. I didn't see it."

"And Giuseppe?"

He looked away. "I really don't know, signora. When it happened, Pietro and I were already in this cave."

He still had his hand on her knee. It felt raw and hot. Of all the ways to make a man speak, this was the most certain, but as he pushed his hand under her dress, Helen got up.

"Sit down," he said softly. He waited a few seconds, then he pulled his pistol out and pointed it at her. He didn't say anything. He just held the pistol, and while Helen looked at his feverish face she felt the blood beat in her temples.

She didn't really believe he was serious, but she didn't know him well enough to quell her fear. For a few seconds she didn't know what to do, but as she was about to give in to her fear, she caught the sudden uncertainty in his eyes.

"If you kill me," she said calmly, "you will never get away from here. Tell me who killed my husband and I will sit down again."

"Are you honest?" he asked suspiciously. He now looked like a small excited boy with the urge to put his hand under a woman's dress, and if she let him do it, she would finally have certain knowledge. It wasn't much, measured against the goal toward which she had already gone so far.

She sat down, took her cigarette case out of her pocketbook, and offered it to him. He took a cigarette greedily, let her light it for him, and inhaled the smoke hastily. He put the pistol back under the blanket.

"Was it Giuseppe?" Helen asked.

"It wasn't me who told you," he muttered. His hand was already under her dress, but she hardly felt it. Her only reaction was satisfaction mixed with hatred. She stopped him when his hand had gone too far.

"Just once, signora," he begged. "Just once."

She saw that his eyes were moist. Suddenly, she felt almost sorry for him, but if she let him go farther, he would consider it his privilege in the future. She stood up.

"We didn't mention that," she said.

"You promised to sit down next to me," Salvatore said. His face now looked as repulsive as it had the evening before. Perhaps it wasn't that simple to make him her ally against Giuseppe.

Salvatore went on begging. "I can't do anything to you, signora, just look at my legs, I can't even move them. Do you want to see my legs?"

There was a sound in his voice which she didn't like. But before she knew what he was going to do, he had pulled the blanket away, and for half a second she saw his naked body, from the bony white legs up to the sharply protruding hip bones. She turned away, went into the cave, and sat down in the dark on a crate. She was still sitting there when Piera came in five minutes later.

"Did he annoy you, signora?" she immediately asked.

Helen shook her head. It was pointless to talk about it with Piera, and moreover it revolted her.

"I am going to get water," Piera said. "If you want, you can come with me." She picked up her bucket and went back outside; then she looked at Salvatore. He had pulled his blanket over him again, and he had a half shy, half satisfied smile on his face.

"What did you do?" she asked.

"Why don't you ask the signora," he said with a grin.

She turned around to Helen, who was standing behind her. "You can tell me quietly, signora. I'll tell Pietro."

"It was nothing," Helen said.

The girl hesitated. "I can imagine. Come with me, signora."

She led Helen out of the hollow and across the stones to the rocks on the right side of the valley. There they came to a strip of stone which clung to the wall of the valley just below the overhanging rocks. When Helen looked back she saw the side of the mountain above the cave in its entirety. Above the cave it ascended sharply to a peak. It wasn't Monte Soro; she would have recognized it.

They went about twenty feet along the strip of stone before they came to an opening between the rocks. They entered it and crossed a narrow ridge to the west side of the mountain. Here three mountain ridges met. The valleys in between were flat, covered with stones and in a few spots overgrown with dry grass and bushes. Piera pointed below, where between the rocks a large funnel-shaped hole gaped. "That's where we get our water, signora. It comes from a well. If you ever want to go for a walk, you can always come here; only you are not allowed to go farther down into the valley."

Her euphemism made Helen laugh. "I had to go for a walk already two hours ago," she said.

Piera looked stunned. "Mother of God! I never thought of that. Was it bad?"

"I survived," Helen said and laughed.

Piera laughed too. "Men never understand that. You can wait for me here."

"Aren't you afraid I'll run away?"

"Not with you, signora. Do you see that big rock there?"

Helen had already seen it: a huge piece of stone connected with the mountain by a very sharp ledge, the walls of which dropped vertically into the depth.

"From that point one can see the road and the valley," Piera said. "If you wanted to run away, you would have to go the same way you came last night. Vito would see you before you even got to the road."

"Is he sitting on the rock?"

"Yes. I'll be back in a moment, signora."

Helen looked after her as she quickly and easily climbed down to the hole and vanished behind some rocks. When she came back shortly after with a bucketful of water, her face was red with the effort. She put the bucket down and sat beside Helen on the warm rock. Her dress was a bit too small for her; she pulled it all the way up without embarrassment and fanned herself with a dirty handkerchief.

"Pietro discovered that well only a year ago," she said breathlessly. "Before, we always had to bring the water in cans. You can use it for bathing too, signora. You can stand in it all the way up to your stomach, but it is very cold. Are you hungry yet?"

"No."

"We are eating rabbit with cauliflower today. The rabbit is fresh. Pietro shot it this morning. Nobody is better with a gun than he."

"Do you like him?" Helen asked and stared at Piera's long sun-tanned thighs.

Piera blushed a bit. "He used to be a nice guy, signora, but since he's been stuck here he's been almost as impossible as my brother. It's like a disease. I don't know what Salvatore told you before. You don't have to tell me, but two years ago he wouldn't have done a thing like that. It's about time we got out of here."

"Well, I guess I came at the right moment then," Helen said with a smile.

Piera nodded seriously. "You are like a gift from heaven, signora."

"I'm so glad," Helen said.

The girl blushed again. "I say stupid things."

"Why do you say that?" Helen asked. "I understand. Were your other brothers older than you?"

"Yes. Ciro would be twenty-four now and Caspare would be twenty-six. Salvatore didn't have to become a soldier. He volunteered. My mother didn't want him to, but we were doing badly then. Pietro told us that it wasn't dangerous at all for a soldier in Sicily, and when Salvatore volunteered he got some money, good food, and he could also bring something home."

"Then Pietro made your brother do it."

Piera smiled. "He didn't have to make him do anything, signora. Salvatore always looked up to him. Pietro had already been a soldier for two years and he often came home on weekends. Now he feels guilty because he thinks he shouldn't have let Salvatore become a soldier after all."

"I see," Helen said. She understood better now, and while she was looking at Piera she wanted to ask if she was going to marry Pietro. Somehow the thought was unpleasant. It was crazy, but she couldn't resist the feeling. After all, Piera was an extraordinarily pretty girl, and while the fact that she wasn't wearing anything under her cheap dress might affirm Pietro's judgment on the women of Chiesa, it might also have advantages which she, Helen, could not quite fathom. With a hairdresser and a more suitable dress, she would have made quite a stir in Toledo, Ohio, and she seemed to be thoroughly aware of it. At least she never missed a chance to parade her body as if to show that a woman did not need a bank account and good grooming to please a man. But what man, for heaven's sake, she wondered with annoyance. Pietro?

She stared up at the small white clouds sailing across the sky. "Pietro told me he shot a man in Palmigano," she said after a while.

Piera looked up quickly, "When did he tell you that?"

"Before we arrived here."

"He surprises me," Piera murmured and stared ahead of her. "Men are often comical, signora. He didn't say a word about the man for a year; then one night he put a pistol in his pocket and left. The day before he had been in Nicosia to see the doctor once more. He had tried to convince him to visit Salvatore, but the doctor always refused. At that time, Salvatore had terrible pains. He often cried out all night. Pietro would sit beside him and stare at him. It's strange, signora, but . . ." She stopped herself for a moment and then she continued. "Perhaps you will laugh, but once Salvatore knew the man was dead, his pain almost stopped."

Helen knew it was pointless to argue. "Has he never seen a doctor?"

Piera shook her head. "There's no doctor in Chiesa. Vito knows about herbs and he has nursed him. None of us thought he would pull through because he had a terrible fever and was unconscious for eight days. Pietro thinks it's a miracle. Do you believe in miracles, signora?"

"I never thought about it," Helen answered vaguely. "Has Vito been with you long?"

"He often worked for us when my father was still alive. Since Salvatore and Pietro came here, he has brought them everything they need. Often when the Americans and carabinieri were checking the roads, Vito still got through. He knows every path in the mountains."

"How old is he?"

"Nobody knows, signora. He came here ten years ago, no one knows from where. There are some old people who say they saw him creep out of a crack in the rocks and the rock closed behind him."

Piera stood up and led the way with her bucket. She hadn't quite reached the gap in the rocks when she stopped and looked back.

"What is it?" Helen asked.

Piera put her finger on her mouth and listened; then she put the bucket on the ground. "Run to Salvatore," she said. "But not down the valley. Vito has a rifle and he can hit a fly."

"Don't you want to tell me . . ."

The girl interrupted her impatiently, "Don't ask now, signora. Wait for me with Salvatore."

She quickly turned around and followed the west wall of the mountain up to the small ridge which led, a thousand feet away, to the pillar-shaped rock. With its edges and teeth it looked like a gigantic coxcomb.

Helen stared after her until she realized that Piera was climbing up to the ridge. She was startled. She could understand Vito climbing along it; it probably took as much instinct as power and courage, and Vito seemed to her to be a creature of instinct anyway. But for a girl it seemed impossible. She waited until Piera had reached the foot of the large rock and climbed past the first tooth of the ridge, then she could no longer watch. She set off for the hollow.

As she reached Salvatore he was just putting his pistol back under his blanket.

"You might have been a carabiniere," he said with a grin. "I'm waiting for one to show up. I have been waiting for two years. Did you hear the buzzard?"

Helen stared at him.

"I have ears like a bat," he said. "First the buzzard cried twice, then Piera sent you here. Vito should show you how he does it. Pietro can do it too, but not as real as Vito."

Helen was confused. Perhaps she hadn't heard anything because she had no idea how a buzzard cried. "What does it mean?"

"Carabinieri."

She had expected it, but it was a shock all the same.

"Don't get excited," Salvatore said ironically. "They are still on the road. If they came to the valley they would almost certainly turn back when they got to the slopes with the stones."

She didn't know why he was so certain. If the carabinieri really got this far, there was no reason why they would not have a closer look this time.

Salvatore seemed to guess her thoughts; he pointed to some large rocks at the edge of the hollow. "All we have to do is roll one of those down," he said. "The carabinieri, if there are any left after that, wouldn't have the slightest desire to climb any farther. Have you ever seen a stone avalanche?"

She shook her head.

"We tried it," Salvatore said. "It was as if the whole mountain was moving. Why don't you sit down beside me?"

Helen didn't answer.

"I hadn't meant to scare you," he said ironically.

If he hadn't told her that the carabinieri were here, she would have gone back into the cave; but her restlessness was greater than her disgust and she decided to wait for Piera's return. She couldn't spend her days in the cave simply because of Salvatore; and it was ridiculous to be so put off by a silly adolescent. At the time of her escapade with the governess she had been three years younger than he was now, and she had looked without shame at things much worse. Probably it was the sight of his white skeleton-thin legs which had repelled her so. The rest she was used to—even though it might be appropriate for a woman from a "better family" in Toledo to be shocked and to run away, if only from her own excitement.

It wasn't as hot as before in the hollow; a cool wind, smelling of the sea, was blowing from the mountains. It made her think of Bentley. Since she had come here she hadn't missed him for a moment. What was more, she had almost been relieved not to have him near. Two days ago she had been afraid of being in love with him!

She opened her pocketbook and pulled out her cigarettes. Sensing that Salvatore was looking at her, she asked, "Do you want one?"

"If you give me one."

She went over to him and watched him take out a cigarette. He had thin bony fingers with black ridges under his nails.

"Will you tell Pietro?" he asked.

"What?"

"That I annoyed you."

"If you do it again." She sat down next to him in the deck chair. "Tell me why you and Pietro want to share the money with the others?"

"Pietro will explain it to you," Salvatore said. "If I had had my way . . ." He stopped and drew on his cigarette.

"It's a lot of money for just you and Pietro," Helen said. "I don't see why you have to buy a tractor for Giuseppe."

"He helped us," Salvatore muttered.

"With the holdup?"

"Even before."

She saw that he didn't want to talk about it. Perhaps he was now sorry that he had betrayed Giuseppe, by telling her that it was he who had killed her husband. She crossed her legs and watched the chair's awning over her head flutter in the wind. "Piera thinks your friends are only thinking of themselves," she said.

"They didn't used to," Salvatore said peevishly. "It all started with Antonio. He wanted to help get me away from here and he persuaded Giuseppe and Lucio to pull some tricks. At that time Giuseppe wasn't talking about a tractor. But those hundred thousand dollars have gone to his head. They have all gone crazy."

"Couldn't they have helped you in another way?"

"How?"

"I thought Giuseppe had money."

"When a man in Sperlinga has money, signora, it simply means that he isn't starving to death. Giuseppe has five acres and a couple of dozen goats and sheep. How much do you think they are worth?"

"You told me before that he had more goats and sheep than he could count."

Salvatore grinned. "He isn't a very good counter. We have five goats at home."

"And Antonio?"

"He has four children. If he had money, he would send them to Palermo to school. He would like to see them do better than he's done. Antonio isn't stupid, signora, but now he's gone as crazy as Giuseppe and Lucio. If they suddenly got a lot of money, they would act so crazy that the carabinieri would immediately smell a rat. Pietro also thinks . . ."

He stopped and listened. "It's Piera," he said.

Again Helen hadn't heard anything, and it was quite a while before Piera appeared. She was alone, dragging her bucket of water along. When she stepped into the hollow she wiped the sweat off her forehead with her hand and set the bucket down next to the entrance of the cave. There was something changed in the look on her face.

"Have they gone?" Salvatore asked.

She didn't answer him. Turning to Helen, she said, "I have to talk to him, signora. Please sit at the table in the meantime."

Her voice sounded different too, harsh and commanding. Helen was tempted to answer her sharply, but she remembered in time where she was and walked away. From where she sat she could hear them whispering. A moment later Piera got up and vanished into the cave with the bucket. Salvatore frowned, staring straight ahead.

"You can sit next to me again," he said finally. "Your friends have gone. I guess they must think you're a princess or something. Otherwise they wouldn't have sent a hundred carabinieri into the mountains."

Helen was startled. "A hundred?"

"A hundred mounted carabinieri," Salvatore said, impressed.

"Which way did they go?"

"Toward Fratello."

"That's no use to me," Helen said.

Salvatore howled with laughter. "No, it sure isn't!"

# 21

After ten miles the road led straight over a low, densely overgrown mountain top. At the highest point Bentley saw a man in the light of the beams. He was standing on the side of the road, and although he was at least two hundred feet away, Bentley recognized him immediately. He accelerated and saw the man leave the road and vanish into the bushes. At the spot where he had last seen him, Bentley stopped the car and got out. The man did not show himself, so Bentley took the suitcase out of the car, put it down, and stared hesitantly around him. Then a voice from behind him said, "Are you armed, signore?" Bentley shook his head. He didn't move. A minute later he felt himself being frisked.

"A little formality," Pietro said gently and went to the car. He turned off the lights, picked up the suitcase, and turned again toward Bentley.

"Walk down the road a little, please. My friends and I have to ask you one more favor. You have nothing to fear."

Bentley obeyed. In spite of Pietro's calmness, he was no longer quite certain that he had done the right thing by leaving the pistol in the car.

As the walked along the road neither one spoke. After about two hundred feet they came upon another man. He was standing in the entrance to a narrow path which vanished somewhere in the bushes. Bentley recognized him too.

"Good evening, Signor Bentley," he said with a smile and lifted his hat in a salute. "You are punctual."

"Officers are always punctual," Pietro said.

"Especially American officers," the other man said. "That's why they won the war."

"Let's not talk politics," Pietro said and led Bentley another hundred feet down the path while the other remained on the road.

They came to a clearing with only a few twisted little trees. There were three horses there and next to them, too much in the shadow for his face to be seen, a man was crouching.

Pietro gave the suitcase to the concealed man and then said to Bentley, "The signora has given us a check. She asks you to cash it for her. Will you do that?"

He was a bit smaller than Bentley and he was not holding a weapon this time. Bentley looked over to the man with the horses.

"Good friend of mine," Pietro said. "As long as his skill as a knife-thrower isn't challenged, he wouldn't hurt a fly."

There was nothing to be done and Bentley knew it. He also realized what check this was, and that the gang had not only understood his plan but was even using him. If he hadn't been so furious, he would have felt something like admiration.

"For how much?"

"Three thousand dollars, made out in your name. We will let you know when and where you can hand over the money. Here is the check."

Bentley put it away. "How long are you going to keep the signora?"

"Not longer than necessary. Is it true that her father is coming to Chiesa?"

"How do you know?" Bentley asked.

Pietro smiled again. "I have my sources. If her father should arrive within the next few days, please tell him not to worry about her. She's feeling quite at home with us."

"I don't think he would be satisfied with that," Bentley said with suppressed anger. "You may think you are very clever but you have gone too far this time."

"You don't understand the situation," Pietro said very politely. "We didn't want to talk to the signora; the signora wanted to talk to us. She has offered us a deal and we have accepted it. As soon as it's finished she can go where she wants to."

"It is your deal and not the signora's. She offered you ten thousand dollars, not fifty thousand."

Pietro stared past Bentley at the solid wall of vegetation. "You may not believe this, but we don't want any more money than she will give us voluntarily."

Bentley shrugged. "Voluntarily, because she has no choice."

"You make another mistake, signore. When I say 'voluntarily' I mean just that. Did you already talk to the carabinieri?"

"No."

"I thought you had," Pietro said, still staring into space. "Someone in Sperlinga saw a whole company of carabinieri ride by. I can only guarantee the security of the signora as long as our security is not in danger."

Bentley was startled. "A whole company?" he repeated.

"I imagined that you already knew," Pietro said, finally turning toward him. "Didn't you talk with the lieutenant last night?"

"He realized we had vanished," Bentley answered. He wondered whether the gang got all its information from Signor Rigido alone.

"I understand," Pietro said. "What did you tell him?"

Bentley looked at the horses again. As far as he could tell in the dark, they were not saddled. They were little shaggy creatures with long manes. They stood motionless. The man crouched beside them was smoking, covering his cigarette with his hand when he drew on it to prevent his face from showing.

"Nothing that could endanger you," Bentley answered. "If I wanted to, I could go to the nearest American command post. There are plenty of American soldiers in Sicily."

"We know that," Pietro said. "Your soldiers don't give us gray hair. I want to make you a proposition, Signor Bentley. If you see to it that the carabinieri leave us in peace for eight days, we will send the signora back to Chiesa at that time."

It was more than Bentley could have hoped for. "What guarantees do I have?"

"I am your guarantee," Pietro said in a final tone of voice.

"The carabinieri are not just looking for the signora," Bentley said.

Pietro laughed. "Well, in that case, they can give themselves another eight days. You are an American, Signor Bentley. If you wanted, there wouldn't be carabinieri left in Sicily within twenty-four hours. I am now taking you back to the road."

He walked over to the man by the horses and whispered something to him, then he led Bentley back to the road. The other man was sitting there, waiting.

"That was quick," the man said. "Did you discuss everything?"

"Everything," Pietro said. "The signore will get us the money, Antonio."

"He is a gentleman," Antonio said, satisfied. "All Americans are gentlemen."

"There you go talking politics again," Pietro answered. "From here you can find the way alone, Signor Bentley. Cash the check tomorrow, and wait until you hear from us."

"Wait till you get a postcard," Antonio said with a laugh.

Bentley could still hear him laughing as he walked back to the car, breathless with anger. Before he had set out he had racked his brain over a plan to outsmart them, but now, after talking to them, he realized that it was senseless. The way they had arranged the meeting, a man alone hadn't a chance. He could have notified the carabinieri, but apart from the danger to Helen the chances of succeeding would not have been very impressive. Until the last moment the gang hadn't told him where they would meet, and he would have needed hundreds of carabinieri to close off a twenty-five-mile stretch of road effectively.

As he drove back to Chiesa he started again to doubt Pietro's sincerity. Although he still didn't know exactly who this man was, he was now sure that he was the head of the gang. That didn't make him any more reliable; but for a few minutes Bentley had been tempted to take him at his word about sending Helen back after a week. But the more he thought about it, the more illogical it seemed to him. When, after half an hour, he had reached the steep climb toward Chiesa he had still not made up his mind about it.

About half a mile before he reached the inn he saw four mounted carabinieri standing in the street. They seemed to be waiting for him, and when he approached they dismounted; one of them was Lieutenant Gastone.

"I hadn't counted on seeing you anymore today," Bentley said with surprise. "Where do you come from?"

Lieutenant Gastone smiled. "From a different direction, Mr. Bentley. When I said good-by to you a few hours ago, I didn't think you would go on another trip tonight. When did you decide to?"

"I received a telegram," Bentley said, throwing a look at the horses. He could see that they had recently been ridden hard. "You don't seem to be on a pleasure trip," he continued. "I'll bet you're coming from the same direction as I."

"We have been in Cesaro," Lieutenant Gastone said and stepped over to the car. "And you?"

"I'll tell you in the inn. Were you waiting for me?"

"We saw your headlights." The lieutenant talked quickly to the three carabinieri and got into the car next to Bentley. His uniform and boots were covered with a thin layer of dust and he was wearing a heavy pistol and a leather folder for maps. "I hope the telegram wasn't bad news," he said.

"That all depends." Bentley drove the last few feet to the inn. "I took Mrs. Brazzi some of her things—clothes and other things she needed."

"That's interesting," Lieutenant Gastone said. "Did you talk to her?"

"Not directly. Between Sperlinga and Nicosia two friendly gentlemen were standing at the side of the road. They took the suitcase from me. Come in, Lieutenant." He led Lieutenant Gastone up the darkened stairway. "Did you change rooms?" Gastone asked Bentley as he opened Helen's door.

"As you see." Bentley turned on the light, went to the window, opened it, and sat down. "I like this room better. Do you want a cigarette? The gang wants you to leave them alone for a week. In eight days they are supposed to release Mrs. Brazzi."

"That's news," Lieutenant Gastone said. "Why?"

"I wonder too," Bentley muttered. He now had had time to think about it, and it seemed so ridiculous that he felt like a fool repeating it. Next he would have to bring up the matter of the three thousand dollars, which would make him seem even more stupid. He stared at the lieutenant. "Perhaps it's connected with you, sir. Didn't you march out an entire company?"

Lieutenant Gastone produced a smile, which vanished and then came back again. "You are terribly well informed, Mr. Bentley. May I ask how?"

"You have your own little secrets," Bentley answered. "Why did you march out a whole company?"

Gastone hesitated. Then he pulled out a map and spread it on the table. "For the past forty-eight hours all roads through the Nebrodi have been under observation. They lead through a completely uninhabited and bare mountain landscape. Presumably anyone on these roads going north or south will come out at the other side."

"How do you keep it under observation?"

"By posting men on each side and comparing their observations. Since last night we know that there are people who leave Cesaro but do not arrive in Fratello."

Bentley stared at the map. The road from Cesaro to Fratello led between Monte Ambola and Monte Soro toward the sea. "What kind of people?" he asked.

"I don't know yet."

Of course he knows, Bentley thought. That's why he was so surprisingly indifferent about my news just now and everything I told him. Perhaps he already knows where they are hiding.

This thought created a conflict in Bentley's mind. Helen, after all, had been kidnapped in his presence and he wasn't at all certain that she agreed with him that it was senseless to try to prevent it. Perhaps a woman expected more from a man than sober judgment in such a situation. So far his own performance had not quite equaled his hopes and expectations. The thought that Helen might come back to Chiesa without his help made him more worried than happy. At least he should attempt as much as the lieutenant. Otherwise it would be difficult to face her afterward.

"What are you going to do now?" he asked.

"It depends on you, Mr. Bentley. You must understand that I have too great an interest in this to be negligent."

"Well," Bentley said, "do you see anything better than to accept their offer?"

"I do for me, but I don't know whether it would be better for the signora."

Bentley stared at the map once more. The best thing for him was to gain a week's time. With some luck . . .

"We will wait," Bentley said. "If Mrs. Brazzi isn't back within a week I will bring the local commander in Palermo into the picture. Do you mind if I have one more look at that area between Cesaro and Fratello?"

"On the contrary," Lieutenant Gastone said as he got up. He smiled once more. "I can only recommend it, Mr. Bentley. It's one of the prettiest landscapes in Sicily.

Bentley stared at him. "I expected you to advise me against it."

"I don't seem to have had much luck with my advice, Mr. Bentley. Do you want to go to Nicosia tomorrow?"

"No, I changed my mind."

"I thought so," Lieutenant Gastone said. "In case it would be of any assistance, I will leave the map here. Don't neglect to look at Monte Ambola. It is undoubtedly the highest and most scenic mountain in the Nebrodi."

Bentley remained at the table and stared at the map for a long time. Next to Monte Soro, Monte Ambola was a hill. No one knew that better than Lieutenant Gastone.

# 22

After dark, Vito had come down from his observation post and helped Piera to carry Salvatore back into the cave. For dinner they had had goat cheese, bread, and a heavy red wine. The taste of the cheese had not appealed to Helen and she had eaten very little. Now she was slightly dizzy from the wine. She was sitting alone at the table, watching the stars appear.

During the afternoon she had slept a few hours. Being with Salvatore had tired her; although he hadn't repeated his blunt approaches, it had been an effort to talk to him. He was both childish and cunning. His moods shifted from whimpering self-pity to tough cynicism. She had realized how time and again she had wished for Pietro's return.

Now, sitting alone in the darkness, left with her thoughts, she felt that she had never waited more impatiently for anybody. There were all sorts of reasonable explanations for this. It made sense that she might be nervous about his plan to go back to Chiesa, given the special role he played in her life at the moment, but it still seemed exaggerated that she should be so anxious for him. She caught herself offering various explanations and alibis for his action. But even when she weighed everything in his favor, it wasn't enough to whitewash him. He was an outlaw and murder could not be justified, not even the way Piera had tried to do it.

A noise behind her focused her attention to the entrance of the cave, where Vito reappeared. He sat down, put bread, cheese, and a bottle in front of him. He broke off an enormous piece of bread and a hunk of cheese almost as large and put both in his mouth at the same time. He kept his face turned toward her, and though she couldn't see much in the darkness, she felt that he was grinning at her incessantly. She wondered whether she should go in; after half a day the prospect of more conversation with Salvatore was not appealing. She could have said that she was tired and lain down, but the idea of the dark, narrow cave repelled her. The night would be long enough, anyway.

Vito was a smacker. He washed every bit of food down with big gulps of wine, rubbed his mouth with the back of his hand, and gnashed his teeth while chewing. Luckily, she thought, the two deck chairs were standing in the hollow. This enabled her to get away from him for a little bit. In spite of the late hour, it was still pleasantly warm in the hollow because of the heat still retained in the rocks.

A little later Piera came out of the cave. She sat down beside Helen. "Salvatore asks if you want to come in, signora."

Helen said she had a headache.

"That's the air," Piera said. "We are at almost four thousand feet. Shall I bring you a blanket?"

"I'm not cold."

"I'll bring you one all the same. If you catch a cold, Pietro will hold me responsible. Has he kissed you?"

Helen looked at her startled. "Why?"

"I just wondered," Piera said and went back into the cave.

Vito caught Helen's eye. He sat motionless at the table, his head sideways—a huge bird of prey eying a dove. Suddenly he got up and walked to the edge of the hollow and remained there, motionless. When Piera came back with the blanket, he seemed to whisper something to her. She stood beside him and for a moment they didn't stir. Then Vito uttered some strange sounds and pointed.

"It's Giuseppe and Lucio," Piera said loudly.

Helen became ill at ease. She got up.

"You can stay here, signora," Piera said.

Vito cleared the table, picked it up, and carried it into the cave. A few moments later the two men climbed across the edge of the hollow. There followed what appeared to Helen as another whispered conversation with Piera. Helen saw them all staring at her; then they vanished into the cave.

She sat down in the deck chair and spread the blanket over her legs. She closed her eyes. Giuseppe had killed her husband. Knowing that, she hated him more than she feared him. She heard Vito come back; he posted himself at the same edge of the hollow where he had been sitting when she arrived with Pietro twenty-four hours before. It seemed incredible that it had been such a short time. She felt as if she had been there a week.

She didn't know how much time had passed when Lucio came out. He approached her slowly and sat down.

"Catching some fresh air," he said. He had a thin voice, and he smelled of goats. She remembered how Salvatore had told her that he was completely under domination of his brother. "When do you think the money can be here?" he asked.

"The three thousand dollars?"

"No, the other money."

As she searched for an answer she remembered that Pietro hadn't told them everything. "I don't know," she said.

"It mustn't take more than two weeks," Lucio said, lighting a cigarette. The tobacco smelled of straw and burning leather. Helen turned her face away.

"We won't let ourselves be stopped, signora," he said, staring at Vito, who didn't stir. Although it was impossible that he could be overheard, Lucio lowered his voice. "Don't think that Pietro is the big shot here."

"Why wouldn't I think that?" she asked.

"I just want to make it clear," Lucio said, "that if Pietro wants to do business with you behind our backs, you will have to pay double."

"Should I tell him that?"

"That's up to you. Pietro wants to do everything alone, take the money, and disappear. If it reaches that point, we will have to keep you until you get the money a second time."

She hadn't thought about that. "Are you talking about the three thousand dollars?" she asked finally.

"No, no," Lucio said. "That's just to keep us quiet. He wants to meet your fiancé tonight and tell him to get us the money. If there is a trick behind it, we will find out. Giuseppe and I figured that you might help us, but you must not tell anybody, not even Piera or Salvatore."

Helen felt slightly disturbed but she did not really believe him. If Pietro really wanted to disappear with the money, he could only do so by leaving Salvatore behind, and that seemed impossible. For Salvatore he had killed a man and sacrificed two years; now, when there was finally really a chance of helping him, would he leave him? It did not seem logical.

She decided to stall for time. "How do you think I could be of help?"

"Just keep your ears open. Giuseppe and I are leveling with you and I can prove it."

"How?"

"I shouldn't tell you," he said, staring again in Vito's direction. "You mustn't talk about it. Pietro is the man who killed your husband."

Helen felt surprise, then anger. Pietro himself had never accused either Lucio or Giuseppe—probably so that she wouldn't know who the murderer was—and now these two were trying to put the blame in his lap. It was a dirty bluff. She got up without saying a word and entered the cave. Giuseppe and Piera were sitting at the table. As she came in they stopped talking.

"Are you tired, signora?" Piera asked.

Helen nodded. From the corner of her eye she saw Salvatore on his cot. Giuseppe was in a chair smoking a cigarette. She realized that he was watching her, and she slowly turned to face him. In the light of the blue acetylene lamp his skin looked dirty yellow. With his sunken cheeks, his prominent cheekbones, and little beard he looked like a Latin American. She looked at him for the first time consciously as the murderer of her husband, and she felt her hands moisten.

"I will light a lamp for you," Piera said and stood up. "Did you see Lucio?"

"He talked to me," Helen answered, still looking at Giuseppe.

"I think she likes you," Salvatore said to Giuseppe. "She asked me today if you were still free."

"You must have dreamed that," Helen said.

Giuseppe smiled. "You never know what will happen, signora. Did you have a nice chat with Lucio?"

He had a way of looking at her as if she were a horse for sale. She didn't answer and his face changed. "You don't talk with everybody, do you?"

"Why don't you ask your brother?" Helen said and turned around.

"Stay here," Giuseppe said. He hadn't raised his voice but Helen felt a sliver of fear run down her back.

"You heard her say that she wants to go to sleep," Piera said. "What else do you want?"

"Shut up," Giuseppe said. He turned toward the entrance where Lucio appeared. His thin, mousy face was red with anger.

"It must have been a nice chat," Salvatore said. "Did he propose to you, signora?"

Helen didn't answer.

After a few seconds Salvatore went on, "It must have been more than a proposition. Watch him, signora. When he or Giuseppe see a beautiful woman, they go crazy."

"Don't talk stupidly," Giuseppe said.

Salvatore grinned. "I will talk as stupidly as I want. But I'd also like to talk the way the signora wishes me to. And if the signora wants me not to talk stupidly, then you won't go crazy anymore. Would you prefer him not to go crazy, signora?"

Suddenly he had the heavy pistol in his hand, and Helen saw Giuseppe pale. Lucio, who was standing near the fire lighting a cigarette looked afraid too. "Of course the signora doesn't want that," Salvatore continued. "I just mean that if she wants to go to sleep now, I figure she should go to sleep, shouldn't she, sister?"

Piera nodded, smiling tentatively. "Come with me, signora," she said. She led Helen to the back of the cave and lit the lamp. "Salvatore has never done a thing like that," she said. "You're a good influence on him. What did Lucio want of you?"

Helen suddenly felt weak in her knees and sat down. She wanted to talk about it but she was afraid of the complications. She would make deadly enemies of the men and her own situation would be even worse. "He wanted to know when the money will come," she said finally.

Piera frowned. "That must have been Giuseppe's doing. He wouldn't have asked that on his own. You must be careful with Giuseppe. He is vain and he holds grudges. Do you need anything else?"

Helen shook her head. She was thinking of Pietro again. Later, as she lay in the dark on the mattress that he had dragged up from Cerami for her, she was happy that Giuseppe and not he had killed her husband.

# 23

Once in the night she woke up. She thought she had heard a voice and she lay awake for a while listening in the darkness, but she did not hear anything else and she fell asleep once more. She woke up a second time and he was sitting beside her. She couldn't see him and she had been sleeping so soundly that it took her a minute before she realized where she was. But she knew immediately that it was he and she lay with open eyes without moving, until he bent over her and kissed her. Then he lay down beside her and she felt she should scream or at least say something, but it was as if she had no voice left and his clothes still smelled of sweat and horses, as they had the day before. He lay beside her without touching her and she felt his breath on her face. She moved away from him a bit, so that he would know that she was no longer asleep. She tried to concentrate and remind herself that he had killed a man. Even if there was nothing else with which to defend herself against him, she should at least remember that for a moment. As he put his hand under her neck, she wondered why she didn't at least try to scream, and why she so calmly accepted the idea that there was no way to resist him. All she had to do was call Piera, who loved him, or Salvatore, and for a fleeting second she was determined to do so; but his hand stayed quietly under her head, and she did nothing. Perhaps she had already missed the right moment, for she still did not cry out when he pressed her closer and kissed her neck and touched her shoulders, her eyes, and, again, her mouth. And while he kissed her she felt almost happy not to be alone in the dark anymore and not to have to tremble with desire for him. The feeling became stronger the longer he lay beside her; it was as if his caresses spun her in a fine net which made her powerless against herself. And when he got up and slipped under the blanket with her, she tried once more to think of everything she knew about him and how he had dragged her from Chiesa and beaten her. Perhaps she would have cried out for Piera or Salvatore then if he hadn't immediately pressed her against him once more and smothered her mouth with his kisses. For a moment she couldn't breathe and she twisted her face aside. She felt her nudity and felt his hands on her. She felt her body becoming rock hard at his touch, and she was afraid. But it wasn't the same fear as she had felt with Bentley, and although she waited for herself to start screaming as she had screamed with Bentley, she was afraid to scream, and while she was lying breathless with fear in the darkness, trembling, she suddenly felt Pietro come into her. And then she realized that she hadn't screamed, and she put her arms around him and cried with relief. She cried until the end, and afterwards she pressed her body against him, returned his kisses and caresses until she had gone through it all once more and lost all doubt and all fear. Then she lay with her head on his chest and tried to think, but she was too tired and she fell asleep. When she awoke again, he was no longer there; instead Piera was standing there and Helen saw her smile.

"It's past eleven, signora," she said. "Pietro wants to know if you want to get up."

Helen stared at her until she realized what the girl had said. Then she nodded and smiled back. "I didn't know it was that late. Is it nice weather?"

"It's always nice weather here," Piera answered, looking surprised for a moment. "It's only not nice during the rainy season, but then we won't be here any more. I brought everything in here for you. Pietro has brought your suitcase. Here it is."

Helen stared at the suitcase. She recognized it immediately, but for a moment it seemed a mistake all the same. "Did he get it in Chiesa?" she asked.

Piera laughed. "Pietro can do anything, signora. He had it brought to him by your friend. I hope everything you need is in it. I will now make you your breakfast."

"Did Pietro have his breakfast?"

"Quite a while ago," Piera answered and left.

Helen got up. She resisted the temptation to open the suitcase immediately, and when she was dressed she found that she hadn't tried once to think about the past night. There was no point. It had happened and she couldn't fool herself. She no longer had to act as if she were resisting—which had suited her as little as the contradictory feelings of the past eight days. She felt almost relieved. None of the many new problems which now replaced the old ones had been solved, but she couldn't take things too seriously. She hadn't wanted this, and she hadn't provoked it; under normal circumstances a man like Pietro would arouse in her no more than a slight curiosity. There was no point in wondering whether or not she could have stopped it. She needed Pietro to get away from here, and perhaps she needed him for something else. Many women did it for less and she had learned that it was the surest way to influence a man. Moreover, after the first five minutes she had forgotten who he was and what stood between them. That put her in a better light, she thought. She realized what her friends in Toledo would think of it, but those people in Toledo also held that a little affair was one of the most natural privileges in the world.

She found that she was taking as long as possible to make herself up. She also realized her heart was beating very fast. She had expected him to come in and ask her to have her breakfast. She would have preferred that to facing him with Piera and Salvatore present. They hadn't spoken a word to each other during the night, and she didn't quite know how to behave toward him. Finally, after she had powdered her nose for the tenth time, she had to go out. Piera was standing at the stove, putting the wood in.

"Where do you get the wood?" she asked. "Also in Chiesa?"

Piera shook her head. "No. About a mile from here is a little forest, signora. We have to get the trees half a year in advance so that the wood will be quite dry. Moist wood smokes too much and might give us away."

"I wondered where the smoke went," Helen said.

"There's a crack in the rock above the fire. Pietro and Antonio widened it. It works well when the wind isn't blowing from the west. When it is, the smoke backs up. Your breakfast is outside, signora. I didn't cook you any eggs because it is already so late, and Pietro wants to talk to you."

Helen saw him as she came out of the dark cave and into the sunny hollow. He was sitting next to Salvatore, who was reading another old book. He was carefully groomed, and had on a freshly ironed shirt. She caught his eyes and blushed and he blushed a little too. But he didn't say anything; he just looked at her and smiled with his eyes. Perhaps it would be asking too much of a man from Chiesa to get up and say a few words, but it would have made it easier for her to sit down at the table. When she had sat down and no longer had to see Salvatore's grinning face, Pietro came over. He reached across the table, took her hand, and held it.

"There's something I wanted to ask you last night," he said seriously. "But then I couldn't quite bring myself to wake you up, so I sat beside you for an hour."

"That's not very nice," Helen said.

He nodded. "I wondered about it. That's why I didn't wake you. Are you angry?"

"You should have waked me and asked me," she said. "Do you always do it that way?"

"How?"

"That way," Helen said and looked at him. "What did you want to ask?"

Pietro let go of her hand. "Your friend told me that your father is coming to Chiesa."

"It's not sure. We just thought so."

"Does he know where you are?"

"No, but he could find out in Naples."

Pietro looked away. Looking at him, she was reminded again of her husband. He had the same hair, the same nose and mouth, and now even the same eyes.

"There is something else," he said. "I don't want Piera to find out."

Her first reaction was annoyance. "Are you afraid I'll tell her?"

Pietro shook his head. "You misunderstand, signora. There was nothing serious between me and Piera, but she is very impulsive. She might run to the carabinieri. Since yesterday the road is being watched. We can't use it anymore. I don't give us more than eight days here."

She understood. It was very still around them and suddenly she felt quite cold in spite of the hot sunlight. "What will you do?" she asked after a pause.

"Can you ride?"

"No."

"Then we must think of something else," Pietro said. "In Caronia there is a man who has a fishing boat. He could take us to the mainland."

"When?"

"In three or four days. He has to fix it first. As soon as he is ready, we will go."

"And then?"

"I want to talk about that with you," Pietro said. "But not here. Why don't you eat?"

She had only drunk a cup of coffee. "I'm not hungry," she said and stood up.

Pietro went over to Salvatore and whispered something to him; then he came back to her. "We can go, signora."

They walked toward the well across the stony slope and past the ridge. It was now very hot and quiet. A few clouds were floating across the face of Monte Ambola. They sat down on the warm ground between two rocks. Helen opened her pocketbook, took out her cigarette case, and offered it to Pietro. "You left it on the table," she said.

He smiled. "It's your property." After a moment he lowered his eyes. "I don't want to talk about feelings. For most people a hundred thousand dollars are more important than feelings. Antonio,

Giuseppe, and Lucio want a hundred thousand dollars from you. But before the money gets here, we will have been caught by the carabinieri."

"I understand," Helen said.

Pietro smiled again. "Perhaps not quite. I told them that your friend was to get us the money. We will leave without those three. Salvatore and Piera only count on fifty thousand."

"And you?"

"On ten thousand, as you suggested."

She felt amused. He wasn't the kind of a man to let a hundred thousand dollars get away from him, even if he were seriously in love with her. "I wonder how Salvatore and Piera feel about it," she said.

He shrugged. "That's not your worry, signora. They are both young. At their age people don't think farther than their noses. How long do you need to get the remaining two thousand?"

"A week."

"Then you'll be back in Naples in two weeks," Pietro said. He put his hand in his pocket, pulled out a pistol, and put it in her lap. She immediately recognized it as her own.

"Are you giving it back to me?"

"It belongs to you."

He watched her take out the magazine and check it and then push it back in. "Aren't you worried?" she answered.

He smiled. "That's my risk. I can't always be near you when my friends are around."

"I still don't understand why you're doing all this," Helen said.

"I told you I don't want to talk about feelings, signora. Let's just say that I don't want you to give us away to the carabinieri afterward. As long as we're satisfied with what you offer us voluntarily, you have no reason to inform on us."

"There are other ways to stop me from doing that," Helen said.

He nodded. "Not for me. They are after us because we broke through some locked doors and because we have held up a bank and because we shot a man. The bank escapade was a bust; behind those doors we broke open we found trash, imitations, glass pearls, and five hundred lire. Altogether it was less than three hundred dollars. It was war, signora. Then you came to Piera and offered us ten thousand dollars. When Piera told me, I thought it was a trick. After everything which had gone wrong, I couldn't afford to fall for a trick."

It made sense but she still could not forget that he had asked for fifty thousand dollars in Chiesa. When she reminded him, he shrugged again. "I changed my mind," he said.

"Why?"

"I like you," Pietro said, staring beyond her. Then he smiled. "I thought you knew that already."

She blushed. "You didn't say much."

"Neither did you," Pietro said and took her by the shoulders. Softly he pressed her to the ground and leaned over her. "I liked you when I first came into your room that Sunday."

"You showed it in a strange way," she murmured. She had brought it on herself this time, and she knew it, but she wasn't repelled by his caresses; when he kissed her, she put her hands on his neck and forgot everything they had talked about. He didn't smell of horses anymore and she helped him with her dress, and then it was the same as the night before, except even better. Because this time she could see him and she felt no need to be afraid anymore, either of him or herself, and while she kissed his face and stroked his back and responded to his kisses, she lost all self-control. She had never felt it so intensely with any other man; at the end she cried—because she was ashamed of herself, and because she was happy. After, she lay pressed against him, staring past his shoulder at the mountain. She wished she had never met him.

"What are you thinking?" Pietro said.

She moved away and lay on her back. "Why don't you marry her?"

"Who?"

"Piera."

"She reminds me of Chiesa. Have you been in the castle?"

Helen nodded.

"When the weather is clear, you can see the sea." Pietro said. "Once about fifteen years ago I ran away. I was caught in Cefalù and brought back home. I was half starved. I never tried again."

"Where did you want to go?"

"Anywhere, where it didn't smell of goats, and where women wear underwear. I didn't quite know what an island was at that time. I just knew I was sick of it."

"And what about your family?"

He laughed suddenly. "Family? A family of bums and whores. I had two brothers and five sisters. They are all younger than I. We lived together in one room for twenty-four years until I couldn't bear the sight or the smell of them anymore. Every day our parents sent us to work on other people's land. I am not ungrateful, and I hope they make it to heaven someday, but I doubt it."

"When did you see them last?"

He frowned. "It must have been in May 1943. After that they went to Ragusa. My oldest sister found some idiot who married her and took the whole family in. He must still be kicking himself."

"It sounds likely." Helen smiled.

He talked about it all in a way which made it sound almost gay. She could understand now why he wanted to get away from Sicily; but she couldn't help thinking that for a man like him there wouldn't be much chance of getting ahead somewhere. She thought of Naples and wondered whether he would be better off in a big town. There, too, he would find himself an Antonio or a Giuseppe and go on as before. He would end up in prison or at the gallows. The thought didn't leave her indifferent; the conflict she had foreseen was no longer an indefinite problem in an abstract future.

"What will you do when you have all the money?" she asked.

"Find a doctor for Salvatore."

"And then?"

He didn't answer. His dark face suddenly looked much older.

"Salvatore told me that you don't have any profession," Helen said.

"I'll get by."

"As before."

He shrugged. "I haven't done so badly," he said, putting his hand on her thighs. "Or isn't this something?"

"It isn't everything."

"It is more than that for me," he said. "What's your first name?"

"Helen."

"It suits you," Pietro said. "It is pretty and cool like your skin. I like it when women are pretty and cool like you. I could lie beside you and look at you all my life."

"You would soon get tired of it," Helen said.

"Not in a hundred years," he said. He bent over her and kissed her neck. Even without Piera, she would have been convinced that she wasn't the first woman he had had. He never rushed. He did everything deliberately, almost too deliberately, she thought, but it must be his way, and perhaps it was the only way. And now she didn't satisfy herself with simply responding to his caresses. She provoked them, and she let herself be carried away and do things which she had hardly been able to force herself to do when she was married. Temporarily the inner conflict was obscured. But at the same time it was deepening. She tried to sustain her state of semiconsciousness as long as possible, and she felt an almost painful intensity in making love to him. She found herself believing things which were not really true.

When they returned to the cave half an hour later, she feverishly avoided thinking beyond anything but the fact that she would be with him for another two weeks.

Salvatore received them with a grin. "Piera has asked a dozen times where you were. Was it nice?"

Pietro went over to him. "Was what nice?"

"Nothing," Salvatore said, hunching himself deeper under his blanket. "I was just kidding."

"I don't like your kidding," Pietro muttered and turned back to Helen. She saw that his face was white. Then she heard Piera behind her: "Where have you been so long?"

She was standing in the entrance of the cave staring at Pietro without an expression on her face.

"We had to discuss something."

"It was quite a discussion," Piera said and ducked back into the cave.

Pietro hesitated a moment; then he sat down at the table. Helen looked at Salvatore, who was moodily leafing through his book. "What is he reading?" she asked Pietro.

"The Bible."

At first she thought he was joking, but then she saw Salvatore blush.

"His mother brought it one day," Pietro went on. "He has read it so often he should know it by heart."

Salvatore looked up. "Bring me something else and you can hang this in the outhouse," he said.

"Hang yourself there," Pietro said fiercely. "One day I'm going to leave you to rot somewhere."

"I'm sorry," he said to Helen. "At times I'd like to kill him and myself too."

Helen sat down; then she realized that both men were listening to something.

Salvatore said, "It was once!"

"Are you sure?" Pietro asked.

"Once," Salvatore repeated.

"I had a feeling all morning," Pietro said. "You have to go in," he told Helen.

She stood up.

"I'll explain to you later," Pietro said. "Wait inside."

She still hadn't heard anything but she sensed that something extraordinary had happened. Inside, she found Piera standing at the stove. She looked at Helen and walked out.

The cave smelled of roasted meat. Helen looked in the stove and saw an iron pot standing in the flames. There was a pot of water standing beside it. She sat down on a crate and began to wonder what she was really afraid of. If the carabinieri found them, she could be back in Naples two weeks sooner. In three weeks she could be in Toledo. But what, she thought in the same breath, do I want in Toledo?

Piera came back. She stood silently near the fire, poured some hot fat over the meat, and turned it over. Helen couldn't stand her silence.

"Did you hear anything?" she asked.

"They are in the valley," Piera said.

"Did you see them?"

"Vito saw them; he gave the signal. If he cries just once, it means in the valley."

"What will you do?"

"Ask Pietro," Piera said. She took a handful of spaghetti from a bag, threw it in the water, and looked at the meat again.

Helen sat down again and listened. She felt her heart sinking. It was pointless to fool herself. The way you fell in love with a man didn't change the end result. Perhaps it had happened in the most uncomplicated way because the usual uncertainties hadn't entered it. But she was no longer sure if the same thing might not have happened under normal circumstances. Trying to justify herself once more, she was tempted to compare him to her husband and to see similarities between them, even some which she conjured up herself. Their dissimilarities she attributed to the difference in age. She even succeeded in convincing herself that if Genno Brazzi had been only seven years older, he would not have looked very different from Pietro or, for that matter, any other thirty-one-year-old Italian of vaguely similar stature. It seemed to help her to believe that the two South Italians looked as much alike to her as two Orientals might appear to anyone from Toledo, Ohio. Certainly the social circumstances of each were similar enough. Thus did she manage to justify the fact, to minimize the peculiarity, that she now trembled for a man who stood outside every ethical and social code she had ever learned.

In another situation she might have felt less ambiguous about the relationship, but now she was actually afraid he might be caught by the carabinieri, and this intensified her emotions and made her feel as if she had already been with him for a long and intimate time.

She had lost track of time when Pietro came in. He went straight for the middle cave, where the large crates were standing. A few seconds later he came back and Helen saw that he was carrying a short-barreled automatic rifle.

"Are they coming up here?" Piera said. She was standing at the stove and all the color had drained from her face.

"They haven't made up their minds yet," Pietro said, turning toward Helen. "I don't think they will come up. They are five men and they have field glasses. They're reconnoitering."

"Where are they?" Helen asked. "In the valley?"

"At the bottom of the stone slope."

"If you shoot one of them . . ."

Pietro grinned. "We have something better for them. For someone who doesn't feel like climbing up, it's a long way."

"Can I help?" Piera asked.

"By not letting the meat burn," Pietro answered and walked out.

"He's always like that," Piera said. She hesitated, then she turned toward Helen. "If you want you can eat now, signora; there's no point in waiting for Pietro."

"I couldn't swallow a bite."

"It's the opposite with me," Piera said. "When I'm afraid I get very hungry. I can't do anything about it." She took out the meat and cut off a piece. "Won't you try?"

Helen shook her head.

"Four days ago it was the same thing," Piera said. "Then there were three. They didn't stay long."

She sat down opposite Helen on a crate and put the plate in her lap and picked up the meat. "I love mutton," she said and tore off a piece with her teeth. While she chewed she wiped the fat from her mouth and stared at the entrance of the cave. "I don't like it," she said and put the meat back on the plate and stood up.

"What don't you like?"

"It's taking too long. I don't know why it's taking so long."

"Go have a look."

"Pietro doesn't like that."

"It might be better all the same," Helen said.

She watched Piera go out. She was now so restless that she couldn't stay either. She walked carefully toward the entrance of the cave. She could see a small section of the hollow. She held her breath and listened but could not hear a sound. After a few minutes she couldn't stand it any longer. She stepped outside and saw Pietro. He was lying flat on the ground and staring down into the valley. He had taken a place between two large rocks. She could also see Piera, who was crouching near Salvatore and listening eagerly. When she saw Helen, she put her finger to her mouth and motioned her to go back to the cave, but Helen stayed rooted to the spot and continued to stare at Pietro. She saw the gun next to him and the rocks on each side, and she realized that ten minutes ago those rocks had not been there, and she understood why they were there now.

Salvatore caught sight of Helen and whispered to Piera. Piera shrugged and Salvatore turned toward Pietro. A few seconds passed; suddenly it seemed to Helen that she could hear a voice from the valley and she saw Pietro raise his head a bit. Salvatore was sitting up too, and although no one said anything, she knew that the carabinieri were coming up the slope. She kneeled down where she had been standing, unable to think.

At the same moment the sun went behind a cloud. She looked up and stared at the sky. Clouds from the south were coming up, black with yellow lining, filling the horizon. It became cold in the hollow, and sitting there on the ground and staring at the dark sky, Helen wanted to cry. She heard Salvatore's voice and she saw his face turn gray. Then she heard another voice from the valley and an answer, this time so clearly that there was no further doubt possible. She saw Pietro grasp the gun, pull it toward him, move a bit, and let go of it again. She heard Salvatore whisper: "He's gone crazy. My God!" She didn't understand why he said that, but she knew the reason for Pietro's hesitation: the carabinieri were now so close that their voices were as clear as if they were already in the hollow.

It became quiet and she saw Pietro crawling backward. When he sat up his face was covered with sweat and without color. "They turned around," he said.

It seemed so strange that Helen could only stare. Piera and Salvatore didn't speak either. "They were thirty yards away," Pietro said. "If I hadn't thought . . ."

He didn't go on, but looked at Helen as if he were seeing her for the first time. She understood why he hadn't finished his sentence. It must have been terrible for him to watch the carabinieri coming up the slope without being able to do anything—to lie there and watch them come within thirty yards, waiting motionlessly for a miracle. He couldn't afford to shoot as long as there was the slightest chance for the miracle, because without the miracle, he, Piera, and Salvatore would be lost, even if they had killed all five of the carabinieri.

When Pietro started to come toward her, she remembered that he had ordered her to remain in the cave. He stopped in front of her and looked down at her without speaking, and then very carefully and

slowly he stroked her cheek with the tips of his fingers and smiled.
For a moment she didn't understand the smile. Then she remembered
the pistol in her pocketbook and she realized that for a minute the
carabinieri had been only thirty yards away. She didn't understand
herself anymore.

## 24

There had been no rain, but a thunderstorm sounded in the distance
and the evening was cool. They were sitting outside and Piera put
wine, bread, and bacon on the table. Pietro had been away for two
hours during the afternoon. Helen had unpacked her suitcase. She
hadn't heard anything of the carabinieri anymore, but she still felt
that something had changed. Pietro and Salvatore ignored the incident in their conversation. During dinner they talked about the new
buses to Messina, about the coming rain, about the government in
Rome, about everything except carabinieri. Piera said very little.
Helen realized that she looked sad. Later Carmelo came. Helen
hadn't heard him approach; he was suddenly standing in the hollow.
He talked quietly to Pietro and vanished as softly as he had come. He
was the man Helen understood the least, a lightly built young man,
with an indifferent, rather stupid, face and very black eyes. She asked
Piera about him.

"He is an orphan," the girl said. "His parents died of typhoid
fever, and he lives with his grandmother."

"Was he in Palmigano?"

"No, but he is very fond of Pietro."

Helen smiled. "Like your brother. Why has he impressed them
so?"

Piera looked at Pietro, who had seated himself next to Salvatore and was talking to him. "It's just that Pietro is different, signora. I don't know what it is. He always wanted to leave Chiesa. Chiesa is a prison for him."

"Not for you?"

"I didn't pick it. If it hadn't been for the war I would have a job now in Switzerland. They always need maids there."

Helen remembered that Pietro had had similar ambitions. "Are you too old for that now?" she asked.

Piera shrugged. "No, but it isn't everything to be a maid."

"Especially if one is as pretty as you," Helen said. "Why don't you marry a rich man?"

"In Chiesa?" Piera made a face. "If you find me one, I'm ready! When I was fifteen, I would have married only a man from Rome. My God! How do *you* like Pietro?"

Helen hesitated. It was too dark now to see Piera's face. "Why do you ask?"

"I noticed something," Piera said. She stood up and began to clear the table. When she was gone, Pietro came over to the table in the darkness.

"Piera says she's noticed something," Helen said.

"What?"

"She didn't say."

"Perhaps we called each other by our first names," Pietro said. "I don't care."

She stared at him. "You don't?"

"I noticed something too," Pietro said. "Let's go for a little walk."

She hadn't been alone with him all afternoon and she got up immediately. They climbed out of the hollow and she held on to Pietro. He had eyes like a cat, and he led her surely to the ridge. There he took her in his arms and kissed her until she became weak in the knees and dropped to the ground with him. They did not let go of each other and when they had come to their senses, they continued to hold on to each other for a long time. Then they smoked and Helen asked, "What did you notice?"

"That I'll miss you."

"Is that all?"

"It's enough," Pietro said. He pushed out his cigarette and looked at the sky. "I often wonder why I still go on."

"With me?"

"In general. It's like an avalanche: one stone starts another."

Helen had talked to many men, intelligent men, stupid men, and men who seemed to have memorized an encyclopedia. Usually, after a few minutes, she felt as if she understood them clearly. Pietro was different. She couldn't put him in a category. She couldn't even decide if he was intelligent or not. Their talk was as sparse and haphazard as the landscape of the Nebrodi. Bentley was witty, cynical, and in a sense original, but she could not find those qualities in Pietro. He spoke very little; he seemed locked within himself. She couldn't talk to him the way she would normally talk at this stage of a relationship. Yet she did not feel hamstrung or uncertain in her emotions. It was enough for her to be near him and to know that she did not have to worry about him at this particular moment. It wasn't much for a cultivated lady from Toledo, even if she considered only her barest needs. She had thought about it for two hours that afternoon without reaching any conclusions. Perhaps the explanation lay beyond normal considerations. Perhaps the unity and sympathy, which she could feel but not analyze, was enough

She put her head in his lap and looked up at him. "What do you expect from me?" she asked quietly.

"From you?"

"Yes."

Pietro laughed softly. "Two thousand dollars."

"Is that all?"

He waited for a while. "It doesn't matter what I expect," he said. "When I got out of school, I expected a chance. I walked my legs off for that. What *should* I expect from you?"

"Perhaps your chance."

"By taking a hundred thousand dollars from you? I think the risk is bigger than the chance."

Helen nodded. She was still lying in his lap. "I wasn't thinking about money," she said.

He stared at her with surprise. Then he laughed again. "You mean I should propose to you?"

She didn't answer. Of course it was absurd, but not more absurd than the fact that his laughter annoyed her. Most of the complications in her life might have been avoided if she had been more prepared to compromise. After all, an affair didn't have to become a matter of the soul, but she had never been able to keep the two apart. Her main problem was really nothing more than her inability to be immoral in the conventional sense of the word. Her curiosity and her erotic sensitivity made it easy for a man to become a problem for her. Up to now she had been protected only by a lack of opportunities. Her position in Toledo had saved her from most problems as long as she hadn't looked for them. The meeting with Bentley, however, had already sufficed to open doors to all sorts of things; perhaps with him she had exhausted her capability to resist, and the next temptation had to be fatal, even if it hadn't been Pietro.

She felt a moment of despair, and casting about in her mind, she thought of Giuseppe. He was really the cause of everything. He had shot her husband, and thinking about this while she rested her head in Pietro's lap, she began to hate Giuseppe with even greater intensity. As with Bentley she constructed a high wall of hatred. It didn't solve any problems, but at least it diverted her from thinking about the consequences of her relationship with Pietro.

It became colder. She shivered and reached for her clothes. While she dressed, she could feel Pietro's eyes on her. Of course he wouldn't hesitate for a second to marry her. Nothing better could happen to him, and she wouldn't have to worry about any unpleasant surprises in Toledo. He would be in a completely strange environment and dependent on her. Perhaps something could be made out of him. She could dress him according to her own taste and teach him good manners—change him the way she had changed Genno Brazzi. Her father would find him a job. No man could be too unintelligent to become at least the head of a department if he had McShane's protection! But there must be less complicated ways for a woman in Toledo to fight her boredom than by making herself a protectress of the moral order. After all, marriage with Pietro was a little hard to imagine, and her father would never accept it. But why not? she then went on thinking. He had accepted Genno. I am not very consistent; I'm crazy, she thought to herself. Marriage with Pietro is the last thing in the world I want.

She concentrated again on Giuseppe. He had not only killed her husband, but also the bank clerk, and he was the most important man for Lieutenant Gastone to catch.

For a moment she had forgotten Pietro's presence. He had not interrupted her thoughts. In fact, it was extraordinary how little he intruded on her thoughts. She smiled, and sensed that he knew she appreciated it.

"What amuses you so?" he asked as she sat down beside him.

"You do."

"I don't like that," he said.

She laughed. She bent over and kissed him; it was the first time that she had kissed him. "Piera will notice our absence," he said.

"Aren't you afraid anymore that she will let herself walk into the hands of the carabinieri?"

He shook his head.

"Why not?"

"I thought of something else," Pietro said.

It took her a moment to understand what he meant. "Apart from the fact that you will miss me?"

"Yes."

"May I know what?"

Pietro said slowly and calmly, "I'm afraid they already know where we are."

"You mean they already know where we are hidden?" Helen asked, astounded.

"I thought about it all afternoon," Pietro said. "There's no other reason for them to turn back thirty yards from the hollow."

"I don't understand," Helen muttered.

Pietro nodded. "I didn't understand either, but now I realize that they just didn't want to put you in danger. As long as you are here they don't want to attack us. They just want to show us that they know where we are."

"Wouldn't that endanger me from their point of view?"

He hesitated. "I'm just guessing," he answered. "I don't know what they expected from doing it. Maybe they just want to scare us. But if I'm right, we have to get out of here as quickly as possible."

"How do you expect to get out if they know where we are?" she asked.

"There's another way out. If tonight . . . I almost forgot," he muttered.

"Forgot what?"

"Three thousand dollars. I would guess your friend withdrew the money today."

"You mean you want to meet him once more?"

"I have to. Antonio and Giuseppe . . ."

He stopped again and thought. Helen put her hand on his arm. "I don't want you to go to Chiesa again," she said. "Do you need those three thousand dollars immediately?"

He didn't answer.

"If there's no hurry," she said, "I could have it sent to me together with the two thousand. Or do you have to share it with Antonio and Giuseppe?"

"That was the plan."

"Then let them go to Chiesa," Helen said impatiently. "I will have five thousand dollars sent to me."

"I don't like that," Pietro muttered.

"Why not?"

"I would rather forget the whole thing. If it weren't for Salvatore . . ."

"I'll pay for his operation," she said quickly.

At that moment she would have promised him a hundred thousand dollars without thinking.

"I'd still rather forget the whole thing," Pietro said. Suddenly he pulled her to him and kissed her mouth, her eyes, her whole face. He caressed her breasts, her body, her hips; finally he pulled up her dress and started kissing her until she began to lose her senses and moan. Then he suddenly let her go and stood up. "It only makes everything worse," he said breathlessly. "Do you want to go back to Chiesa?"

She was still lying as he had left her, half naked and in a trance, and when she didn't answer, he leaned over. "Do you want to go back to Chiesa?" he repeated softly.

"When?"

"Now, tonight."

She sat up and looked at him. "And you?"

"Don't worry about me," Pietro said. "I asked you if you want to go back to Chiesa."

Helen thought of what he had said about the carabinieri. He obviously didn't know what he was doing anymore. She stood up, straightened her dress, and looked for a cigarette. When she had lit one, she said, "I've never been in a fishing boat before. How long will it take?"

Pietro turned away. He put his hands in his pockets and stared at the mountains, which were now clearly visible in the rising moon. Then he turned toward her and said, "Six to seven hours."

"I'm not a very good swimmer," Helen said.

"If we drown, we'll drown together," Pietro answered. "I can't swim at all."

He picked up his jacket, put it on, and took Helen by her arm. "Come, signora. I have to go to Caronia tonight and I will think of you the whole way."

"What do you want in Caronia?" Helen asked.

"To see how good a boat it is. When the sun comes up tomorrow we'll have Italy in front of us. Come." He led her in the moonlight through the rocks to the slope. Then he suddenly stood still and listened. Helen held her breath. "We have visitors," he said.

"Giuseppe?" she asked.

"It was Antonio's voice, and if Antonio is there, Giuseppe and Lucio are near. If I only knew . . ."

She felt frightened. Giuseppe and Lucio had been there the night before too. Why was it so extraordinary?

"What does it mean?" she asked.

"Well, I sent a message to them in the afternoon, through Carmelo, not to come. Well, let's go and say good evening."

In the hollow the moonlight was not as bright as on the ridge, but Helen recognized the three men all the same. They were sitting with bottles and glasses. Carmelo had come too; he was in the deck chair next to Salvatore. A moment later Helen also made out Piera standing next to the cave. All of them were staring at her intently. No one said a word. They sat motionlessly. It was a ghostly scene, interrupted finally by Antonio's cough. "We've been waiting half an hour for you," he said, his voice even softer than usual. "We want to talk to you, Pietro."

"I wouldn't know about what," Pietro answered. To Helen he said, "Go ahead, go in. It won't take long."

"You never know," Giuseppe said.

Pietro silently watched Helen pass the three men at the table, then Carmelo, then Salvatore, and then Piera. "You too," he said to Piera. Piera shrugged and followed Helen into the cave.

"And now business," Pietro said to Carmelo. "Didn't you tell them not to come today?"

"They have a suggestion to make," Carmelo said.

Pietro sat down at the table. "What kind of suggestion?" he asked slowly.

"The carabinieri," Antonio answered. "They are watching the road."

"That's why I sent Carmelo. You weren't so stupid as to use the road."

"No. We found out from a bus driver in Nicosia. There are still more carabinieri coming. We would be safe in Rocella."

Pietro frowned. "Why Rocella?"

"Giuseppe knows a reliable man there. For two hundred dollars he can get us a house. It's at a good spot."

"Complete with bath?" Pietro asked.

Antonio leaned back. "You don't like the idea."

"No."

"Why not?"

"Too risky," Pietro answered. "How do you propose to get Salvatore there?"

"How did we get him here?"

"That was six miles," Pietro said. "Rocella is thirty miles away and, besides, the signora has never been on a horse."

Antonio took a little sip from his glass. "I wonder if we still need her."

"What do you mean?"

"Just what I said. When the money comes the matter is over. Or do you have something else going with her?"

"With whom?"

"With the American woman."

"Maybe," Pietro said.

Antonio nodded. "I thought so. Giuseppe and Lucio don't see why the only thing we should share is the money."

"How about you?"

"I don't see it either," Antonio said. "Perhaps she'd even like it. I've heard of American girls who take on at least six at a time."

"Where did you hear that?" Pietro asked. "In church?"

The men grinned.

Pietro stood up. "Is that all?"

"Not quite," Antonio said. "This was a good hide-out as long as we could get here without trouble."

"I didn't ask you here. There were times when you didn't show up for three months."

"We wouldn't have had to show up at all," Antonio said. "None of us would have had to dirty one little finger."

"Except me," Pietro said.

"I didn't say that."

"You're playing the wrong card," Pietro said. "You didn't dirty your fingers just to be nice guys. You helped because you were scared shitless that the Americans would get your names out of Salvatore and me. They knew there were eight of us in Palmigano."

Antonio examined his fingernails. "That's what I'm talking about," he said. "We're just as much involved in this mess as you and Salvatore. Take Giuseppe. If they catch him, he's had it."

"That's his problem. Nobody asked him to shoot the clerk. If he hadn't, Salvatore and I would be just where we are now, only they wouldn't be after us for that too. People like you shouldn't be allowed to handle guns."

"Does that include me?" Giuseppe asked quickly.

Lucio put his hand on his arm. "Don't get excited. You know as well as I do that you didn't want to kill a man."

"I don't care what he wanted," Pietro said. "If he doesn't have the guts, he should have stayed home. Besides, that bank was Antonio's idea."

"You had no better ideas," Antonio muttered. "So you don't want to go to Rocella?"

"No."

"Then one of us will stay here."

Pietro stared at him. "Why?"

"The American girl is as important to us as she is to you. Giuseppe, Lucio, and I will change guard every two days."

"No, you won't," Pietro said.

Antonio moved his chair back a bit. "And why not?"

"Different reasons. I don't want the carabinieri at my throat because of you."

"We aren't beginners," Giuseppe said sharply.

Pietro whistled. "Yes, you've demonstrated that, all right. If you switch off every two days, the carabinieri will be here within a week. Why do you think Vito is still at his post? Only eight hours ago the carabinieri came up the slope. They stopped thirty yards away from us."

The man stared at him. "How many were there?" Antonio finally asked.

"Five. They came without horses and they went away to the south across the ridge."

"From Monte Ambola?"

"I guess so."

Antonio stood up. He went to the edge of the hollow and stared off at the ridge which ran from east to west. "That's one more reason to go to Rocella," he said.

"If he is telling the truth," Lucio said.

Pietro turned toward him. "What?"

"Nothing," Lucio said. He looked fearfully at Pietro, who walked around the table and stood behind him.

"What may not be the truth?" Pietro asked.

Giuseppe came to his brother's aid. "Leave him alone. None of us has seen the five carabinieri. And even if it's true, we can still change guard at night. I don't care."

"I don't either," Lucio said. "If you have nothing to hide, Pietro, you won't mind someone being here."

"We don't need any snoopers around here," Salvatore said, speaking for the first time.

Pietro walked over to Antonio, who was still standing at the edge of the hollow. "How long have we known each other?" he asked.

"When there's a woman involved," Antonio answered, "you can't

200

know your best friend long enough. Giuseppe and Lucio don't trust you."

"And you?"

"I tell you what," Antonio said. "Go to Rocella and the whole matter is solved."

"I wouldn't consider it," Pietro said.

"Then give us the woman. We'll take her to the same spot where her husband is lying."

"There's always time for that."

"Yes, until she runs away. All you have to do is let her out of your sight for a moment. She speaks Italian as well as you and me and she isn't stupid. I'll bet she knows everything about us—our names and where we live."

"Just how naïve do you think I am?" Pietro asked.

Antonio shrugged. "That has nothing to do with it. She picks up things here and there. There's more at stake for us than for you. If I'm lucky I'll be on the Municipal Council in October. But Giuseppe will be hanged if they catch him. Think about him. He's lost ten pounds since that matter with the bank. And he doesn't like it that you're the only one who has fun with her. Give him a break. Let him have a shot at her too. Maybe it will bring him to his senses. We figure that he should stay here tonight."

"Until when?"

"The day after tomorrow I'll take his place."

"You're sure you want to wait that long?" Pietro said.

Antonio looked coldly at him. "If I didn't have a family, I would do it now."

He turned away and went to the table. "Let's go," he said to the two men. "If I'm not welcome I don't want to hang around."

"We agreed that I would stay here," Giuseppe said.

"I don't want trouble," Antonio said. "You do what you want." He emptied his glass, turned around, and climbed out of the hollow. The two men waited a few seconds, hesitatingly; then Lucio got up. His thin face was white with anger. "Come on," he said to his brother. "Now at least we know where we stand."

"You make me weep," Salvatore said.

They did not answer him but walked past Pietro on their way out. "You may be sorry," Giuseppe said in a hoarse voice.

Pietro nodded. "If I have the time." He watched them climb out of the hollow and follow Antonio. At the same moment Carmelo stood up from the deck chair, walked over to Pietro, and stared after the two men. His dark face was expressionless.

"We will wait ten minutes," Pietro said to him. "Make sure they leave." And then to Salvatore: "You won't have much sleep tonight. Vito must stay at his post and I need Carmelo in Caronia."

"Tell Piera to bring me two more blankets," Salvatore said. "How long do you plan to stay away?"

"I want to be back before it gets light," Pietro answered. He sat down. Carmelo waited ten minutes and then ascended the slope.

"I'm surprised," Salvatore said. "Antonio is behind this; not Giuseppe. Giuseppe doesn't have enough imagination. I hope it will all work out."

"Why not?"

"If the boat isn't ready . . ."

"I promised him a thousand dollars," Pietro said. "You think you can manage?"

"To Caronia?"

"Yes."

"I'll have to. How long will it take?"

Pietro thought a moment. "At most three hours," he said. "We follow the Fratello. The valley is narrow but easy for riding. Watch her while I'm gone."

"How far did you get with her?"

"Far enough for our purposes," Pietro said and stood up, and went into the cave. Inside, he talked with Piera, who was sitting on a crate, looking discontented. "You have to go to Vito. He can't leave his post tonight."

"He didn't sleep much last night," Piera said.

"I know. As soon as we reach Caronia, he can sleep as much as he wants. Give Salvatore two more blankets."

"Is he staying there?"

"It's better. I don't trust Antonio." He looked at her. "What's the matter with you?"

"Nothing."

"Yes, I can see that," Pietro said. "Don't bother me now; I have enough troubles."

Helen was already lying down when he went to her. She was dressed in light blue pajamas which he hadn't seen yet. When he looked at her he saw that her eyes were red. He sat down and took her hand. "Were you crying?" he asked.

She shook her head.

"I can see it," Pietro said. "Why?"

She didn't know herself. She had been lying down in the narrow cave thinking about everything, and the tears had come to her eyes.

"Perhaps you should have gone to Chiesa after all," Pietro said quietly.

"No. That's not it."

"What else."

She was silent.

"I love you," he said quietly. "Did I tell you already?"

"Not that clearly."

"It doesn't come as easy to me as to other men. If I didn't love you, I wouldn't be crazy enough to want to send you to Chiesa." He took an edge of her pajamas between his fingers. "What are these called?"

She told him.

"They're pretty," Pietro said. He went to the table, turned the lamp up, and sat down beside Helen again.

"Suppose Piera comes in," Helen muttered.

"I sent her to Vito." He bent over her. While he kissed her, she remained completely passive. It worried him more than her red eyes. "Why did you cry?" he asked again.

She looked away. "It has no meaning."

"It has to me," Pietro answered. He stared at her. He wouldn't have felt as worried if he hadn't had to go to Caronia. As long as he was near her he felt certain of her. "Carmelo is waiting for me," he continued. "Would you rather I stayed here?"

"Is he going with you to Caronia?" Helen asked.

Pietro nodded. "We need three more horses for tomorrow evening.

I thought I could find another way, perhaps a cart, but there's no time."

"How are you going to get me to Caronia?"

"You will be on a horse with me."

She laughed. He didn't understand and frowned.

"What's the matter with you?"

"It reminds me of something," Helen said. Then she thought of something else. "I never noticed your horses. Where are they?"

"Three miles from here. In an enclosure."

"Isn't that dangerous?"

"No. There are always horses around belonging to all sorts of people. You can come and get them and take them back without anybody bothering. Officially, the enclosure belongs to the municipality of Cesaro, but nobody minds. It's too far from the village. How do you open these?"

"I thought Carmelo was waiting for you."

"Carmelo likes waiting for me," Pietro said. He had discovered a snap and didn't talk for a minute. Then he asked her why she didn't have any children.

"How do you know I don't have any?"

He smiled.

"We hadn't been married long enough," Helen finally said, blushing. During the first year she had wanted to avoid giving the impression that she had been forced to marry Genno Brazzi, and afterwards she had concentrated exclusively on making an important man out of him. Children would have been a distraction. Besides she had never been sure that she really wanted them. She took Pietro's hand. She wasn't in the mood for him and she tried to stop him by asking, "Is Carmelo coming with us?"

"Yes."

"Vito too?"

"No. Vito would die of homesickness. You could give him a castle but he would still die. He needs the people who believe in his magic, and the people here do."

"Seducing their children?" She saw that that annoyed him.

"They are too young," he said impatiently. "He has his fun and they do too."

"Strange fun," Helen said.

He frowned. "I don't like it either, but that's the way Vito is. But why talk about it. Let me look at you."

"What can't you see?"

He was smiling again. "Your back. I like you even better without the pajamas. Turn over."

She didn't like the way he said it, and she didn't move.

"What is it?" he asked quietly.

"Why?"

"Because." He pulled his hand away from hers and tried to turn her over. She resisted, and he suddenly became mad, and took her by her shoulders and pulled her over. For one moment she saw his furious frown, then she saw nothing, but only felt his hands caressing her brutally.

It wasn't like before. She felt it was humiliating and primitive, and she resisted until he hurt her. The pain forced her to give in. She heard him cough, she felt him breathing on her neck, and lying with her eyes closed, pressing her face to the pillow, his lovemaking did not excite her. Her only reaction was disgust mixed with disappointment. Then she felt him suddenly let go of her again and sit up. He didn't do what she thought he would. He remained motionless beside her, and when she turned over again he laughed shyly. "I didn't mean to hurt you," he said. "Are you angry at me?"

She didn't answer. She looked at him and it suddenly seemed almost incomprehensible to her that she had ever felt anything for him.

"It's just that I am so crazy about you," he said. "Did I hurt you?"

She shook her head.

"You are beautiful," he said. "When I look at you, I lose my head. Shall I wake you tonight?"

"If you want to," Helen said, not wanting to annoy him again.

"Like last night," he said. He kissed her softly and left the cave.

Outside in the hollow, Salvatore was alone. Pietro had been with Helen for a quarter of an hour, and Carmelo had not returned.

"I don't understand it," Salvatore said. "Perhaps they saw him."

"Carmelo knows how to be invisible," Pietro said. He went to the edge of the hollow and stared at the empty valley, now clearly lit by the bluish moonlight. "Piera is staying away too."

"But she only just left, Salvatore said.

Pietro turned around. "What?"

"She left just before you came out. Didn't you see her?"

"I told her to go fifteen minutes ago," Pietro said. He sat down next to Salvatore and lit a cigarette. It dawned on him what had happened and he felt the blood rush to his head. "She is becoming difficult," he said, "You must keep an eye on her."

Salvatore stared at the moon above the mountains. "That's easily said. When she finds out what you are after . . ."

"I don't know what I'm after," Pietro said. "It all depends."

"I like your plan to go to Caronia," Salvatore said. "Then we could stay together."

"I will send for you all."

"For my mother too?"

"If you want."

"She wouldn't survive it," Salvatore said. "I can't let her sit around Messina at her age."

"She would be well off with her brother."

"Well?" Salvatore said.

Pietro said impatiently, "I thought we had discussed this all before."

"True," Salvatore muttered. He had thought about it all day long and he had liked it less and less. "It's a stupid feeling I have," he went on. "I had pictured it all so nicely to myself, Switzerland and all that. I mean the three or four together. If you don't go to America, that is. Couldn't you tell her to stay with us?"

"Where, in Switzerland?"

"Yes."

"I don't know where I stand with her. Maybe she has . . ."

"If the money . . ."

"If it were just the money, I wouldn't care. I've never really known what I wanted. First I thought of a good job in Palermo, then of a good job in Switzerland. When you have lived in Chiesa for twenty-eight years you look at the world from a stable. And when you live in a stable, a job in Switzerland is the best thing you can imagine. Shall I tell you what it really is?"

He bent over, took Salvatore's hand, and held it in front of his face. "Dirty nails. I've tried ten thousand times to imagine what there is in the world besides Sicily and Switzerland. Now I know."

He went to the edge of the hollow. Looking down, he saw Carmelo climbing up like a cat; half a minute later he jumped into the hollow.

"You've been a long time," Pietro said. "What happened?"

"I lost them," Carmelo said breathlessly.

Pietro frowned. "Where?"

"On the road. They suddenly vanished."

"Like I told you," Salvatore cried. "They saw you go after them. How far did you follow them?"

"Up to the side road which leads to the enclosure."

"We're not sure they left their horses there," Salvatore said.

Pietro remained motionless for a moment, then he said to Salvatore, "I can't stay here. Carmelo can't either. Can you manage alone?"

"If you bring me my rifle."

"You'd bring the carabinieri here with the first shot," Pietro said.

He went back to Helen. She was lying as he had left her, but she had pulled the blanket back over her legs. He picked up her pajamas from the floor and smiled. "Did you know I was coming back?"

She was annoyed but she managed to return his smile. She hadn't known he was coming back; lost in thought, she had just forgotten about her pajamas.

He sat down beside her and stared at the floor.

"Is there trouble?" she asked.

"I don't know yet. You may not get much sleep. It's possible that you'll have to get up very quickly. Would you mind sleeping in your clothes tonight?"

She was startled. "Why?"

"You might have visitors."

"The carabinieri?"

"No, hardly," Pietro said, putting the pajamas down over her legs.

"I was thinking of Antonio. He and Giuseppe and Lucio are around somewhere. If they come back while I'm not here, you will have to go to the ridge with Piera and hide there. I will send straw and blankets up. You'll be safe on the ridge."

"Did you fight with them?" Helen finally asked.

He was smiling again. "Not directly. It's just that they've guessed that we're up to something and they don't see why we should share just the money with them."

She was suddenly sorry that she hadn't accepted his offer to go to Chiesa.

He guessed what she was thinking, "I'm glad you didn't go to Chiesa. You would have run right into their hands."

That idea made her tremble. "Can't you stay here tonight?" she asked.

He shook his head. "I thought about it, but if I don't go to Caronia tonight, the boat won't be ready. Don't worry, they won't look for you on the ridge."

"They will ask Salvatore."

"He won't say anything."

"And if they force him?"

Pietro sat quietly for a moment, then he stood up and went into the outer cave. She heard him opening a crate.

She found herself waiting for him to come back and realized that she had just been trying to convince herself to despise him. She'd better not forget again that without him she would be at the mercy of Antonio and Giuseppe. But she had also better stop idealizing him and seeing him differently from what he really was. He was a man from Chiesa, and a man from Chiesa would always act as he had earlier. He was inscrutable, moody, and in the last analysis just as primitive as Giuseppe and Antonio. That he had offered to let her go back to Chiesa was as contradictory as many of the other things that had happened during the past twenty-four hours. Of course it was absurd for a man in his position to renounce a hundred thousand dollars, but it was no more absurd than her own reactions.

She couldn't think it through clearly, but she decided not to be so easily swayed in the future.

He came back after about five minutes. "I remembered that we had a dozen American hand grenades somewhere. Don't forget to get dressed before you fall asleep. Piera will wake you in time."

"And if they find me all the same?" Helen asked.

Pietro smiled. "That wouldn't be too good for Antonio."

# 25

It was pure chance that Antonio had noticed Carmelo. At a curve in the valley he had told Giuseppe and Lucio to go on ahead. He had been crouched behind a rock when, suddenly, he had heard a small clatter of stones hitting each other. He turned around and looked at the slope. Then he ran after the two men so fast that he caught up with them before they had reached the road.

"Carmelo is behind us," he said. "I almost expected it."

"Why?" Giuseppe asked.

"I'll explain later."

They walked along the middle of the dry river bed between the steep walls until they came to the crossing. They went through the main valley and climbed along the stones up to the road, which looked in the moonlight as if it were covered with snow. Before they went on, Antonio stared at the eastern wall up the valley with its straight sides and rocky top.

"I don't think he can see us in this light," Lucio said.

"Vito has eyes like a cat. Follow me."

He led them across the road. They followed the many curves between the mountains; after about five hundred yards they came to a deep gorge. Huge rocks towered at its entrance where Antonio was waiting. It was a good spot because from there they could observe the road without being seen. They didn't have to wait long. After two minutes they heard approaching steps and a moment later they saw Carmelo pass by. They waited a while and then they returned to the road.

"I don't understand any of this," Giuseppe muttered. "Why is he spying on us?"

Antonio didn't answer. He stood with his hands dangling at his sides for a few moments, and then he started off in the direction they had come. The others followed him without asking any more questions. Two hundred yards further on, Antonio left the road and headed into the valley. Here Vito could not see them anymore. After they had gone about five hundred feet, they climbed the eastern wall, which was in shadow, until they came to a huge rock which stood out against the sky like a beckoning finger. From this point they could see not only the entrance to the side valley but also a large part of the main valley and even the road, which curved by sharply to the right and ascended the bare mountain slope to the north.

The men were panting from the steep climb. They dropped to the ground and stared across the dark valley. The opposite wall was bathed in moonlight, and above it Monte Ambola stood as white as if it were frosted.

"She reminds me of Mount Etna," Giuseppe said. "Now, why did you think Carmelo was spying on us?"

Antonio laughed softly. "I had a hunch. Didn't you notice anything?"

"I've noticed a lot of things tonight," Giuseppe answered. "The woman must have turned his head; he acts crazy."

"Not just his head," Antonio grinned. "I tell you she's a real bitch, that one."

"When you think of all we've done for him," Lucio said. "That's no way to treat friends, to chase us like dogs."

Antonio nodded. "He's up to something. He barely sat down at the table with us before he was up again. All right. He didn't have to agree with us. That's his business, but when a man is in such a hurry, he's up to something."

"Do you mean . . ."

"I don't mean anything," Antonio said quickly. "I don't even mean what you think I mean. I'm going to stay right here and not get off my ass until I know what I mean. Listen, that stupid bastard is coming back!"

The men turned their heads at the same time. Carmelo was clearly visible, coming around the bend. He wasn't moving as fast as before; they watched him climb down and vanish.

"I never could stand the guy," Giuseppe muttered. "I could never figure out what goes on in his head. What do we do now?"

"Wait," Antonio said. "Who's got a cigarette for me?"

Lucio gave him his tobacco pouch. "Don't make it too thick. I haven't got much more."

"In four weeks you'll be smoking fat cigars," Antonio said. "Did you ever figure out how much you can buy with fifteen thousand dollars?"

"It will be thirty thousand for us," Giuseppe said. "Lucio and I are putting our money together. First we'll get a tractor. I asked about the dollar rate today. I'm not a stupid guy, but I couldn't even figure it out in lira."

"Where did you ask about the dollar rate?" Antonio asked.

"From a schoolteacher."

"In Sperlinga?"

"Where else?"

"You're an idiot," Antonio said softly. "A triple idiot. Do you want to be hanged?"

Giuseppe looked guilty. "I don't know why you're getting so excited."

"He doesn't know," Antonio said, "Holy Madonna! He doesn't know." He started screaming. "Because you don't have a trace of brain in your head! Today you're asking the schoolteacher about the dollar rate and in a couple of weeks you're going to buy a tractor! In a few days the schoolteacher will read the story of the hundred thousand dollars. What do you suppose she'll think?"

"He's right," Lucio said nervously. "You shouldn't have asked."

Antonio threw his cigarette away. "You're both fools," he said. "If you buy a tractor, there will be about three hundred people in Sperlinga who will figure out where you got the money for that tractor."

"Let them," Giuseppe muttered, but he added uncertainly, "I don't care what people think."

"What they think?" Antonio said impatiently. "The carabinieri will come. All they have to do is watch whatever man spends more money than he earns. You can buy a villa in Rome as far as I am concerned, but no tractor."

"What would I do with a villa in Rome," Giuseppe said. "Would you go to Rome?"

"I didn't kill anybody," Antonio said.

Lucio sighed, "We should have done like Frank and Filippo. They got out in time. What do we care about Salvatore? That bank job was for the Mafia, not for people like us."

"You weren't so tender with the Americans."

"That was war, man," Lucio said. "It's not even fair to talk about it anymore. Nobody invited them here to liberate us."

"Those things are usually not done by invitation," Antonio said. He turned to Giuseppe. "Do you understand?"

"It's easy for you," Giuseppe said unhappily.

"Why? If they catch us they'll find out exactly how much of it was my idea. Pietro will put all the blame on me."

"I fired the shot."

"Well."

"Well, nothing. It's not my style."

"It's not mine either," Antonio said. "I'm not a Mafia man."

"You didn't do it on purpose," Lucio said. "We can all testify to that."

"They won't ask," Giuseppe said.

"The trouble is, you're all wetting your pants," Antonio said. "And even worse, Pietro knows that you're wetting your pants, and the worst of all is that I was stupid enough not to realize what he was up to."

"I wish Salvatore had kicked the bucket that time," Lucio said. "It's all his fault."

"If he had we wouldn't be about to lay our hands on a hundred thousand dollars. There's two sides to everything. Ever since Pietro and Salvatore have been here we haven't had a quiet minute. Frank and Filippo are in Nicosia; they're out of reach. They've got no relatives and they could afford to get away to Naples. Carcai hasn't been heard of in two years. I'll bet he's gone too. I would have done the same. What's keeping you in Sperlinga?"

"That isn't anybody's business," Lucio muttered. He looked at Giuseppe, who looked away from him. "Giuseppe wants to get married."

"He can do that in Rome or Naples. Why not take her along?"

"Her parents won't let her."

"Then look for another one," Antonio said. "For thirty thousand dollars you can find as many pretty wives in Naples as you want."

"That's not the problem."

"What is?"

Lucio hesitated, then he went on. "It's easy for some people, like Pietro for instance. I'm not sentimental, but to just leave everything behind?"

"Your sheep?" Antonio said. He spit on the ground. "How many sheep do you think you can buy for thirty thousand dollars?"

"It's not just the sheep."

"What else?"

"Everything," Lucio said. Then he saw the carabinieri.

First there were three of them. They were proceeding slowly in the moonlight along the curve of the road. They reined their horses for a moment and surveyed the valley before they continued. A moment later, about a hundred and fifty feet behind, others appeared. Lucio counted twenty-five of them. They came single file, the dusty road muffling the beat of their horses' hoofs—a long, seemingly endless row, soundless, disciplined, and awesome.

Lucio stared at them and he felt the sweat come out on his forehead. He turned and looked at the pale faces of Giuseppe and Antonio, who were watching tensely. The shadow of the valley wall hid them, but involuntarily they pressed themselves closer against the rock. Now the carabinieri were on the same level as they were. They could hear the soft clang of weapons, the breathing of the horses. They were only two hundred feet away. The head of the column reached the side valley. For a few seconds it seemed as if they were going to leave the road, and at that precise moment the hoarse cry of a buzzard sounded through the night and was echoed from farther away, and the three men saw the carabinieri put their heads back and stare into the moonlit sky. But they passed the side valley and, a minute later, the road and the valley lay abandoned in the moonlight.

Antonio's breath sounded like an emptying tire. He bent over and looked for the cigarette he had thrown away, found it, and lit it once more. His face looked completely exhausted.

"I'm getting old," he said and tried to grin. "What's the matter with you all?" he asked.

Giuseppe stared at him. "Where are they going?" His voice sounded cracked.

"I have no idea. Perhaps to Fratello, perhaps not. The main thing is that they have passed."

"I won't hold out much longer," Giuseppe muttered.

Lucio wiped his face. "It was bad. I don't know . . ." He stared in the direction the carabinieri had vanished.

"What don't you know?" Antonio asked when he had pulled himself together.

Lucio didn't answer.

"He's thinking about the American girl," Giuseppe said. "I wouldn't want to be involved either."

"With what?"

"With what?" Giuseppe repeated. "The bank matter is enough for me."

Antonio gave him a cold look. "Do you want your thirty thousand dollars?"

The two men didn't answer. They sat quietly until Lucio went on: "Perhaps we're misjudging Pietro. We could always depend on him before."

"As long as there was no women involved," Antonio answered. "I don't think you quite understand what it's all about. For thirty thousand dollars you can buy fifteen tractors."

Giuseppe grimaced. "What good is that if we can't even buy one. We have to find another way to stop the woman from talking."

Antonio nodded. "Do you know of one?"

"Perhaps Pietro does."

"Perhaps," Antonio said.

Giuseppe didn't like his tone of voice and he looked suspiciously at him.

"But if he knows one," Antonio said, "he will put the money in his own pocket. *I* don't know of a way. I don't usually believe this kind of thing," he went on, "but there was a woman in Cerami ten years ago; she was a fortune teller; she told me that I would have a lot of money some day."

"They always say that," Giuseppe said.

"Not this one. She told a friend of mine that he would die soon, and a week later he fell from his horse and was dead."

"Yes, there are such things," Lucio said.

Antonio nodded. "I wasn't too excited about this at first," he said. "But now I'm in it up to my ears, and I'm going to stay with it to the end. How about you? Before we came to Palmigano, no carabinieri would have looked at you twice. You did your work and on Sundays you went to church. Now that's all over. You can hang or you can get rich. What do you prefer?"

There was a silence and each of them got lost in his own thoughts. When Lucio looked up again he saw two men on the road. They were walking from the side valley. He recognized them immediately. Antonio and Giuseppe had now seen them too. They sat without moving, watching the two reach the road and come nearer.

"Pietro and Carmelo," Giuseppe whispered. "Is that what we're waiting for?"

Antonio laughed in the dark. "Yes, sort of. Must be an important matter."

"Why?"

"They know the carabinieri are near. Vito gave the signal."

The two men were now on their level. They were walking rapidly, and they quickly vanished around the nearest curve.

"They're going to the enclosure!" Giuseppe hissed. "Now, what the hell do they want with their horses in the middle of the night?"

"Maybe they're going after the three thousand dollars," Lucio said.

"In Chiesa?" Antonio thought for a moment and shook his head. "I don't think Pietro is that stupid. They would walk into the hands of the carabinieri. We agreed to wait at least three days before we contact the American."

"I don't like this," Giuseppe said.

*215*

Antonio grinned. "Nerves?"

"It has nothing to do with nerves!" Lucio said. "Something's wrong. I'd like to know where those twenty-five carabinieri went. What are they looking for in Fratello?"

"You're driving me crazy," Antonio muttered. "If you don't want to sleep in the mountains . . ."

He stopped and stared into the valley.

"What's wrong?" Giuseppe asked.

"I thought I saw a man."

"Where?"

"Down there. Coming down from the ridge."

They stared at the wall of the valley. Giuseppe was about to accuse Antonio of seeing things when he saw the man too. He was scrambling down the steep wall. When he got to the road he stopped for a moment, looked around, then walked along the road quickly, climbed down to the bottom of the valley, and vanished from sight.

Antonio got up. For the past half hour he had been ready for any surprise, but he had not expected to see Lieutenant Bentley.

# 26

After his exchange with Lieutenant Gastone at the inn, Bentley had spent a restless night. The next morning he drove to Nicosia. He cashed the check, made some purchases, and returned to Chiesa in time for lunch. In the restaurant he had a short talk with Signor Rigido and asked him to bring lunch to his room. When the innkeeper came up a half an hour later he found Bentley leaning over a map. He put down the tray and stared over his shoulder. "Are you going up into the mountains, signore?" he asked in a hoarse voice.

Bentley folded the map. "Where would *you* look for them?"

"For whom?"

"I didn't know you were such a hypocrite," Bentley answered. "Please bring me some chicken, a dozen eggs and hot coffee for my thermos bottle."

Rigido did not leave the room. He stood and watched Bentley eat his fish. Finally Bentley looked up at him and asked, "What are you waiting for?"

"I know that area," Rigido answered. "You shouldn't go there alone, signore."

"Why not?"

"You should leave it to the carabinieri."

Bentley leaned back. "What should I leave to the carabinieri?"

"I don't know if I understood you right," Rigido muttered, "but if it's about the signora . . ."

"Are you getting pangs of conscience?" Bentley asked.

"It's not my business, signore, I have my work and my living, and I could act as dumb as all the people here."

"That's just what you've done so far," Bentley said. He started to eat again. "What are you driving at?"

"You shouldn't go into the mountains alone," Rigido repeated. He sat down and folded his hands. "You should stay here. You won't . . ."

He didn't finish his sentence. Bentley stared at him. Then he took a little sip of his wine. "What makes you think I won't find the signora?" he asked quietly.

As the innkeeper did not answer, he leaned toward him. "Do you know where she is?"

"I am an old man, signore."

"That's no answer."

"It's the best I can do. At my age one has to accept things."

"What things?"

"Everything. I grew up in another time. We didn't know any better then."

"What didn't you know any better?"

"Look at me, signore," Rigido said. "In all my life I have been in Palermo twice and that's all. I don't even know Naples. But the young people don't accept that the way I do."

Bentley nodded. "I guess I understand. You probably think it's right that the young people now hold up banks, kill men, and kidnap women. Please fix my things. I want to leave in half an hour."

Rigido shrugged and stood up. "You want your eggs hard or soft, signore?"

"The same as always," Bentley answered. "My thermos bottle is on the washstand."

When the innkeeper had left the room, he opened his map again. To Monte Ambola was about thirty-five miles along the road. Even if he had to drive slowly, he could be there in two hours.

He got up and looked at his face in the mirror. He had only slept a few hours and he looked terrible. One more reason to end the uncertainty; even if his trip didn't lead to anything, it was better than hanging around and wondering. The longer he had been separated from Helen, the more he tended to gloss over their bad moments. Once back in civilized surroundings, she would feel different about him. Even a strong woman like Helen Brazzi must be depressed by a place like Chiesa, the same way he was. He washed his hands, changed his shirt and went to the window to look at the sky. Black clouds were drifting against the mountains and sudden gusts of wind drifted dry leaves along the stony stretches of their base.

These were probably the first signs of the coming rainy season. Nothing seemed worse than the prospect of winter in Sicily.

He went to his suitcase and took out a pair of military boots, congratulating himself for bringing them. He took out his raincoat, filled the pockets of his jacket with ammunition, and left the room. Rigido was waiting for him in the restaurant.

"It looks like a storm," the innkeeper said. "Don't you want to sit it out here?"

"It won't bother me in the car," Bentley answered. "Please bring my things out." He went to the car, checked the tires and the water, and unlocked the doors. As always at this time, the square and the streets were lying empty. Only the two cats were there, sitting on the well's edge.

Rigido brought the thermos bottle and a large bag. "I wrapped everything, signore," he said, looking up at the sky. "Perhaps you are lucky. It looks as if it is drifting west. I would suggest that you take a bottle of Marsala along. The coffee won't be enough."

"It can't do any harm," Bentley said. "Why don't you bring two."

He got into the car, started the engine, and waited for Rigido to bring the bottles. Rigido put them in the back and then he came to Bentley's door. "How long are you staying away, signore?"

"That depends on your friends," Bentley answered. "Do you want to come along?"

Rigido shook his head violently. "Not for ten thousand dollars."

"Now why did you say ten thousand?" Bentley asked sharply.

"It's a round number," Rigido answered and stepped back. "Have a good trip, sir."

Bentley drove off. In the rearview mirror he saw the innkeeper standing motionless under the trees, staring after him. He looked perturbed.

Half an hour later Bentley arrived in Cerami. There was little traffic: a few donkey carts with indifferent-looking men; and beyond Troina, two men on horses, the bus from Nicosia, a shepherd, and a pedestrian. In the fields on both sides of the road men and women were sitting and resting, drinking from bottles, and eating their food.

As Bentley traveled east, the mountains became higher and more rugged. The road climbed steadily and led over a pass. Ten miles beyond Troina he came to a side road leading to Cesaro, narrow and with a barely readable sign. The road climbed so steeply that Bentley had to drive in first gear. The map listed the altitude of Cesaro at almost four thousand feet; he reached it with a boiling radiator. There were not more than a few hundred little decrepit houses of gray stone, nestled between three bare mountain tops which were silhouetted sharply against the blue sky. The dark clouds had vanished to the west. In the dirty village streets, goats and pigs rooted around and a few ragged children stared at the Fiat.

As Bentley passed the last house he happened to look to his right. Against the wall of the house half a dozen carabinieri were leaning. They held automatic weapons and they pretended to ignore the car.

Bentley grinned. As long as Lieutenant Gastone had a chance to become police president of Rome he, Bentley, had nothing to fear.

The road continued climbing between the mountain peaks. In the distance a new pass appeared, flanked by mighty mountains glittering in the early afternoon sun. The wilder the landscape became, the worse the road. In some places it was not more than a path with deep holes and bad ruts. When Bentley reached the pass, he sighed with relief. The entire panorama of the Nebrodi was spread out before him, with Monte Soro in the middle, Monte Pelalo alongside of it, and, so close he felt he could touch it, the mighty cone of Monte Ambola.

Bentley got out of the car. The water in the radiator was boiling again. He kept the engine running. A square stone with an inscription which he couldn't decipher stood beside the road. He sat down on it and scanned the road descending through a wild labyrinth of peaks and ridges. He calculated that he was close to the eastern foothills of Monte Ambola. He looked once more at the map and realized that it was still five miles. On the pass it was no longer so hot. A fresh wind blew from the west. Bentley looked again at Ambola. He guessed that from its peak he should be able to see all the valleys between Soro and Pelalo. The night before, Lieutenant Gastone had said that it was the highest mountain in the Nebrodi and he must have meant something by saying that. Since Bentley had seen the six carabinieri, he was sure that Lieutenant Gastone was following every move he made.

He returned to the car. For the next fifteen minutes he had to drive cautiously. At times the road descended at almost a twenty per cent grade, and when he finally reached the valley the sharp smell of burnt rubber filled the car. Then the driving became somewhat easier. The road followed the valley, which gradually widened and turned north. To the right of it was a dry river bed, its banks overgrown with bushes.

After four miles Bentley noticed a stony road leading diagonally up the western wall of the valley. It looked reliable. He stopped the car and made sure that that road was wide enough for it. If he were right, the road should lead to the eastern approach to Monte Ambola; the farther he could drive, the better. The climb didn't seem to be more than about ten per cent. He continued.

It was easier than he had thought. In several places he drove over ruts left by carts, which seemed to prove that the road did not lead to a dead end. It did become narrower, and it bent in a hairpin curve toward the opposite direction; Bentley had to get out to push a large rock aside. Farther on he could see the top of Monte Ambola. A second hairpin led him back in his original direction, and a few yards beyond he passed an imaginary line defining the valley wall.

Bentley braked. Looking left, he could see the huge face of Monte Ambola. Its top stood against the sky like a truncated pyramid. From where he stood it could not be more than an hour on foot. Then he looked once more at the road ahead, which led down into a hollow and vanished behind a curve. To the right of it was a ravine with perpendicular walls.

On both sides of the road rocks were piled high, but after some searching he found a place where he could leave the car. It would be pointless to stay on top of the mountain after dark, and so he took only his pistol, his raincoat, his thermos bottle, and one of the chickens Signor Rigido had wrapped for him. He put it all in his raincoat and rolled it into a pack, which he slung over his shoulder. He wouldn't have to worry about the car because he would always be able to see it from the top of the mountain. Looking around once more, he set off. If he had looked more carefully, he would have seen the five carabinieri, who were sitting on a small ridge a thousand feet away, watching him through field glasses. When he turned around and started climbing, one of them got up and began to follow him.

For the first few hundred feet Bentley made good progress; then he came to bushes which grew so thickly that he had to struggle to get through them. Beneath the bushes the ground was furrowed as if it had been plowed with a giant machine. Bentley repeatedly lost his footing; he lost time and began to perspire. He had only one free hand, which made the going even more difficult, and his pauses to rest became longer and longer. When he had gotten through the undergrowth he found himself facing another valley, which dipped deeply between where he stood and the naked mountain beyond. The floor of the valley was strewn with huge rocks and it took him more than half an hour to get to the opposite side.

Bentley was now so close to the summit of Ambola that he felt sure that he would encounter no further difficulties, but the path up was so steep that it made him lose his breath. When he finally reached the top, he was so exhausted that he fell panting to the ground. To the northwest was Monte Pelalo and to the right of it the huge mass of Monte Soro. Behind, at the horizon like a blue shadow, lay the blue sea. He could see Etna again too. Its cap was wrapped in dark mist that covered the upper third of the mountain. Between Etna and the western part of the island, which was covered with clouds, an enormous lonely labyrinth of mountain world stretched to the horizon. In the foreground stood Soro and Pelalo, valleys radiating from their faces in all directions. Bentley could see the floors of most of them, but the valley where the road along which he had driven was hidden from view. From where he stood the Fiat looked like a black bug sitting motionless in the grass.

Bentley rested until he had caught his breath, then he opened the thermos bottle and poured himself a cup of black coffee. He set it next to him on the ground and looked around. The stony mountain top was almost completely bare. As the sun was already far down in the west and the wind was blowing even sharper, Bentley decided to keep on his jacket, although he could feel the perspiration running down his back. He was sorry he hadn't brought his field glasses. They would have been useful here, but when he had been in Naples last he had not expected to find himself on the top of Monte Ambola looking for bandits.

He began to feel hungry and ate part of the chicken he had packed. After eating he felt so tired that he would have liked to go to sleep; but he was afraid he would miss something. When he had scanned the terrain for more than an hour, he began to suspect that there was nothing to miss and that he might as well have stayed in Chiesa. He wondered more and more what he had expected from this expedition. If there was any point in sitting on Monte Ambola, surely Lieutenant Gastone would have posted some carabinieri here. The fact that he hadn't probably meant that Gastone already knew where the bandits were hidden; perhaps he was just trying to keep Bentley out of the way so that he wouldn't interfere with his plans. His promise not to do anything definite before next week was not necessarily to be taken seriously.

The temperature had dropped. Bentley wrapped up his thermos bottle and the rest of his food. Earlier he had planned to spend the night in the mountains, but now it seemed to him that he was wasting his time. If he wanted to get back to his car before dark, he had better hurry. He felt resigned about his failure. After all, there wasn't really much he could have done in Chiesa either. As a matter of fact, since Helen had gone it didn't make any difference where he spent his time. He missed her more and more.

When he stood up, he caught sight of three men on horses. They were so far away that first he thought his eyes were tricking him, but he stared until he was certain. They were coming from the west across a bare stretch of land, and as near as he could tell, their trail would lead them to a valley parallel to a ridge. In the beginning twilight they were not clearly visible. They were going slowly, and when they finally reached the valley, Bentley lost sight of them.

He weighed possibilities quickly. It was not necessarily suspicious for three men to be crossing the mountains on horseback. In this country every man on horesback took the shortest route; perhaps the three men were going to the coast. Still, Bentley clung to the belief that it was unlikely that the bandits were hiding anywhere but in the mountains, so as long as he wasn't sure that they were going to the coast, they were suspicious. Normally one would assume that a traveler would hurry to get out of the region before dark, and these men were moving slowly. Bentley decided to establish their destination. He couldn't go by car, and since it was getting dark so quickly, he had to do the most obvious thing. He decided to descend the mountain's northwestern wall. The road he had left the car on appeared to lead in the direction of the hidden valley also, but since it curved south before reaching it, it served no great advantage. Besides, he was worried about a ravine north of the mountain. If he couldn't get through that, he would have to go all the way around and lose a lot of time. He decided to gamble on the short cut.

The northwestern wall had no shrubbery and it was also not as ridged as the eastern wall, where he had come up. Most of the way he made good time, and when he reached the valley where the road ran he had not spent more than about ten minutes. A comparable stretch had earlier taken him almost two hours. He crossed the valley and climbed a slope covered with stones. Then he came to the ravine. As he had feared, it was impossible to cross it at this point. It was about a hundred feet wide and just as deep. He followed the southern edge west. As he walked along he found that it became steadily wider but also less deep, until it finally assumed the shape of a shallow trough and could be crossed with ease. The sun was at the horizon—a soft red disk; in about fifteen minutes it would be too dark to see the three men. To reach the valley where the men had disappeared he had now to turn northwest again. He had not quite reached the valley when he heard the sound of hoofbeats against rock. He stopped and dropped to the ground.

It was only the roughness of the terrain which had prevented Bentley from seeing the three men sooner. They were now so close that it sounded as if they were coming directly at him. He pressed himself closer to the ground and pulled his pistol from his pocket. Then he realized that the sounds were getting fainter. He got up and, running with his head down, moved to a little rise nearby. It was now almost dark, but he could see the three men clearly. Staring after them, he realized that he was trembling from head to foot.

Until a minute earlier he hadn't believed that he had found three members of the gang. Such luck did not seem possible to him. If the three went on in the same direction, they would reach the ravine at the same point where he had crossed it; then they could go either east or south. In either case it would be useless to follow them. It was also possible that they might see the car, become suspicious, and turn around. In that case it would be almost impossible to hide from them in this bare landscape. Having reached this point in his thoughts, he took the shortest way back to the ravine. There he sat down and waited. It was now completely dark, but the contours of the landscape appeared sharp against the sky. A little later the moon began to rise. He was surprised that he hadn't thought of it before. In half an hour there would be enough light to recognize a man on a horse at a thousand feet. He looked at his watch. The three men had had to cover about three times as much distance as he had, but they should show up any moment now. If they didn't, it would mean that they had gone south and he could return to Chiesa.

The time he had figured to reach the ravine had already past, but he waited on. Suddenly he heard the sound of their voices. About half an hour had gone by.

If they had tried to, they couldn't have surprised him more. They had re-emerged right below him, at the bottom of the ravine. It was too dark there to see them. It didn't seem possible to him that they could have gotten there with their horses, even if they had dismounted and led them. They must have left them at the edge of the ravine, and there was only one reasonable explanation for that.

He stood up, forgetting to pick up his raincoat. Now that he was sure of the identity of the men, his main thought was to stay near them. As long as they stayed in the ravine, that couldn't be too difficult.

The moon became brighter by the minute and he made fast time, moving along the north edge of the ravine to the point where his car stood on the opposite side. There was now enough light to see it clearly. Further along he came to the point where the ravine met the valley and the road. Now all he had to do was climb down to the road and wait for the three men to reach it.

The descent wasn't too difficult. He stuck to the side flanking the valley, and then it struck him that it would be wiser to descend just far enough so that he could keep an eye on the men. He didn't know which way they would turn when they reached the road, and he didn't want to run the risk of meeting them.

He climbed down the wall about halfway, then he crouched to watch the entrance to the ravine. It wasn't likely that the gang's hideout was hidden right there. It seemed too obvious. Surely Lieutenant Gastone and his men had searched that area completely.

To his surprise, the men reached the road not less than five minutes later. That seemed to prove that this wasn't the first time they had followed this trail. They stood still for a moment and looked around, clearly visible in the light of the moon. They were still too far for Bentley to see whether he could recognize any of them. When they turned north, they did what he had expected them to do, but now he made his first mistake. Instead of going directly down to the road and following them at a distance, he decided to keep them in sight from the ridge of the valley. He realized this was impossible when he had followed it for about three hundred feet and it became too steep. He could only proceed on hand and foot and he quickly lost sight of the men. After ten minutes he gave up. He sat down, trying to catch his breath, and decided to wait for their return. He had no way of knowing if they had stayed on the road, so there was little point in following them blindly. Moreover, it was so light now that the danger of being seen by them was considerable. He felt he could be satisfied with what he had achieved so far. If the men hadn't been near their destination, they wouldn't have left the horses behind. Perhaps it would be even better to wait until morning before continuing his expedition. In the meantime he had better reconnoiter his surroundings.

It crossed his mind that he might be stalling to gain time and courage. He didn't feel very brave; in fact he had never been quite as afraid. Leading an experienced company of infantry soldiers against an enemy position was one thing, but running around alone in a wild and mysterious landscape behind a gang of outlaws was something else again. For the first time since Helen had gone, he wondered whether his desire for her was worth his dying. No question that she was extraordinary but, after all, what man in the heat of love doesn't think his woman extraordinary? And, he mused to himself, you're not exactly an adolescent who thinks that it's for all time. There are dozens of types, and this one only seems special right now. In fact, there are over thirty million women in the United States; the chance that you'll meet another one like her is not as small as you think. Sure, she has money, looks, and other assets, but there's no reason why your number shouldn't come up again. You've been playing hero long enough. Nobody's impressed.

Thus his thoughts ran as he watched the road. It was at least another hour and a half until he saw the three men again, and when they appeared he couldn't tell where they had come from. They were walking rapidly. He lost sight of them every now and again, and where he was sitting he couldn't be sure of where the entrance to the ravine was. He now had to decide either to go back to his car or to look around some more. To do the latter he would have to go down to the road, and he didn't like that idea. With the moon above the valley it was dangerously light, although the opposite wall of the valley was in deep shadow. For that reason Bentley had not yet seen the small valley that bisected the larger one no more than two hundred feet away. Now, looking in that direction, he saw a pillar-shaped rock projecting above the ridge of the valley, but he paid no particular attention to it. Only the road was clearly visible in the moonlight. It ascended toward the north and Bentley remembered that his map showed another pass somewhere in that direction.

The three men had now definitely vanished from his sight. He felt sure that they had reached the ravine and were going to get their horses. He was now beginning to feel a nagging hunger and thirst. He made up his mind to return to his car and think out his next move there.

He stood up. Almost at the same moment he saw a man appear on the road. He seemed to be in a hurry, but before each curve he slowed down. He appeared to Bentley to be trying to catch up with the three men without being seen. Immediately Bentley forgot his hunger and thirst. He sat down once more and watched the man until he disappeared in the shadows along the opposite side of the valley. Five minutes later he reappeared. Bentley got a good look at him this time. Suddenly, he left the road and vanished.

For the next half hour he saw the twenty-five carabinieri enter the valley from the south and go north, he heard the cry of the buzzard, and he saw the two men pass by under him and vanish in the opposite direction. Then nothing happened for the next half hour. Now only one question was burning in Bentley's mind. He couldn't go back to his car before he had found a satisfactory answer. The sight of the carabinieri had given him renewed strength, but as he descended to the road he felt like someone walking on very thin ice. He crossed the road quickly and headed north, walking in the shadow beside the road. Two hundred feet beyond, he reached the place where the valley wall suddenly opened into the small valley which bisected it. The road turned into the smaller valley at a ninety-degree angle. Now Bentley realized how the men had disappeared and reappeared with such suddenness.

As he looked into the smaller valley he felt his heartbeat quicken. He was tempted now to try to solve the last riddle, the location of the hide-out. He stood for a moment debating with himself. He was about to go into the small valley, when he heard a sound at his back. He turned around. For a split second he saw the three men approaching him in the dark. He began to run. He did not remember his pistol until he had reached the opposite wall of the valley. Then he realized that the three men were not following him. He dropped to the ground, completely out of breath. He looked back into the valley. The men had vanished.

It was the second time in his life that his courage had failed him, and he made no excuses for himself. The sight of the three men in the dark had made him lose his head, exactly as the German counterattack at Palmigano had. But worse, he had made the gang aware of his presence. They had plenty of time to take countermeasures and he didn't even dare think what they might do. He had to get in touch with Lieutenant Gastone as quickly as possible; he should have done so half an hour ago, before he climbed down to the road. It was incredibly naïve of him to have hoped that he could deal alone with a group of heavily armed men. He was appalled by his own stupidity.

Since he had scrambled up the western wall of the valley, now once more the ravine lay between him and the car, yet he decided to take the long way around. Nothing in the world would have made him go down to the road again. It was not impossible that the men were waiting for him somewhere in the dark, watching his every move. It was probably only fear of alerting the carabinieri that had prevented them from shooting at him. The sound of shots would have carried many miles in the mountains.

The farther he climbed the wall, the steeper it became. For the last hundred feet he had to crawl. He felt the perspiration running down his back again, but he didn't stop until he had reached the ridge. From there he proceeded toward the ravine. He could orient himself by the northern, moonlit, wall of Monte Ambola. His path led across a stony field to a flat valley and then once more up a slope. He didn't take time to look for his raincoat. His expectation of finding the horses at the end of the ravine was disappointed. Perhaps they had somehow led them in and tethered them there. He climbed across to the other side and proceeded toward his car. The worst part was now behind him and he could move faster. He was terribly hot and had to keep wiping the perspiration from his eyes. His feet burned as if he were walking on hot coals.

He was only half a mile from his car when he heard the shots. They followed each other so quickly that it was impossible to count them. After a short pause two more answered another weapon. Their echo lasted for several seconds and the silence that followed hurt Bentley's ears.

Breathlessly he stared into the night. He had been so startled that he had failed to trace their direction, but he felt sure that they had come from across the valley, more or less where he figured the hide-out of the gang to be located. He started to run again.

## 27

After Pietro had left the cave, Helen got dressed. She felt wide-awake and she sat on her bed until Piera came in.

"I thought you were already asleep," the girl said. "Aren't you tired?"

"No."

"I'm always tired," Piera said, sitting down at the table.

Helen sensed that Piera's words were intended as more than light conversation. She had worried about talking to the girl. But now she decided that she might as well face it. "Is he still here?" she asked.

"Pietro?"

"Yes."

"Do you want something from him?"

"I want to know if he's here," Helen answered quietly.

Piera shook her head. "He left. You *talked* with him a long time today." The way she stressed the word talk, made Helen blush.

"I talked with your brother too."

"Not as long as with Pietro. With me he only talks now and then."

"That's too bad," Helen said coldly.

The girl smiled. "I don't think you're sorry, signora. Perhaps he talks better with you than with me. Did he mention me?"

"Perhaps."

"What did he say?"

"Why don't you ask him yourself?"

Piera's face hardened. "I will, signora. I'm just surprised at you."

"Why?"

"That you can talk with him so well."

It was more than Helen had expected. She searched for an answer and almost smiled at herself. "You are ignoring something," she answered.

Piera looked at her.

"You forget that I'm not here voluntarily. You obviously can't imagine that I would rather have stayed in Chiesa."

"Oh, yes, I can," Piera said. "I can imagine quite well. Did Pietro threaten you?"

"With what?"

"I wouldn't know. With Giuseppe or Antonio. I mean if you don't do what he wants."

"What Pietro wants?"

"Yes."

"We didn't talk about that," Helen answered. "It wouldn't have made much difference; as long as I'm here, he can do what he wants without threats. Can I go out for half an hour?"

"If you want to." Piera stood up. She waited for a moment. "I think you are right, signora. I wouldn't have thought about it twice if you hadn't been married to a Sicilian."

Helen stared at her. "What does my husband have to do with it?"

"I thought you knew," Piera said and walked away.

It was a minute before Helen understood what she meant. She got up and followed her. She found her in the first cave, wrapping up straw in a blanket.

"Did you know my husband well?" Helen asked.

Piera shrugged. "The men are all the same here, signora."

"My husband was an American."

"A Sicilian in America is still a Sicilian. You wouldn't even be able to make an American out of Pietro."

"What makes you think I want to?"

"I just thought," Piera said and went back to her packing.

"May I help you?" Helen asked.

"No. If you want to do something, talk to Salvatore. He's had a bad day."

She took the bundle under her arm and left the cave. When Helen followed her out, she had vanished.

Salvatore greeted her with a grin. "Piera told me that you couldn't sleep. Did she tell you about the carabinieri?"

"Which ones?"

"They were on the road," Salvatore said. "Twenty-five of them. One more beautiful than the other. Piera and Vito counted them." He was covered with a blanket up to his neck. Helen sat down beside him.

"Where did they go?"

"They didn't tell Vito."

"Can't you sleep either?"

Salvatore stared across the hollow at the mountains. "I've seen this view for two years now, but tonight I thought I couldn't stand it anymore. Do you want a blanket?" He didn't wait for her answer, and put a blanket across her knees. "It's easy to catch cold at night," he said. "When I was fifteen I had pneumonia and I'm careful now. Did you have trouble with Piera?"

"Why do you ask?"

"I just thought. Perhaps she thinks that you want to marry Pietro. Do you?"

"Did he discuss it with you?"

"With me? I'm not his mother. He didn't even tell me what he's going to do with me. Did he tell you?"

She didn't answer.

"He's not stupid," Salvatore went on. "Once he gets free of this, he'll be a millionaire. In school he was always the smartest kid."

"How do you know?"

"In Chiesa people know everything about each other. They know what you say at confession. Three years ago I went to confession for the last time."

"You should go again," Helen muttered.

"What about you?" he asked with a grin.

Helen blushed. As she lit a cigarette he reached out his hand.

"Do you have another one?"

She held out the case for him. In the suitcase that Pietro had brought there had been a fresh supply of cigarettes. Bentley had been very considerate. He had forgotten nothing that she might need. It was almost painful to think that he had packed it for her.

"Tell me something," she said. "Has Pietro told you that he would be a millionaire if he were free?"

"Pietro?"

Helen nodded patiently.

"Possibly," Salvatore said. "I'm not sure. It is important?"

"Perhaps," she said. "Do you like him?"

Salvatore looked up at the sky. "I would rather stay here another two years than . . ." He fell silent.

"Than what," Helen asked.

"Nothing."

"Has your sister gone up to the ridge?" she asked him.

"She's carrying a few things up," Salvatore said. "I don't think Antonio is coming back. He can't know that Pietro and Carmelo have left."

"He might have seen them. Pietro told me that they're still around somewhere near here."

"Vito would see them," Salvatore said. "Are you Catholic?"

She smiled. "What makes you suddenly ask that?"

"Just a thought," Salvatore said. "Sometimes I think I will never get away from here."

"You shouldn't feel that way."

"Perhaps. How old are you?"

"Thirty."

"When you were twenty, could you imagine you would ever be thirty?"

She laughed. "I never thought about it."

"I often do," Salvatore said. "Perhaps I have no imagination. I can't imagine it."

Helen was silent. She felt like putting her hand on his arm.

"In the beginning it was bad," Salvatore went on. "Now I don't know anymore. I might miss this place one day. Once we're out of here, Piera is going to get married, Pietro has his own plans, and my mother won't live much longer."

"There'll be other people."

He shrugged. "If it had been up to other people, I would already be dead. Do you know what the priest said when Piera wanted to bring him here? He said he had to think of the people. He said he had a cold and a bad cough."

"They are not all like that," Helen said.

Salvatore ignored her. "A bad cough," he repeated. "I almost cried when Piera told me. The poor bastard. One day he'll be late for his own absolution because of a bad cough."

He laughed softly and looked up at the sky. When Helen looked at him, she thought she saw tears in his eyes. She touched his arm. "They're not all like that," she repeated. Salvatore nodded.

"Piera says the same, but I never met the other kind. Did you?"

"I've never been in your position."

"Then you wouldn't know," Salvatore said. "Once you are dependent, then you'll know where you stand with people, the way I do."

He seemed to become aware for the first time that she had her hand on his arm. He felt for it and stroked it, then he drew it under the blanket and pressed it against his body.

For a second she resisted, but then she conceded to herself that her resistance was silly considering all he knew about her and Pietro. She had ignored more significant opportunities to resist; what she was doing now was only a gesture of compassion. Everything she had done until today had really only been done out of self-interest. She had never given in because of a feeling of pity, nor even from calculation or real love. She had given in because she hadn't been strong enough not to give in. That was true with Pietro, and it was true with her husband. She still thought of her marriage with Genno Brazzi as resulting from her incapability of resisting and only afterward had she started to love him. And now that she had the strength to resist—because no strength was needed to resist this half-paralyzed boy—she voluntarily did not resist; for the first time in her life she wasn't thinking of herself. This was her first contact with a man for which she did not have to reproach herself, because she had not done it for herself.

Salvatore didn't move and she stayed patiently beside him until he suddenly ended it. He continued to hold her hand, and when she looked at his face, she saw his eyes sparkle as she had never seen a man's eyes sparkle before.

"Will you like me better now?" he asked seriously.

"If you promise never to do it again," Helen answered.

He nodded. "Pietro would kill me. Don't tell him about it."

"I won't."

"I knew you were not that way," Salvatore said, still holding her hand. "You don't have to be afraid anymore, signora. As long as I can kill a man, nothing will happen to you or me. Can't you stay with us?"

"That wouldn't be a good idea."

"Well," he muttered, "do you want to go back to America?"

"That's where I live."

"I will never get to America. The doctor in Palermo thinks that even after an operation I won't be able to walk."

Helen looked at him. "I thought he never saw you."

"Pietro described where the bullet is and told him that I can't move my legs. The doctor thinks that something has gone wrong with my back and it can't be fixed because too much time has passed. Pietro didn't want to tell me, but I listened secretly once when he described it to Piera. They thought I was asleep."

"That doctor is an idiot," Helen said. "He has no right to make a statement like that. He would have to check carefully and take X-rays."

"That's what Pietro says," Salvatore muttered. He let go of her hand. Then he yawned. "I'll find out soon enough. If it's true I will just put a bullet through my head. I think Piera is coming."

It was another thirty seconds before Piera appeared in the hollow. She was breathless and excited. "Vito has seen a man," she cried.

Salvatore grinned. "On the Monte Soro?"

"Don't make jokes," she said. "He came from the other side of the valley. He ran back the same way a few minutes later.

*234*

"So much the better for him," Salvatore said indifferently. "Was it a carabiniere?"

"He was not wearing a uniform. Vito thinks something in the valley made him return."

"Perhaps he saw you," Salvatore answered. "Did he see him again?"

"No."

"Then we don't have to get excited. Perhaps he was after his sheep. Why would a man run down a mountain and then up?"

"I don't understand either," Piera said. "Vito says that he doesn't like it."

"He's just trying to act important. Since he's in love with you, he sees his own grandmother sneaking around the mountains."

Piera looked at him sharply. "Have you been drinking?"

"Why?"

"I just wondered," Piera answered. Then she asked Helen, "Has he been drinking, signora?"

Helen shook her head. If it weren't so absurd, she would think that Piera had guessed something had happened in her absence. But why absurd, she asked herself. The girl was certainly a sharp observer—or perhaps it was instinct. For women in this part of the world instinct was as important as brains.

While Helen was thinking about it, she saw the three men. They came into the hollow without their shoes on. Antonio was smiling softly, with his pistol in his hand.

# 28

Bentley had gotten away only because he had crossed the road at a point within sight of Vito. Antonio had thought of it just in time and held the other men back. They watched Bentley quickly climbing the wall of the valley until he vanished between the rocks.

"Are you sure he is the American?" Giuseppe asked, hoarse with fear.

Antonio nodded. "I'm sure. As sure as I know that the carabinieri will be here within eight hours."

"We should have bumped him off. Why didn't you let us shoot him?"

"Because then it would have taken only half an hour for the carabinieri to come," Antonio answered. He dropped to the ground and stared at the spot where Bentley had vanished.

"Why are you sitting down?" Giuseppe asked rapidly. "We have to get out of here."

"Where to?" Antonio asked.

Giuseppe stared at him, then he sat down too.

"I can think better when I sit," Antonio said. "He came by chance, or maybe he knows the hiding place."

He couldn't have been so lucky," Lucio muttered.

"Then he knows it's our hiding place," Antonio said. "Let's assume that. What would you have done in his place?"

"Gotten the carabinieri."

"I wonder," Antonio mused, "whether there is any connection between him and the twenty-five carabinieri."

Giuseppe got up again. "I'm beating it," he said. "I can be in Messina tomorrow morning."

"And then what?" Antonio said. He got up slowly. "If I beat it, I have to have my family come after me and start all over again somewhere else. I couldn't do that for less that fifty thousand dollars. We don't need a hundred thousand dollars now; we need too hundred thousand. Come on."

Giuseppe took hold of his arm. "Where are you going?"

"To get the American woman. We'll go to Rocella with her."

"Count me out," Giuseppe said.

Antonio turned to him. "That's your business. The less money you have in your pocket, the sooner you will hang. What do you want to do in Messina, polish shoes? You can't even do that. Your name will be on every wall."

He turned around and started off toward the side valley. When he reached the slope leading down to the dry river bed, the two men came after him.

"You'll never make it," Giuseppe said, panting. "Salvatore won't let us take her."

"We don't need his permission," Antonio said.

"When Pietro comes back . . ." Giuseppe began.

Antonio stood still. "I've heard enough from you," he said softly. "Either shut up or beat it."

"Let's go, Giuseppe," Lucio said softly.

Antonio blinked. "He should have calmed down in the bank. It's too late now. How do you think I feel?"

He walked away from them again.

"He's gone crazy," Lucio said to Giuseppe. "Believe me, it's madness to take the American woman to Rocella now. You have to prepare a thing like that thoroughly."

"We don't have time for that."

"Do you want to . . ."

Giuseppe interrupted him. "I don't want to listen to your nonsense anymore. You hear me?"

"Yes, Giuseppe," Lucio said.

"I'm sick of it," Giuseppe continued. "Antonio knows what he wants. He is ten times smarter than Pietro."

Lucio didn't answer. Descending the road with his brother, he felt deadly afraid.

Antonio was waiting for them at the foot of the slope. "Take off your shoes," he whispered. "Salvatore has ears like a rabbit."

"How do you want to go up?" Giuseppe said. "On the right hand side?"

Antonio looked up the slope. The eastern part of it was in the shadow of the mountains. He nodded. "Piera may be watching. We'll leave our shoes here."

"Can't we think about it for five minutes?" Lucio asked.

"Why not," Giuseppe said. He let himself fall to the ground with a sigh of relief. "How are you planning it, Antonio?"

"It depends on Salvatore. When we tell him that we want the American girl . . ." Antonio fell silent for a moment. "Vito must have seen Bentley. Maybe they know already."

"Then they'll really be on the alert," Giuseppe said. "We shouldn't have gotten into this."

Antonio sat down too. "If you want to look at it that way, we shouldn't have gotten into it in Palmigano."

"In Palmigano there was no woman involved," Giuseppe said. "Women always make trouble."

"Wounded people too," Antonio said. He took a little bottle out of his pocket, opened it, and took a long drink; then he gave it to Giuseppe and Giuseppe gave it to Lucio. When they all had drunk Antonio put the bottle back.

"I wasn't told that we couldn't kill wounded American soldiers. Why did they give us guns, I'd like to know. I don't really know what the Americans think war is all about."

Antonio grinned. "There is some kind of law there."

"A law?" Giuseppe asked.

"It's too complicated for you," Antonio said. "Do you still have the watches?"

"They are buried."

"You should have buried your tractor too," Antonio said. "You may not need it. I've always wondered how it feels."

"How what feels?"

"To be hanged."

"Oh stop it!" Giuseppe said.

"I've never had a wristwatch," Lucio muttered, getting up.

"Where are you going?" Antonio asked.

"I want to get it over with," Lucio said determinedly. "It's all the same to me now."

"Did you ever feel that way before?" Antonio asked, surprised.

"You're afraid," Lucio said and he started climbing the slope in his socks. Giuseppe stared after him.

"He's really gone mad."

"He's a good man after all," Antonio said. They followed Lucio at a short distance, moving stealthily. Near the top they found Lucio waiting for them. At the same moment they caught sight of Piera. She was running from the western ridge down across the moonlit part of the slope. They watched her until she had disappeared into the hollow.

"She must have been with Vito," Giuseppe muttered. "Do you think she saw us?"

Antonio wiped the sweat off his forehead. "She hasn't seen us. Come on."

When they had gone twenty feet farther, they heard voices. They walked more carefully. In a few seconds they were close enough to hear the words. They crawled the last few yards. Finally Lucio climbed into the hollow, Giuseppe and Antonio right behind him.

Salvatore saw them a second after Helen had given a little cry, because Piera was standing between him and the men. He reached under his blanket, but when he saw Antonio's pistol pointed at his stomach, he kept his hand where it was.

"I hope we are not interrupting," Antonio said with a little laugh. "Isn't Pietro here?"

"He's sleeping," Salvatore said.

Antonio didn't stop laughing. He stepped around behind Salvatore and held the pistol against his neck. "Have a look what he's got under his blanket," he said to Giuseppe. And to Helen: "You are up late, signora."

Helen didn't answer. Dizzy with fear, she watched Giuseppe go over to Salvatore and pull at the blanket. "If you do that, you'll be dead," Salvatore said in a level tone of voice. "I have a hand grenade."

Giuseppe dropped the blanket. "He has a hand grenade," he said to Antonio.

"I heard him." Antonio frowned. "It's possible. Let Piera do it. The signora can help her. Come here." His last words were directed to Helen.

When she didn't move, Lucio gave her a push, which made her stumble forward.

"You too," Antonio said to Piera.

The girl obeyed. Now they were all standing around Salvatore's deck chair, Piera on one side and Helen on the other side, with Giuseppe and Lucio behind him.

"Take the blanket away," Antonio said to Piera.

Salvatore let Piera remove the blanket. "You will die for that," he said without looking at Antonio.

"We all have to die one day," Antonio said. He looked at the two hand grenades and the pistol resting between Salvatore's legs.

"Take that stuff away," he said to Giuseppe. "Next time we come here I will bring you some lead soldiers to play with."

"He's got something in his hand," Lucio said dubiously.

Antonio smiled. "Is he not wearing pants because of you, signora?"

Helen didn't answer him.

"I know I'm not your type," Antonio said suddenly, "but you'll have to get used to me." Then he told Piera, "Take that thing out of his hand."

"Pietro will kill you," Piera said.

"Why don't you wake him up," Antonio replied.

"You pig," Piera said. She bent over Salvatore. "It's no use. Give it here."

She took the hand grenade from him and handed it to Giuseppe, who put it on the ground with the other grenades and the pistol.

"Now we can talk in peace," Antonio said. "But first . . ." He went over to Piera and hit her several times quickly with the back of his hand. She didn't make a sound. When he stopped, she took out her handkerchief and pressed it against her mouth.

"That's for calling me a pig," Antonio said softly. "Nobody's going to call me names anymore." He turned to Lucio. "Take her into the cave and watch her."

"Fine," Lucio said. Now that everything was going so smoothly, he was very pleased. He pushed Piera ahead of him into the cave.

"What about the American?" Giuseppe asked.

"You can go ahead down the slope with her," Antonio answered. "One more moment."

He sat down next to Salvatore in the other deck chair and looked at him. "We are taking her with us," he said quietly. "Where is Pietro?"

Salvatore didn't answer.

"We saw him and Carmelo leave," Antonio continued, "and we've seen the American. He tried to get into the valley; when he saw us, he ran away. You may have the carabinieri here tomorrow. When is Pietro coming back?"

"You won't get away from him," Salvatore answered, pulling the blanket back up over his legs.

Antonio nodded. "We don't want to get away from him. On the contrary, we will wait in Rocella. Tell him to ask for us there. Tell him to go to Signor Gaja. Where is he?"

"He will tell you himself," Salvatore said.

"Perhaps Piera will tell me," Antonio said and stood up.

He looked at Helen, who was standing motionless, pressing her pocketbook against her breasts.

He found Piera sitting at the table.

"Watch her," he said to Giuseppe and went into the cave.

He found Piera sitting at the table.

"She tried to open a crate," Lucio said, pointing a pistol at her.

"Which one?" Antonio asked.

Lucio showed him the crate.

"That's the one with the rifles," Antonio said. He looked in it and went back to Piera. "Where is Pietro?"

She turned her face away silently.

"Stand up," Antonio said.

Piera obeyed. "Giuseppe has always liked you," Antonio said. "Shall I send him in?"

"I don't know where Pietro is," she muttered.

He stared at her with a frown and then he went out again.

"Piera tried to get a rifle," he said to Giuseppe. "Tie her up somewhere. Maybe to the bed."

Giuseppe grinned broadly. "What else?"

"That's up to you," Antonio said shortly. "Hurry up."

"I'll kill you if you do anything to her," Salvatore said. "I swear I'll kill you."

Giuseppe grinned again and disappeared into the cave. A moment later they heard Piera scream. The sound came from far away. Salvatore groaned and struggled to climb out of his deck chair. When he didn't succeed, he fell back with tears in his eyes.

"As God is my witness, I didn't want that," Antonio said. "Where is Pietro?"

He looked again at Helen who was standing still, her face gray. "Do you know, signora?"

She shook her head.

"We'll find out," Antonio said. "Come with me." He dragged her by the arm into the cave. Piera had stopped crying. Giuseppe appeared from the inner caves. He was pressing a handkerchief against his chin and swearing. "She's worse than two dozen mules," he said. "If you want to tie her up, you'll have to knock her out first."

"Where is she?" Antonio asked.

"In the last cave. It's pitch-black. She threw something at me."

Antonio nodded. "Yes, I guess she would. And Lucio?"

"He's making sure that she doesn't get out and get a rifle."

"I'll take care of her," Antonio said. "Take the lady down and wait for me where our shoes are. I'll send Lucio after you."

He let Helen's arm go and went into the inner cave. A moment later Lucio came out. "Go ahead down," he said, throwing an anxious look at Salvatore, who was lying motionless in his deck chair. "Is your chin bad?"

"It's bleeding," Giuseppe said. "That girl has the devil in her."

"I don't even want her for free," Lucio muttered. He turned to Helen. "Go ahead. If you play tricks, you'll be sorry."

He pushed her to the edge of the hollow, and then he suddenly stumbled back. Salvatore had picked up a heavy stone, thrown it, and hit him in the small of his back. Helen turned in time to see Giuseppe hit Salvatore in his face with both fists. Lucio was standing still, pressing his hand against his back, where the stone had hit him. There were tears of pain in his eyes. Helen started to run.

She had covered a short distance before Lucio started after her, but because he was running in his socks on the sharp stones, he could not move fast enough to catch her. She ran toward the western wall of the valley. Giuseppe, realizing where she was heading, tried to cut her off, but without shoes he couldn't run much faster than Lucio. Still, Helen knew that she had no real chance. She had no plan; she had just run away, heedless and without calculation. She could feel her legs giving out. She was out of breath.

She managed to reach the ridge. There she stumbled and dropped her pocketbook. She stopped, picked it up, and turned around. In the bright moonlight she made out the figure of a man approaching her. When he saw her, he slowed his pace and approached her cautiously. She hoped that it would be Antonio or Lucio, but it was Giuseppe. As she watched him coming closer, she felt a wave of nausea. She stood motionless, unable to move a finger; now she could already see the grin on his face. The sight of his half-closed eyes and the yellow skin over his cheekbones made her want to run, but her feet would not obey. She wanted to scream but she had no voice.

When he was ten feet away from her, she thought of her pistol. She took it out of her pocketbook and let her pocketbook drop to the ground. Without realizing what she was doing she undid the safety catch. Perhaps she would not have fired if he had given her time to think, but she did not even have time to think about her hatred, which had swelled in her over the past twenty-four hours. She felt herself reacting mechanically. She took her finger off the trigger when the magazine was empty. She had fired eight shots; two had missed but she didn't know it. All she knew was that Giuseppe's form was pitching forward, and Lucio was behind him in the distance, stepping slowly back in fear. She turned around again and ran, along the ridge half crazy with fear. She couldn't see Lucio, but she heard him scream, and she had never heard a human voice sound like that. It sounded like a dozen people screaming.

She did not realize that it was the echoes in the mountains which made his voice reverberate, nor did she understand for a moment that she had reached a part of the ridge that was too narrow to be crossed. She stopped and suddenly realized where she was. She felt like a tightrope walker. Her stomach turned and she heard Lucio's screams coming closer behind her. After another sixty feet, she felt too dizzy to go on.

For the next ten seconds she felt more fear than she had ever felt before. Then two shots rang out. She thought that Lucio had fired the shots and she anticipated the impact. Suddenly it became quiet around her. Then she heard steps. She opened her eyes, turned around, and saw Vito running toward her.

She stared at him in utter bewilderment until she realized that he was carrying a rifle and that he had fired the shots. In the distance she saw Lucio running away. She looked back at Vito, who said something to her in his incomprehensible language, and he pointed back with the barrel of his rifle. She understood that he wanted to take her back to the cave, but now that she was no longer running for her life, she found herself unable to take another step on the narrow ridge. She shook her head. He said something again, this time impatiently, and when she didn't react, he stepped closer and picked her up like a child. It did not occur to her to resist. He was walking effortlessly along the narrow rock while Helen clung to his neck. She could hear him muttering his strange language, but she was no longer afraid of him. When they came to where the rock widened, he carefully put her down. Then he saw Giuseppe lying on the ground. He walked quickly over to him and looked at him.

Helen had forgotten all about Giuseppe. She remained motionless and watched Vito turn him on his back and feel his pulse. Then for a seemingly endless time he stared at her. Finally he walked toward her, bent down, and picked up her pocketbook. A few yards farther he bent again and she saw that it was her pistol he had picked up. He held it out for her. She must have dropped it after firing the shots; she couldn't remember. He pointed at the pistol and then at her, and Helen nodded mechanically. Then he pointed at the pistol and at Giuseppe and Helen nodded again. His mouth opened in surprise, and she wished she could explain to him why she had killed Giuseppe, but she couldn't find the words. Now that she could think clearly again, she felt strangely isolated from everything that had happened in the past half hour—as if it had been only a nightmare—and not even the corpse could move her beyond tired indifference. She felt neither satisfaction nor horror. Fifteen minutes earlier she would have been unable to look at a dead man, but she had felt such deadly fear that now she could feel nothing. She did not even feel that she was really alive. Then she heard a sound like the hoofs of many horses, growing louder until it sounded like thunder, then fading to the whisper of distant surf. Next to her, Vito said in a completely clear voice, "Holy Madonna, you have started an avalanche."

# 29

After Lucio had left the cave, Antonio took the lamp and went after Piera. On the way to the innermost cave he found her dress in shreds. He picked it up and went on. Inside he found her sitting on Helen's bed. She had put a blanket around her.

"Who took your dress off," Antonio asked. "Giuseppe or Lucio?"

She gave him a contemptuous look. "Nobody took my dress off. They tried to hold me. What do you want?"

"A little chat," Antonio said. He put the lamp down, took a chair, and sat down so close to Piera that his knees touched hers. "You could have saved yourself all that trouble," he said. "I don't like to be lied to. Where is Pietro?"

She didn't answer.

"I don't have much time," Antonio said softly, "but I don't want to run any risks. It's my own head that's at stake. What do you think is more precious to me, my own head or yours?"

"You won't do anything to me."

"Why not?"

"Pietro . . ."

"Pietro is sick of you, if you haven't noticed. He has something better. And she's still new to him. You don't have anything new to offer, do you?"

He watched her face change. "I always thought you were an intelligent girl, but you haven't a chance against the signora. Where is Pietro?"

He waited a moment, then he hit her on the mouth. He stood up, pulled the blanket away, and bent over her. He stared at her and sweat broke out on his forehead.

"You wouldn't dare," she said.

Antonio smiled, took her by her shoulders, and pushed her onto her back. He sat down beside her. "You are beautiful," he said. "Black and hot like espresso. Pietro is stupid."

"He'll kill you," Piera said.

"When I take the signora with me," Antonio said, "I will give him a thousand reasons to kill me. Why don't you cry?"

"You won't do anything to me," she said again.

"Well," Antonio said, "maybe I'm not in the habit. It's a mortal sin, after all."

She didn't answer.

"I was just reminded of something," he said, looking at his hands.

There was a silence.

"So you won't tell me where he is?"

"In Caronia," Piera said.

He stared at her with surprise. "What's he doing there?"

"He wants to rent a boat."

"A boat?"

Piera nodded. "He wants to leave tomorrow evening."

"Where to?"

"He never told us."

"He wouldn't have told you tomorrow evening either," Antonio said. "He would have vanished with the American woman and let you rot somewhere."

"That's why I'm telling you," Piera said. "I heard the way he talked with her tonight."

"About what?"

"Just in general," Piera said.

Antonio smiled. "If she's that sharp, she won't mind us taking her to Rocella. Giuseppe and Lucio aren't married yet. You don't mind, do you?"

Piera suddenly had so much hatred in her face that she was hardly recognizable. "I will burn a candle for each time they take her," she said. Then her face softened again. "What did I remind you of?"

"That I have a wife, but not much fun," Antonio said. "The doctor says that she is anemic. That I have four children, a house, nine acres, fifteen goats, and myself. As soon as she goes to bed, she falls asleep."

"Is that why you lost the habit?"

"No," Antonio said. "I guess I just want to be able to look the children in the eyes."

"You're lucky," Piera said. "I wouldn't have cared."

"I saw that."

"Really?" She stared at him. "I don't care about anything. Maybe someday I will shoot him."

"He is no man for you," Antonio said. "You either get used to this life or kill yourself. Pietro is the kind of man who won't get used to it. Was he your first?"

"Yes."

"And the American?"

She didn't answer.

"He was a nice guy," Antonio said thoughtfully. "It's really strange."

She looked at him.

"His wife is now doing to you what you did to her," Antonio said. "Does she know about it?"

"No."

"Still it's strange. Would you have married him?"

"Maybe."

"Then you'd better be glad that he tried to run away from you first," Antonio said. "Imagine if he'd still been here when she showed up. He would surely . . ." Antonio suddenly stopped.

"What is it?" Piera asked.

He didn't answer, but when she looked at his face she was startled.

"Wait for me," he said and ran out.

In the hollow Salvatore was sitting upright in his chair. "Where is Piera?" he asked.

Antonio stood still and looked at Salvatore's bloody face. "What's happened here?"

"I asked you where Piera is," Salvatore repeated.

"Who was firing shots?" Antonio asked.

Salvatore grinned with his swollen face. "Did anyone fire shots?"

"Two rifle shots," Antonio said. "Was it Vito?"

"Why don't you ask Lucio?" Salvatore said. "I heard him screaming like he had a knife in his belly."

Antonio stared at him for an instant, turned around, and quickly climbed out of the hollow. Immediately he saw Lucio coming down from the ridge, running along the slope. He didn't stop when Antonio called his name. He looked as if he had lost his head. Antonio stared after him, and he felt his knees tremble. Without turning around, he ran after him. In the hollow, Salvatore rolled himself out of his deck chair, choked back a cry of pain, lay still a moment, and then, dragging his naked legs lifelessly behind him, pulled himself on his elbows across the hollow.

It took him a full minute to cover the fifteen feet to the edge, driven only by the strength of his fury. When Piera emerged from the cave, he had already rolled two large rocks over the edge of the hollow down the slope, and was heaving at a third. The sight of his half-naked body struggling with the stone startled her, and she screamed and ran to him. She stared past him down the slope, and she saw the two men clambering frantically down, Antonio near the bottom, and Lucio almost at the edge. Then she heard the sound of the quickly growing avalanche. She saw Antonio stop and look back, and she saw Lucio racing into the valley. Then she could not see anything anymore, but she continued to stare at a gathering cloud of white dust. Finally she turned to Salvatore. He was lying on his belly, pressing his face against the ground and his hands against his back.

She kneeled beside him and tried to move him, but she lacked the strength. While she was still trying, Vito climbed quickly into the hollow. He dropped his rifle and bent over Salvatore. A moment later Piera saw Helen at the edge of the hollow. She stared with a mixture of hatred and surprise at Helen's pale face.

Helen did not notice. She watched Vito turn Salvatore on his back, and she recalled how he had turned Giuseppe over the same way. When she saw the blood on Salvatore's face, she felt sick. She watched Vito pick him up and carry him into the cave, followed by Piera; then she became so dizzy that she had to sit on the ground. She tried to cry but her eyes remained dry. She was still sitting when Piera came back. She heard her steps and lifted her head. The moonlight had faded somewhat, but it was still light enough to see the face of the girl. It was without expression. "He only fainted," she said to Helen and sat down beside her on the ground.

For the first time since she had fired the shots at Giuseppe, Helen felt something like relief. "He looked terrible," she murmured.

Piera nodded. "Giuseppe did that. Why didn't you run away?"

"When?"

"You were alone for fifteen minutes," Piera said. "You could have reached the road in twenty minutes. You might have found your friend there."

Helen looked up at her. "Is he here?"

"Antonio, Giuseppe, and Lucio saw him when they were in the valley. He got away. Why didn't you run away?"

Helen could not answer, but she knew why she hadn't. She was surprised that the thought had never even entered her mind. Piera did not seem to expect an answer, and went on. "You couldn't have been afraid to run away. You weren't afraid to kill Giuseppe. Where did you get the pistol from? Did your friend send you the pistol in your suitcase?"

Helen remained silent.

"I know where you got the pistol from," Piera said. "And I also know why you didn't run away. You lied to me, signora."

At any other time Helen would have lost her patience, but now the girl's words didn't even annoy her. "Then why are you asking me?" she said indifferently.

"Do you mind?"

"I would only mind asking Pietro why you wanted me to escape."

The girl colored. "I didn't say that."

"It was clear enough," Helen answered. "I felt ill. Perhaps that's the reason I didn't run away."

"Do you still feel ill?"

Helen hesitated. She could understand that Piera did not believe her, but she felt she must not let herself be pushed to rash action by a twenty-year-old girl. It would bother her for the rest of her life if she failed to understand what attracted her to Pietro. No other man had had her so easily. To no other man had she ever delivered herself without strings attached. She did not feel ready to think clearly yet, but she had an instinctive feeling that more was at stake for her than getting to Chiesa a few days earlier. It was not so much a matter of her relationship with Pietro; it was for herself alone. She was determined for once in her life to gain a clear insight into herself.

She answered Piera in an indifferent voice. "Your brother didn't know I had a pistol. I could have left an hour earlier."

"I thought so," Piera said. "Are you in love with Pietro?"

Helen was thrown by the directness of the question. "Perhaps."

"You don't know for sure."

"No."

"If you didn't know for sure," Piera answered, "you wouldn't be here."

"You can put that differently. If I did know for sure, I wouldn't have to be here anymore."

Piera stared at the ground and finally said, "Only an hour ago you told me you would rather have stayed in Chiesa."

"True."

"And yet you didn't run away?"

"True," Helen said again.

"So," the girl said, "why don't you admit that you like it."

"Like what?"

"When he undresses you."

Helen opened her pocketbook and realizing that there were no cigarettes in it, closed it again.

"I watched you this evening," Piera said. "I am not as stupid as you think."

"It doesn't take much brains to snoop," Helen said. "If you were really clever, you wouldn't have told me."

"Why?"

"You figure that out for yourself."

"I am not as clever as you are, signora," the girl said. "I say what I think."

"Yes, I see that," Helen said. She wondered why she did not simply walk off.

"Before you came here," Piera continued, "there was no fighting. It all started with you."

"I'm not here voluntarily."

"You wanted to talk to Salvatore. Why did you come to Chiesa? You must have known that your husband wasn't alive."

"I didn't know."

"You should have known," Piera said. "You haven't heard from him in two years. I'm not saying this because of Pietro; I know him better than you. We know that many American women come here for what you really did. Why would you have married a Sicilian otherwise!"

This time Helen did get up. She felt a desperate craving for a cigarette.

In the last cave a lamp was burning. Helen opened her suitcase, took out a pack of cigarettes, and sat down.

She felt appalled at how simple it could be to kill a human being. She hadn't fainted and she hadn't cried. She had cried when Bentley had tried to take her, but when Giuseppe had fallen down she had not uttered a sound. She had thrown up ten minutes earlier, but that was because she couldn't stand the sight of blood. She could shoot a man, but she couldn't stand blood. She wondered what kind of person she really was. She hadn't cried either when she had gotten word that her husband was missing, and since that moment she had become hardened to the misfortunes of other people. She had only been occupied with her own hatred and her own loneliness.

The thought that she had behaved so callously now seemed as incomprehensible as the thought that she had killed a man. In both cases a part of her seemed to have stepped aside to watch the rest of her. But if she was neither the woman who had only focused on her own feelings in Toledo, nor the woman who had killed Giuseppe, the question remained who she was in reality.

And then there was still the nagging question of Pietro. Being with him presented no problems: the person who was with him seemed to be entirely herself. She had often felt the same in the past—with the governess's friend and with Genno. Only Bentley did not fit into any pattern.

Her thoughts were leading her nowhere. She decided that she had more important problems to attend to. She still didn't know what had happened in her absence, and she was worried that she hadn't heard anything about Lucio and Antonio. The thought of Lucio screaming at the sight of his dead brother and the possibility that he might walk into the cave made her jump up. In the hollow she could at least run away as she had done earlier. In the cave she was in a trap.

Standing up, she noticed a piece of material on the floor and she recognized it as part of Piera's dress. It was the dress she had worn before the three men had come to the hollow. The sight of it increased her nervousness. She picked up the scrap of material, put it on the table, and went to the adjoining cave. Salvatore was alone, lying on his stomach, his face on his arms. A blanket covered him to his shoulders. He did not move. She stood for a while undecidedly. She could hear no sound anywhere. She went out into the hollow. Piera had vanished and Helen's nervousness turned to fear. She climbed quickly up on the rim of the hollow and looked down into the valley. The avalanche had hardly left a trace; only a little of the slope was more even than before. At the bottom Helen caught sight of Vito and Piera. They looked as if they were searching among the stones. She sat down on the edge of the hollow. If her guess was right, there was nothing further to fear.

A short time later Vito and Piera appeared at the edge of the hollow. Piera walked past her without a word, but Vito sat down beside her, propped his rifle between his legs, and pulled out a tobacco pouch.

He was still wearing the same dirty cap and hunter's jacket as when she had first met him. As he rolled himself a cigarette she remembered that it was because of her that he could not return to Chiesa—and he had saved her life. She was sorry now that she had felt the need to talk about him to the carabinieri. "Where is Lucio?" she asked him.

He shrugged with a grin and pointed down the slope.

"Is he dead?" Helen asked.

He shook his head, and she was almost relieved although she didn't know why. She looked toward the western wall of the valley where somewhere in the dark Giuseppe was lying. For the first time the memory of what had happened made her shiver.

"I haven't thanked you," she said. "I don't know what would have happened without you. Did you fire at Lucio?"

Vito shook his head again. He took up his rifle, pointed it toward the sky, and grinned. She understood that he had shot in the air.

She looked at her watch. It was almost midnight. The moon was setting behind the mountains and it was rapidly getting darker. The temperature had dropped sharply and she felt frozen. Vito seemed to notice and pointed with his thumb toward the cave. She shook her head, but he got up, went into the cave, and came back with a blanket. He put it over her legs and sat down again beside her. In the dark his face seemed much less repulsive. Suddenly she found herself looking at him as good. With his black beard he reminded her of an apostle. She could not remember which one.

She noticed that he had finished his cigarette and she offered him one of her own. He lit it, but after one puff he threw it away. He pulled her pistol out of his pocket. She recognized it in spite of the darkness. He took out the magazine and removed the safety catch. He looked impressed. When he offered it to her, she waved it away. "You can keep it," she said. "I give it to you."

He looked surprised. He pointed at the pistol and then to himself. Helen nodded. Nothing in the world would make her touch it again. "Take it," she repeated, "it's yours."

He grinned and put it in his pocket.

"I didn't want to kill him," Helen said. "He came after me, and . . . I don't remember what happened." She felt a great need to talk about it with somebody, and although she wasn't sure that Vito understood, she was glad that he was sitting there listening. It would be terrible to be alone now.

"I wanted to get away," she continued, "and then as I saw . . ." She fell silent. It was ridiculous. Why was she trying to justify herself? She knew what she could have expected from Giuseppe. Pietro had made it clear enough. Neither Antonio nor Lucio nor Giuseppe had any reason to let her go back to Chiesa alive. They would have silenced her the way they had silenced her husband. Her feeling of guilt could not be connected with Giuseppe's death. Perhaps she should not have provoked this encounter after all. Perhaps she should have listened to Bentley and gone back to Naples. Everything she had done had been wrong, and now there was Pietro. With Giuseppe dead there was nothing to divert her thoughts from him. No hatred. No more alibis.

She stared at Vito, who continued to sit silently and motionlessly. He was the only man alive who had ever done something for her without asking for something in return—the only person who would never ask any foolish questions or gossip. She asked him if he had known her husband and he laughed—it was the first time she had ever seen him laugh—but he did not answer her.

"We were married for three years," she told him. "I don't remember ever fighting."

He was probably the first man to whom she could talk un-self-consciously, because she felt sure that he hadn't heard the story of the governess. With almost everyone else she had the feeling that this incident in her past made her attractive.

"We wanted to have our honeymoon in his country," she said, "but then the war came and we had to postpone it."

She paused and continued the counterpoint of her thoughts. In most cases she had known exactly why men were drawn to her. They had heard that she could resist no one. She had heard it long enough and often enough to believe it herself.

"Perhaps it took too long for him," she went on in her one-sided conversation with Vito. "One day he told me that he wanted to be there when our soldiers landed in Italy. I guess I'm the only woman who didn't try to stop her husband from going."

She had started to fear men. Finally it had become an almost irresistible urge to run away as soon as she was alone with a man. It had only changed with Genno Brazzi.

"When I heard that he was missing," she said, "I felt that the ground had been pulled out from under my feet. Do you understand?"

She looked at Vito once more and saw that he was nodding. Then she realized that she had been speaking English to him the whole time.

# 30

Once Bentley reached the Fiat, it took him less than ten minutes to reach the main road. He had decided not to look for the hiding place any longer, and to get to Lieutenant Gastone as quickly as possible. Nevertheless he now drove north. When he had heard the shots, his only thought had been to end his doubts. He now feared the worst for Helen, and no other consideration entered his mind.

It did not come as too great a surprise to Bentley when he came upon Lieutenant Gastone about a half a mile from the place where he had left the three men. In fact, for the first time seeing the lieutenant gave him an unalloyed feeling of relief. Clearly recognizable in the headlights of the car, he was standing in the road with three carabinieri. Even before Bentley had stopped, he was at the side of the car, saying with unusual sharpness, "Turn off your lights!"

Surprised, Bentley obeyed and said with annoyance, "Would you mind telling me . . ."

"Certainly." Lieutenant Gastone had regained his usual polite little laugh. He opened the door for Bentley. "We are waiting for visitors and your lights could scare them off. Did you have a pleasant day, Mr. Bentley?"

"Did you hear the shots?" Bentley snapped in reply.

"I think they could be heard all the way to Fratello," Gastone answered. He made a signal to the three carabinieri and they vanished into the dark.

"Are your people doing the shooting?" Bentley asked impatiently.

"No."

"Then I don't understand why you don't do anything. We have to look for Mrs. Brazzi."

"That's all I've been doing for forty-eight hours," the lieutenant said. "Follow me, Mr. Bentley."

"Where to?"

"To my headquarters. They're right near here."

He led Bentley off the road through the dark to the bottom of the valley and from there through a gap in a cluster of rocks. After a few steps the gap widened into a space. In the middle, around a big fire, half a dozen carabinieri wrapped in blankets were lying on the ground and sleeping. Their horses were standing in the background shadows next to a windowless wooden hut.

"Headquarters?" Bentley asked.

Lieutenant Gastone laughed. "Yes," he said. "I've lived in worse places, but I'd prefer something better."

"I see," Bentley said. "You're afraid that your complexion will suffer from the sun."

"You sound rather irritated," the lieutenant said.

The inside of the hut was surprisingly large and clean. There was a makeshift table with an acetylene lamp. Straw was scattered on the floor.

"We brought the straw and the lamp ourselves," Gastone said. "But when the weather is dry, my men prefer to sleep outside. So do I. Do you want a drink, Mr. Bentley?"

"No."

Bentley sat down on a bench and looked at the lieutenant. "I'd like to know what you're going to do to help Mrs. Brazzi."

"Last evening you insisted that I don't do anything," the lieutenant answered and sat down too. "Are you worried about the shots?"

"Aren't you?"

The lieutenant hesitated. "Let's say that I know what happened," he said. "My men more or less observed everything and what they didn't I can figure out for myself. It's quite possible that you saw some of my men."

"And what were you after?" Bentley asked.

"What do you mean?"

"By sending me up Monte Ambola. Surely there was something behind that."

"I'm not sure exactly where the gang is hidden. All I've wanted to do for the past two days is make them uncertain."

"Did you succeed in that?"

"I think I did," the lieutenant said. "I figured that they would leave their hide-out as soon . . ."

"I see," Bentley answered. "And you're waiting for that?"

"Yes. And we will catch them when they do."

"And the shots?"

"As far as I can figure it out there was some kind of internal conflict. There were three men. They tried to get back to their hide-out half an hour after they had left it. I think we'll know more in an hour."

"Do you want to . . ."

"I could have made my move last night," Gastone said. "The problem is to find the right moment. When I commit myself I may create great danger. I told you I don't know exactly where they are hidden. This is not negligence, Mr. Bentley. As it stands right now it wouldn't take more than ten minutes to find them."

Bentley was silent. He was impressed by the lieutenant's manner. Finally he asked, "What part did you think I would play?"

"Your own. Since you wanted to look around, I thought I should at least put you on the trail. I think you have done the signora a great favor."

Bentley looked suspiciously at him.

"I'm quite serious," Lieutenant Gastone said. "To see you here must have upset the gang more than seeing the entire company of carabinieri. I don't think it's a coincidence that those shots were heard after they had seen you."

"Did you know that those three would show up tonight?" Bentley asked.

"Yesterday there were five of them," Gastone said. "Coming from different directions. It was just an experiment, that's all. We've been lucky."

If the lieutenant had observed the three men, Bentley thought, he must have also watched his hasty flight. "I hope you're not wrong," he said. "I mean about the shots."

"Did you hear the avalanche?" the lieutenant asked.

Bentley frowned.

"There was an avalanche of stones. It happened while you were moving along the road. Something went wrong among those men. How many shots would it take to kill a woman?"

"Stop it!" Bentley said.

"I meant to reassure you, not scare you," the lieutenant said. "Of course there is risk. It wasn't absolutely safe to send you to Monte Ambola. I hoped that you would be seen by the gang but I didn't want you all to meet. Otherwise I wouldn't have gambled. You were a bit reckless, you know."

"Yes, I know now," Bentley said. "They showed up suddenly behind my back."

"Yes, that's what I figured. My men couldn't see exactly, it was too dark at that spot. They only spotted you again when you had crossed the road and started coming back up the mountain."

"I wondered why they didn't shoot at me."

"Perhaps it was too risky. They knew we were near. If you had stood still . . ."

The lieutenant stopped speaking and listened to a sound outside the hut. "That's for me," he said hastily. "Please wait a second."

He vanished. Bentley was tempted to go after him but decided against it. He was too tired to get up again. It had been twelve months since he had had so much exercise. He felt an irresistible urge to lie down for a moment. He went over to the straw. Although he had meant to stay awake, he fell asleep immediately.

When he woke up again, it was clear daylight outside. The lamp on the table was still burning. As he looked around, everything came back to him. He heard a strange noise. It sounded like the women of

Capua when they kneel at the shore of the river and beat their laundry on the stones. Wondering what it was, he got up.

The ache in his muscles had become worse; he felt as if he had been beaten from head to toe. As he stumbled to the door, the strange sound suddenly stopped, the door opened, and Gastone appeared. He looked as fresh as if he had slept for twelve hours.

"They told me you were awake," Gastone said. "Did you sleep well, Mr. Bentley?"

"Who told you?" Bentley asked.

"One of my men heard you get up."

"What's going on?" Bentley asked. He tried to walk past Gastone, but the lieutenant politely restrained him.

"His name is Lucio Canepa," he said quietly. "My men will send him to Cesaro and check on him. He's a loser—as teachable as a goat. I ordered breakfast for us. Just wait five minutes."

"Do you treat all your prisoners that way?" Bentley asked.

The lieutenant lit a cigarette. "All police have their own methods —the American police too. He's a dirty little criminal who tried to tell me a stupid story. By tonight he will tell me the truth."

Bentley sat down. "What did he tell you?"

"It's not worth talking about. My men saw him leaving the valley during the night. They lost him in the dark; then at dawn we found him hiding behind a rock. He claimed he was going home with his brother. On the way they were attacked by bandits and his brother was shot, but he managed to get away."

"You're right so far," Bentley said. "That's one of the weaker stories I've heard. Where was it supposed to have happened?"

"He can't remember anymore, he says, but he will soon enough. The only thing true about his story is his dead brother."

"You mean . . ."

"Yes," the lieutenant said with a smile. "It happened the way I had guessed. Now, let's have breakfast."

A tall, very young-looking carabiniere came in, put a little basket on the table, and started to unpack it.

"This is Sergeant Tasca," Lieutenant Gastone said. "If you want to be friends with him, just call him Ciro."

"Hello Ciro," Bentley said.

259

The sergeant smiled. "Signore."

"He doesn't say much," Lieutenant Gastone said when the sergeant had gone. "His father was an undertaker. What do you think?"

Bentley looked at the gleaming china, the white bread, the butter, the jam and the prosciutto. "How do you manage it?" he asked.

"You'll have to ask Sergeant Tasca," the lieutenant said, undoing his belt, "He arrived from Fratello a few minutes ago. The china is my own. I like to live the way I am used to. But start, Mr. Bentley, you have earned it."

Bentley hesitated. He looked at his dirty hands, felt his stubby chin, and stared at the pink face of the lieutenant. "How long did you sleep last night?"

"I didn't at all. I got used to doing without sleep for forty-eight hours. I have an uncle in Turin who gets along on four hours a night. You still have straw in your hair, Mr. Bentley."

"I should have washed and shaved," Bentley said. "When I look at you I feel as if I hadn't seen a piece of soap in a month."

The lieutenant smiled. "Don't feel embarrassed because of me. I'm used to things like this."

"Strange that I never liked you," Bentley said. "I used to think that you were absolutely cold."

"That often happens to me. It doesn't bother me. Do you want sugar?"

"Two lumps," Bentley said. "Do you have any brothers or sisters?"

"No. You?"

"No."

"We have something in common," Gastone said. "It's hard to be an only child. I guess you'll be going back soon."

"We're waiting for repatriation in Naples."

"Come back in three years," Gastone said. "You won't recognize it. Come and visit me. I will show you Rome."

Bentley smiled. "I don't think I will be back in Italy so soon."

"Don't you like it?"

"I'm a regular soldier," Bentley said.

"You will be my guest, Mr. Bentley. I still live with my parents. The house is so big there is room for a whole company."

"Are you that rich?" Bentley asked, and then he was sorry he had said it.

The lieutenant answered, "We are not exactly poor. My mother is a shareholder in her brother's factory in Turin. He made a lot of money during the war. If Mussolini . . ."

"Yes," Bentley said, "Why don't you go on?"

"I don't think you'd be interested. You have a different idea about him."

He was interrupted by Sergeant Tasca, who came in to report. They talked so softly that Bentley could not hear them. A look of satisfaction came over the lieutenant's face. "Our friends have come back," he said to Bentley. "Do you remember the two men who were walking toward Cesaro last night?"

"Did you arrest them?"

"No, they would have been missed. I cannot risk that because of the signora."

"Won't they miss Lucio?"

"I don't think so. It's the third man who bothers me. Lucio only talked about his brother. He wouldn't admit that there was a third man."

"What do you plan to do now?" Bentley asked.

"We will close off the valley. When it gets dark, I will pull back my men and see what happens."

"And if nothing happens?"

Lieutenant Gastone stood up. "Then something may happen to-morrow. We have time. Do you have to go back to Chiesa?"

Bentley hesitated. He doubted that after all that had happened the gang would still try to contact him, but he did not want to discount the possibility entirely. And his desire for a bath was greater than his fear that something would happen in his absence.

"Do you expect anymore surprises before tonight?" he asked.

The lieutenant shook his head.

"Then I'll go," Bentley said. "If you don't mind I'll come back late in the afternoon. Will you be here?"

"If I'm not here, you'll find Sergeant Tasca. Come. I'll take you to your car. We pushed it off the road."

The front of the hut was still in shadow. Only the upper part of the

rocks was bathed in the cool light of the morning sun. The carabinieri were nowhere to be seen.

The Fiat was standing in the shadow of the eastern wall of the
valley, partly hidden behind a rock. "Our friends might have become
suspicious if they'd seen your car," Gastone said. He stood and
watched Bentley start the car.

"One thing I don't understand," Bentley said. "What's a man like
you doing in the carabinieri."

The lieutenant smiled. "The only childhood wish my parents never
fulfilled was a good pistol."

"I'm not sure you'll get very old," Bentley said and drove off.

It took him an hour and a half to get to Chiesa. On the way he
did not see a single carabiniere. Stopping his car in front of the inn,
he saw Rigido standing in the doorway. His face looked so relieved
that Bentley was almost touched. He got out and went over to him.

"I want to take a bath," he said. "Have your friends been here
again?"

The innkeeper did not react.

"I guess they haven't," Bentley said. "I brought you back your
eggs and one of the chickens. You can eat it yourself. I'll pay for
it."

He went up to Helen's room, opened the window, lit a cigarette,
and stared at the mountains in the sunlight. Rigido came in with a
small tub.

"How do you want the water? Warm?"

"Hot," Bentley answered. The innkeeper had something on his
mind and Bentley turned to him questioningly.

"It's the two bottles of Marsala," Rigido finally said. "Should
I . . ."

"You can drink them to the health of the signora. But please wait
until I've had my bath and my dinner."

An hour later, sitting and having his dinner, Bentley felt revived.
"Have you ever been on Monte Ambola?" he asked Rigido.

The innkeeper shook his head. "We don't have time for things
like that. Did you have success?"

"Success with what?" Bentley asked.

Rigido left the room.

After his dinner Bentley lay down on the bed and thought. He hadn't achieved anything, yet he was not dissatisfied. He'd been lucky —first to spot the three men, and second to get away from them. He had taken more risks than most men would. Then he realized with mixed feelings that he had felt the same in January 1944, when he came back from a reconnaissance and Captain Green had told him that he had been two miles behind enemy lines without having noticed.

He fell asleep. When he woke up he found Rigido standing by his bed.

"I knocked," the innkeeper said. "You didn't hear."

Bentley looked at his watch. He had slept almost three hours. If he wanted to get back to Gastone before dark, he had better hurry. "What is it?" he asked.

"Somebody wants to talk to you and he says it's urgent."

He thought of Helen's father and quickly got up. "An American?"

Rigido shook his head. "No, a simple man, signore. He has hurt his arm."

"Send him in," Bentley said.

He quickly put on his jacket and sat down. A few seconds later the door opened.

"You . . . How . . . " Bentley almost shouted.

Antonio smiled. "It's my lucky day," he said. He pushed the door shut behind him and looked around.

"We are alone," Bentley said. Although he had only seen Antonio in the dark, he had recognized him immediately.

"You have a good memory," Antonio said. He was barefoot, his jacket was dirty and torn, and he held his right arm pressed against his chest. "May I sit down?"

Bentley pointed at a chair. "Did you have an accident?"

"If you want to call it that." Antonio sat down heavily on the chair and put his arm on the table. "If you could get me a glass of water?"

Bentley got him one. As we watched him drink it he thought of their last meeting at the dark roadside between Sperlinga and Nicosia, and he guessed who the third man had been last night. "Did you come for the money?" he asked.

Antonio nodded. "If you have it here, sir."

Bentley was impressed with his coolness. "Aren't you being a little reckless?"

"I thought about it," Antonio answered. "If you make trouble, you won't be doing the signora any favors. You should be able to figure out what's more important for you."

It could be a bluff, Bentley thought, but there was something about Antonio's manner which made him cautious. "What do you want?" he asked.

"Three thousand dollars and a four-hour head start."

"For what?"

"To get away. If you help me, I'll tell you where you can find the signora tonight."

"We can have your friend tell us," Bentley said. "The carabinieri caught him this morning."

"I know. When they found him, I was a hundred yards away on the ridge."

"Then you also know that we already know where the hide-out is."

"That's why I'm here," Antonio said. "If the carabinieri use force, the signora will be killed. I know an alternative."

"Maybe your friend does too."

"Then you wouldn't be sitting here," Antonio said.

Bentley hesitated. He could risk making a fool of himself by going along, or he could risk criminal negligence by ignoring it. He felt sure now that the gang had no intention of letting Helen go after a week. "How do I know you're telling me the truth?" Bentley asked.

Antonio shrugged, "I have nothing to gain by lying. Once the carabinieri have caught me, it doesn't make any difference to me what happens to the signora."

"They could make you talk."

Antonio smiled. "You haven't much time, signore."

Pursing his lips Bentley got up and walked to the window. The money didn't matter. Helen Brazzi could spare another three thousand dollars. Actually, it was probably a mistake to hesitate.

As he tried to make up his mind, he heard a noise. He glanced out of the window. About thirty feet from the house were three carabinieri standing on a slope. They were armed with automatic rifles and they were staring motionlessly up at him. Bentley suppressed a smile. Gastone certainly didn't take chances.

He turned slowly around, took out his wallet, and removed the money. "Four hours, you say?"

"Yes."

"How will you know that I won't call the carabinieri before then?"

Antonio looked at him. "You are an American officer, signore. If you give me your word, I will take any risk." The look on his face made Bentley feel almost sorry for him.

## 31

She heard him come in, and she knew immediately that it was he. Somehow, something had awakened her and she had been lying in the dark, waiting. She felt him sit down next to her and touch her face, and she asked, "When did you come back?"

"A while ago," Pietro said. "You were sleeping so soundly. I didn't want to wake you. Piera told me that you didn't go to bed until morning. When did you wake up?"

"I don't know." She took his hands from her face and held them. "What time is it?"

"Eleven. Do you want to get up?"

"Yes. Did you succeed?"

"Yes," Pietro said. "We have enough horses and the boat will be ready by tomorrow."

"How is Salvatore?"

"All right. He is as strong as a goat. I knew I could depend on him."

He lay down beside her and put his hand under her head. "Did you sleep in your clothes?"

"Yes."

"Shall I light the lamp?"

She shook her head. Now that he was with her, she could not hold anything against him. Perhaps she had waited too long and felt too much fear; she was no longer the same. She felt that something had changed, more than in the past ten years. At the moment she felt that he was as important to her as anything in the thirty-two years of her life.

"Salvatore told me everything," Pietro said. "Did anything happen with Piera?"

She hesitated. "What makes you think that?"

"She's in a terrible mood. Look, I admit that I had my eye on her once, but there was really nothing between us. That only happened when we came here. Two years are a long time if you have to spend them this way."

"You don't have to explain it to me," Helen said.

"I should have explained yesterday. You make it too easy not to. I never even hinted that I would marry her. Salvatore can be my witness."

"I believe you," Helen muttered. She was really glad that he had said all this. She had been upset by her last conversation with Piera.

"She wasn't always like this," Pietro went on. "During these last two years there were plenty of times when she went her own way and didn't bother about me. Tell me, is it very difficult to learn English?"

Helen laughed. "I don't think so. Do you want to?"

He turned on his side and began to stroke her hair. "I've been thinking about it since last night. Even if you wanted to marry me, you couldn't stand me for long, I don't think."

"Why not?" Helen asked.

"Imagine a civilized woman like you with a man like me. You'd always have to hide me from your family and your friends. But I'd be satisfied just to get to America. I know a few words of English and I'm not really stupid. I'd do anything to get away from here. I would work my hands off."

"Is that all you've decided?"

"That's one side of it. I don't want to talk about the other. Where is the town where you live, north or south?"

"North."

"I will find a job in the south," Pietro said.

"Why?" Helen asked after a pause.

Pietro sat up and lit a cigarette. "I have never been a burden to anybody, not even my parents. I never want to use a person. Is that enough?"

It wasn't. She knew why he had said it but it was superfluous, and he had not answered the most important question. "I'd like to know about the other side of the matter," she said. "The one you don't want to talk about."

"Do you want to hear that I would miss you?" he said.

"Would you?"

"It's the only thing I'm afraid of."

Helen was thinking. As long as she lived in Toledo it was hopeless. She had always wanted to live in California, but she had never made any serious plans to leave Toledo, even though there was nothing to keep her there but her father.

The thought made her feel immensely relieved. It would no longer be necessary to "make a big man" out of Pietro. A son-in-law of McShane would make his way in California well enough. Her father made regular business trips to Los Angeles, so he must have his connections there. She was sure she could manage to defend marriage with Pietro, the way she had managed with her husband; her problem was that she was not quite sure that she wanted to. What made it even more difficut was that her emotions changed every hour, and she had not been at all prepared for this conversation. She thought that they would first talk about what happened last night, and it made her nervous that he was ignoring the subject, although she was a little grateful too. In fact, he was behaving as if it were the most natural thing in the world for a woman to shoot a man.

She looked at him. Every time he drew on his cigarette she could see his face. He was younger than she and at an age when a man starts to think seriously about his future. It would help him to have the right woman.

"Where is Piera?" she suddenly asked.

"Outside."

"Are you sure?"

She saw that the question had startled him. "I just asked because she eavesdropped on us last night," she said. "Did she tell you?"

"I noticed myself," Pietro said. He got up and lit the lamp. "She won't eavesdrop anymore. How did you know, from her?"

"Yes."

"So you did have trouble with her," Pietro said.

Now with the light on, Helen could see that he was tired and dirty. He looked at her. "It's a pity about your dress. Piera can iron it for you."

"I can do that myself. What time are we leaving tonight?"

"As soon as it's dark. That's the best time. Do you want to wash?"

She nodded.

"I'll get you some water," Pietro said and left.

Helen stood up. Her dress was too heavy for the weather anyway, and she decided to put on another one. She waited until Pietro came back with the water.

"It's almost cold," he said. "Piera let the fire go out."

He put the water on the table and went over to her. "I didn't get a chance to shave yet. Do you mind?"

"As long as you don't kiss me," Helen said. But she did not mind when he kissed her. She put her arms around his neck and looked at him. "What did you do with him?"

"With whom?"

"With Giuseppe."

"Vito took care of that," he said. "Don't worry about it. He would have been hanged someday."

"I didn't want to shoot him."

He shrugged. "It's easier than one thinks. When I saw you the first time and when I found the pistol in your pocketbook, I was sure that you would never hesitate to kill a man."

"Then you knew more about me that I did," Helen said. There had been no point in bringing it up.

"I will come back when you have washed," Pietro said.

In the hollow Carmelo was watching the valley, holding an automatic rifle. "Anything happening?" Pietro asked.

Carmelo shook his head.

Pietro stared past him to the right wall of the valley, where he saw Vito on guard.

"If nothing happens in the next hour," Salvatore said, "I'll believe it was all coincidence that the carabinieri were here."

He was lying in his usual place under the awning. Next to him, Piera was sitting, her face pale. Pietro turned toward her. "Fix some breakfast for the signora. She doesn't know anything. I will tell her myself."

The girl stood up and went into the cave without a word.

"Why haven't you told her yet?" Salvatore asked.

Pietro sat down and lit another cigarette. "We'll tell her that we saw the carabinieri for the first time just now."

"Why?"

"It suits me better."

"If it's not a coincidence that they're here, we'll never make it to Caronia tonight," Salvatore said. "Maybe they caught Antonio or Lucio."

"Maybe," Pietro said. He threw his cigarette away and went back into the cave. Piera was standing near the stove. "Did you talk to her?" he asked.

She shook her head.

"If you have anything to say to her in the future," Pietro said, "check with me first. It's not that definite that you'll ever get away from Chiesa."

"It's not that definite for you either," she said.

He grinned. "From Chiesa . . . no doubt about it."

Helen was sitting on her bed completely dressed. "I didn't know if I should come out," she said.

Although she had on more makeup than usual, she still looked very tired. She was wearing the orange dress with the short sleeves and Pietro stared at her for a moment before he sat down. "You can wear what you want," he said. "You'll always look good. How do you do it?"

She smiled. "Just like the women in Chiesa. Have you got problems?"

"Does it show?"

He was one of those men who hid his feelings, but she could sense something from the way he touched her. "It's just a feeling," she answered.

"Well, you can trust your feelings. The carabinieri are back." She paled. "Where?"

"The whole valley is full of them. Vito told us. I'm assuming that they'll move on during the day."

He didn't sound convincing.

"You may be eating breakfast in Chiesa tomorrow," he said.

"I'd planned to eat breakfast on the mainland tomorrow," she replied.

"Me too. Your eating in Chiesa tomorrow morning is just one of two possibilities. We'll know more tonight."

He went out with her to the hollow, where Helen immediately noticed Carmelo with his gun. She was startled.

"We're not going to shoot," Pietro said. "Maybe a few warning shots, so they'll know we're not sleeping. If they wanted to come up, they would already be here."

"Can you see them?"

"No. They're in the lower half of the valley."

"They may come closer," Salvatore said. "Did you sleep well, signora?"

Piera was sitting next to him again and she stared at Helen with hostility. She was smoking; it was the first time Helen had seen her with a cigarette. Helen looked from Piera to Salvatore. His right eye was almost closed by a large swelling. His lips were swollen and covered with scabs. Helen remembered that Giuseppe had done it.

"I know I've looked better," he said happily, "but Giuseppe looks even worse."

"Shut up," Pietro said. He looked quickly at Helen, who sat down, opened her pocketbook, and pulled out a cigarette. She was pale.

"You should drink your coffee," Pietro said. "It will get cold."

"I don't want it."

Pietro sat next to her and filled her cup. "Nobody is worth starving for; not even me," he said. "What do you want on your bread?"

"Just butter," she said.

As he offered her a piece of buttered bread, Piera stood up quickly and went back into the cave.

"She still has things to do," Pietro said. "We want to take some of our things with us tonight. Sugar?"

Helen shook her head.

"There's not much more I can do at the moment," he went on with a smile. "Maybe I'll get some more sleep. I didn't get much last night."

"Can I go to the well later?" Helen asked.

"No. What do you want to . . ."

He fell silent. Then he stood up, went to Carmelo, and talked softly to him. "I'll take you over," he said to Helen, coming back to the table.

"You're crazy!" Salvatore said.

Pietro didn't answer. He waited for Helen to finish her bread.

"Is it dangerous?" Helen asked.

"Not for you," Salvatore said before Pietro could answer.

"Then I'll stay here," Helen said.

Pietro took her arm. "Come!"

"If they see us," Helen said, "they'll know where we're hiding. Isn't there another place?"

"Not for a woman," Pietro answered. He helped her over the edge of the hollow and led her across the sunny slope to the large rocks. He walked close beside her and kept watching the valley. When they had crossed the slope, he wiped the sweat off his face. Vito welcomed them with a broad grin. "He's amazed," Pietro said.

"At what?"

"At me. Please hurry."

Giuseppe was no longer lying there. She noticed as soon as she reached the ridge. When she came back five minutes later, Pietro was standing beside Vito, staring down into the valley.

"We shouldn't have done this," Helen said. The thought that she had exposed him to danger almost made her sick. No other man would have taken such a risk for such an absurd reason. As they walked back she took his hand.

When they had only twenty more yards to go, he said, "We made it. Somebody seems to like us."

When they reached the hollow, Salvatore and Carmelo stared at them.

"Relax," Pietro said. "I'm going to shave."

"For the carabinieri?" Salvatore asked.

Pietro went into the cave.

"He wouldn't have done that for me," Salvatore said. "Why don't you sit beside me, signora."

Helen did. She looked at Carmelo, who had taken up his post again. "Do you think they've seen us?"

"We'll know tonight," Salvatore said. "What do you care."

"If I didn't, I wouldn't be here. Last night your sister and Vito gave me fifteen minutes to get away."

"If I tell that to Pietro," Salvatore answered, "he'll burst into tears." He looked curiously at her. "Did he give you the pistol?"

"I don't want to talk about it any more," Helen said.

"I didn't mean it that way, signora. Quite the contrary. Shall I tell you what I thought when Piera told me the story. I thought what a pity it is that you're not my mother."

The remark surprised her. She felt herself blushing. "I guess that should make me proud," she finally answered.

"No, it shouldn't." Salvatore did not look at her. "I know that you're ten years too young for that, but in ten years you'll look exactly the same as you do now. You can marry Pietro. I'm not against it anymore."

"How do you know I want to?"

"Don't you love him?"

Helen was silent.

"I know it's none of my business," Salvatore said. "I'd just like to know what will happen to him in case . . ."

"In case what?" Helen said quickly.

"Perhaps it's too early for that," he went on. "I'm not worried about Piera. She will find some sucker who will help her and our mother too. It's easy for a girl. All they have to do is look good. I used to think that she and Pietro . . . I mean, it would have been fine with me to have him for a brother-in-law. I would have liked him more than all the others. But I don't think she would have been the right wife for him."

"Why not?"

Salvatore looked up at the awning. "I'm not sure. She doesn't fit with him. To me he always came second to God only. And . . . well, she's just my sister."

Helen didn't answer.

"Maybe I'm crazy," he said, "but if the carabinieri show up again, I won't involve him. I promise you that."

"I don't understand," Helen said.

He grinned. "You're too beautiful to understand."

## 32

It was still daylight when Bentley reached the quarry. He drove the car off the road behind the rock where it had been hidden earlier and went to look for Sergeant Tasca. To his surprise the hollow was empty and the hut, too. He climbed back up to the road. There was no one there either, and he looked around nervously. He had just decided to go back to the car, when he caught sight of Sergeant Tasca appearing around a corner. When he saw Bentley, he stopped for a moment, then came quickly to him. "Have you been here long?" he asked.

"Two minutes," Bentley said. "Where is Gastone?"

"I'm to take you to him. I didn't expect you so early."

"That surprises me."

The sergeant smiled. "The lieutenant will explain it to you, signore."

As they climbed the steep road in the gathering twilight, Bentley asked, "Have you known the lieutenant a long time?"

"His father; he was a general in the carabinieri."

"Lieutenant Gastone's father?" Bentley asked.

The sergeant nodded.

"He didn't tell me," Bentley said. "Is he still alive?"

"Yes."

The sergeant's tone of voice discouraged further questions. After two hundred feet, they passed a gap on the left side of the road.

"That's where I was sitting last night," Bentley said, pointing it out. "What happened to the horses of those three men?"

"I don't know, signore," the sergeant answered.

They were only a few minutes away from the point where the two valleys met. Bentley looked around carefully. It was here that he had met the three men the night before. It now seemed incomprehensible that he had not seen them earlier. At least he should have heard their steps on the stony ground.

They left the road and climbed the narrow side valley. After a few dozen steps they met the first group of carabinieri. They were sitting around in small groups behind a large rock. They were all tall young men, with sun-tanned faces and dark eyes which looked at Bentley curiously. To the point where the valley curved to the left, he counted at least fifty of them. Then he saw Lieutenant Gastone. He was standing at the curve, scrutinizing the mountain ridges with his field glasses. When he heard footsteps, he turned around.

"You must have flown," he said, surprised.

"Why?" Bentley asked.

"Because you were in Chiesa only an hour and a half ago. I hope you had a fruitful conversation, Mr. Bentley."

Bentley checked his irritation in time. He stared past Gastone. "You must pull back your men immediately," he said.

Gastone nodded. "In ten minutes, Mr. Bentley. Do you see anything?"

"Where?"

The lieutenant pointed up the slope. "It's always the same thing; they climb up and vanish."

"Underneath the wall," Bentley said, "there must be some openings. If that boy told me the truth, we only have to deal with four men and Salvatore's sister. And Salvatore doesn't count; he's paralyzed."

"If you were an Italian," Gastone said, "I would try to get you to join the carabinieri. Did you get your three thousand dollars back?"

Bentley smiled. "How did you know about all this?"

"It's nothing special. We have a radio connection with Fratello. It's just a phone call from there to Chiesa. Excuse me a minute."

He went over to Sergeant Tasca and talked to him. Bentley stared up at the slope once more. It was so steep that he had to strain his neck. He felt his heartbeat quicken. Gastone addressed him again. "What else did you find out?"

"They want to take Mrs. Brazzi away tonight. They want to take her to Italy in a boat."

"You made a good investment," Gastone said. "Come with me, Mr. Bentley."

"When did your people see him?" Bentley asked as they climbed up the valley together.

"As he entered the village; he was acting suspiciously."

"Then they could have arrested him before he got to the inn."

"They could have, but I thought it would be more useful to have him talk to you first. I was counting on the gang trying to contact you once more."

"I wasn't," Bentley said.

Everything had happened fast. Only three minutes after Antonio had left him, a sergeant of the carabinieri had come in and given him back his money. When he reached the square in front of the inn, it had been standing empty in the sunlight. Rigido had vanished too.

Bentley and Gastone passed the first carabinieri. Sergeant Tasca left them.

"He's a good man," he said. "Is he a Sicilian?"

"Most of them are," Gastone said. "Since the war ended we've gotten so many applications that we can pick the very best. There are people who have been fighting the Mafia for five years. They are under General Luca in Palermo."

"Are you?" Bentley asked.

The lieutenant only smiled. "How many people do you suppose, Mr. Bentley, have lost sleep because of the signora?"

"Well, I'm just as bad off," Bentley muttered. "Where are you taking me?"

"To my advance post. You'll see."

The advance post was a rock about fifteen yards high which stood at the foot of the southern wall of the valley, near the entrance to the side valley. It was a good choice, because from it one could see everything on the road as well as the entrance to the side valley. Behind the rock, five carabinieri were huddled together. Two of them were operating a radio. When they saw the lieutenant, they took their earphones off and looked up at him. Bentley had already observed how much respect his men had for him. While the lieutenant talked to them Bentley looked at the radios. They were German, and their directional aerials were pointed north.

"They're war loot," Gastone said. "The Germans left them behind. If we had a dozen more, I could do all my work from my bed. Can you manage fifteen minutes without me?"

"I've managed twenty-nine years without you," Bentley answered. "What do you want?"

"I have to post my men in their new places. Please wait for me here."

Bentley didn't feel like getting into a conversation with the five men, so he sat down in front of the rock and watched the lieutenant walk away. It was getting darker rapidly, and Bentley lost sight of him. Then he heard a dull sound of boots on stone. He saw the carabinieri marching out of the valley in a long file. Some of them continued north, while others began to climb a steep wall across the road, and a third group turned south. Bentley counted about thirty men. Part of the company must have stayed behind in the side valley. He guessed that these were earmarked for the most important role in the lieutenant's plan.

Now with the resolution so near, his feelings were mixed. Even the thought that he would see Helen again in a very short time didn't evoke any clear reaction, probably because their meeting would be complicated by so many problems and unpleasant memories. He feared it as much as he relished it. If all went well, Helen Brazzi would within twenty-four hours face the choice of returning to Toledo or traveling to Naples with him, and after all he had gone through with her, it would be sanguine to have illusions about her decision.

When Lieutenant Gastone finally reappeared in the darkness, almost an hour had passed. "I thought you were bringing Mrs. Brazzi with you," Bentley said.

"I would have liked to," Gastone answered and vanished behind the rock.

When he came back again, he sat down beside Bentley. "It doesn't quite work out the way I had thought," he said. "Cigarette?"

"Have one of mine," Bentley said. "I hope you'll get it straightened out."

"Some of my men got lost in the dark," Gastone said after he had lit his cigarette. "I had to look for them."

"How did you distribute them?"

"It wouldn't make much sense to you. I don't have the feeling so far that I've overlooked anything."

"I'm not trying to tell you how to do your job," Bentley said. "You're counting on them coming down the slope?"

"Yes."

"I don't know the area . . ."

"I do, Mr. Bentley. I don't deny that three experienced men could do almost anything, but they can't get very far no matter what. They have to think of the signora."

"Not just her. Salvatore can't walk. He has a bullet in his back."

"Whose bullet?"

"I couldn't find out."

"Do you have any idea?"

"A guess, perhaps," Bentley said. "It's not important."

"What else did Antonio tell you?"

"That he'd never been in Palmigano. Did you get anything out of Lucio?"

"No."

"Antonio impressed me," Bentley said. "If I'm correct, Mrs. Brazzi was guarded by only two men during the past night."

"You didn't know that last night," the lieutenant said.

"Of course not." He felt he had scored a point and it pleased him. "I'm just curious," he went on. "Why did you let those two men walk by this morning."

"General Luca wanted it that way."

Bentley had suspected as much. "Do you get your instructions from him?"

"He works on the Mafia," Gastone answered. "When there are difficult decisions to make, I consult him. This case is a one-in-a-hundred chance for me, Mr. Bentley. I can't afford any mistakes."

"I understand."

"Perhaps not completely. My father and General Luca were in the same service and have known each other more than fifty years—a real lifetime friendship, though they've had their misunderstandings, mainly over politics. The Fascists retired General Luca but not my father. Today it's just the other way around. But it hasn't ended their friendship."

"I understand," Bentley said. "Is that why you're here?"

"Luca wanted to give me a chance. Neither he nor I could have known two weeks ago how big a chance it would be. If it all comes out well, they will remember my name in Rome. They will remember my father's name at the same time."

"You think they might then reactivate him?"

"Yes. Does that surprise you?"

Bentley hesitated. He remembered what Lieutenant Gastone had said about Mussolini. He hadn't sounded too hostile toward him. He was a little more complex than most boys from Toledo, he thought.

He was thinking of something appropriate to say when the lieutenant stood up. "I am waiting for one more message that should have been here now," he said.

"Why don't you send one of your men?"

"I'm too nervous," Gastone answered and Bentley could tell from his voice that he meant it. Gastone walked away. The moonlight had not yet reached the valley. The sky was clear and full of stars, but it was pitch-black where he sat. In the silence Bentley heard the voices of the men behind the rocks—scraps of sentences. It reminded him of nights during the war, of the weary waiting for the next morning, for the next attack. He had almost forgotten how on such nights he had wished that it would all be over. Now that it had been over for quite a while, he was no longer pleased. He did not know how much time had passed when he suddenly heard steps. Their sound came from the right. A few seconds later he heard Sergeant Tasca calling his name breathlessly. He stood up. "I'm to take you to the lieutenant, Mr. Bentley," he said, panting. "The signora is back."

For a moment Bentley was sure he had misunderstood him. "Are you talking about Mrs. Brazzi?" he asked.

"I don't understand it either," Sergeant Tasca said.

# 33

Late in the afternoon Carmelo noticed the lieutenant for the second time. He was standing on the right side of the curve in the valley with field glasses to his face. Two men came up to him and Carmelo watched them talk and look up the slope; then they all three vanished.

He waited a minute before he turned to Salvatore. When he saw that he was asleep, he called Pietro from the cave and told him what he had seen.

"Are you sure one of them was the American?" Pietro asked.

"I would have recognized him at twice the distance," Carmelo said. "I had a good look at him when he came to see Piera the first time."

Pietro went to Salvatore and waked him. "The American was here again," he said.

"That's no reason to wake me," Salvatore muttered. "Did you see him?"

"Carmelo did. He was standing with the lieutenant, looking up."

"Where is he now?"

"Back down in the valley. I'm sure now that they caught Lucio or Antonio."

"Then they know everything."

"I guess so," Pietro said. He sat down. "Where was Antonio standing when you started that avalanche?"

"About in the middle of the slope. Lucio was at the bottom. I can't believe that Antonio got away. It would be enough if Lucio got away."

"If we want to be in Caronia before dawn, Carmelo had better get the horses. In an hour at the latest."

"Yes. I can also count," Salvatore said. He lit a cigarette and said, "I knew it already early today."

"What?"

"That we wouldn't get out. We waited too long. Last night would have been the right time."

"Why didn't you speak up?" Pietro said.

Salvatore looked at him. "I'm not blaming anyone. If Carmelo can't get through, you have to try it without horses."

"That's just half of it. Can't you think of anything better?"

"You?"

"I don't want to talk about funerals as long as there's no one dead. Do you think that's the reason I've been sitting around here for two years?"

Salvatore nodded. "Yes, precisely. Enough is enough. You should have given up a year ago."

Pietro shrugged. "You make me weep," he said and got up. He went into the cave where Piera was busy packing clothes and other items in a large bag. "You can stop," Pietro said. "We're leaving it all here."

Helen was lying awake on her bed. When Pietro came in, she sat up quickly. "Have they gone?"

"The carabinieri?"

"Yes."

"Why would they go?" Pietro said. "They're here just for us." He sat down and smiled at her. "It looks as if you're going to have breakfast in Chiesa tomorrow after all. Your friend is back."

"When?"

"Five minutes ago. Will you marry him?"

"Neither him nor anyone else," Helen said hoarsely.

Pietro nodded. "Then you won't mind saying good-by to us all."

He left her and went out again. Salvatore was talking heatedly with Piera. When they saw Pietro, they fell silent.

"I'm interested," he said. "What were you talking about?"

"She's getting on my nerves," Salvatore said. "She wants me to tell her how we are going to get out of here."

"Why don't you tell her?"

"Perhaps she can grow wings and fly out. Give me something to drink."

"You shouldn't drink," Piera said. "Your stomach can't take it."

"He has to take a lot more today," Pietro said. "That wall is a hundred feet high."

Piera turned pale. "Which wall? Along the road?"

"Yes."

"But it's impossible," she said.

"Do you know another way?"

She didn't answer.

Pietro took the bottle from the table, took a sip, and said to Piera, "Get us something to eat. It will be dark soon."

He leaned his head back and took a long drink from the bottle, and passed it to Salvatore.

"What about the horses?" Piera asked. "Is Carmelo getting them?"

"If the carabinieri let him through. Would you like to discuss it with them?"

She turned around and went into the cave.

"It won't be long," Salvatore said, looking at the colorless sky. "What happens to the signora now?"

"I haven't decided." Pietro took the bottle and brought it to Carmelo. "Piera wants you to get the horses," he told him.

"I heard." Carmelo turned, took a drink from the bottle, and handed it back. "I'll go across the wall."

"And after that, when you reach the horses?"

"I don't know yet."

Pietro stared at his dark face. "We can always try. Where will we meet?"

"You figure it out," Carmelo said, turning toward the valley once more.

"Why not where we keep the firewood?" Salvatore suggested. "They won't expect you in that direction."

"Us," Pietro said.

Salvatore stared at him. "They won't expect you in that direction," he repeated.

"Cut that stuff out," Pietro told him. "I need my head for more important things."

He sat down beside Carmelo and stared in front of him. When Piera brought the food out, he went back to Helen once more.

She was still sitting the way he had left her. In the light of the lamp her face looked painted white. "Why did you say that?" she asked immediately.

"What?"

"That it wouldn't be difficult for me to say good-by."

"Is it difficult?"

She didn't answer.

"Well, that's what I want to talk to you about," Pietro said sitting down. He took her hand and held it. "There wouldn't be any point to it anyway," he continued. "I don't know if we'll get through; they have posts everywhere. As soon as it gets dark, I'm taking you down."

"Down where?"

"To your friends. What do you want to do, go back to America?"

Helen looked at him. For two hours she hadn't been able to manage a clear thought. "Don't you want to come too?" she asked.

"Yes."

"Then why don't you?"

Pietro stood up. He walked into the middle cave. When he came back he put a pile of paper currency in her lap. "It must be four thousand five hundred," he said. "I spent five hundred on the boat and the horses."

She looked at the money and then at him. "What am I supposed to do with it?"

"It's yours. When they catch me, I don't want to have it in my pocket."

"I'll tell them that I gave it to you."

"Why? It would only complicate things for you."

Helen took the money out of her lap and put it down beside him. "Where will you land?"

"I'm not sure. I know a man in Bagnera."

"He won't do anything for you without money. What will you use for money?"

He did not answer.

"You must keep the money," Helen said with determination. "You will need it for Salvatore. Where is this Bagnera?"

"Why do you want to know?"

"We could meet at your friend's house."

"Impossible," Pietro said quickly. "I don't even know if he's still there."

"Then I'm going to meet you in Caronia," Helen said. As usual when she had made up her mind about something, she refused to consider it further. It had been a difficult decision. She wasn't quite sure she would have made it that quickly under less pressing circumstances. Now there was no time left for reasoning, and she acted straight from her feelings.

"When will I meet you?" she asked.

Pietro looked away. "I didn't think it mattered that much to you."

"We discussed that already." She smiled. "I'm afraid that I have no other choice."

Pietro stood up. "I have to think about it. Piera is waiting for us with the food."

"I can't eat now," Helen said. "And I don't want to see Piera. Not now."

"Wait for me here then," Pietro said. When he came out into the hollow, it was getting dark. Carmelo was sitting at the table eating. "It's about time for me," he said. "Did you think it out?"

"I can't think of anything better," Pietro said. He looked at Piera, who had taken Carmelo's post, and asked her, "Do you see anything?"

She shook her head.

"Stay on the road to Troina for a mile and a half," Pietro said to

Carmelo. "If they stop you, tell them that you are taking the horses to the market in Nicosia."

"Good," Carmelo said. He took another sip from the bottle, wiped his mouth, and got up. "Shall I send Vito over?"

"No, he has to keep his eye on the carabinieri. If we haven't gotten to you by midnight, don't wait any longer."

"Don't even think that," Carmelo said and went over to Salvatore. "If you want my tobacco . . ."

Salvatore grimaced. "Keep it for your grandmother. Or does she smoke cigars?"

"I feel like you," Carmelo said and climbed out of the hollow.

"What did he mean by that?" Piera asked.

None of the men answered her and she left her place and went over to Pietro. "How do you want to get Salvatore over the wall?"

"The Americans have promised him a helicopter," Salvatore answered. To Pietro he said, "I don't know why you're making such a fuss. They'll take me to the nearest hospital, operate on me, and then send me to my mother. If you feel like it, you can send me a postcard."

"What are you two talking about?" Piera demanded.

Pietro climbed up to the edge of the hollow, paused for a moment, and then went off down the slope.

"Where is he going?" Piera asked.

Salvatore shrugged. "To Vito. He wants to be certain."

"About what?"

"Don't act stupider than you are," he answered. "Do you have a helicopter?"

She looked at him, then sat down. "If you stay here, I stay here."

"No, you don't," Salvatore said. "If they catch you, they'll put you in a dirty prison filled with whores. They can't do much with me. I haven't killed any Americans and I wasn't in on anything else. Pietro is different. They have half a dozen reasons to hang him."

"What about the signora?"

"I guess he'll send her away."

"To the carabinieri."

"Where else?" Salvatore asked.

Piera didn't answer.

"He's not the only man in the world," Salvatore said. "It wasn't such a big thing."

"If she hadn't come along, he would have married me."

"You just tell yourself that."

"I shouldn't have told him about her," Piera said. She felt so full of hatred and disappointment that she started to cry.

Salvatore cursed. "Stop that! She would have found him without you. You don't have to go with him if you don't want to. Go to Messina and take care of our mother. She needs you more than he."

Nothing else was said between them until Pietro came back. "Take Vito something to eat," he said. "He's starving. Don't forget the bottle."

The way she was slumped at the table annoyed him. "What's the matter with you?"

When she did not answer, he asked Salvatore, "What did you talk about?"

"She wants to stay here," Salvatore said. "How does it look?"

Pietro sat down. "Vito climbed down a way. Some of them have left. The others are hidden in the valley."

"Hidden?"

"Yes."

"Then they know we're trying to get out," Salvatore said.

"It looks that way."

Pietro looked at Piera. "Why do you want to stay here?"

She still did not answer.

"If it would help Salvatore, I would give up my hand."

"Keep your hands for the signora," Piera said. "What kind of deal did you make with her?"

"What are you talking about?"

"Don't bluff me. Antonio and I knew from the first what you were after."

"What was I after?"

"You want to marry her," Piera said. She gathered some food from the table and went off to Vito.

Salvatore cleared his throat. "It was a shock for her. She counted on the money. What's the real story? Are you two meeting?"

"I haven't asked her yet."

"You'd better. In an hour it will be too light to get across the road. I don't know what you're waiting for."

Pietro went in to Helen. She saw his face and stood up quickly. "What's the matter?"

"Nothing. Put on your coat. It's getting cold."

"What should I take?"

"Just your pocketbook. The carabinieri will get your suitcase." He helped her with her coat. He was still very pale.

"You're not telling me everything," she said.

He shook his head.

Salvatore received them very gaily. "I hope you had a nice time with us, signora. Will we see you again?"

"Tomorrow morning," Helen said. "Where's Piera?"

"With Vito. Why? Do you want to say good-by?"

She smiled.

"Oh, well," Salvatore said, "we'll all meet again tomorrow morning anyway." His voice sounded strange.

She went over and shook his hand.

"I'd rather have a kiss, if you don't mind," he said. "Only I have a swollen mouth."

"I don't mind," Helen said and bent over him.

"You taste of peach jam," Salvatore said.

She turned back to Pietro, who was standing motionless. "We haven't agreed where we'll meet."

"I'll take you part way down," he said. "Hold on to me."

The descent was difficult in the dark. Helen realized that they were not taking the direct route. Instead they turned toward the left wall of the valley. The rocks were not as big there and it was easier to walk.

They had gone about three quarters of the way when Pietro stopped and stood still. "You can do the rest alone," he said softly. "Would you mind very much waiting half an hour?"

"Here?"

"Yes. We need a little time. As soon as the carabinieri see you, they will come up."

"I'll wait an hour," Helen said. "Where do I meet you?"

"You must go to Fratello first and then follow the coast to Caronia. I will be standing by the road at five o'clock."

"Where?"

"Three hundred yards before the first houses. Do you have money?"

Helen opened her pocketbook. As she was about to take some out, he held her hand. "It's better if you keep it. You may change your mind before tomorrow morning."

"I know you need it," Helen said and closed the pocketbook. "How will you get to the road?"

"Across the ridge."

"And Salvatore?"

"We're three men," Pietro said. "We'll manage."

"What should I tell the carabinieri."

"That we sent you away."

"Nothing else?"

"That's up to you," Pietro said.

When Helen looked at his face, she realized that she had hardly talked to him for the last three days. She had not done much but ask and answer questions, and she knew it was not just the problem of language. Nonetheless, it seemed to her now as if nothing remained to be said that had not already been said.

She moved her head and stared past him at the black silhouettes of the mountains. "I hope it's nice weather tomorrow," she mumbled.

"I don't think the weather will change," Pietro said.

"Is it a large boat?"

"It even has a cabin."

"I look forward to it," Helen said with tears in her eyes.

When he kissed her, she pressed her body against him. "It will work," he said. "Without you, we'd go to hell."

He released himself from her embrace, turned around, and climbed back without stopping once. He did not look around either.

Salvatore and Piera were waiting for him in the hollow. He walked past them into the middle cave. He opened the crate with the rifles. It held six semiautomatic American carbines, wrapped in blankets and properly greased. He took one, filled his pockets with ammunition, and went out.

"What do you want with the rifle?" Salvatore said.

"I have a plan."

"To marry your signora?" Piera said. She was sitting on the ground next to Salvatore.

Pietro went close to her. "Are you coming?"

"No."

"She isn't quite with it anymore," Salvatore said. "Her father started the same way. Don't you want to talk to Vito?"

"Why?"

"I figured," Salvatore said, "by the time you'd be back that maybe she would have changed her mind."

Pietro looked down at him. "If you mean that it's better . . ."

"You don't have to come back for me," Piera said.

"It's better in any case," Salvatore said. "Don't forget the map."

Pietro climbed out of the hollow.

"What map shouldn't he forget?" Piera asked, but then she understood.

Salvatore grinned. "I hate all this good-by business," he said.

It was quite still in the hollow. Salvatore stared across the mountains, which were becoming clearer against the sky.

"Is he meeting her?" Piera asked.

Salvatore did not answer.

"I can imagine," she said. "He wasn't even after the money."

"That's not true," Salvatore said. "He couldn't know in advance that he would fall for her. Maybe he could have pulled off the whole thing alone. He just needed us to make it look more real."

"To make what look more real?"

Salvatore grinned again. "He fooled you all. The only one who understood anything was Antonio; Giuseppe and Lucio would never have understood."

"I understood something," Piera said. "What would have happened if she hadn't fallen for it?"

"We would have kept her in Italy until her father sent the money." He shook his head. "I would never have believed that he could have gotten so far."

"That he could have gotten her to meet him tomorrow?"

"No one else but he could have pulled that off," Salvatore said, his voice filled with admiration.

"She isn't with him yet," Piera said, getting up.

He stared at her. "Where are you going?"

"To talk to Vito."

"You stay here," Salvatore said and took her arm. "If you try to spoil it for him, I'll never speak to you again," he said.

"You're stupid," she said.

"O.K., go ahead, but Vito isn't there. Pietro took him with him. Nobody knows the mountains better. Sit down!"

She obeyed.

"He couldn't have done it any differently," Salvatore said. "If everything had happened the way he wanted it, we would all be in Italy tomorrow evening, and the signora would have kept us in style."

"That's what you think."

"That's what I know. I couldn't beg him to stay and I can't beg you to go, but if you don't go, my dear sister, they'll put me in a hospital and you in prison."

"I don't care," she said.

"But I care. I want you to visit me in the hospital, and you can only visit me if you're not caught. Go to Carmelo. He'll take you to Messina."

"But he's waiting for Pietro."

"He'll wait for nothing," Salvatore said. "Pietro just sent him away to protect himself. They'll get to Caronia better on foot than on horseback. If Carmelo had found out that you wanted to stay with me, he would have wanted to stay himself. Go to him!"

"I don't want to," Piera said.

Salvatore sat up. He had only a few minutes left and he knew it. "You're acting like an old woman. "I don't need any more nurses. I'm sick of being washed and babied by you. Do you understand?"

She did not answer. He went on, almost screaming. "I know you'll miss it. You must be sorry that I'm your brother."

"You're crazy," she said. "Why would I be sorry?"

"Why?" Salvatore asked. "Because you like it so much. Do you think I don't know why you run around me half naked all day, why you want to wash me all the time, and why you sit on my bed at night?"

She looked terrified. "What are you saying?"

"Maybe I am crazy," Salvatore said. "If I weren't crazy I would have done what you wanted me to do long ago. Sister or no sister, I would have done what you've been waiting for me to do." He bent over and put his hand on her hip. "Pietro knows what's going on with you. He wanted something better than a girl who's even willing to make it with her brother."

Piera stood up. She could hardly talk. "Why do you say that?"

"I wanted to tell you long ago," Salvatore said. He felt the sweat on his face. "But you would have run away. Now I don't need you anymore and I don't care if you know or not. You can still have what you want, if you're quick. What shall I do for you?"

She felt as if she were going to hit him, but instead she ran away, sick with disgust.

Salvatore smiled and wiped the sweat off his face. When he could no longer hear her steps, he pulled the pistol from underneath his blanket. He took the catch off and waited alone in the dark for the carabinieri.

## 34

In the dark, Bentley recognized Helen first by her coat. Until that moment he had not believed that she was back. Then he heard the sound of her voice, although he did not understand what she was saying. Nor was he aware that he was holding her hand. He stood next to her and stared at her face. He could have stood like that all night. Then he realized that Lieutenant Gastone was looking at him. He let go of her hand and said quietly, "I couldn't believe it."

"Me neither," Gastone answered. "You must help me, Mr. Bentley. The signora refuses to answer my questions."

"That's not so," Helen said. "I told you that I gave my word that the carabinieri wouldn't come up until half an hour from now."

"Just a moment," Bentley said, but the lieutenant interrupted him. "We respect your promise, signora. I'm just asking you to tell me if they've already left and which way they're going."

"I don't know."

"How many of them were there when you left?"

Helen turned to Bentley. "Do you have the car here, Clyde?"

"Yes."

"Then please take me to Chiesa now. I'm tired."

"You're making a big mistake, signora," Gastone said.

Helen turned her back on him. "Come, Clyde."

As they walked down through the dark valley, small groups of carabinieri ran by them, and in back of them they could hear the sharp voice of the lieutenant giving orders.

"He'll never forgive you," Bentley said, taking her arm. "I still don't understand."

"Why I'm back?"

"Yes." He laughed. "When I gave Pietro your suitcase, he told me that he would keep you for a week. His friend—the one who was in the car with us—came to the hotel today to ask for the three thousand dollars. He almost convinced me that they were taking you somewhere."

Helen realized that he must be talking about Antonio. She forced herself to speak in an indifferent tone of voice. "Where is he now?"

"With the carabinieri. Lieutenant Gastone caught him. He said that they never intended to let you go. Is it true that they wanted to send you to Italy tonight?"

"I don't know anything about it," Helen said. "And I don't want to talk about it now."

It seemed to Bentley that she had changed in some indefinable way—even more aloof, yet strangely close. As a matter of fact, he felt as little like talking as she did. He was glad to have her near him again. As he walked with her with his hand under her arm, he could feel the warmth of her skin through the thin material of her coat.

It took them fifteen minutes to reach the larger valley. Here the moonlight was already bright, and when they walked up to the road, they could hear the sound of many boots.

Helen stopped and looked back. About a hundred feet away a group of heavily armed carabinieri were streaming out of the side valley. They turned north and vanished into the dark.

"In ten minutes this place will be crawling with carabinieri," Bentley said. "Gastone has commandeered half an army."

"Where is the car?" Helen asked.

Bentley took her arm again. "We have to walk a bit more."

They came to the spot where Helen had gotten out of the Fiat three days earlier. She remembered how Pietro had looked at her shoes and torn off the heels. It seemed to her as if it had happened weeks ago. She was wearing low-heeled shoes now, and they were once more on the road to Chiesa. But she felt as afraid as she had three days ago, perhaps even more. At the same time, her fear was tempered by a strange feeling of unreality. She felt as if she were about to wake up from a long dream.

"Did you find out anything about your husband?" he asked.

She nodded. Earlier, when she had been sitting alone in the dark, she had realized that she had never asked about his grave. Worse, she had not even thought about him for the past twenty-four hours. She had come all the way from Toledo and simply forgotten about him. The fact that it had happened two years ago was no excuse. Only a few weeks ago she had fought against the thought of his death. Now that she knew that he was lying somewhere under a heap of stones, it seemed not to touch her anymore. She had slept with another man— kissed him and held him—as if she had never been married to Genno Brazzi. The living were nearer than the dead, and her fear for the living man whom she loved was stronger than the sorrow for a dead man she had once loved. It was all so justifiable, and yet so terribly tasteless. It made tears come to her eyes, and for a moment a feeling of contempt for herself weighed even heavier than her fear for Pietro.

She became aware of Bentley's voice again. "That was stupid of me," he said.

"Why? You never doubted that he was dead."

"Will you have his body moved to the U.S.?"

"As soon as I find out where he's buried."

"Don't you know?"

"No."

"It should be possible to find out," Bentley said. "We have two members of the gang."

"Two?"

"The carabinieri got the first one earlier today," Bentley said. "His name is Lucio Canepa. Do you know anything about the shooting last night?"

Helen did not answer. She felt relieved that the avalanche had not killed either of the two.

"I forgot you don't want to talk about it," Bentley said. "I'm sorry, Helen."

"Lucio should know where my husband is buried."

"Leave it to me. I'll speak with the lieutenant. It's somewhat complicated. You have to make an application for his transport. Until all the formalities are . . ."

"I know about it. I found out before I left."

"It's simpler for a living soldier," Bentley said. "When they sent us over, there were no formalities for the relatives. How did you get over here, by plane?"

"On a freighter."

"It would have been more comfortable in six months. Normal passenger traffic . . ."

Bentley suddenly stopped. Twice before he had had the feeling that they were not alone on the road. Now, looking over his shoulder, he saw four carabinieri. Helen had seen them too. "What do they want?" she asked.

"It's your bodyguard," Bentley said. "Gastone doesn't want to run any more risks. I'm glad you're here, Helen. Or did I say so already?"

He had not, but she had felt it. She was also aware that he had taken many risks for her, and she wished that he hadn't. For three days she had hardly thought of him, and only now did she recall their last being together. Her feelings were ambivalent. It was like meeting an old friend who reminded her of things she would rather forget. At the same time, she felt strong sympathy for him. He was similar to her in many ways, and she had no doubt that he would make an entertaining and loyal friend. But after all that had happened a real friendship was unthinkable. He would never yield to mere friendship. She made up her mind to discuss their relationship as soon as possible.

At the car, Sergeant Tasca and another carabiniere were waiting. Bentley had seen the sergeant just before he had seen Helen again. "How did you get here?" he asked.

"The lieutenant's orders, signore. We are to come with you."

"That's unnecessary," Helen said. "Tell the lieutenant that we can find the road to Chiesa alone."

"I'm sure," the sergeant said. "But I have orders to come with you. I am responsible for your safety, signora."

Helen turned around to face the four carabinieri who had followed her. They were now standing at the edge of the road staring at her. She considered them for a moment and then said to Bentley, "You're an American officer, aren't you, Clyde?"

He nodded. "If I haven't been suspended in the meantime."

"Then get rid of these people for me. I didn't ask the lieutenant for this."

She opened the car door, got behind the wheel, and started the engine.

"You heard," Bentley said to Sergeant Tasca. "Mrs. Brazzi insists on going without you."

The sergeant shrugged. "I'm sorry, sir, the lieutenant ordered me."

Bentley lost his patience. "You're forgetting who I am," he said rudely. "I'm here under the direct orders of the Supreme Commander of the American Army. Do you want to lose your post?"

"The lieutenant . . ."

"Tell him to consider his father," Bentley said and went to the car. As he opened the door he heard the shots, first two, then another, and then a whole series. The carabinieri had heard them too. They all stared in the same direction.

Bentley waited with his hand on the door of the car until there was silence again, then he got in next to Helen. She seemed not to have noticed. The motor was making too much noise inside the car. Helen put the car in gear and steered it onto the road. The sergeant had made no further effort to follow. As the car approached the four carabinieri they stepped aside and let it pass.

"It's ridiculous," Helen said. "He treats us as if we were his men."

Bentley said, "I don't think he'll try again. Why are you so opposed to them?"

She couldn't explain. "He could at least have asked me. Please give me a cigarette."

"Do you happen to know what time it was when you got to the lieutenant?" he asked casually.

"Half past ten," she said immediately. "Why do you ask?"

"I'm interested," Bentley said. Gastone had waited at least a half an hour before sending up his men after all. "Was Gastone there when you came down?"

"No. There were four carabinieri. But he wasn't far away. It couldn't have been more than ten minutes before he came."

"He must have been surprised," Bentley said. "I wish I could have seen his face. It must have been a bad moment for him."

"Why do you think so?" Helen asked.

Bentley laughed. "Here he had the chance of a lifetime to save you from those bandits. I'm glad I'm not in their shoes, but there is something I don't understand . . ."

"What don't you understand?"

"It's not important," Bentley said. For some reason he did not want to mention the shots to her.

As he looked at her he wondered what she had been through. He wanted to ask her if they had treated her well, but he decided to respect her wish not to talk about it. Her reappearance was as mysterious as her entire behavior. She did not look as if she had been through some terrifying experience.

He watched her as she drove the car up the dark pass. For a girl from Toledo she drove with an amazing certainty. It had surprised

*295*

him earlier. "What are you going to do now?" he asked. "Are you going to wait until they find your husband's body?"

"No."

"If you want, I can take care of it. Do you have any idea of the place?"

"Not exactly. It must be near Sperlinga. Do you know the town?"

He nodded. "A cave town. Before the Army reached Palmigano, we were there for two days. Don't you mind the driving?"

She did mind, but it was helping her fight her anxiety. "I'll tell you when I'm tired. Clyde?"

"Yes?"

Helen hesitated. Although she had prepared what she was going to say, it was difficult. "I'm leaving tomorrow morning." Her voice sounded hoarse. "I don't want you to ask me where I'm going. It only concerns me. I'll tell the car rental people where they can pick up the Fiat. Do you still have the three thousand dollars?"

"Of course," Bentley said mechanically.

"Then you can pay our bill with Signor Rigido and for the car, if there's still any money due. I'll leave you a thousand dollars. I'd like you to stay around until they've located my husband. Do you think they could . . . until they transfer him, put him in . . . I mean . . . find a decent place for him?"

"We have two war cemeteries on the island," Bentley answered.

"That would be fine," Helen said. "I don't know how long I'm going to stay away. We may not meet again. Is there some American post near here where you can leave me a message?"

"Yes, of course." Bentley watched her steer the car through a hairpin curve. "How about the town commander in Palermo?"

"That's good. You can leave a note for me there. Tell me if they've found my husband. As soon as I'm back, I'll handle his transport. Please don't make a face, Clyde. I'm not crazy. If you really meant the things you said in Chiesa, then you'll have to take me as I am. I don't want to discuss it with you or the carabinieri. Now you may give me another cigarette."

Bentley did not want to discuss it either. He felt exhausted. He was suddenly convinced that there was some man behind all of this. From that moment on he could not think of anything else.

*296*

Two miles beyond Cesaro he took over the wheel. She had suddenly stepped on the brake and said that she had to sleep for half an hour. But she did not sleep. He could tell, even though she did not move for an hour. They had passed Cerami, which seemed to hang against the mountain wall in the bright moonlight, when she uncurled herself, opened her pocketbook, and started fumbling in it.

"Are you looking for a cigarette?" he asked.

She nodded.

He gave her his pack. "Where is your suitcase?"

"The carabinieri will find it," Helen said.

"Won't you need it if you leave tomorrow morning?"

She had not discussed it with Pietro, but she felt sure that she could buy whatever she needed once she was on the mainland. "Perhaps they'll still bring it."

"When do you want to leave?"

"Two o'clock."

"In the middle of the night?"

"Yes."

Bentley was silent. It was useless to try to make her change her mind. But his suspicion was growing stronger, and as they drove up the steep road to Chiesa, he began to wish that she had not come back.

Under the dense trees in front of the inn it was pitch-dark. He drove the car up to the well and turned off the engine. "Do you have your car keys back?" he asked.

Helen shook her head. She hadn't thought of it either. Pietro must still have them in his pocket.

"The papers are in the glove compartment," he said and handed her his set of car keys.

At same moment he saw in the lights of the car two carabinieri. They were standing with automatic rifles in the archway of the village street, staring at them. As Bentley got out of the car they came over. One of them touched his cap. "Forgive us, signore. Is that the signora who was missing?"

"Yes."

"Then she was freed?"

"Yes. She has freed herself," Bentley answered. He took a step toward the inn, but the carabinieri held his arm.

"We locked the door, signore. Here is the key. Where did they find the signora?"

Bentley turned to him and took the key. "Where the lieutenant thought she would be. Isn't Rigido here?"

"We arrested him."

"Why?"

"Lieutenant's orders, signore. We have arrested more than twenty men in Chiesa."

"But that's crazy," Helen said. She had come around from the other side of the car. "Why?"

"Lieutenant's orders," the carabinieri repeated. "They are suspect."

"I know precisely that they had nothing to do with it," Helen said to Bentley. "This is just ridiculous."

"That's not all that's ridiculous," Bentley muttered. He went to the inn, unlocked the door, and put on the light. "I almost forgot," he said. "I moved into your room."

"Didn't you like your own?"

"It was too quiet."

Helen looked at him but said nothing. Up in her room, she took off her coat and looked around. "Nothing much has changed here," she said. "You can stay here; I'll take your room."

"Why?" Bentley took her coat and hung it up. "You'll have to pack your other things. Are you hungry?"

She nodded.

"I'll see if I can find something," Bentley said and left the room.

Helen looked around the room again. Here everything had started. It was here that she had first met Pietro, and she recalled how he had hit her and forced her to dress in front of him. And now she wanted to leave voluntarily, in the middle of the night, to go to a strange town to meet him. She wanted to get into a fishing boat with him and go on to another strange town and strange people. It would be exactly the same as in the mountains. She would feel the same fear and have the same problems. Nothing would change, neither the fear of the carabinieri nor the fear of Piera's jealousy. It would all go on just as before.

She did not understand why, but during the few minutes that she waited for Bentley to return she remembered a hundred different things which she had totally forgotten in the past few days: the many contradictions, the almost insoluble problems which stood in the way of marriage with Pietro—the problems of a relationship with a man who in twenty-four hours would be on the wanted list of every police office in the country. It was useless and she had known it, but she had not wanted to know. She had forced it from her conscious mind.

It was as if she was waking from a hypnotic trance, as if with each breath she took of the familiar atmosphere of the hotel room she regained a portion of her capacity to be sober, and to consider her actions without sentiment. No longer could she barricade herself behind such emotional walls as her hatred for Giuseppe or her passion for Pietro. In a fleeting moment she felt herself thrust helplessly into a situation which she considered beyond her strength and far beyond what she wanted to risk for the sake of a man. After all, it was completely absurd to want to go to California with Pietro. No American consulate would give a visa to a man wanted not only by the carabinieri but also by the military police. It was a fact of life which could not be undone or ignored, yet for the past few days she had ignored it completely—the fact that not only Genno Brazzi but many other American soldiers had been slaughtered.

She walked over to the mirror and looked at herself. Her face had hardly changed. Only the blue shadows under her eyes hadn't been there four days ago. She wouldn't get much sleep tonight either for she was about to pile the ultimate absurdity on all the others. In spite of her plan being without justification and without hope and against every rational argument, she was still determined to drive to Caronia. There were a dozen simpler ways of meeting Pietro. If he wanted to see her again, he could easily wait for her in Bagnera, whether or not his friend was still living there. But she hadn't thought of that. She had been too afraid for him to think of a better solution.

She heard Bentley on the stairs and stepped away from the mirror. As Bentley came in she was sitting on a chair with her legs crossed, smiling. "Did you find anything?"

"He has everything locked, even the refrigerator. I guess he didn't trust the carabinieri."

"I wouldn't either," Helen said. "I'm not hungry after all."

Bentley put a bottle and two glasses on the table. "Me neither. Do you want to drink something?"

"What is it?"

"Marsala."

"All right, to keep you company."

"I've figured to keep the room for a few days," she said. "I'll just take whatever will fit into my bag and leave the rest here."

"I thought you weren't coming back," Bentley said.

Helen hesitated. It had been an impulse; she couldn't explain it. "I'm not quite sure," she said. "I have to think about it. If it's still my room, they can put my suitcase here."

Bentley sat down. "For how long?"

"Until I send for it, or until I get it myself." She took a sip from her glass and looked at Bentley. "I haven't been easy on you, Clyde."

He grinned. "Nor I with you. But you can't blame a man for falling in love, can you?"

"You should have known it wouldn't lead to anything."

"Do you always know, when you're falling in love?"

She didn't answer.

"I'm really sorry for you," he said. "You always meet the wrong men."

"Not every time," she said.

He nodded. "You're thinking of Genno Brazzi. Looking at it objectively, you had as much bad luck with him as with anyone else. If not, you wouldn't be here tonight. Don't worry. I'm not going to ask you where you're going tomorrow, but considering everything I know about you . . ."

"What do you know about me?" Helen asked.

"Quite a lot, and I'm not even thinking of what you told me yourself."

"Perhaps you're just imagining it."

"Imagining what?"

"People often imagine that they know something about someone

*300*

else," Helen answered. "What does one know, even about oneself? I'll admit I like you, Clyde, but in a different way."

Bentley shrugged. "I want it to be the way it usually is between a man and a woman. What I don't understand is why with you it's so difficult one day and so easy the next. A few days ago you lay and slept beside me all night. I asked myself whether you were quite normal. Maybe I'll spend the rest of my life trying to figure out who you really are. The stupid thing is that I can't help feeling that it could have all been different if I were only half as clever as I think I am. Do you think it's really impossible that we'll ever get together again?"

Helen said nothing.

"It doesn't have to be today," Bentley continued calmly. "I'll wait ten years for you if I have to. I know that I won't find anything better in the meantime. I'd even wait for you if my chances were a hundred to one—but you have to guarantee me that one chance, otherwise it's useless. What do you think?"

Helen looked at him with moist eyes. "I would like to, Clyde."

"What would you like to?"

"I would like to be able to guarantee you that."

"Fine." Bentley stood up. "Now I'll let you get some sleep. Do you have an alarm?"

She shook her head.

"I'll wake you," Bentley said. "I've been sleeping like an old woman lately anyway. Is one thirty early enough?"

Helen nodded. She watched him go to the bed, take his pajamas, and go to the door. "I'm sorry," she said. He stood and looked at her.

"I'm sorry you sleep like an old woman," she said.

Bentley grinned. "You will one day too. Good night, madam."

She heard him go to the other room and open the door. It was all like four days ago, but it was somehow different. He had become a complete stranger. Now all she had to do was pack, dress, and wash. Since she had come to the inn, she hadn't been able to rid herself of the feeling that she hadn't washed in months, but she couldn't gather the energy to do it. She sat motionless at the table. She did not realize that time was passing or that she was crying.

When she finally got up, took her traveling bag from the cupboard, and began to listlessly throw her things into it, an hour had gone by. Her most important possessions were in her suitcase; she could not decide what to take. After she had spent some time putting things into the bag and taking them out again, she gave up. She undressed, washed hastily, and put on her morning coat. Then she turned off the light and lay down on the bed. She felt so wide-awake that she did not even try to sleep; she felt her heart beating. No sound came from Bentley's room. She felt as if she were all alone in the inn.

After ten minutes she could no longer bear it. She got up, went to the table, and lit one of Bentley's cigarettes. Then she heard a noise. She froze until she heard footsteps on the stairs; then she went to the door and locked it carefully, and waited. The footsteps went along the corridor; she heard Bentley's voice and the voice of Lieutenant Gastone; then there was a knock on her door. She waited a few seconds, turned the key, and opened the door a crack.

Bentley was standing there. "The lieutenant wants to talk to you," he said. "He says it's very important."

"What does he want?"

"He wants to talk to you. Or would you rather not?"

"No. Tell him to wait a moment."

She locked the door again and walked over to the mirror. Her heart was beating so fast that she could hardly breathe. Before she called Bentley in, she sat down at the table and lit another cigarette.

He brought the lieutenant with him. "Did you sleep?" Bentley asked.

She nodded while she looked at Lieutenant Gastone. Even before he opened his mouth, she knew that he would have bad news for her, yet her voice was even and quiet. "A strange time for a visit, Lieutenant. Won't you sit down?"

"I'd rather stand," he said.

Helen felt the blood rise to her face. "Don't you want to apologize?"

He stared at her. "I thought you would at least apologize," she said; and then she addressed Bentley, "Or isn't that the custom here?"

The lieutenant frowned. "You didn't give me time," he said finally. "Moreover, I'm in a hurry. I brought Salvatore's sister. She has something to say to you."

This was worse than she had thought, and she held her breath for a moment. "Where is she?"

"Downstairs. Can I bring her up?"

"What does she want?"

"She only wants to tell you something, signora. We caught her when she tried to get to her brother. He had taken a shot at one of my men."

"Where is he now?" She finally asked.

The lieutenant shrugged. "We didn't know who it was in the dark and we shot back. I will send her up."

He had already been gone several minutes when Helen found herself still staring at the door. She looked at Bentley. He was standing motionless beside the bed.

"I'm sorry about the girl," he said. "Do you want me to stay here?"

"Is he dead?" Helen asked.

"They must have fired twenty shots at him. I heard it as I got into the car."

"Why didn't you say anything?"

"I didn't want to scare you," Bentley said and left the room.

Helen didn't stir until Piera came in. When she saw her face, she was sure. "Sit down," she said. "What happened?"

"He did it on purpose," Piera answered.

"Why?"

"He wanted them to kill him."

"I don't understand," Helen said. "Where was Pietro?"

"Gone."

Helen stared at her. "Did he leave without you?"

"Salvatore wanted it that way. He sent me away too, but I only went as far as the ridge. I wanted to be near when the carabinieri came."

"Couldn't Pietro have taken you with him?"

Piera did not answer.

"Then what happened?" Helen asked.

"I saw them come up the slope," Piera said. "There were shots and when I ran to him, I ran right into their hands. They wouldn't let me go. Are you meeting Pietro tomorrow morning?"

"Yes."

"Your husband was with us for three months," Piera said. "Pietro kept him because he liked him. Antonio and the others were against it. They thought that your husband would change his mind one day."

"About what?"

"He had promised not to run away. He had told us that he never wanted to go back to America, and that he had always wanted to live in Scordia one day."

"I don't believe that," Helen said. "I don't believe that he said that."

Piera looked away. "I don't care if you do or not. He told me that he was going to get a divorce from you. I liked him too. I wasn't interested in Pietro then. Three months later your husband wanted to leave and he took a rifle out of the crate, but Pietro was quicker."

She paused a moment and then went on. "I won't tell the carabinieri because I don't want them to hang Pietro. Your husband was the cause of everything. He told Pietro too much about America, and how simple it was for a Sicilian to marry a rich woman because the men in America are not real men. He made quite an impression on Pietro. Pietro completely forgot about Salvatore and me. He was always talking to your husband. I think he liked your husband even better than Salvatore, but then your husband decided to run away and squeal on us. If all this hadn't happened, Pietro would never have thought of marrying you. It was all that talk that hypnotized him. Shall I tell you what your husband said about you?"

Helen said nothing. She felt as if she had died.

"Maybe I better not tell you," Piera said and got up. "We laughed at you, signora, your husband most of all. I don't believe everything he said about you anymore. I never heard you cry out when Pietro was with you. If you want to, you can marry him. I don't need him anymore."

She walked to the door. As she came out into the corridor, Bentley left his room. He stared after her as she walked stiffly to Gastone and the two carabinieri who were waiting for her on the staircase. Then the lieutenant came over to him. "Is it true that the signora wants to leave tonight?"

"Who says that?" Bentley asked.

"The girl. I sent for a car from Nicosia to bring her to the signora in time. If it's all right with you, I'd like to talk with her once more now."

"With Mrs. Brazzi?"

"Yes."

"Give her ten minutes," he said and went back in to Helen.

She was still sitting the way Piera had left her. When Bentley saw her face, he had to clear his throat before he could speak.

"I heard everything," he said, going to the window. He opened it and stared out into the darkness. "If I were you, I wouldn't kill myself over it," he said. "Other people have gone through worse, God knows."

"I thought you didn't believe in God," Helen said. Her voice was completely subdued.

It was always the same. He would never know what she really felt.

"I could have figured it out myself," she went on, "if I had been quiet and thought about it for five minutes. Maybe I did know. Please close the window, and wait for me in your room until I call you."

"I don't want to be responsible for leaving you alone," Bentley said, still looking out the window.

"Before I consider killing myself," Helen said, "I will try to think of a more original solution. I want to think things out on my own, Clyde. Unlike you, I believe in God and immortality. Now, for Christ's sake, please get out of here."

Bentley conceded. Outside he leaned against the door and looked into the impatient face of the lieutenant. "She needs a bit more time," he said. "You can't handle a thing like that in ten minutes."

"What are you talking about," Gastone said.

Bentley grinned. "You may think it sounds foolish, but I think Mrs. Brazzi has just discovered herself. What else do you want anyway? You can serve your general the signora and three heads on a silver platter. Isn't that enough?"

"There are still three heads missing," Gastone said. "I don't like to do things halfway."

"Yes, that's what impresses me so," Bentley said. "If I am not mistaken, you'll get them too, and without lifting a finger. You must just learn to wait. Can I reach you somewhere within the next hour?"

The lieutenant hesitated. "How long will it take?"

"It's hard to say with a woman. At the moment Pietro's head is hanging by a little thread. When the time comes, all you have to do is catch it."

"I'll be down in the restaurant."

"Good," Bentley said. "Rigido didn't lock up the wine."

He watched the lieutenant go down the steps. When he turned to go to his own room, Helen came out. She was dressed and her face was as strange as before. "Come in," she said.

Bentley followed her. She must have dressed the moment he left the room. Somehow he wished that she had taken longer. "What time is it?" he heard her ask.

He looked at his watch. "One."

"Is the lieutenant still here?"

"He's waiting downstairs. He wants to talk to you once more."

Helen sat down. "You have to drive me to Caronia. Do you know where that is?"

He thought, then shook his head. "Where is it?"

"Near Fratello. Do you have a map?"

Bentley got the map from the desk. "Why don't you leave it to the carabinieri?" he asked.

"You wouldn't understand. Give me the map."

He handed it to her. As she unfolded it he stood behind her.

"Here it is," she said, pointing at a place on the map. "How long do you think it will take us?"

Her strange tranquillity made Bentley's scalp tingle. "The shortest way goes through Cesaro. At least three hours."

"Then we have to leave in half an hour. Tell the lieutenant. Tell him that I want him to come along."

Bentley had half guessed. "Are you sure you know what you're doing?" he asked.

"What?"

"I guess you're going to hand over some men to him."

"Just one. He will be standing on the street at five o'clock. You'll see him," Helen said and stood up. "Discuss it with the lieutenant. I want to be alone for half an hour."

"I wouldn't do it if I were you," Bentley said and left.

Helen sat down on the bed again and let her thoughts run on. She could not get beyond a certain point. She felt as if she were going in circles, as if some superstructure in her mind collapsed every time she built it to a certain point. She began to feel as if the room was spinning, the bed, the furniture, and finally the whole house. The pain in her chest became stronger and stronger. It felt like a lump of ice pressing against her ribs and cutting her breath. Then it seemed as if it had frozen her completely, as if she could not feel or think anymore. She went over to the mirror and looked at herself again. Her eyes were dry and her face was pale and reposed. She was sure she did not look as tired as two hours ago.

She decided that when she came back from Caronia, she would move to a hotel in Palermo and take a few days rest. She would send a card to her father saying that everything was fine and that he should not worry. Perhaps she would go to Rome or Venice. Anywhere, she thought.

Bentley came in again and said, "The lieutenant thinks we can't do it in three hours. He will follow us."

"Does he have a car?"

"Yes. There will be another one in Cesaro. Do you want to put your coat on?"

Helen nodded. Gastone was waiting for them in the restaurant. "It would be less dangerous for you, signora—" he began, but Helen interrupted him: "I will show you where he is; the rest is your business."

"It'll get light at five o'clock," Bentley interjected. "He'll see the other car and get suspicious."

The lieutenant looked at Helen. "You leave that to me, Mr. Bentley. If the signora will only tell us more or less where they . . ."

"You will see," Helen said and walked past him to the door.

Bentley came after her. The square in front of the inn was full of carabinieri. They respectfully stepped aside for Helen and looked curiously at her, but she never noticed them. "You drive," she said to Bentley. "Do we have enough gas?"

It was typical of her to think of a thing like that at such a moment, Bentley thought. "I filled the tank," he said.

A police jeep was standing under the gray arch as they drove up the narrow street. It followed them after they passed it.

"If I only knew how to help you," Bentley muttered.

Helen did not speak. She stared through the windshield at the scenery. Bentley fell silent too.

The police jeep was still behind them when they reached Cesaro an hour later. They drove along the village street; there was not a soul in sight. The houses looked gray and abandoned. As they left the town, they passed a huge truck which was standing beside the road with its lights off. Bentley looked around and saw that it was full of carabinieri. In the rearview mirror he saw the jeep stop and then follow them again. The truck started to follow them. Lieutenant Gastone had certainly planned everything well.

Now they had come to the most difficult part of the road. The heavy truck could not make good time, so Bentley had to slow down. On earlier trips they had not taken more than an hour and a half to get to the side valley; this time it took almost two hours. He remembered the landscape well, although the moon had set and it was very dark now. Helen must have recognized it all too, but she never turned her head. She sat as motionlessly beside him as when they had driven to Chiesa.

They drove over two more passes before they reached Fratello, then the road dropped steeply toward the sea. Dark orchards and trees flanked it. When they reached the coast, the sky was turning gray in the east. They saw the sea stretched in a black plane to the horizon; the air smelled of blossoms.

"We will be in Caronia in half an hour," Bentley said. "Do you still not want to tell me where you're meeting him?"

"Before Caronia," Helen said. They were the first words she had spoken since she had gotten into the car.

Bentley looked in the rearview mirror. The jeep had just reached the coastal road, closely followed by the truck. "Perhaps I'm crazy," he said, "but I don't feel pleased by this."

"Do you want to get out?" Helen asked.

He shook his head. "You know I don't want to get out. I just don't know why you're taking this risk. If you really want to see him hang, you could do it more simply. This isn't like you."

"You've misjudged me before," Helen said.

It was now almost dawn, and Bentley switched the high beams to the parking lights. The jeep had fallen farther behind; there were many curves in the road and Bentley lost sight of it often. On his left side the landscape was slowly emerging in the dawn. There were steep mountain walls with bright villas, geranium gardens, steep staircases, and old blossoming trees and flowers. The sea was changing too. The gray-black shapeless mass became a glittering metallic surface, and where it met the pale sky at the horizon, a touch of purple appeared.

"It reminds me of something," Bentley said. "It reminds me of the three hundred men who died during the invasion. It was a morning like this. That must be Caronia there. You don't have much time left."

"Time for what?" Helen asked, but Bentley was silent.

She had already seen the place herself—a picturesque panorama of houses huddled together and stretched up the mountainside. To the left on a cone-shaped mountaintop lay the village proper, with a cathedral which glowed pink in the early light of dawn. And then everything changed.

When she saw Pietro standing at the side of the road, the car was not more than thirty feet from him. She recognized him first from the way he was standing, his body slightly bent over, his arms hanging limply. Where he stood, the road was flanked by a small orchard—stubby, gnarled trees weighed down heavily with fruit. The Fiat rolled on at the same speed, but it seemed to her as if the distance between them was not becoming any less. She could see his face now, his curly hair which grew low on his forehead, the expression of disbelieving amazement verging on fear in his dark eyes.

And while she was looking at his face, holding her breath, and while the distance between them remained the same, as if she were watching him through the wrong end of a telescope, his face suddenly seemed blurred and for two heartbeats it was no longer Pietro standing at the side of the road but Genno Brazzi. She heard herself call his name. She heard her own voice as if it were the voice of a stranger from far away, and then she was no longer even sure that she had heard it. And while she was still looking at him, she suddenly could not see him anymore. Then she realized that the car was standing still. She looked at Bentley, whose face was ashen. "Why did you stop?" she asked. It was her own voice once more.

And at the same moment that he saw the jeep appearing around the curve, Bentley released the clutch and the car started again. The truck with the carabinieri appeared. A moment later they reached the orchard and he watched them pass it. He had to look back to the road, which was now curving, toward the harbor.

It was just a small harbor with a few fishing boats and a single pier sheltering the boats against the sea. People were already stirring, and returning fishermen were dragging baskets to the shore, lowering sails, and hanging nets out to dry. There was nothing extraordinary about the harbor and Bentley hardly looked at it. He turned toward Helen. Her face was wet with tears. He felt for her hand and held it.

"You're just beginning," he said to her.

They drove through the village and then down the road to San Stefano. Two miles farther on the jeep passed them and Lieutenant Gastone signaled them.

"I guess you'd better think up something," Bentley said, stopping the car. "You didn't see him or something."

"You do it," Helen said. The tears were gone from her face.

She watched him get out of the car and meet Gastone halfway between the jeep and the Fiat. They talked briefly, and then they both came over to her. The lieutenant looked pale and tired.

"Perhaps you made a mistake, signora." he said. "Where were you supposed to meet him?"

"One mile beyond Caronia."

"From Fratello?"

"Yes."

The lieutenant stared at her. No man had ever showed her more clearly what he thought of her. "He didn't mention a specific place?"

"He wanted to stand on the street."

"Perhaps you didn't see him."

"Or he saw me," Bentley interjected. "Mrs. Brazzi can't do anything more for you, lieutenant. It's up to you to find him now."

"If he's here, we'll find him, Mr. Bentley. What are you going to do?"

"I guess Mrs. Brazzi wants to go back to Chiesa."

"Then I'd suggest that you go by way of San Stefano. Otherwise you'll have quite a number of stops."

"Why?"

"We are closing the coast," he said and then he turned to Helen. "I would be grateful, signora, if you would wait for me in Chiesa. I have some more questions to ask."

She nodded.

"That's very kind of you," Gastone said. He turned around and went to the truck, which had stopped behind them.

"I still don't give Pietro a prayer," Bentley said. He got into the car and drove off.

"How far is it to Palermo?" Helen asked.

Bentley thought. "About a hundred miles. Why?"

"I'd like to ask you to take me there."

"Now?"

"Yes."

"But the lieutenant . . ."

"I don't want to see him anymore," Helen said. "Tomorrow I will go on to Naples. Would you mind bringing my things to Palermo before then?"

Bentley didn't answer.

"Please," Helen said.

"Of course," Bentley muttered. "It's just so sudden."

"I didn't know myself," Helen said. She avoided looking at the sea, which was now slowly turning blue in the light of the rising sun. "Did you see him?" she finally asked.

Bentley nodded. He wished he could feel contempt for her but he could not. "I knew," he said.

"What did you know?"

"That you couldn't do it. You were never completely sure. That's why you wanted us to come along and that's why you didn't want to give him away beforehand."

It wasn't the first time he had really understood her, and it still did not make her feel anything special about him. Since a few minutes earlier she had felt strangely insulated from everything. She felt as if she had left part of herself behind, and the farther they went west along the coast road, the stronger this feeling became.

"I guess I'm glad it happened this way and not some other way," Bentley said.

"Because you don't know everything," Helen answered.

He stared at the coast in the morning light. All its colors were now emerging. "I can imagine. I wouldn't have gotten any satisfaction either. On the contrary, it might have hurt more. Do you still want to look for your husband in Sperlinga?"

"Ask Piera, she must know where he is. I'd like them to bury him in a war cemetery. I don't want him transported to Toledo."

"You may regret that later," Bentley muttered.

"No, that's not the reason," Helen said. "He always belonged here. Do something for Piera; she couldn't help herself. And I'd like Salvatore to have a decent grave. Leave some money here."

"How much?"

"As much as they want. You don't have to return any of it."

She didn't speak for a moment and then she looked out of the window. "You may not find me in the hotel tomorrow," she finally said. "So there's no point in waiting for me."

Bentley nodded. "I expected that." It hurt him as much as usual. "Perhaps I'll visit you someday in Toledo," he said. "Would you throw me out?"

"You'll have to look for me in California."

"Do you want to? . . ."

"I wanted to go five years ago. Don't you like California?"

"It's a big place." He was wondering why she had told him. It wasn't much but it was something he could live on for a while. "What will you tell your father?" he asked.

She turned her head and looked at the landscape, and this time it didn't make any difference anymore. She tried to imagine how it would look on the beach in San Diego. "I will tell him I took a few weeks' vacation."

Bentley laughed dryly. "It must have been hell for you," he said.

"Oh no, not hell," said Helen.